Both Sides of the Blade

Volume I of the Qualthalas Quandaries Quadrilogy

RYAN MCLEOD

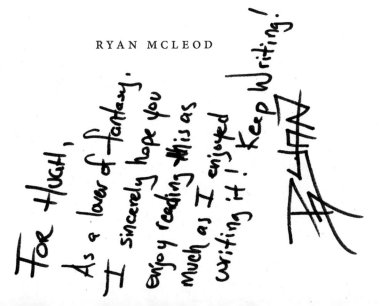

For Hugh,
As a lover of fantasy,
I sincerely hope you
enjoy reading this as
much as I enjoyed
writing it! Keep writing!

 FriesenPress

One Printers Way
Altona, MB R0G 0B0
Canada

www.friesenpress.com

ISBN
978-1-03-913120-0 (Hardcover)
978-1-03-913119-4 (Paperback)
978-1-03-913121-7 (eBook)

1. *FICTION, FANTASY, EPIC*

Distributed to the trade by The Ingram Book Company

Both Sides of the Blade

Prologue

A CROWN PRINCE BE BORN

In response to the touch of the moon elven sage, the quantemporal sands of the Sanctus Orb swirled and shifted within the confines of the artifact's diamantine structure. Bound by the will of Ithrauss Suh'Min Tenebril-Durath, the orb served the ancient Archmaster of Divination, as he prepared for an augury, gazing beyond the device, out the window of his laboratory. From his tower upon Antiqua's silver moon, he viewed the planet far below upon a backdrop of stars, including the giant blue sun of the system which blazed far beyond its horizon.

With the practiced ease of centuries dedicated to mastering the intricacies of the arcane device, the old elf's fingers, weathered yet highly dextrous, traced sigils of augury upon its smooth facets in preparation for the divining soon to commence. Usually inert, now the prophetic dust stirred subtly inside the relic, revealing the patterns of fate woven into the very fabric of time and space. Ithrauss' hands worked in unison to create arcane patterns and symbols, lines of softly glowing blue and orange light trailing behind ink-stained fingernails, invoking the power of the orb at his command. In particular, the venerable moon elf, silver-grey eyebrows furrowed in concentration, focused his intent upon the cosmic thread of his grandson: soon to be *born*, the upcoming Crown Prince of the Kingdom of the *Sillistrael'li.*

The Sanctus Orb glittered in response, stationed upon its amethyst and platinum stand, which itself lay enshrined atop an ornate, rune-inscribed table in Ithrauss' personal chambers. Coupled with the wizened elf's incantations, the raw mana infused in the structure of the orb activated, awakening miniscule silvery strands encapsulated within the shifting dust inside. This set the forthcoming augury in motion; though Ithrauss, despite his tens of thousands of years of experience, had no precognition of the chain of events it would soon reveal.

In the former High King's masterful hands, the orb became a powerful tool for remotely scrying upon the planet's two existing moons and into the dealings of the various, mostly human Kingdoms scattered upon the surface of the world below. Among his peers, Ithrauss was unanimously regarded as the most experienced Divination expert in all of Antiqua even without the orb's significant aid. Utilizing its immense capabilities, the sage could peer into the invisible strands that wound from the immutable past and through the ever-changing present to observe deep into the possibilities that entwined the future of its focused subject. These unique abilities aided in accurate predictions, even regarding theoretical subjects; neither time nor dimension were of significance to the artifact's power. With care, Ithrauss' fingers glided across the smooth, cool facets of its surface: the gentle caress of an old friend.

The orb was a relic of ages past, *ancient* by Ithrauss' reckoning, according to the multitude of rigorous tests he had once performed upon it before attempting to harness its powers. Every seam in its hardened diamond composition was magnetically fused through a process that defied all that Ithrauss understood about magic. Raw *mana*, the force which powered most forms of Arcanist spellcasting, inexplicably bound the individual facets of the orb's crystalline structure into its roughly spherical form. Through experimentation, Ithrauss had also discovered that the orb could grow or shrink, theorizing it could even change shape and dimension, which likely held the key to explaining its impossible capabilities.

Through centuries of research, Ithrauss confirmed that the Sanctus Orb originated from Antiqua, and dated back to the Second Cycle: a period forgotten by any but the most learned of sages. In this age, one hundred and sixty-six thousand years in the past, the collective human race of the Neph'al had been seeded upon Antiqua by enigmatic sources. In its ignorance, the ambitious, and comparatively complex society nearly obliterated the entirety of the world using cataclysmic powers and devices. The few records exhumed which survived the period referred to Antiqua as, 'Gaia the Paradise Planet' and indicated relative global prosperity up until a major turning point in its history. What little knowledge of that critical moment the Moon Elven archives held, gleaned from archaeological digs performed deep within the planet's crust, led Ithrauss to believe the Sanctus Orb's original purpose was to provide military advantage to its possessor.

. Once sufficiently translated, the scattered documents revealed that a significant threat to the planet came in the form of extraterrestrial creatures using advanced technology that facilitated travel between the stars in giant craft. These warlike, conquering beings powered their ships with materials plundered from resource-rich worlds, and Gaia was a prime target for their incursion. Only by some miracle of cooperation between the races and factions of the time was the threat repelled, and the Sanctus Orb purportedly vanished, taking along with it the aggressive alien race, mysteriously averting some catastrophic disaster which would have torn the planet apart.

The great relic had come into the venerable elf's possession many centuries past, but the memory of the event was so bizarre and striking that Ithrauss' face creased in a smile of vivid reminiscence. The orb was transferred to the old sage by an enigmatic archmage from another time strain; it was conceivable that the man belonged to another dimensional reality altogether. The strange *Ma'Jai* had stumbled into his laboratory, emerging from a sudden and inexplicable black vortex of chaotic energy, coughing through crimson-stained lips, his robes smoldering as if recently charred by fire or lightning. With a cry of alarm, Ithrauss called immediately for a Sae'Ret-ii Clerist, one of the powerful healers of the moon elves, and prepared warding spells, not knowing whether this was an attack or just a teleportation mistake. The blue-robed intruder merely waved a dismissive hand in disdain at the elf's precautions as he choked out a few words, flecks of blood spattering the silvery cloth clutched tightly to his face.

"*The Boy Who Would Be God* cannot..." the mage attempted to speak through a coughing fit that wracked his body, and he laid a scorched hand upon a nearby table for support while his chest heaved. Ithrauss feared the man may carry a strange disease, but after a moment, the Ma'Jai steadied his ragged breathing and continued, "Do not let him make *my* mistakes." Another fit took him, but when it finally abated, he straightened, yet still avoided revealing his face, hidden beneath the folds of the runed and tattered hood. Stronger now, his voice came as a declaration which somehow Ithrauss knew was of great significance, "Your grandson and this *being*... their lives are entwined..." Once Ithrauss nodded in acknowledgement of the bizarre statement and bid the Ma'Jai to continue, the azure-robed man pressed a scintillating, multifaceted diamond orb into Ithrauss' grasp. Then, nearly collapsing from the exertion, he began to intone arcane words with perfect inflection and tone: powerful magic the venerable sage, with all his millennia spent studying the art, barely comprehended. The palpable, unimaginable force of mana the figure before him possessed was staggering; this was certainly the most powerful Ma'Jai that Ithrauss had ever encountered but… *what did this all mean?*

"Please," the elven sage begged of the man whose touch felt as if plagued and burning with fever, "your injuries need attention and…" he paused to convey his sense of confusion, "I… do not *have* a grandson." Ithrauss' words fell short as the grey-haired Ma'Jai focused his countenance upon the bewildered sage and fixed his remarkable eyes upon the elven Diviner for a fleeting moment as he drew back the charred hood, allowing the elf to finally see his face. The old sage gasped sharply, and his knuckles turned white as he clutched the nearby desk from the shock inspired by the mere sight of *those eyes*! The incredible eyes that locked with his were cosmos themselves, filled with galaxies of endless stars, encapsulated in the irises of an otherwise human appearance. Never had Ithrauss seen their like, and never again would he in subsequent years, until he reached the afterlife, when he once again met the Celestial traveler. There, in an altogether different dimension, beyond the Plane of Death where some of his kin went after their bodies finally expired, did he and the Ma'Jai sit and converse of the events that unfolded after their fateful meeting.

Afterwards, Ithrauss never spoke of the Ma'Jai himself, nor of how he had come to possess the Sanctus Orb, even to his guild-mates, who knew better than to press the secretive master for information he would flatly decline to give. *Those eyes* spoke of sublime knowledge that should never be spoken aloud, conveyed by a being who understood things beyond the ken of mortals. Before being enveloped by a summoned portal of blackness and stars that shifted and formed at his bidding, the mage had leaned in and clasped Ithrauss by his robes, almost apologetically. In a low, conspiratory tone, the Ma'Jai dispelled the moon elf's earlier confusion regarding the High King's lack of progeny with two simple words, "You will." With a final, sardonic smile that reminded Ithrauss of a serpent, the cryptic wizard disappeared, leaving the Sanctus Orb in Ithrauss' shaking hand as the solitary memento of the event.

The fading memory served as a poignant reminder of the purpose of his current undertaking, and dismissing the reminiscent thoughts, the Lord Overseer of the *Twisted Strings* guild fixed his intense ice-blue eyes at the stirrings encapsulated within the Sanctus Orb. The ancient elf absorbed all his focus into the device, analyzing with a practiced gaze the subtle patterns formed within the prophetic sands. The powdery dust weaved and churned inside the transparent diamond structure before seeming to finally settle. The repetitive rippling resembled something one might see in a remarkably simple, yet painstakingly crafted Zen-Garden, denoting the careful preparations made before the child's impending birth. Each minute variation of the central swirl exaggerated slightly as it reached the breadth of the globe, indicating to the Scion of Divination that his grandson's destiny would have great impact upon his people, a direct parallel to the silvery threads spread out within the sands themselves. The subtle intimation Ithrauss felt, scanning the orb with eyes well-attuned to magical variations, was akin to the wake made by a pebble thrown into a pond.

Master Ithrauss realized he had spent the last few minutes unconsciously pacing his laboratory in reminiscence and moved slowly yet possessed of a dextrous grace that belied his age. He paused to run his fingers along a wet spill pooled in a semicircle upon a smooth wooden table covered in alchemical apparatus, clenching his jaw at the disarray of his laboratory. Everything within the chamber was horribly unorganized; the ancient elf had been neglecting mundane chores during the preparations for his grandson's emergence ceremony. Soon to be born under the sign of the ascending crescent moons, the child would be Crown Prince to the *Akir'Aelyph-Ana'ii*: the elven dynasty which Ithrauss himself had once ruled over as High King. Centuries after their race made the ascent to colonize the silver moon, Sillis-Thal'as, Ithrauss had abdicated his throne, and passed rulership onto his eldest son. Nearly a thousand years had passed since.

For the Sillistrael'li, the ceremony had become an event of the highest magnitude – Adamon Thriun'Ir-Tethrind Aeth'Akir, present High King of the moon elves, had not sired a child in all his years of sovereignty. Though the King was far from old by their standards, his people had begun to question the possibility of a successor to the crown. They loved their King; he was a man of conscience and wisdom, strict and swift in command, but compassionate and intelligent too. However, during his dominion, the Sillistrael'li had become an isolated society, and there were the stirrings of talk that their ruler needed to accept that the moon elves were not truly alone, even secluded as they were upon Antiqua's silver moon. The advent of the Neph'al's rapid advancement on the world below implied that one day soon, the elves could have unwanted company on their acquired homeland. Ithrauss' musings were again swiftly broken, this time by a faint crackling noise emanating from the Sanctus Orb.

Inhaling sharply, Ithrauss' tired but observant eyes snapped to a nearly imperceptible pattern emerging within the depths of the sands, visible as slight striations along the bottom and sides of the diamond globe. "What is *this*?" he almost hissed aloud, gilt-runed robes creasing as he dipped his head to observe closely the underside of the orb. "Amazing," he mouthed silently, "the strands are *still* moving..." Ithrauss snaked his head, inspecting closely the new formations inside the depths of the orb, creases forming at the corners of his mouth where a rare, bewildered smirk passed across his lips. Even by Aelyph'en standards, Ithrauss was incredibly old, counting his years in the many tens of thousands. Few things could surprise the sage, especially considering his vocation was that of *Divination*: the magical art of prophesy and probability. His hands stretched out to follow the pattern in the sands, and then his lips parted in an expression of utter awe. Hundreds of times Ithrauss had gazed into the shifting dust, drawing wisdom and information from the ripples and surges made as he plied his arcane craft upon it. What he now witnessed was without precedent.

Coursing sands riddled through with snaking lines of silver began to curl throughout the globe, reaching, branching, rejoining paths, diverging and converging in a pattern that his perceptive eyes struggled to analyze. Was *this* indicating what the Ma'Jai had spoken of those hundreds of years now past? The sands' initial uncharacteristic stirrings from within were enough to make him take note, but now the changing colours and seemingly unending capillaries they formed were something wholly new. Had Ithrauss been weak of constitution, he may have had a heart attack; indeed, he could feel quickening palpitations thrumming in his chest as an exhilaration raced through his very essence. The unending design revealed by the orb conveyed to Ithrauss a perfectly clear message. The very fabric of time and reality was written in the essence of this individual about to enter the world, the soon-to-be Crown Prince. His grandson could *shape* Destiny.

Streaking past clattering beakers and tomes scattered throughout his laboratory, the ancient elf moved with such fervor that he seemed possessed. Hurriedly, Ithrauss gathered up his velvet robes, and drew its hood over his beaming face as he burst through the door of the tower. His feet skidded to a halt for a second upon the smooth granite landing outside his study. Seeing the radiant stars within the night sky, gathered as a backdrop to the planet far below, took his breath for a moment and he steeled his purpose at the gentle reminder of the greater scope of the universe. This upcoming being, his grandson, would travel amid the countless suns of the cosmos; he would be unbound to this world by the very nature of his birth.

Foremost, Ithrauss needed to contact the agents belonging to his cryptic order, the *Twisted Strings*, and then immediately after, give a report to the High King himself. From what he could glean from the Sanctus Orb, the old elf surmised that Adamon should understand the weight his heir would inevitably bear. The child possessed immense potential; he must possess purpose and direction and receive careful guidance in the utilization of his royal birthright. Though the youth would have to grow to see his hundredth year before its bestowal, Ithrauss was now confident in his decision to begin the lengthy preparations required. It would be the first time in millennia that the sage would inscribe an Aeth'Akir with the power of the *Masque of Myriad Minds*; one of the ancient secrets the master kept hidden for its potency was so great.

"Grandson," he intoned, smirking a knowing, secret smile, "what wonders will you weave…"

Chapter 1

AN UNCEREMONIOUS BEGINNING

The rough *crunch* of a flailing body hitting earth startled a group of horrified onlookers outside the well-known smithy on Lowton Avenue. Cackling as he spat blood upon the hard-packed earth and cobblestone of the street, the Aelyph'en known as Qualthalas Ithrauss Aeth'Akir clutched his aching ribs, ready to vomit. The roguish elf noted with cold clarity that the gigantic oryk (who had tossed him like a skipping-stone) was now drawing forth from the baldric on his back – a heavy, serrated claymore. A savage, bloodthirsty look played upon the bestial face of the figure towering over his victim and the huge man smiled maliciously at the plight of the comparatively miniscule elf at his feet. A meaty, clawed hand gripped the moon elf roughly by the nape of his torn, grey cloak, and a massive arm hauled Qual up suddenly, jerking the pale-skinned elf upright to the creature's impressive eye level. Legs dangling, Qualthalas looked furtively side-to-side and reached instinctively to his scabbard, found it empty, and swore in moon elvish. A disgustingly toothy grin erupted into a vicious sneer upon the monstrous oryk's maw as he then spoke to the hapless vagabond.

"Look like this the end for Elfie-man," he issued in guttural, broken Mithrainian, the common language of the continent. Clearly, the huge orykan man was preparing to do something much nastier than break a few ribs. The giant blacksmith, father to Qual's lover Kaira, was intent upon *murder*. Each crescent of the blade's edge gleamed menacingly as the massive brute pressed the weapon dangerously close to the squirming elf's face. "Blood-Saw is making pritty elf-head off on ground." The tall oryk released the moon elf, who fell in a heap onto the hard soil aside the worn brickwork of the nearby shop. Adjusting his grip on the huge saw-toothed blade with both his rough, grimy hands, Baergrenth "Blackhand" raised the weapon, execution-style, high above Qualthalas' exposed neck. The heavy musculature of his grey-green skin rippled impressively in preparation. Salivating at the wicked thoughts of decapitating this Aelyph'en rogue in a bloody mess, the monstrous hulking figure's eyes blazed in murderous ecstasy, belying an inner nature that hungered for violence and slaughter. A few onlookers, stunned at the early morning scene, could only gasp or turn away. None of the meek individuals was brave enough to call out, nor stupid enough to try to stop the ferocious orykan smith, whose strength and hot-tempered nature were legendary in the district.

"So, I don't suppose we could… cut a deal?" the scrambling elven man muttered, still chortling slightly under his breath, despite the bleak situation that was becoming more dire with every passing second. It was still early morning, and in this part of the city, the guards rarely made more than a few passing patrols. Expecting any help from the cowardly peasants caught up in the scene or the street urchins peering out from the dusty alleys was folly as well. Looking up and brushing a stray lock of silver-gold hair from his eye, his characteristically smooth skin now rough and caked with blood and grit, Qual's jaw clenched ever so slightly as he directed a pained expression of mocking hurt to his attacker. Qualthalas prided himself on never 'losing his head' in this kind of situation and vowed silently that he would not allow this monster to make that figurative statement false in a more literal sense.

"I've got gold crowns, you know, and more than a few gems along with it. I'd be willing to bargain them to keep my pretty head in its rightful place atop my shoulders." He enticed the old blacksmith, knowing the impossibility of swaying this vendetta against him with the promise of wealth. The rakish elf raised an eyebrow and looked directly at his would-be executioner to gauge the effectiveness of his statement. Certainly, the oryk didn't take to the generous offer; in fact, Qual's words had incited an even more intense rage within the blacksmith poised to deliver a killing blow. Strangely enough, the reaction was precisely Qualthalas' intent. The ever-calculating mind of the elf was setting a dangerous plan in motion; one he desperately hoped would work. His life and possibly many others could depend on it.

"Elfie thinks can bargain daughter's virtue for *money*?" the monstrosity growled, as spittle and foam issued forth between Baergrenth's clenched teeth as he shook with fury. Incensed that the impetuous elf would even consider putting up coin against his pride and perceived family dishonour, the beast slowly lowered its massive sword. "No. Blood-Saw no cut off elf-head. Not *enough* punish. Now, Elfie… will learn… new meaning for *PAIN!*" Having said that, the oryk flung aside his greatsword, and raised an iron-plated boot, bringing it swiftly down on the prone elf, trying to smash his ribs to splinters.

"You know," Qualthalas managed a ragged gasp, winded from the powerful kick dealt to him, forced to pause long enough to catch his breath as the words choked up in his throat. He was lucky that his leather jerkin was enchanted to cushion blows and turn aside blades. Without it, he would have been fortunate to even *survive* such a brutal stomping. Qual put a hand down to steady himself upon the rough dirt and broken cobblestone and continued weakly, "I... wasn't the one who stole your girl's virtue, my *large* comrade." Pausing for just a second, with a sideways glance as if conspiring with a captive audience, he smirked deviously, adding, "Another had been there long ago–*many* others, in fact, if I am not mistaken. Ask around the tavern she works at. Kaira's a *popular* young woman."

That ought to do it, Qualthalas thought with satisfaction. *If that little performance fails to trigger the transformation, then I shall resign from the Bards' College.* A slow, razor-thin smirk crept its way up the left side of the elf's pale lips, as it was apt to do when he was up to mischief. There was no damn way Qualthalas was resigning, nor was he resolved to perish this day. The barbaric oryk, unable to control the bestial urges welling deep within himself, released a frenzied roar that echoed through Lowton Avenue. If Qualthalas' suspicions and investigations were correct, all the nearby gawkers were about to make an unsettling discovery. Another hair-raising, purely primal howl erupted from the hulking creature's throat. Taking advantage of the momentary distraction, Qualthalas' keen, almond-shaped ice-blue eyes scanned the nearby dirt and debris for *Ithrin'Sael-I-Uiin*. His ensorcelled rapier, known as "Mourning-Song" in the common tongue, *had* to be laying somewhere close. It was swiftly becoming time to drop this charade and make his play. A glint of light amid the contrasting gloom of the street caught Qual's eye, coming from the area outside a nearby alehouse, only a short dash away.

The marvelous blade had been cast to the ground earlier, beside the tavern's carved oaken door, and now lay beside a trough meant for watering horses whilst the patrons inside quenched their own various thirsts. It was a magnificent sword indeed, forged of a unique alloy of rare materials: titanium, mithril, adamantium, and tantalum. The metallurgy involved in the enchanted weapon's crafting rendered Ithrin'Sael-I-Uiin nearly indestructible, feather-light, and highly flexible: the perfect traits for a rapier. These metals had been folded together many thousand times over in the legendary Aelyph'en smithy known as the Midnight Forge. Though its existence had faded mostly into obscurity after the moon elves relocated their kingdom high above Antiqua, the few blades still in circulation upon the planet were regarded by master weapon-smiths as unparalleled in construction and quality. Qualthalas' rapier was razor-edged and capable of penetrating solid stone as if it were butter and coming out unscathed.

The unnatural sound of cracking and shifting bones issuing from the oryk's twisting and rippling body snapped Qual's focus back to the scene at hand; he regained his senses and prepared his next move. Ornate, etched runes danced along the surface of the weapon: ebbing and glowing in dark green, indicating the danger that the weapon sensed in its vicinity. The ancient wielders of Ithrin'Sael-I-Uiin had placed meticulous levels of enchantment throughout the layers of the blade as they fought countless devious creatures. Through the thousands of years since its creation, sorceries were designed and implemented to detect and exploit vulnerabilities as the blade attuned its capabilities to best combat its wielder's foes. Sizzling, black-veined arcane symbols indicated the presence of a lycanthropic shapeshifter, though the horrified onlookers were already keenly aware. Mixed expressions of revul-sion and fear washed through the crowd like a crashing wave as they witnessed the dreadful transformation. Though none of the rabble had seen a werewolf before, all recognized the howling, crimson-eyed beast in their midst. Huge and utterly terrifying, possessing wolven claws upon its misshapen fingers and snap-ping jaws that could tear a man in half, the lycanthrope passed a terrible, bloodshot gaze fervently across the stricken crowd. It finally spotted Qualthalas, who now stood tall, no longer playing the cowering scoundrel.

Hand outstretched towards his gleaming rapier, Qual whispered in moon elvish, "*E'threiss.*" At this command, the weapon vanished from the ground, suddenly in-hand, shimmering, threatening, and poised to strike. Qualthalas leveled the tip of the blade at Baergrenth, or rather, the thing that was *once* Baergrenth. The roguish smirk previously upon his face had melted into a grim, solemn expression; Qualthalas regretted the inevitability playing out in front of himself and the crowd. There was no hope of cure for this one, now. The curse ran so deep it had become an integral part of the once proud orykan man; his blood was forever tainted, and it condemned the man to a deepening madness that would worsen the longer he continued to live.

The grievous wounds inflicted by a were-creature posed a risk of transferring the lycanthropic infection to any victim fortunate – or rather *unfortunate* enough to survive a vicious attack. Normally, once infected, these poor souls would change form only on the six nights where the planet's two moons were full in their cycles. Certain magics and alchemical infusions, if applied swiftly enough, could treat the horrible condition, and reverse the magical disease. However, one such as Baergrenth, whose curse had become incurable, was capable of transformation through sheer will or if triggered by powerful emotion. Termed "Ascended Lycans" as Qual's research had led him to discover, these creatures would only *descend* further into madness and destruction as the curse was woven anatomically, changing the structure of the entire being so infected.

Weeks prior, upon learning the nature of his lover's father quite by accident, Qualthalas had sought the consultation of an ancient practitioner of the Druzaic Conclave who conversed with him at length regarding prognosis for this type of curse. A primordial force of nature, a Dryad she was – one of the spirit-sages of the trees and animal kingdoms – and her expertise in the area was without parallel. The conclusion, which *Kana-Tovara the Wizened* explained to the stunned elf in stoic terms, was that a swift death was the most reasonable and peaceful solution possible. Short of a true divine miracle or complete genetic restructuring, there was no return from the perpetual, increasing urge to kill. The horrific eventuality was that surviving victims would continue to spread the curse, and rampantly. Though he was not sure what a 'complete genetic restructuring' entailed, Qual knew that *divine miracles* were in short supply. With sad recollection, the druidess informed Qualthalas of a time long past, when her duty to the natural order compelled her to act against an entire community who had harbored infected lycanthropes for years. The story was grim, and painted a horrifying picture that Qual swore he would not allow to happen to the people of Morningmist. He had thanked the dryad matron for the information, and resolved himself to carry out the necessary resolution, which led him straight to the smithy and the confrontation now taking place.

"If it's any consolation, I was only jesting about your daughter." Qual intoned, bringing his rapier to bear as the snarling creature advanced with menace, spittle and froth flying from its fanged face. It raised a massive, wickedly clawed hand and swiped viciously at Qualthalas' cheek. He deftly sidestepped and Mourning-Song flashed in the dim light of dawn, piercing the werewolf's forearm twice in precise lightning thrusts from the experienced elf's swordplay. The werewolf howled as wracking pain shot up its arm; the blade had attuned, affecting the creature as if made of the purest silver: the bane of all lycanthropes. Qualthalas continued his empassioned speech, "Kaira is *truly* a fine girl, and as luck would have it, not affected by your unfortunate curse. I am deeply sorry to have to end you this way, old oryk."

If it cared; if there was any vestige of the man behind the bloody fury of the slavering *thing* now bearing down on Qual, there was certainly no sign of it anymore. Beyond animal savagery, there was a deep-seated malevolence to its wild and deadly swings. *Swings that are all too near my throat*, Qual coolly noted as he sidestepped a raking strike that would have ripped him to shreds. Frowning, ducking and maneuvering to a position at the creature's flank, Mourning-Song made a whip-like sound as Qualthalas slashed a crosscut with two swift snaps of the wrist. He had inflicted a bloody gash in the creature's midriff, weakening it certainly, but the creature registered no sign of slowing its terrible assault.

Qualthalas backstepped, raised the rapier's hilt high, but kept the tip low defensively as he gauged his target. It was clear that the brute sought more than just murder. It lusted with an evil urge for wanton *slaughter*. The thing before him needed the ecstasy of spraying blood upon the ground and reveled in the terror it impressed upon the few paralyzed onlookers remaining: those who were too horrified to run away. The very existence of such an aberration was an abominable horror and this was why Qual steeled himself with an intense look, now meeting the swiftly advancing creature's steps. Kaira and the entirety of Morningmist's population depended on the werewolf's destruction before it could spread the curse and cause an epidemic. As Qualthalas brought the rapier to bear, he could hear it humming as the runes inscribed upon the gleaming blade flared to match his determination. He could not back down. No. It must end soon.

Although it was not a specialty of his, the well-traveled elf did dabble in Combative Thaumaturgy: the school of evocative magicks whose aim it was to inflict woeful damage upon a foe. Recalling a few words of elemental fire and the tones and verses needed to expel said energy, Qual incanted swiftly. The syllables sounded like he was spitting or cursing, *"Threil-sorca nauthrenn o'reth nin-threil'ah,*" and his free hand fluttered, fingers dancing, drawing ancient symbols in the air, all an elaborate part of the spell, which he made seem practiced and natural. Darts crafted of conjured flame formed in a spiraling pattern high in the air above the monster. With his raised hand, Qualthalas motioned as if gripping the spinning motes of fire, then extended two fingers, arm suddenly arcing down from over and behind his head to direct them at the howling werewolf bearing down on him. Even as its claws tore up the cobblestone in a mad rush, the flaming spikes streaked down, leaving smoldering smoke trails as they buried themselves in the slavering beast. With a throat-splitting roar, the werewolf reeled to the side as the fiery shards embedded themselves in its fur and flesh; amber flames ripped through the thrashing creature's torso, setting it alight. The overpowering stench of charred skin and burning fur assailed the entire street as the monstrosity staggered about, howling in severe pain. The scene became too much to bear for several of the shocked townsfolk, who finally regained enough sense to flee terrified into their homes.

Although it seemed a telling blow, Qualthalas intended the attack merely as a distraction for his next move. Rough cobblestone broke apart as the elf skip-stepped back to give himself distance from the monster, and he glanced at his gloved hand as he slipped a small vial out of a case on his belt. He nodded with satisfaction at the swirling pearl texture and violet colour of the mixture, crushing the glass in his fingers. The liquid vaporized and enveloped Qualthalas with a pearlescent sheen; his image shimmered momentarily as three more blurred and shifting outlines sprang forth. The illusions swirled through each other in a distorted, almost hypnotic pattern, mimicking the rogue's appearance and movements.

The werewolf tried to focus on his prey, but everything was chaos to its heightened senses. The creature's flesh and fur smoldered, nostrils snorting at the pungent odour; the throbbing rush of blood pounded in its ears amid the screams of the panicked. Worse was the constant high-pitched whine of the sliver of silver the elf-man was flashing around. These distractions were impossible to ignore, and now it could scarcely make out an opponent who seemed to be in four places at once. Still, the werewolf thrashed at the closest vision only to find its claws sweeping through empty space, though the image remained, swirling as if made of smoke.

Repeatedly it clawed, raking vicious arcs, deadly enough to kill any mortal man in a single swipe, yet no satisfying snap or crunch occurred. Everything was completely ineffective. A rough growl emerged from deep inside its throat, anger and frustration coupled with unfathomable cursed rage flowing forth. "Kill, *kill*.... **KILL!**" was the only repeating thought within the remains of the blacksmith's fractured mind; a once proud oryk now reduced to a slavering killing machine. And then, in the next instant, there were no thoughts at all, no more rage, no fury or frustration, no bloodlust. Buried to the hilt under its jaw and protruding upwards through the top of its charred skull, Ithrin'Sael-I-Uiin glistened with Baergrenth's thick red blood. Qual's hand twitched, clenched tightly around the rapier after making a snapping twist, the deathblow that released the creature from its curse and from its miserable life. Still standing, the mighty oryk's muscles rippled; his arms convulsed involuntarily one last time, then hung at Baergrenth's sides limply and his body crashed to the ground at the weeping elf's feet.

A raven screeched from its rooftop perch, as if to signify the end of the disturbance at Lowton Avenue Smithy. A blazing sun was making its way to the horizon, streaks of azure and silver reflecting off wispy clouds in the distance. Although he had accomplished what he set out to do: what he *had to do*, there was the aftermath to contend with, namely in the form of his lover, Kaira. Qual gritted his teeth and let out a weighty sigh. There would soon be hells to pay.

Chapter 2

TROUBLE FOLLOWS TROUBLE

Snarling viciously through curled lips, Kaira slammed Qualthalas'
head into the polished hardwood of the bar once more for good
measure, her knuckles cracking as she pressed his face down, her
tear-filled eyes blazing crimson. She released him roughly and
stormed away. A barstool blocked her path and Kaira sent it flying
with a kick that shattered it upon its impact with the bar top. One
of the nearby locals dodged the splinters that flew past his rough,
pockmarked face. The beautiful and fierce half-oryk woman
halted and she spun around; the barkeep and the few patrons in
the Painted Pony Taproom winced for Qualthalas, though none
stepped up to intervene. They knew Kaira. The rakish elf was on
his own.

"Maybe I was incorrect…" The elf parted swollen lips to spit
blood on the barroom floor. It hit a stray beer-soaked peanut
discarded by one of the patrons earlier. Qual admired the sheen
of the lacquered and freshly polished floorboards briefly, noting
that they were oddly blurry in his right eye. Kaira had introduced
that side of his face to the counter repeatedly during her initial
tirade. He had come to the bar to take her aside and explain that
her father, Baergrenth, was dead and that it was at his hands, but

apparently, she had already heard the news. Before Qualthalas could utter a single word of condolence, she had greeted him with a closed fist and then proceeded to hurl him about the bar, much to the chagrin of the owner, who had dared not intercede. Qualthalas continued his trailing statement partly because it was not in his nature to stop talking when he probably should, and partly to rile his off-and-on lover. He knew she needed to take her anger and grief out on *something*; it might as well be him. Suggestively, he finished with, "...perhaps you *do* have the taint of your father's curse. Such fury you possess; we should have you tested."

The enraged half-orykan girl was on him in a flash; this time the press of cold, curved steel greeted the elf's neck – her knife flying from its belt sheath into her deft hands, scraping against his throat in mere moments. At the back of the bar, someone gasped. The barkeep and part owner, an old dwarvish man everyone called 'Merry' croaked, "Kaira, maybe you should put the cutter away..." Merry wore a frown of concern, and he tugged at his shaggy grey beard as he ventured a hesitant step forth, but his voice trailed off at the blood-red glare the girl flashed at him. Her dark makeup was streaked, and tears streamed down her face. The anguish inside continued to boil out and Kaira tried to speak, but the biting reply choked up in her throat. She emitted a low moan as the desolation of her emotions cascaded out amidst the churning rage she felt inside. Kaira steadied herself against the bar top and took a moment to breathe. Finally, her words came out in stark contrast to the explosive display minutes ago, calm, and plain, "*Why*, Qual?"

The gleaming blade still at the elf's throat glistened with a wet line of blood that trickled down its sharp edge onto the fine Steel-Oak bar top. The counter had thankfully been unharmed by the several jarring impacts of the beleaguered bard's head. *Small miracles*, Qualthalas mused as distorted visions of the world spun around him. Slowly the elf rose and pushed precariously against the pressure his lover still exerted on the blade. It hurt, but Kaira relinquished as he straightened up, which allowed the dizzy elf to rise, and he stared: *squarely at her large breasts.* An obvious, lecherous grin erupted on Qual's face. She caught the look and rewarded the stupefied rogue with a backhand hard across his cheek, thoroughly disgusted that he could think like *that*, at a time like *this*. Reflexively, she slapped him again, harder this time, and the orykan woman hissed as her dangerous fury boiled to the surface. Kaira's knife returned to Qualthalas' neck, and she tipped the edge slightly so that it pressed against the pulsing vein below his jaw. Swallowing, the elf chuckled nervously. Kaira grinned with malice as a bead of sweat stung Qual's bloodied eye. Several long seconds hung in the stillness of the room as everyone present watched in frozen silence, locked in the scene while they worried the moon elf might meet his end at the hands of his lover. Qualthalas' mouth opened and closed several times, as if an explanation or apology was forthcoming while he struggled for words, but nothing escaped his lips until Kaira leaned in to look him directly in the eyes.

When Qualthalas finally whispered a response, his tone became intimately soft, his demeanor somber as if a switch had been flicked and he was a different person altogether. He put it simply, "You *know* why, my love." Qual's glittering silver-blue eyes were downcast as he spoke, but lifted to meet hers, which were stained with a mixture of black eyeliner and salty tears. Qualthalas locked her eyes in his gaze, and in that instant, Kaïra knew that everything leading up to this had been a talented performance. The elf's eyes revealed only the torment of his previous decision; his lip quivered slightly, betraying the truth he rarely spoke. After he saw Kaira had acknowledged his true feelings, Qualthalas carefully obscured it all behind the practiced wall of emotional and mental masks that protected him. His customary smirk reappeared as the rakish elf ran a hand through his unkempt hair, which had spilled out of its neat braid in the altercation. He took care to brush aside the knife still touching his neck. It was not difficult though. Kaira's grip on the weapon was limp, and as her arm went down to her side, the blade clattered to the floor. She began to sob openly. "I'm sorry, Qual," she started, and a wracking gurgle issued forth as she sputtered, "I... I know what he *was*."

"Take her out of here, Qual; she's got the rest of the week off," came the soft voice of Merry from behind the bar, "and take her somewhere *nice* too, ye scoundrel." He continued, raising his voice so the cringing elf was sure to hear, "The barstool's going on your tab, too, *incidentally*." Merry was already heading around the bar with heavy steps, gathering up the broken bits of the fine chair. He shuddered at the thought of a kick hard enough to break Steel-Oak, named such for its grey tone and the resilience of the wood. It was damned expensive too, but though Qual had the demeanor and appearance of a rogue, vagabond, or ne'er-do-well, Merry knew very well how deep the moon elf's pockets were. He was sure the bard would cover the costs, plus probably some more.

Qual hovered a few moments when he reached the taproom doors with Kaira in tow, nodded solemnly, making sure to catch Merry's eyes as they departed. The look was one of reassurance as he guided the broken lass to the exit of the Painted Pony, flicking the latch with his leather boot and kicking it open in one motion. With a return nod from Merry, the pair left, and the inn filled with its usual chatter as the patrons resumed their gossip. They would all have stories when they finally made their ways home this afternoon, and word was already spreading like wildfire about Kaira's father: blacksmith and werewolf, slain by *Crescent-Moons*, the Sillistrael'li elf.

The two slipped through the alleys and thoroughfares alike, crossing in between the now bustling streets of Morningmist, remaining silent throughout the long walk. Winding a way along cobbled paths, betwixt shanty shops and corner markets the pair strolled, largely ignoring the backdrop of the city as it passed them by. Qualthalas had no inkling of their destination; Kaira seemed to be wandering of her own accord, listless; not once did the sullen orykan woman glance up at the Floating Flames of First Avenue, which usually delighted her. She paid no mind to the hawkers who uncharacteristically avoided her and her companion as they wandered around Blind Deals Bazaar. Kaira's only vision was an inward one, where she was remembering her father, strong and proud in his younger years before the curse took him. She recalled with a sharp pain in her heart how he slowly succumbed to deeper anger and fits of violence. What he could have become – a ruthless lupine killer, Kaira understood; the very thought threatened to unhinge her, so she pushed it away and slowly became aware of her surroundings.

Kaira turned her tear-stained eyes sideward to Qualthalas, who had remained uncharacteristically silent as he patiently let her lead him in a seemingly random set of directions for nearly an hour. She dearly loved the elf though she would never admit it, even having fantasized once or twice about settling down in a gigantic apartment with him somewhere in the Marble Maidens district. She had fleeting dreams of the pair spending their nights between silk sheets for the rest of life, but she knew it was pure fantasy. Kaira knew that even if he felt the same desire, her elven lover would never settle down. Qualthalas was *driven* by some purpose underlying the carefree veneer he wore; she had watched the devious elf poke his prying nose into any secret he could uncover. The roguish moon elf was on a mission of some sort, but exactly what it entailed... she had never been able to pry out of his lips. Qual was the consummate liar. Always there was a riddle or misleading answer off his tongue when asked *why in hells* he had descended from the Silver Moon to Antiqua proper. *Why* in particular had he come to the Mithrainian continent; *why* take up residence in Morningmist... His answers ranged from idiocy like, "The paper is of such fine quality here," to enigmatic and annoyingly poetic riddles such as, "Shadowy secrets kept by none, and told by all, thus shall lead me to the Darklord's Hall." That word, 'Darklord,' unsettled Kaira whenever he spoke it, but the elf's glib tongue always deflected any further probing.

Qual noticed that the woman's mind was finally wandering from the grim fact that he had just killed her father: her *werewolf* father. *Well,* spoke his inner voice, *you could console her with the fact that the thing you killed little resembled a man anymore. No,* he continued internally, *better let her find distraction in other things, see where-in-the-hells we are going to end up, find a quality inn-room and...*

A whistling sound followed by three concentrated points of agony in his right shoulder shocked Qualthalas suddenly back to reality. *Darts – poisoned or magical,* his mind registered instantly. The situation became rapidly apparent to the elf: following from the bar throughout their long walk, the assailant had been waiting for the precise opportunity to strike. Locked in Qualthalas' mind were defensive incantations he was able to cast the instant he sensed imminent danger; the precision of the unexpected strike had bypassed the elf's guard. Only a professional killer employing psionics or the like could have penetrated Qual's defenses in such a manner. Purposefully they had chosen this moment to assail him when he was distracted and his thoughts unclear, lost in his concern for Kaira.

Qual buckled and went down on one knee, bracing himself with both hands on the stone at his feet; his rasping breath was difficult and forced. His heart began to race, and in the next instant felt dreadfully sluggish. His silver, almond eyes turned towards Kaira, who seemed to be speaking in slow motion. A delirium spread inside his fevered head, and with a giddy chuckle, Qual tried to tell the girl she sounded like a grunting boar. Darkness filled with hellish nightmares descended upon Qualthalas as he envisioned the recurring terror of ripping off mask, after mask, after mask before a mirror, only to find he possessed no face underneath...

Kaira reached for her companion as he babbled something incoherent about a boar and went down – *hard* – onto the paved stone. "What in blazes, Qual?" she hissed and shook him roughly, but upon finding him completely limp and unresponsive, Kaira hauled the inert elf onto her shoulder like a sack of barley. Something metallic pinched her; it felt unnatural poking out somewhere around Qual's shoulder, but she dared not take the time to inspect whatever it may be. Instead, the half-orykan barmaid wheeled to the side, seeking escape down the nearest refuse-filled alley. Kaira pulled her curved knife from its sheath, glanced furtively back the way they came, and scanned the nearby windows and rooftops. High upon a dark stone balcony, she spied the stereotypical 'shadowy figure' receding from view on the third floor of a nearby apartment.

Etched upon the tall building's gold-and-marble plaque were the words, "The Blackstone." Kaira committed the name to memory and took careful note of their exact location before taking her unconscious elven lover swiftly through the alleys. Ahead, she was forced to dodge a few ravenous Clackerbirds as they squawked and dove at her from the trusses. Physically, the strange avian creatures posed no real threat. The small birds' four ridged beaks lacked the strength to cause anything but minor cuts and scrapes, however, oft-times they carried disease, which is why Kaira took care to avoid further attacks. The next one that swooped at her lost its head in a flash from her dagger's bite. The narrow alley reverberated with an eruption of clacking from the jittering and flexing of multi-jawed beaks as the remainder flew off in a panic. The torrent of sound – for which the birds were named – grated on Kaira's ears another few seconds before it finally receded. The dusty and thankfully empty alley seemed safe, for the moment at least.

Kaira saw the three darts protruding from Qualthalas' right shoulder as she laid the elf gently against the adjacent alley wall. Thanks to years spent as the blacksmith's daughter, she recognized the purple-veined metal of the spiral needles embedded in her lover's still form. *Iridite*, employed by hunters and assassins both, could innately bear toxins and chemicals due to its tubular internal structure. Exquisitely crafted, these were the tools of a *killer*. "Qual... no," Kaira choked as her voice cracked, but she steadied herself and gathered her wits. Turning her cheek to Qual's nostrils, she was relieved to find that the elf still drew breath: deep and slow as if in a slumber, though no amount of shaking could wake him. *At least he seems stable*, she thought, once again scanned her surroundings and prepared to make a break for the lengthy and notoriously winding avenues of Middletown. Maybe she could lose any pursuers in the complex series of corridors and bustling shops therein. Friendly territory was nowhere near to her. True safety might be a long way off. Perhaps it would be better to hide somewhere nearby...

Kaira spied a door with a latch and keyhole tucked into a sunken recess in the clay-and-stone walls of this building, just a scant few steps deeper into the alley. Kaira heaved Qual the short distance, dropping him on his side as he snored loudly. Qual chortled, and a hand limply batted the air as if dismissing something or someone. A few garbled words left his lips, something that sounded elven to Kaira, but it was as if Qual was in a lucid, drunken slumber.

Bastard is probably enjoying his poisoned state, she noted crossly, *and here I am picking a lock in a back alley in Middletown.* She had gathered up some tools of the thieves' trade over the years, and though she seldom put them to use, Kaira had gained a level of proficiency in popping locks. In and down she twisted the first steel pick, hearing a satisfying click as the tumbler was set. A few more of these successes almost brought a smile to her lips.

Almost, had it not been for Qual's now-annoying elvish banter with himself. He seemed to be babbling something in drunken moon elven, and… *answering himself,* though the words were lost to her. She had tried to learn, but the tongue of the Sillistrael'li was a tricky language, carrying many abbreviations for more complex words, which meant different things in each context. Though she understood many of the basic terms, like *"greetings," "where is the lavatory,"* and *"fuck off",* the intricacies of it were too much for Kaira to sit patiently and listen to Qual's attempts to instruct her in its flowing verbiage. That, and he was not a particularly good teacher. She smiled at the memory, and when the lock popped gratifyingly, she hauled him through the doorway, and took a careful last look down the alley to check for observers. There was nothing. She silently shut the door behind them after retrieving her picks, re-locked it from the inside and looked around the musty surroundings, her half-orykan eyes swiftly adjusting to the still blackness. *Momentary safety,* she thought…

Chapter 3

INTIMATIONS OF EVIL

Only darkness and quiet greeted Kaira in the chill of the room. She hated the feel of the place, whatever it was. Even though they were hidden away from prying eyes and the place was relatively secure, (at least she'd hear the lock opening if anyone had managed to follow her), there was a palpable tension in the air, and it felt more than just a play of her tumultuous emotional state. A lurking danger permeated the area, deadly, delicate... *subtle*. In addition, she disliked absolute darkness. Even though by grace of her racial ancestry Kaira could see clearly – she *was* half-oryk – everything in the inky darkness appeared grey and muted in tone. The shadows blended in a way that contributed to the uncomfortable sensation gripping her stomach. If it had not been for the randomness of their flight down the alleys, Kaira might have felt this all an elaborate trap. *Nevertheless*, she thought, *who could have predicted we would come in here?* Kaira might have kept running down the alley or picked another building for all anyone – including her – may have guessed. No, it was impossible. Perhaps she just felt edgy because Qual's previous *annoying* banter had stopped suddenly, and he was unnaturally quiet, much like the velvety silence that surrounded her.

Again, Kaira leaned close to Qual, her delicate but strong hands made their way to his neck to check for a pulse, and she felt the dried blood in a line under the elf's jaw where her knife had cut him earlier. A tear threatened to roll down her cheek as a confusing jumble of tumultuous emotions flooded her. She kept the panic welling inside at bay though. Qual's breathing was still extremely slow, and she noted a faint but even throbbing rhythm from beneath his skin. He felt exceptionally warm though, and sweaty, but if he had a fever, it was mild. *It was probably something to do with the poison*, she presumed.

Suddenly remembering that Qualthalas still had three darts protruding from his shoulder, she gasped. Kaira was no medic. Was it proper to pull them out or leave them in? She was accustomed to leaving anything sharp in a wound until it could be properly dressed, to avoid excessive blood loss upon removal. Unfortunately, (or was it fortunate?) she hadn't seen a lot of battle in the last few years, and the girl wondered if the same held true when dealing with a poisoned weapon. It might be better to pull them out. After all, the darts functioned to puncture armour and administer their foul toxins, not to cause blood loss.

Deciding it was the right thing to do; Kaira drew a deep breath and took hold of the first dart. It made a quiet shucking sound as she gingerly removed it from Qual's shoulder. She drew the stained shirt aside and inspected the area for blood, relieved to find no sudden gush after pulling out the first of the three weapons. Kaira quickly yanked the remaining two darts out and jerked aside Qualthalas' leather doublet to have a better look at the wounded area. She raised an eyebrow at the peculiar lack of fresh blood at the site where the darts had, only moments ago, protruded from Qual's shoulder. The dart-holes had closed swiftly, sealing the three wounds before even a drop could come out. Was it some spell of his or could it be some innate magic within the darts, in order to prevent the poison's removal? Either way, worrying about the result was probably pointless. The effects had been instant, and even though Qualthalas was still out cold and unresponsive, the roguish elf seemed stable. She might just have to wait it out. Maybe it was time to have a look around and plan their escape...

They were in a nondescript brick-walled room. A sturdy desk accompanied by a single wooden chair sat pressed up against the southern wall to her right, some parchments scattered upon its surface. She noted a bland poster or picture that hung at an odd angle above the desk, chained to the wall. Other than an over-turned metal bucket that lay a few feet from the desk and what she presumed was a scrubbing brush beside it, the room was quite barren of any adornment. The excessive cleanliness of the whole place worried her because that indicated the area was often occu-pied, and this made Kaira even more nervous. *Could the usual inhabitants be nearby?* Kaira frowned at the thought. She certainly had enough of trauma and trouble this day. She wanted to get the hells out of here and to safety; she wanted a warm bath and then a warm bed, and then to just cry herself to sleep and not worry about Qual and the constant mischief that followed him every-where... to not think about her father...

Kaira choked on a sob that made her chest heave. There were three more aftershocks before she could control them and though she made barely a sound, Kaira worried that someone might hear her movements and investigate. It was midday, so unless this was a warehouse or after-hours establishment, there must be people inside somewhere. She gathered her wits and began to footpad slowly to the desk, when her heart leapt into her throat, and she froze. *Something brushed her ankle!* Terrified it was a diseased rat or snake, Kaira reflexively drew her leg up and stomped down hard. If they had remained undetected thus far, the scream of pain that Qual issued forth at having his hand broken surely alerted anything within the building – and probably the surrounding three blocks – to their presence.

"*Dre'ith, lir'aithe quai-pah,*" Qualthalas cursed in moon elven, cradling the crushed hand to his chest, finally able to speak clearly. Hazily his mobility and vision had returned; he had reached out to Kaira, trying to speak, but nothing had come from his lips. He watched in terror as she raised that powerful leg, trying vainly to get his hand out of the way, then closed his eyes as her heel came down. "Stomped me like a gutter-rat…" he growled indignantly through gritted teeth, brushing away the tears of pain and shock, certain at least two of his fingers were broken. Kaira had damned hard boot-heels! Qualthalas tried standing unsuccessfully and pitched over into the wall with a resounding *thud.* Kaira scrambled to help him, stifling her surprised gasp. "Quiet, Qualthalas!" she hissed under her breath. "I'm not sure where the hell we are, but we might not be alone in here… at least not much longer, thanks to your shouting."

In protest, Qual rebutted, "Shouting elicited… *by the heel of your boot*, I might remind you." The elf stared at her suspiciously for a moment and with his undamaged hand poked at her belly with the remark, "Did you gain some weight?" Already Qual's *charming* sense of humour had returned. Kaira gritted her teeth and scowled for a second, but relief washed through her, and she smiled, albeit sickly, at the fact that the elf was regaining his senses. *It will always be like that with him,* she mused, curling an arm under the wounded elf's shoulder to steady him. She helped Qual make his way to the chair by the desk, with another glance at the overturned bucket off to the side. The faint edge of something underneath caught Kaira's attention; it appeared to be a marking on the floor. Maybe it was an inscription? Setting Qual's backside squarely on the chair, Kaira steadied the elf with one arm to ensure he did not collapse, and then reached for the bucket…

The silver-shod tip of a rapier scabbard suddenly blocked her reach. Kaira raised a confused eyebrow at Qual, who unsheathed Mourning-Song just enough to reveal a deep red glow and she clearly heard a humming sound emanating from the blade. "What the...?" she mouthed silently, drew her hand back to her belt, and fumbled with the clasp on her sheath. With an unsteady hand, Kaira brought forth her dagger. *Qual's rapier senses something evil in... a bucket? Is this standard fare for all the nondescript warehouses in Middletown?* The sturdy half-oryk woman glanced back and forth from the bucket to Qual. His grim, uncharacteristically serious expression alarmed Kaira, however she remained still and continued to observe. The elf wore a thoughtful scowl and his brow furrowed as he motioned her aside with his free hand and began to reach into a hidden pouch in his doublet. Qualthalas visibly winced and bit his lip at the careless motion, barely stifling a cry as the pain from his broken fingers came rapidly back. He would have to do something about that.

A light, lyrical verse came out of Qual's lips as he cradled his injured hand in the palm of the other while a soft golden light flowed through his fingertips. Kaira felt entranced any time she watched him use this kind of magic: Song-Magic. The elf was a bit of a dabbler in many forms of spellcasting, claimed proficiency in a few schools, and was notably skilled when it came to Enchantment in particular. Bardic magic though, rated Qualthalas at a whole other level; his proficiency made even the stodgy wizards stuck up in their musty towers take him seriously. He had yet to meet his better when it came to the weaving of this Celestial form of spellcasting. Qualthalas could strum a lute, finger a harp, play a flute, dance, and sing, while weaving extremely sublime, powerful magic through the chords and notes. When he cast bardic spells, it was as if things fit into their places, thoughts and feelings felt much more real; everything made *sense*.

In the Sillistrael'li tongue, he intoned a healing verse: "I'ihil-no thraes; so tauh-minh'u-auh eyah-ir, Auri-il-to suraes; Tar'a-auh hinh'u'eyah-ir, Su-ril-to, I'ihil-raes." Translated to Mithrainian, the spell became, *'Fly to me swiftly, light, and carry away pain, restore my might, soothe like rain.'* The verse carried rhyme and cadence in both languages. In fact, therein lay the secret to lyrical song-magic. With an increased understanding of how the syllables related and how, in other languages – especially the ancient ones – if the composition of words still made sense, they carried a truth that empowered them; made them magical. Qualthalas understood nineteen different languages, both contemporary and ancient, and meticulously translated a variety of his verses such that he could weave this spell in eight of them. This made even a rudimentary casting increase doubly in magnitude. Even the renowned Sae'Ret-ii Clerists of his people envied his skill; with years of training and medical practice, most could not heal a wound as swiftly as Qualthalas was capable.

As the radiance coursed through his outstretched fingers, the bones in Qualthalas' crushed hand reset seamlessly and painlessly. Luminous motes of healing energy repaired the internal lattice formation surrounding the marrow. His tendons and muscular structure were restored undamaged, perhaps even minutely better than before. The bloodied and bruised tissue surrounding the muscle became whole: supple and strong again in moments. Soon after, the soft surface of Qual's skin became smooth and taut, free of blemish or scar. It was widely accepted that magical healing could provide increased natural longevity to mortals. Sages who studied the obscure history of the moon elves postulated that the ancient progenitors of the race had utilized restorative magic so extensively through the millennia of their evolution that it provided them with the near immortality they purportedly possessed. Strangely, though, Qualthalas knew of only perhaps thirty of these ancients living in the Sillistrael'li kingdom, the eldest of which, like his grandfather, were tens of thousands of years old. Qual was only aware from historical accounts of a few that had died from 'natural' causes and it led him to wonder where some of the others could be dwelling. Even considering the low birthrates of their race, there certainly should have been hundreds, possibly even thousands of elves who were that long-lived by now. The current dynasty was so old that Qualthalas assumed that most of them had disappeared of their own accord. Perhaps the ancient moon elves had journeyed to other planes of existence, however, even considering that possibility, why were there no records of their current exploits or whereabouts? Qualthalas felt it odd that his grandfather had never discussed such things with him, and it occurred to him it was equally strange he had never thought to ask.

His thoughts off on that tangent, Qualthalas broke from his musing when Kaira hissed in warning, pointing upwards to the rafters. The elf smirked, wishing his lover had not looked up. She saw what Qualthalas had earlier observed whilst he lay paralyzed, forced to stare at the room's ceiling. Countless cruel crimson eyes within silvery strands of spider silk hung there, motionless and silent, waiting for something to release them to sate the irresistible thirst for the warmth that flowed through the veins of the two figures below.

"So, let me reiterate my disapproval of your plan to overturn that bucket and expose the sigil underneath, thereby releasing these… *lovely creatures,*" the elf declared, extending his arm with a flourish along the breadth of the suspended things. The performer in him was all showmanship, but Kaira's face twisted in utter revulsion for the mass of unmoving creatures above. Perhaps he would see her panic after all. Qualthalas had mercifully decided to omit the fact that they were, more accurately, hundreds of *undead* spiders. Why quibble over the trivial details anyway?

The thirsty vampiric arachnids were not of primary concern to Qualthalas – after all, unless that sigil was disturbed, they would hang in suspension indefinitely – it was moreso the underlying intimation that these creatures were part of an elaborate trap. Although any sufficiently powerful diabolist or warlock could create such a magical ambush, the meddlesome elf had a sinking feeling that he knew exactly who was behind this predicament. To be more precise, Qualthalas felt the hand of the shadowy individual he was pursuing through his prying investigation of Morningmist: a dark power insinuating itself into every facet of the political structure of the decadent city. In the deadliest of secret cabals, and among the few scions scattered across Antiqua who guessed at the extent of his power, the very mention of the indigo elven Darklord's name spread fear: Zhiniel Al-Nistir Szord'Ryn – the *Soulharvester*.

Chapter 4

THE TRUTH ERASED

Hand mended and hurt feelings brushed aside, *for now, Kaira,* he thought indignantly, Qual again reached into the secret pocket woven into his leather doublet, to bring forth an ampoule of silvery liquid. Rather, it was a translucent mixture infused with silver strands that pulsated and writhed as they wormed their way through the fluid, seemingly alive. Though not truly *living* in the strictest sense, the strands possessed an infusion of natural magical energy with a specific purpose. Qualthalas hoped his suspicions were wrong; perhaps the diminutive identification worms (as he termed them) would become inert or display the banner of some hedge-wizard in the employ of one of Morningmist's merchant guilds. The elf gingerly opened the stopper and watched as a few drops of the hard-to-procure substance hit the floor near the overturned bucket atop the magical sigil that controlled the deadly spider trap. Qual's hopes faded when the strands immediately transformed to an indigo hue, and the liquid reformed into a symbolic marking that prominently portrayed a nine-chained flail protruding from a broken spider web. Qualthalas forced out a heavy sigh.

"Well, that settles it," he muttered bitterly as he capped the vial, absentmindedly tucked the precious liquid back into its hiding place, then gazed pensively at the mark upon the floor. Qualthalas scowled and scratched at his chin, not bothering to explain his vague statement further. A bewildered and still shaken Kaira propped him up with one arm; her other hand remained tightly wrapped around the handle of her knife. She looked to the faintly glowing mark quizzically, then back to Qual, and cocked her head to the side, clearly annoyed at the dubious silence of her motionless companion.

Kaira felt a deep urge to slap the perplexing moon elf silly, as if it would do any good. After staring at him expectantly for another tense few seconds, Kaira lost patience and blurted out her thoughts, "Would you *mind* letting me inside that rats-nest of a brain for a moment and explain to me what the Hells this all means?" She twisted the elf's smaller frame to confront him directly, putting her face directly in front of his, to inspect Qual's expression. The calculating, contemplative look upon the elf's face spoke volumes to Kaira, and she let out a gasp of sudden realization. "This is *it*, isn't it? What you always hide – this means something to that *mission* of yours that you never talk plainly about; this is the thing you conceal from everyone…" she paused to emphasize the final two words, "…even *me*."

Qualthalas gave her a sheepish half-smirk and his customary shrug of casual dismissal, as if the matter was merely a trifle. He opened his mouth to speak, but Kaira was not interested in giving him the chance to spout yet another half-truth to her. The proud half-orykan woman drew back her leg, growled and made as if she was going to kick something with *tremendous* force. Qual bit his tongue and winced, fearing the pain she would inflict, until he realized that she was aiming at the bucket on the floor. His almond-shaped eyes went wide. "Kaira…" he started, in an alarmed, warning tone. She met his eyes, and the ice-cold serious look she displayed told Qual that she was not at all bluffing.

"*No, you e'ghek-Kha – don't.*" she warned him, emphasizing each word (*especially* the Orykan curse-phrase) as it left her lips. Her tirade continued, "I will *launch* that Gods-Be-Damned bucket if you don't start talking, Qual, and whatever you vomit forth will contain truth in this matter: *fact*, if that can even be had from you. Why are we here?" Kaira's voice trailed off as a much more specific question for the *cornered little rat* presented itself. "No, better yet…" she paused and narrowed her eyes dangerously, to make it clear she would not tolerate further deflection, "…*who* planned this; *who* set this trap?"

With a twist and a step back, Qual turned away before he spoke. Kaira imagined it was because he was about to tell a stupendous lie, but in truth, Qualthalas desperately fought to conceal how shaken his revelations had made him. He started speaking plainly, almost casually, but as the moon elf continued, his voice rose and at times faltered as if he was choking on ash.

"You've heard of the Indigo Elves, Kaira? Once, my ancestors and they were of one people, you know." Qual began with a wistful tone, which soon became a rolling crescendo. "The dark matriarchs of the Daemon-Queen Ennetra that scheme and plot from deep within the bowels of the planet – mere legends, right?" The sarcasm on his lips practically dripped off them as he continued. "No one has seen or heard from them in centuries, so they stay in the storybooks and scary-tales that humans tell their children to keep them quiet." In a voice that imitated a mother threatening her child for disobedience, shrill and condescending, he preached, "*If you don't eat your peas and carrots*, the *Dark Ones* will snatch you up and take you to the centre of the earth to devour your soul!" He chuckled at this, but the sound was both biting and bitter.

Qualthalas paused, waiting for her to respond, raising a hand for silence when the skeptical sigh she exhaled indicated she was not taking him seriously. To Kaira, it seemed like Qual was going off on a *bloody tangent* – was he *really* intending to inform her that the subterranean elves were staging an imminent return to the surface, soon to wreak inescapable destruction on the world? Really, Qual was starting to piss her off... except even as she began to mouth a protest at his ridiculous ranting, he continued in a rising tone, fervent in his speech.

"Have you ever heard of *Fiends*? Not the kind that would steal your coinpurse or cheat at cards, mind you, not even the kind of fiend that kills paupers in a back alley or sells concoctions to the desperate. I speak of the kind they write of in religious texts and the like; *Fiends* proper – ones who subvert mortal will and bargain in souls. The intellect of these profane creatures rivals the Celestial beings – Gods, Angels and the like: Archdevils." Qual paced from one end of the room to the other as he spoke; his agitation became infectious. The pale elf's face scrunched up into a scowl and he was tapping the tip of his rapier incessantly on the tile floor, a habit he rarely displayed except when alone and pondering.

At this outburst, Kaira cocked her head to the side. This ranting was completely uncharacteristic of the usually jovial, never-serious elf. He was bordering on fanaticism, his mannerisms conveyed panic – was he *Gods-Damned* serious? Where was he going with this tirade? She glanced upward at the daemon-eyed spiders and then to the runes peeking out from under the bucket and relaxed her foot. Kicking that bucket over was never in her plan, but apparently the bluff had worked *too* well.

Now Kaira wondered if she even wanted the elf to continue talking. She did *not* like where this was going. It sounded nothing like the kind of 'serious' that one would associate with any of Qualthalas' usual dealings. Previously, 'serious' entailed trouble that ranged from confrontations by former lovers to petty theft, larceny, and the odd break-in to a noble's mansion or two. Minor things like charming the chambermaid of a certain *Lord of House*

Ravantheos and going through some of his documents... she was still not sure what that had been about, but she did remember the wild tryst the three of them had in the noble lord's luxurious bedchamber. Great fun, that. This did not speak of a fun kind of involvement at all. This sounded like *World-Changing-Serious* – impossible from Qualthalas.

"Shut up, Qualthalas." Kaira displayed an unamused scowl, but the intensity of his narrowed eyes and the twitch of his eyebrow worried her. He looked *angry*. She bit her lip and took a slow step back, observing his peculiar and uncharacteristic mannerisms. Qual's normally unflinching hand grasped Mourning-Song so tightly that the silver blade vibrated visibly. As if deaf to her words of rebuke, he spoke on, "Did you know that Archdevils can actually *breed* with the mortal races?" His voice trailed off, and he spoke quietly now, as if quoting text, "...an engineered product of the union of the *Infernal* and the *Cursed*." Qual looked at Kaira; it seemed his diatribe had ended, but the elf made one final statement to her. "I pursue the shadowy undercurrents, the whispers and subtle hand of an indigo elven half-*Fiend*, one bent on the domination of our whole world, Kaira." Then, she watched a sudden softness grow in Qualthalas as he whispered into her ear, "*Sae'iss-Serenh.*"

Confusion washed through Kaira as Qualthalas brushed her cheek reverently with his fingertips. She inhaled something sweet, subtle, and beautiful, and then her memory of the last few minutes – all of Qual's rantings – vanished. Unfortunately for the devious elf, the spell placed Kaira's mind roughly back to the moment when she realized that something serious was indeed afoot. Qualthalas turned away from the stormy eyes of his lover. Unabated, and with narrowed eyes, she inquired, "What in Hells is this all about Qualthalas? *Why* were we led here... no, *who* led us here into this trap?" She gripped the elf's cloak and spun him around, somewhat puzzled amid her frustration – *was he facing her only a moment ago?* Holding him before her, Kaira locked eyes with her long-time lover, friend, and partner. Unblinking, he replied, "I haven't the slightest clue what this is all about, my dear. We'll have to figure it out together." He smiled pathetically. Strangely, she believed every word.

Qualthalas probably had more enemies than he could ever remember. His stories abounded with run-ins with thieves, nobles, wizards, and monsters. Kaira finally removed her fist from her hip, leaned back and stifled a chuckle, matching his half-smirk with her own. Qual admired her figure for a moment, the strange beauty that captivated him: those full, charcoal-painted lips complete with elongated lower canines (*they* had taken some time to get accustomed to, especially in the tender moments), the tone of her grey-green skin, which was smooth, but tightly muscled. She wore her hair in short, tight curls of auburn: the cut of a warrior-woman. The reddish-brown eyes with those dark, impossibly long lashes – even with the remnants of her streaking eyeliner staining her cheek, she looked beautiful. His fingers traced a line down her slender neck.

His eyes lingered on Kaira's *giant* bosom. Qual ducked this time as the slap came at him fast. It was playful though: she had caught him taking his time looking her over and enjoyed it. The seductive, suggestive magic he'd used to suppress her memory had the additional effect of removing her inhibitions. Cloak still gripped tightly in her hand, Kaira roughly pulled Qualthalas backwards and hopped up to sit atop the table, her legs spread wide; they invited him into their embrace. She tugged him into the crushing grip of those powerful thighs and felt him startle. Her eyes drew his soul in, and he was powerless under her own charming magic. This was certainly not the time or place for this kind of attention, but *what the hell?* The two had often made love in far stranger circumstances.

Chapter 5

SUBTLE HAND OF THE SOULHARVESTER

A scowl, divided into equal parts disgust and intrigue, played upon the sinister face of Zhiniel the Soulharvester as he observed the lovemaking antics of his prey through use of a scrying screen. Before him, the images flashed in clarity upon a gigantic crystal apparatus that resembled a large and ornately adorned octagonal mirror. The huge device rotated clockwise slowly, marking the passage of time, magically suspended a few metres above the cold obsidian floor of the chamber. Its housing, carved from interlocking pewter and bone designed to resemble an intricate spider's web, came to a razor point of meteoric adamantium at each of the octagon's edges. When inert, the crystal appeared as a perfectly smooth, opaque iridescent material and emanated a chill aura that would freeze living flesh if one dared touch it. Upon activation, it crackled with energy and radiated a searing heat in contrast to its inactive state, revealing any attuned location, person, or object its master willed.

The artifact was a marvelous prize, earned by destroying the *Sacrificial Sanctum* of one of his rivals, Archpriestess Kaereth-Re'Unan, a merciless templar of the dark Daemon-Queen,

Ennetra. The abyssal Demigod's clergy were notoriously ruthless and cunning. Re'Unan, as their uncontested matriarch, was the prime example of wanton abuse of the powers granted by a corrupted immortal. The mighty Temple of the Black Circle was generally uncontested, except by the most cunning and ambitious of the Sovereign Syndicates; the influential and factional rivals that simultaneously ruled and warred ceaselessly within the deep elven citadels.

With a mirthless smile the once-renegade indigo elf recalled the look of shock and rage expressed by the *'Highest Priestess'* when he, the *'Upstart Necromancer'* stormed unabated into her vestibule. Incredulous that a lowly male arcanist dared profane her sanctum with his tainted presence, Re'Unan wore an expression that would change many times over in the Soul Harvester's subsequent siege upon the grand temple over which she presided. Fourteen hundred years had passed since, yet Zhiniel smirked cruelly at the distant but poignant memory. The event proved a pivotal turning point in his rebellion and subsequent bloody conquest of the indigo elven metropolis, *D'zurien-To'th*.

The Darklord had begun the confrontation by casually pitching an armoured, decapitated head before Re'Unan's feet. The dark priestess recognized the ornately sigiled obsidian helm: it belonged to her dedicated bodyguard who had served, in the matriarch's own words, as *'The Manifest Voice and Fist of my Will'*. The macabre *thing* had rolled several times, landing sloppily on the polished stone floor of the shrine, scraping and clanking before it came to a rest only a few metres from her throne. Re'Unan stared at it, her face becoming expressionless, as the necromancer approached the steps leading to her dais.

"You deserve better company, *Matriarch*." Zhiniel spat as he boldly strode forth, his war-flail painting the floor in the blood of her followers as it dragged by his side. The nine lengthy chains snaked along, following the powerful necromancer, chattering, and scraping across the ground behind him. An acid smile reached across his lips as Zhiniel finished his short speech, "That is, you *would* have deserved better company, *Kaereth*, had you fully grasped the ramifications of denying my earlier proposal. It was non-negotiable." His powerful plated gauntlet raised the massive flail out to shoulder height, its chains slick with dark blood that dripped off the curved barbs adorning each link. As if to emphasize the point, Zhiniel snapped his wrist, sending a spattering of crimson across the adjacent wall. The chains shook violently, and the wicked edges of each of the nine heads gleamed, still thirsty.

He wondered in what way she would react... though he cared not. Regardless of her response, the fate of the Archpriestess was sealed, and Zhiniel would savour killing her so much more than the slaughter of her followers and favored bodyguard. Would she start the confrontation with words, weapons, or divine magic? She wielded them all with might and skill, mercilessly destroying or dominating any obstacle in her path to the throne, until she had finally reigned as uncontested Matriarch of Ennetra. Terribly beautiful, powerful, and resplendent in the red and black silken robes of her order, Re'Unan stood, intimidatingly tall compared to the upstart before her. Beyond her considerable reputation, she presented a striking figure of authority. Re'Unan's devotion to her own ambition was admirable in Zhiniel's estimation; conversely, he had nothing but contempt for the Daemon-Queen she relied upon to fuel her power. Zhiniel anticipated with delight this encounter: this *display*, since the moment he had planned it. At length, Re'Unan broke the long silence the two shared as they faced each other, addressing Zhiniel as she might a servant or a spoiled child.

"*Upstart*, your brash intrusion comes as a welcome surprise, despite what you may think. The monotony of rule must be broken on occasion by a radical such as you." The high priestess caressed the cool surface of her throne, the seat of power over all Ennetra's clergy, before continuing, "It serves to teach others that subordinates who forget their place in the weavings of the web need to be made examples of, every so often." Though her words were ice-cold, Zhiniel detected a decided edge in her voice, a slight quivering that belied an uncontrolled rage building behind her callous demeanor. The Soul Harvester's assault upon her Sanctum was an insult: a direct challenge to her position and the accepted way of life their race had adhered to for millennia, under the thumbs of the highborn masters of the Syndicates and the cruel ministry of the Black Circle.

The Darklord remembered clearly, how her knuckles whitened as her half-mailed fist clenched, imbued with daemonic force. Chaotic energy pulsated with each word as it left her blood-painted lips. The crushing weight of her might sprung forth with crackling flames in the form of a titanic maul, which the Matriarch of Ennetra gripped tightly in those terrible clawed gauntlets: the hallmarks of the Daemon-Queen's high priestesses. From his early life, Zhiniel was intimately familiar with the merciless touch of similar devices used for torture, sacrifice and pleasure alike. Closing her eyes, Re'Unan formed a dark prayer in her thoughts to give praise and a promise of blood offering to the Daemon-Queen she so fervently worshipped. Once she reopened them, her entire painted countenance shone with fanaticism and dark faith in herself as Ennetra's champion. Unflinching, the younger indigo elf necromancer met the evil priestess' gaze patiently, knowing she would continue her speech. He bided his time, relaxed as he gathered mana through meditation, cycling spell formulae through his thoughts while she would prattle on.

"You believe, *erroneously*, that your power is greater than that of the Black Circle. If anything, oh, self-appointed *Soulharvester*, you have bolstered the will of the Sovereign Syndicates and the Temple to band together to crush you. You have made our union *stronger*." With that last intonation, Zhiniel watched as the highborn priestess grew slightly in stature, seemingly vested in power by her evil queen. The fact that he had forced the Temple of the Black Circle to form an alliance with the Syndicates pleased Zhiniel immeasurably; it was undeniable proof of the level of threat he posed to their existence.

Indeed, the Temple and Syndicates reaped extreme power at the price of sacrifice and subservience to the Lords of the Nether Realms; however, Zhiniel would bow to none. The greatest liability of the evil church was, in his estimation, its dependence on the investitures bestowed by a Demigod that constantly demanded blood offerings and unwavering devotion. It was no true power, only a borrowed strength; a characteristic he considered a detriment. This he knew; *this* he would prove to the arrogant female who stood unchallenged by any power, save his own, for centuries.

The Darklord felt a growing malevolent presence as it approached from somewhere beyond the cold grey wall of the chamber to his right. He sensed an unnatural disturbance of the psyche: a void within the spiritual currents of the area. The sensation became a torrent and then there was an unmistakable heat emanating through the stone; beyond this plane entirely was its origin. A brief merging of two dimensions, as the thing gated in, caused a reaction in the natural rock of the cavern; already it became red hot and started to bubble. He recognized the aura, which to his attuned senses veritably reeked of the seething chaos of the Abyssal Planes. A daemon approached. Whether it was a summoning of hers or simply bound to service, Zhiniel could not ascertain, but undoubtedly it protected the evil priestess and was here to slay him. He focused and smiled internally, for he too had the means to call upon otherworldly entities to do his bidding.

The necromancer narrowed his eyes at the priestess and sneered with derision. Zhiniel's flowing robes and chain armour swept to both sides as he purposefully took an arcane channeling stance, his feet planted firmly upon the chamber floor. The Soulharvester recalled a high magnitude summoning formula locked in his mind while simultaneously he performed the complex series of hand gestures required to unleash the magical energy of the ritual. *"Nya'leth So'aeari Oaniss-Drah,"* he uttered in the cold voice of death embodied, slamming the palm of his hand down to curse the ground at his feet. Frost formed in rings filled with necromantic symbols amid a great trigram adjacent the necromancer, drawing an undead spirit of immense potency from its home in the negative dimension to the material world. *Yrrigothu the Frozen Shadow* it was called; a name feared by any who studied the darkest of arts, for it was a lord of the undead, commanding legions of lesser spirits through its sheer dominant will. The Elder Void-Wraithe coalesced, nightmarish, dark and terrible, as the very shadows of the room were drawn into its shifting, nebulous form. Jagged black runes and the scent of musty decay surrounded the entity as it fully entered the plane.

Zhiniel addressed the creature with a deep measure of respect, "I trust you to deal with the wretched daemon that approaches." Eyes like ruby shards glittered with malevolence from within the cold empty space of the wraith's face as the necromancer continued, "As your prize, I permit you to harvest the soul energy of the daemon and that of any other creature foolish enough to challenge you." Zhiniel paused while the creature acknowledged the contract with a vague nod of approval and a sound like tortured screams issued from its form. "After your feast, I bid you: return to your demesne and inform your peers that the sanctum was sundered utterly, and its inhabitants will be theirs to reap. I will personally deliver the essence of its slain matriarch to the Eight as completion of my end of our contract."

Zhiniel's gaze passed from the writhing torrent of shadowy souls to the wall nearby. Searing heat rolled from the red-hot stone as the minotaurean monstrosity burst forth, reducing the cavern wall to molten slag at its feet, so intense was the abyssal fire wreathing its colossal form. Though impressive, Zhiniel knew the creature was no match for the potent Void-Wraithe. As a lord of its kind, Yrrigothu commanded abilities beyond those of lesser undead spirits. Its reach extended into other planes of existence, slipped past barriers with its incorporeal form and devoured soul energy with a voracious appetite for both life and mana. Formed from raw chaos, fire, and pure destruction, the daemon's vitality bore a tantalizing scent. The horrific thing lowered its forward-swept black horns and spit fire from its sulfurous nostrils in challenge to the deathly spirit, who writhed with malicious delight. Tendrils of shadow snaked out to envelop the daemon, while the abyssal creature tried to phase partway back to its home plane in defense against the attack. Satisfied, Zhiniel turned his attention back to the Archpriestess.

Re'Unan raised an eyebrow in disbelief and scoffed openly. Although thoroughly impressed that the younger necromancer possessed the influence to call upon such a being, she obviously felt Zhiniel's assumption of victory in this endeavor an overestimation of his own power. "You forget, *young Master Szord'Ryn*, that I am capable of commanding untold force, through the magnificence that is Ennetra!" Her voice rang with power when she spoke the name of the Daemon-Queen whose dark blessings infused her with spiritual might. She cared not for the fate of her daemon protector and ignored the furious battle between it and the Void-Wraithe. She would deal with it in time, after she forced the rebel to his knees and made him beg for a swift death. Re'Unan glanced wickedly at the decapitated, helmed head that Zhiniel had so conveniently tossed at her feet; far superior to these underlings would be the aid of another of Ennetra's High Clerics.

Re'Unan spoke Daemonic words of divine supplication and extended her fingertips toward the jet-black helm that lay cold on the stone nearby. The Matriarch raked her clawed gauntlet across her forearm, offering her own vitality in solemn sacrifice to the Daemon-Queen. Her blood drenched the obsidian throne, flowed like a stream to the lifeless head before her, darkened to crimson as it enveloped the entirety of the helm. At Re'Unan's command, the lifeless thing levitated, and the lithe, naked body of a beautiful indigo elven woman began to re-form from the neck down, brought back to life through immense force. Her eyes rolled back in the ecstasy of absolute self-satisfaction as the daemonic power of her Demigod mistress coursed through the Archpriestess. Ennetra's will brought the body and soul of the slain elven woman back to the corporeal realm once more. Nevertheless, when she brought her visage triumphantly to meet that of Zhiniel Szord'Ryn, her expression turned to suspicious shock. He had begun to cackle an evil, maniacal, mocking laugh that chilled her soul.

"Resurrection is indeed a remarkable boon your Daemon-Queen has granted you for your sacrifice." Zhiniel spoke, cruelly, sarcastically, after his laughter abated. "As you just said, you truly are capable of wielding untold force, through the *magnificence* that is Ennetra." Zhiniel's hollow and derisive repetition of her earlier praise for the Demigoddess echoed through the chamber and the Darklord bore a frown of mock sympathy as he continued. "It is unfortunate for you, that she deigned to permit that power to course through you, dear Kaereth. You fully believed you were returning your *dear* high cleric to life when in fact, you have done *me* a service."

Zhiniel gently extended his gauntleted hand to caress the bare shoulder of a woman whose eyes matched his own in their intensity and furor. Casting the obsidian helm aside to reveal her long scarlet hair, the indigo elven warrior turned directly to face the Archpriestess, smiling wickedly. *What deception was this?* The evil Templar stepped back as panic struck. *This was not her bodyguard!*

Taking a bold step forward, the Soul Harvester rebuked his rival for her foolish assumptions and her inability to predict his cunning, "You are undone, you egotistical *Slae'Lilith-Pah!*" Zhiniel spat the barbed insult with vengeant wrath. "Bear witness to the return of my Dark General, the *Dreadheart* Zaeliar'a Szord'Ryn."

Zhiniel had successfully manipulated Re'Unan into resurrecting *Soulthorne*, his sinister concubine. Zaeliar'a was a betrayer of the entire indigo elven society, having pledged her fealty to the Darklord when he made his bid for supremacy over the Sovereign Syndicates and the Temple of the Black Circle. She was by his side the lightless day he delivered his chilling ultimatum upon the obsidian steps of the Sacrificial Sanctum of Ennetra. "Serve me in life... or in death," were the shocking words Zhiniel had delivered to the assembled delegates of the Syndicates and to Kaereth-Re'Unan herself, in the centre of the city. The underground labyrinthine metropolis of D'zurien-To'th housed three hundred and twelve indigo elven consortiums, noble and lesser, each pledging loyalty to one of the Sovereign Syndicates or the Temple of Ennetra. In the years after his astonishing and seditious decree, the Syndicates' agents, bolstered by the might of Ennetra's Templars, managed to capture, and execute Zaeliar'a publicly for rebelling against the law of their society by openly serving the revolutionary necromancer. Zhiniel had summarily vowed to the entirety of D'zurien-To'th that she would return to wreak vengeance upon the Syndicates and the Temple. Moreover, here in the flesh she was – returned to the Darklord's side by the power of the Archpriestess herself. The joint wrath of Zhiniel and Zaeliar'a soon laid waste to Re'Unan and the clergy of her Sanctum in the hours that followed.

The Darklord shifted his focus back to the present as the memory faded into the dark recesses of his calculating mind. He observed in earnest, annoyed and still incredulous as, in the throes of passion, the moon elf nearly kicked over the bucket covering the sigil-trap. The Soulharvester would not allow happenstance and carelessness to be the death of his enemy; Zhiniel's meticulous plans for the elf lord were far too important to allow him to die with his pants around his ankles. Long ago, he noticed Qualthalas' attempts to counter some of his subtler plots upon the continent of Huromithra, and the Soulharvester developed grand designs for the unsuspecting bard. The roguish elf was undoubtedly nosy and an annoyance, a liability in that respect; however, Zhiniel knew how vital the *Crown Prince of the Moon Elves* could be to his endgame. Thus, he crafted intricate schemes, allowing the heir to the Akir'Aelyph-Ana'ii dynasty to thwart some of his agendas, if only to keep abreast of Qual's position. Zhiniel fed Qualthalas' suspicions through years of manipulation, led him into plots of intricate weaving, to position himself to take the elf's considerable soul energy for his own, and if possible, subvert him as a willing servant. Failing that, the pale elf would make a powerful undead ally, if his meddling ever necessitated killing him outright. Perhaps by then, Zhiniel would have learned more of the Crucible of Souls, the cosmic forge in which the supreme entity known only as 'The Balancer' could constitute and engineer the *Four Cornerstones of Existence: Mind, Body, Will and Self.*

The Darklord sighed an impatient breath. The delay compelled him to further deploy his agent to force Qualthalas further into the depths of the labyrinth below the warehouse. This was taking too long, and the indigo elven ruler had pressing matters to attend. Zaeliar'a had recently returned from the deep, well-hidden realm of the magma gnomes. He recently dispatched her to retrieve a coveted artifact: a tablet of powerful magical and technological energy and purpose. From another realm where magic was subtle, unseen – and largely dismissed as fable – the object held the key to understanding the fusion of advanced energy manipulation and the incarnate force of magic. Zhiniel employed teams of devotees and subjugated captives to unlock the secrets of several similar objects sought and acquired over hundreds of years. This object possessed a unique characteristic he needed; it held the capability to link all these technological marvels buried in the past and unify them in conjunction with the sublime power of magic.

It was a potential that demanded decades of intense study for, in this world, the technology required to utilize the object simply did not exist–yet. However, Zhiniel knew that once he possessed the artifact and began to unravel its secrets, the time investment would yield the path to his ascension. Considering the thousands of years already spent in the pursuit of forbidden knowledge and power, the dedication required to reverse-engineer the device was of little consequence. He could afford patience in this pursuit. The necromancer supreme sat at the verge of pulling the final lynch pins remaining that would topple the establishments of the surface world; he had assured conquest hundreds of years prior. Now, he was simply biding his time.

With what he had already gleaned from the devices and facilities excavated from ruins and remains of civilizations from eons past, the Darklord had developed technology far superior to anything dreamed of by the most ambitious of human scientists. Already he had implemented blends of engineered bio-enhancement supplemented by potent arcanism and necromancy in countless test subjects, and now he commanded several operatives outfitted and trained in their use. Eventually, this tablet would bridge a critical gap he had yet to overcome in truly combining the art of the arcane with the science of technology. The object held fundamental data on methods of seeding vast superuniverses with the necessities to produce superior, dominant life forms. Unlike the mortal races of Antiqua, purportedly forged by their respective progenitor Gods of myth, these engineered creatures existed purposefully: meticulously *crafted* by the hand of their creators. The very building blocks of matter and soul were once manipulated and injected by alien beings whose true power and purpose the Darklord only theorized. Zhiniel felt it his manifest destiny to become that form of being: he sought a supremacy beyond the power of the Gods, and this ambition knew no bounds.

Zaeliar'a had sent detailed reports conveying the successful retrieval of the tablet in her latest missives. In addition, she had managed to capture a magmic gnome referred to as *the Maguscientist*. Named Candremig Arcostronophix Galflagwindel in the long-winded, titular naming convention of their species, the creature was highly regarded as the chief researcher in something called 'dimensional barrier grafting'. *Soulthorne the Dreadheart* as all his legions referred to her – *never* failed him. Even her legendary capture and subsequent death those fifteen hundred years prior; a calculated risk she had proposed to Zhiniel as a ploy to give the Sovereign Syndicates and the Temple of Ennetra a false sense of strength. The disparate groups needed to feel as if they were gaining ground against the powerful necromancer; she knew their arrogance and underestimation of his power would prove the downfall of both establishments. To show them utter defeat despite their combined forces solidified Zhiniel's death-grip on the entirety of D'zurien-To'th and toppled the outdated societal structure holding back advancement. Zaeliar'a demonstrated that her faith in him was *literally* great enough to overcome death.

Zhiniel, though truly heartless, genuinely appreciated her zeal. He admired her unwavering capacity to dedicate herself to his service. He knew it was something he was incapable of – *serving*. However, the utter devotion she held for him was different from the mindless obedience that most masters demanded. No, Zaeliar'a saw the wisdom in attaining his ambitions, dedicated her thought and will to his goals, and that strength of purpose gave her immense power. He never forced her intent or subjugated her will, and this simultaneously puzzled and intrigued the necromancer immeasurably.

The Darklord concentrated on the crystal mirror before him and touched its ice-cold surface with the tip of his long, slender index finger and incanted a few words of unbinding, "Tereth-Ren'Nia Areh Oruo-*Cassat*." The last syllable seemed to echo in the obsidian room as the magic traversed the vast distance between his location deep within the crust of Antiqua, to the warehouse in which Qualthalas and Kaira remained trapped. The effect gradually unraveled the sigil suspending the undead arachnids above the two suddenly panicking lovers, who were now scrambling to retrieve their garments, hastily making their way towards the only apparent exit to the room – a trap door in its furthest corner. A sliver of a dour smile etched upon his face, Zhiniel Al-Nistir Szord'Ryn leaned in and whispered, "Make your way to the cheese, little rat." He then turned on his heel, the woven chains of his robe sweeping behind him as he exited the scrying chamber, satisfied.

The *Soulharvester*, Zhiniel Al-Nistir Szord'Ryn

Chapter 6

LIES FORGIVEN

Frantically, the mostly naked pair scrambled towards the far corner of the room, as an overwhelming horde of red eyes began to creep like a curtain unraveling, down the wall. It was truly a jarring sight: something from a phobic nightmare. Some dropped directly onto the floor, chittering and hissing; others slowly drifted down on barely visible silver strands to form an unliving sheet of tiny black bodies and innumerable crimson pinpoints of light. Gathering and swirling as a single mass, the tide of death-spiders marched in unison towards the warm, living blood they sensed in the pair of creatures before them, driven by unquenchable thirst.

As Kaira backed up, panic took hold, a defenseless feeling seethed in the pit of her stomach and manifested as a choked-out scream she could not suppress. As she released the wail of terror, the mass of skittering arachnids rushed forth in response. Her heart raced, booming in her chest like it would explode – and the knife she held shook unsteadily in her hand. The dagger would be useless against the tide of evil that crept ever closer, and most horrifying of all was the sheer *multitude* of glowing blood-red eyes that fixated on her. Present was a hungry, burning hatred of life in all the countless thousands of them. Kaira searched her lover's face to gauge his expression. It was calm. Qual's lips parted slightly as he controlled his breathing, steady and rhythmic, his eyes intent upon the horde but not frantic at their advance.

Qualthalas managed to retain some measure of composure, and though images of being sucked dry of all his blood flew through his imagination, he remained stoic and prepared swiftly. Stronger than abstract fear was his resolve to overcome these things and find the underlying cause of the plot lain upon them. The moon elf placed a firm, reassuring hand upon Kaira's bare shoulder, which quelled her panic – momentarily. As the nearest of the creatures leapt at him, Qualthalas dispatched the thing with his humming blade; the remainder paused briefly, which gave the elf just enough time to weave a spell. Deftly the bard made a circular set of steps, chanted lightly while the silvery tip of his ensorcelled rapier danced and glinted, tracing intricate arcs and arcane lines of warding in a small radius surrounding the cornered pair.

"Safe, at least for a few minutes…" the bard winked and assured Kaira softly, as the markings etched upon the floor began to glow a deep bluish hue, "… let us at least *clothe* ourselves before we are consumed by these things? I'd prefer my corpse be *presentable* when it's found." The rakish elf chuckled at his own grim jest. Kaira simply glowered at him as she rushed to pull on her garments and attach her belts and pouches. Her dark eyes showed an underlying desperation, mixed with an abundance of annoyance that Qual could even joke about a situation so dire. "You really *are* an idiot, aren't you?" she said incredulously, to which her companion gave an overemphatic shrug and simply smirked stupidly. *I might as well look the part*, Qual thought. The grin on his face spread as he carefully and – *slowly* – adjusted his breeches and took care to tie the strings such that the lacing was in good order. He dipped low to gather up his doublet, and casually patted it down to make sure it was free of dust. With a frown, Qualthalas fingered at a slight tear in the seam of golden threading near the garment's shoulder, and he cast a critical glare at Kaira.

"I think you ripped one of my better shirts." he accused, feigning indignation. Qualthalas felt that keeping Kaira mad rather than panicked a good move and wore a pouty expression as he glanced at her, gauging the reaction. Kaira's icy stare left nothing to guess. *Mission accomplished*, he thought. Donning the last of his garb, the elf turned his attention to the growing radius of spiders, which swarmed full circle around the pair, kept at bay by his simple enchantment of warding. Mourning-Song continued to emanate the crimson glowing runes along its blade, indicating evil: specifically of an *undead* variety. Qualthalas knelt low, peering at the horde of blazing eyes, their hue matching that of his magical rapier. "Well now, my little scamps, what *shall* we do about you?" He questioned the hissing and rearing creatures as if addressing a crowd of children at a whimsical performance.

Kaira openly scoffed, "Yes, Master Entertainer, what *shall we do* with your admiring fans? Perhaps you can sing them a ditty, or play your flute and charm them out of town?" She stared down to where his backside tempted her increasing ire. She had to fight the urge to kick Qual's rump and send him tumbling into the throng of spiders. *That would serve him right, careless, carefree little elven prick...* Kaira scanned the room again in depth, eyes searching for an exit to this horrible place. Her eyes drifted to the desk and chair with papers scattered atop, and the poster that hung cockeyed above it upon the wall. One of its chains was broken and dangled to the side, still attached to the plain wooden frame. A careful inspection would require a closer look, especially in this darkness, which for now seemed impossible.

She hoped fervently that Qual was just playing at something and had a plan for disposing of the disturbing vermin. Kaira had no innate fear of arachnids, but they *were* disgusting. Her nose crinkled at the familiar scent of death emanating from the little furry, multi-eyed things. *Weren't spiders often minions of the Indigo Aelyphen race?* The thought came to her unbidden, as if there was some underlying reason she should associate them this way, though the rationale felt clouded, and she pushed it to the back of her mind. Qualthalas' mental charm was still actively suppressing her memory. Shaking the thought off, she shifted her attention back to the wall. Finally, she spotted the faint outline of a crack behind the picture that she hadn't noticed before.

Kaira started to say, "Qual, there may be something..." but he completed her sentence, "Behind the picture on the wall? Yes. I was staring at it during our *earlier engagement.*" Qual cocked his head back at her slightly, winking charismatically. "Still puzzling a way to get back over there, my dear, don't fret," he stated, rummaging through an impossibly deep pouch on his belt. The elf's free arm worked around, buried up to the elbow in the dimensional space magically stitched into a concealed flap within the otherwise normal-looking container. Handy items were these for a roguish sort; Qual had picked this one up for a considerable sum through a secretive guild known as the *Cutpurse Consortium,* a rather lofty name for what was essentially a small band of thieves operating primarily in Morningmist. However, the group's proficiency and underworld reputation *did* set them apart from common rabble and came recommended to him by several trusted associates. *Though at times, I wish I had purchased a smaller version,* he thought as he rummaged through the pouch's contents. By touch, it was difficult to distinguish which velvet-lined roll of magical vials he needed, and this vexed Qualthalas every time he needed something in a desperate situation like this one. Again, he vowed to organize and mark the objects it held – *when he had time,* of course.

"Aha!" Qualthalas exclaimed at last, as his slender fingers closed around the familiar shape of the vial containing the substance he needed. Qual's exuberance melted into a sour frown as a few of the death-spiders tested the barrier with their forelegs. The first of the creeping things reared up with its appendages outstretched, touched the barrier, then emitted a tiny popping sound when it was summarily incinerated with a bluish flare. This elicited a bone-chilling simultaneous hiss from hundreds of the vermin as they leapt back and crawled all over each other. Then, warily, a vast multitude crept back to the barrier, unable to resist the command of their master. *Press forth*, came the insistent mental command built into the binding spell Zhiniel had used in the ritual of their creation. Against any self-preservation instinct the creatures may have possessed, they began to creep forth in unison, zapping and popping one-by-one as they marched to the deadly ring, concentrated on a single point. Soon they were crawling atop each other, the mass growing steadily taller as they formed a wedge. It would not be long before the arachnids' efforts would weaken the barrier enough to penetrate it.

Bemused, Qual let the words slip, "His command certainly has influence upon you little devils…" Instantly, he regretted opening his mouth (a rare occasion, to be sure.) Qualthalas bit his lip while his eyes darted slyly to see if Kaira overheard his comment. Fist on her hip, composure regained and ire imminent; the elf could feel the woman's hot breath over his shoulder. Normally he would welcome the feeling, however, a raging storm approached. Presently, he might not be able to quell further inquiries: memory manipulation was a tricky thing. The more she had reason to question facts regarding the conversation suppressed in her mind, the more the fog surrounding it would lift…

"Qual," came the tense, flat voice that meant Kaira was suspicious. Of course, he recognised this tone well; he must have heard her use it hundreds of times. *Let's be fair*, Qualthalas considered, *most of what I do is sideways in some way, shape or form. Perhaps she should know the truth.* As if on a rotating platform, Qual lazily turned around and stood to face his lover, ready to admit to everything. The rogue licked his lips, parting them to speak, but before he could utter a word, she put a single finger to them. Her eyes drilled painful holes in him. Qualthalas withered under the sheer weight of the volumes soundlessly conveyed in that one moment: anger, pain, frustration, and disappointment, feelings of betrayal, sorrow… and love. It penetrated every one of Qualthalas' masks, stabbed him through the heart, and made him evaluate deeply – *everything* – that he had done in the years of knowing her. Guilt washed through him and, defenseless against her silent onslaught, a panging remorse reverberated through the fibre of his being. He was disarmed, vulnerable; his entire visage quivered, and words failed him.

Beyond the shamed rogue's reasoning, Kaira enveloped him suddenly in a tight embrace; a release from torment and self denial was her simple gift to him in this moment. For possibly the first time in hundreds of years, Qualthalas felt… *safe*. The feeling emerged as crystal tears that pooled for a second in the corners of his almond-shaped eyes, rolled down his angular cheeks, and came to rest upon the warm, tender skin of the woman he *loved*.

"I am no Enchanter," he stammered, "'Tis *you* who enchants *me*, Kaira. Mine is just charlatanry and parlour tricks, pale in comparison to the magicks you weave without even speaking." He choked out a sob and weakly croaked, "I'm not rightly sure why you've permitted me to be at your side for so long. I…" He could not continue. There was just too much, and all the glibness and wit he possessed was no longer under his command. He just lowered his head and wept openly. After a few more seconds holding him, Kaira gently pushed him back, meeting his eyes for an instant, before turning his shoulders so he faced away from her, then drew him back in, so he could rest upon her chest as he gasped at the sight all around them. *The spiders!* Where there had been a swarm of potential agony and death moments ago, there was now only blackened soot and ashes in a wide circle around them.

"You are stronger and more caring than you'll ever realize, Qual." Kaira spoke plainly, "you did this – when you finally stopped talking, it happened. The circle spread out, silently and swiftly, and they were no more." She continued to hold him quietly and, sharing his moment of realization, allowed him to regain the composure he had left behind. She knew how important his masks and defenses were, how they allowed him to press through the difficult situations his clandestine mission must have presented. Kaira understood him intimately more in those scant moments; she was younger yet much wiser than the elf, whose years outnumbered hers in the hundreds.

The memory enchantment had dissipated when his first tears fell and as she recalled the whole tirade, instead of her normal fury, Kaira had felt *abashed*. Qualthalas would rather try to protect her from the terrible knowledge he possessed; he would challenge a force capable of world domination, and to that end, would leave his home on the silver moon to find himself trapped here in a dank warehouse with her. That meant more to Kaira than the three words neither of them allowed themselves to speak aloud. She knew that sometimes he just needed her unconditional, silent support, so that was exactly what she gave him, and its effect upon Qualthalas was profound.

Letting go of him finally, Kaira strode to the frame upon the wall. It was time to move forward. Whatever that took, whatever the portent, she would be with him, and he with her. Moreover, should that peril lead them to their demise, she would walk into the darkness by his side, unafraid. Feeling him gazing at her from behind, she looked back over her shoulder in the same fashion that his sly personality would have been proud of and winked charismatically. "You coming?" she questioned, "This puzzle isn't going to solve itself; you know." A thin smirk reached across Qual's face as they both chuckled.

Chapter 7

LADY Y'TASZIAH CAMYLLA DEVILSBRIDGE

A brisk draft flowed in through the open window leading to the veranda outside the well-appointed mansion bedroom of Lady Y'Tasziah Camylla Devilsbridge. The heavy purple-and-gold curtains parted gently as they rippled and waved with a light flapping noise that stirred the noblewoman from her slumber. The smooth skin of her bare legs bristled at the chill; the down-filled covers had slipped off in the deep of the night – that, or she had kicked them off, as she was prone to do. Y'Tasziah's dreams had always been dark, nightmarish, and real. Even as a little girl who wanted for nothing, the eldest daughter of an influential noble house had often dreamt of sinister, shadowy things. This night, the croaky whispers and dark feathers of ravens had plagued her throughout lucid slumber. Their voices screeched a cacophony of warnings: *beast within man, blood of the crescent-moon,* and *footsteps in the labyrinth.* Black wings, beating, like her thumping heart, and sinister phantoms at the edge of her thoughts still permeated her subconscious mind.

The uncomfortable feeling, as her spirit slowly returned from the wispy world beyond, left her paralyzed as she lay there, naked amid pillows and sheets. Soaked from sweat, now cold, Y'Tasziah shivered as life returned gradually to her limbs. She stretched out from fingertips to toes, then lightly tapped her feet around in search of the soft violet slippers that lay somewhere on the smooth marble of the floor. The polished stone tiling, though exquisite, did nothing against the chill permeating the room. Y'Tasziah's eyes rolled back, and she extended a bronze-golden tanned hand lazily out towards the fireplace across the room.

"*Atach-Kauss'h,*" she whispered in *the Gloaming Tongue,* a shadowy language native to the Plane of Eternal Twilight where a black sun hung ever on the horizon of its perpetually dusky landscape. Phantoms and other apparitions drifted through its mysterious world of darkness and unnatural fog. Y'Tasziah's mastery of the ancient tongue came through years of forays into the bleak and dangerous dimension, where she sought tomes held in its crumbling libraries and deep catacombs. Twisting purple tendrils wicked out from her fingertips, reached to the mantle, and crawled down the brickwork to a stack of half-charred wood. The ethereal coils wrapped themselves around a small log and gently laid it upon the andiron. Y'Tasziah focused intently on the strands, and they roiled and writhed as she willed them to take on the aspect of flame. The log lit up immediately, cracking and spitting from the infusion of magical fire, and continued to burn even after Y'Tasziah's invocation evaporated into the nether.

The occultist appreciated the more mundane uses for her sorcery, the same magic she attained through a pact made a decade prior with a being that would only identify itself as 'The Enigma'. Research on the entity proved difficult, for the more she found what seemed solid evidence of its nature and home plane of existence, the more she found equally contradictory information soon after. The fact that it was non-malevolent and capable of hiding its origin so well intrigued Y'Tasziah and she actively sought the being out. Through an involved ritual, performed in a precise time and place detailed in the most ancient tome she possessed, Y'Tasziah called out across the planes to the Paradox Lord, hoping for some manifestation of its great power. When the otherworldly being appeared to her in the form of a magnificent corona of billowing violet ribbons and offered to invest in her a portion of its own essence in return for a piece of hers, she had accepted without pause. Thus far, the sorceress had gained new understanding of the occult arts through the tutelage of the entity who was purposeful and meticulous in its teachings. It appeared to her in conjunction with notable planetary alignments and celestial occurrences such as eclipses and solar flares, then drew her into the Eternal Twilight for what sometimes seemed years, though upon her return, only seconds had passed.

Sighing contentedly at the wash of warmth that flowed through her from the radiant heat of the blaze, Y'Tasziah gathered up her amaranthine lace blanket, and purposefully proceeded to make her bed neatly. In contrast to the other contents of her eclectic bedchamber – ranging from tapestries hung on multi-coloured silken ropes, three dressers with various drawers open or closed (lavish garments spilling out of most of them), to the alchemy station with its vials and potions scattered among parchments of scrawled research – the bed itself was immaculate. An heirloom from her estranged mother, Countess Deneille Esqvaulde, the Steeloak-carved canopy bore elaborate etchings of trees and animals inlaid with platinum all along its thick frame. Intricately carved runes wound around each of its four posts in spirals inscribed with Night-Ink, which remained invisible until the midnight hour when they glowed with a dim silvery light. Y'Tasziah had grown up with that bed, remembered fondly how her mother used to patiently brush her long, raven-black hair. It was upon that bed she had learned to apply subtle strokes of makeup, and shared stories of the silly noble boys who kept insistently trying to woo her. She recalled laughing when she told her mother that she had no interest in men...

Now, it was a man she sought. Not for courtship, those years were long past her, though at thirty-seven years of age she could be mistaken for a maid in her early twenties. Her skin was bronzed and smooth, tightly muscled; she had the shapely body of a young woman, having supple wide hips, a narrow waist and – shaking them before her mirror – *perfect breasts*. Y'Tasziah laughed playfully as she admired her reflection in the tall, ornate mirror upon her favorite dresser. She snatched a hand brush from atop its surface and furiously brushed her long, black hair right down to the tips she had recently dyed a sangria colour. Not yet content, Y'Tasziah carefully gathered up all the stray locks above her left temple and braided them tightly to the back of her scalp; it was a look she had seen some orykan women from the South wearing. She liked the wild, fierce appearance of battle-hardened warriors and decided to adapt the style with her own personal flair, adding rich, crimson-coloured beads mixed with pewter clasps, and as a final addition, three polished tigers-eye gemstones. Satisfied, she made a final spin in front of the mirror and clapped her hands with glee.

Next, Y'Tasziah dashed still naked to the alchemy table; its jars, beakers and mysterious devices jingled and tinkled as she rooted through a few drawers until she found what she sought. "The most important morning potion of all," she beamed and cackled, "The wine!" Uncorking the black phial and briefly savoring its bouquet, a deep flowery scent of lilac and vanilla, she took a healthy draw and whistled in a low tone. This was a strong 'Blynh-brew; it was amazing to think that the Gaub races could make such an exquisite vintage. While it was widely known that their alchemical developments were unparalleled on Mithras, most of the Neph'al (which is what the human races collectively referred to themselves as) thought of the Gaub'Blynh peoples as uncivilized and impish. Prone to mischief bordering on maniacal mayhem, the 'Blynh were mostly avoided or shunned in the 'civilized' metropolis of Morningmist, and moreover throughout most of Mithras. Hence, many of their tribes had slowly migrated to the southern continent of Huromithra over the last century or so. Y'Tasziah took another long swig of the savoury wine for good measure and a healthy glow lit up her cheeks – *who gives a damn what 'civilized' people think, I'll gladly trade with 'Blynh again if it means more of this as a thank-you present!*

Thoroughly pleased with herself, Y'Tasziah skipped lightly back to her dressers and carelessly tossed blouse after blouse aside until one struck her fancy – a semi-gloss reptilian leather bodice, adorned with soft black fur. The garment, when drawn tight, displayed her bosom readily but comfortably, and wrapped around to her back, leaving her belly exposed. She flexed her abdomen, toned but not overly muscular, and rooted through a few more drawers. Y'Tasziah spied a belly-button ring which matched the tiger-eye gemstones in her hair perfectly and eased it through the minute hole which was *again* threatening to close. She'd have to decide whether the decoration warranted keeping the piercing. With certain attire, it chafed horribly, and, in many cases, she felt it was more of a nuisance than it was worth. Her gaze naturally followed her bellybutton down... *lower.* She found herself still neatly shaven in that area, though she expected for this meeting, it was likely unimportant. Y'Tasziah was not interested in this man in *that* fashion, though the *information* he claimed to possess highly intrigued her.

Although... she mused, *I've never had an elven lover... perhaps* – she cut the thought short, giggling, and wondered if elves were also short and slender in *that* area. Though Y'Tasziah was not comparatively tall at a height of one and three-quarter metres, she was still taller than most elves she'd ever met. Most of these had been of the wilder variety: ones who lived in arboreal forests to the southeast and twisted bogs to the southwest. The swamp elves, commonly referred to as 'Poison Elves' rarely made forays to large human cities, except to trade for rarities such as imported herbs and worked metals. The Wild Elves from the forest were a mixed bunch: some remained feral and would respond with lethal attacks when encountered in their territories, while several other tribes could be extremely hospitable. Y'Tasziah had once met a small warband camped by a trade route who had taken it upon themselves to hunt road bandits for reward and salvage. The group invited her to the fireside, shared their strong liquor and broke bread together on the path, and Y'Tasziah had learned a little of their strange ways after traveling with them for a couple of weeks. She kept a carved bone dagger that one of their scouts had given her as a memento of the hunts they shared.

The elf she was to meet was, however, a *Moon Elf* – extremely rare on the entirety of the continent and the world in general. Countless centuries past, the pale-skinned subrace had abandoned the planet itself to live on Sillis-Thal'as, using obscure magic and technology to make the silver moon hospitable. Only a handful of the moon elves descended to Antiqua since their exodus; meeting this one would be an event, doubly rewarding considering the information he possessed.

Fumbling around for the last of her garments, she chose the tight-fitting leather pants that matched her top, cinching them up so they just barely covered her hips. Fingerless black gloves, light stockings, and finally calf-high boots followed a belt with pewter clasp, more as an accessory to which she affixed a tight pouch containing some coin. A few bangles slipped over her wrists, onyx earrings, and lastly, she finished the ensemble with her choker from which hung an arcane pendant formed of natural obsidian, which glistened with the familiar purplish hue of her magick.

She made one final spin before the mirror, nodded at herself in approval, and danced like wind to the veranda, swinging fully open the twin doors as she stepped onto the terrace. Y'Tasziah scanned the courtyard below, taking in the vague scent of plum trees mixed with the sweet aroma of the hard-to-cultivate cherry blossoms, which were soon to lose their blooms. She took pause a moment, gazing over Devilsbridge Estate wistfully. Her mood soon cheered as she made her way to the edge of the veranda. It was time to make her way into the city proper to judge this exotic elf's claims for herself.

A spiral staircase of black hardwood topped with an obsidian railing led to the property below. She hopped atop it, sliding down on her bottom swiftly, lighting on the polished granite walkway with practiced ease. She took note of and cordially tilted her head with respect to the few yard workers in the employ of her House whose morning duties brought them out to tend the trees and shrubbery of the mansion. They smiled and waved; Y'Tasziah was always pleasant with each of them, always remembered their names, and treated each with the same respect she might afford to a noble lord or lady.

Although raised amid wealth, both her birth mother Deneille and her stepmother Lady Coeuryn had instilled in her their deep values and willingness to respect people for their merits rather than their pedigree. Ingrained in Y'Tasziah also were the teachings of her father, Lord Orion Devilsbridge, a high-ranking Knight of The Order – a knighthood whose members voluntarily gave up all land, titles, and possessions before their acceptance. His Lordship and seat upon the Council of Morningmist (even if most considered his family the scapegrace among the Ruling Houses) was, unlike many other nobles, hard earned through decades of unwavering service to the populace. As the only self-made Lord on the Council of Thirteen, Orion's honesty and fairness, coupled with his unconventional and outspoken political views often had House Devilsbridge at odds with half of the other Houses, who seemed adept at keeping their wealth and prosperity above all other concerns.

Y'Tasziah glanced back up at the veranda, pointed and snapped her fingers crisply. At her command, the double doors swung together, shut, and latched with a sharp click. She spun on a heel, and marched steadily, hips swaying provocatively as she sauntered along the pathway that led, winding, through the trees of the estate. As she passed a particularly mature plum tree, her hand snaked to snatch a ripe plum from a low-hanging branch and brought it to her full lips. She bit down into the succulent purple fruit. It was perfectly ripe – not too hard, not too soft, sweet, but still slightly tart; she savoured the taste for a few seconds, before swallowing the first bite of its fibrous flesh. Y'Tasziah had a deep appreciation for simple things like this and took every opportunity to turn normal events into memorable moments.

Her duties to the House could at times be dry, boring even, regarding the official activities her station demanded. Conversely, her off-the-book exploits gave the sorceress no room for idly enjoying life's pleasures, except in the rare cases when they involved a coincidental delicious ruse. Y'Tasziah had the associated obligations of being the eldest daughter of a House Lord, with all its politics and posturing, attending events such as Council Chambers, greeting and entertaining dignitaries from other Houses and even provinces, negotiating contracts with merchants and artisans and the like. Then there was the other role – one that required her to tread in shadows lightly. Y'Tasziah was also something akin to a spy and informant; she delved into the illicit affairs that the other Houses tried to hide, both from the populace and from each other in a silently acknowledged power struggle. The information gathered she reported directly to her father, that he might use her findings at Council – in this way, his House alone kept the others in check.

"Bring their schemes to Light, my daughter..." came Lord Orion's impassioned words many years past, shortly after her birth mother had left the family to pursue her own personal journey. "...by observing with keen eyes in darkness, seeing the truth they hide. Make knowledge your weapon–turn their corruption against them. Let Justice be served upon the wicked by their own bloody hands." Her father was capable of intense, passionate speeches; countless rallies in battle and personal campaigns had proven his charisma and ability to influence reaction. Ingrained in him were the qualities of leadership, strict self-discipline and (contrary to the views of most other nobles) a respect for hard labour; virtues that the Order Knights instilled in each of its members. He was a remarkable man; one that Y'Tasziah truly respected and obeyed, not from fear as many Lords demanded of their children, but because he *deserved* admiration. Her capabilities and methods were assets that her father encouraged her to develop; he even knew of her pact with The Enigma, and though he advised care and caution in dealing with the otherworldly entity, supported her decision to pursue the darker aspects of Occultism.

The information that the Aelyph'en man promised, if it were concrete evidence as he claimed, would shake the foundation of the Council. Lord Orion sought undeniable proof of his suspicions of foul play and direct involvement of the heads of two Ruling Houses in the destruction of former House Zennitarr and the assassination of every one of its members. This knowledge was of utmost importance to House Devilsbridge, and to the prosperity of Morningmist as a whole; information like this could lead to a Conciliatory Reform, which is what her father expressed – in outspoken fashion – at meetings of late. It was his view that the Council had been leading the city into turmoil and decadence over the years.

Wealthy and honourable noblemen who utilized their influence to generate prosperity in the capital city first formed the Council; instead, now he felt the current Houses' greed caused further disparity between the rulers and their people. It became more evident the further one moved from the centre of the metropolis. Morningmist touted itself as the pinnacle – the 'Shining Jewel' even – of Mithrainian civilization, yet there remained a steady increase in criminal elements, poverty, and waste. Never in the early history of the capital were slums or red-light districts present in Morningmist, yet now, nobles consistently avoided Middletown and certain other areas due to their increasing reputations for illicit activity. Further still in the outlying quarters, traditionally reserved for craftsmen, hard-working labourers and producers, there were rumours of kidnappings and several unsolved murders ignored by the city watch.

In her father's eyes, this sort of decay would not stand. In a recent internal referendum, Lord Orion had kept his seat on the Council by only one vote, which could bode ill in the coming year if he were unable to reveal irrefutable proof of his fiery claims of corruption within the Council. The accusatory address he delivered had been a calculated risk, meant to incite any wrong-doers into speaking against him, that he may ascertain who directly opposed his House, and it seemed to have worked. Lord Rathimere had stood, *shaking*, spouting that Devilsbridge was a '*rabble-rouser*', and that Orion should be ejected from his Seat for suggesting the city was less than worthy of its title as Capitol of Mithras. Several of the other Lords rose, barking similar things; they did not appreciate the insinuation that they squandered their wealth. The good of the city was, of course, foremost in their policies, and that Devilsbridge should speak less and listen more. Most of these, Orion dismissed as prideful and infantile outbursts from the pompous Lords, but he watched each reaction in turn, and weighed their words with his shrewd perception. Luckily, when Lord Ravantheos, ruler of the First House of Morningmist, rose and cast a critical eye on his fellows and called for silence, they all gawked.

Ravantheos' words chilled them all, for his voice alone could order the vote it would take to discharge a House from its Council Seat. With an unmistakable tone of cynicism, the broad-shouldered Head of Council rose to address his fellows, "Our friend, Devilsbridge, brings a valid point to these often-pointless meetings." He sighed, and lifted a greying eyebrow at his long-time friend, "Orion. I do not speak often at these meetings, so when I deign to address a single House, know that it is with gravity that I ask – what *specific* evidence do you present? Do you name a House Lord or Lady with these allegations, or are they a blanket accusation that the Council *itself* is a corrupt entity?" Lord Devilsbridge quieted at this, reflecting a moment before his reply. He knew the head of Ravantheos was among the canniest and intelligent of men he knew, and perhaps the only one on the entire Council he implicitly trusted.

They had history together beyond the Council – the man had sponsored the younger Lord's entry into the Order Knights nearly forty years prior, and when Orion had been accepted, Estedar Ravantheos was the one to whom Devilsbridge had signed over all his previous titles, land, and holdings. Knights of the Order swore solemn oaths to serve the populace at large, and unwavering dedication to the Knight-Liege they squired under; a term of acceptance meant legally surrendering everything they possessed to another, as the Order felt its members must be forged from a clean slate. Property, entitlements, and pedigree meant nothing to a candidate's acceptance.

At the time, House Devilsbridge was wealthy, and Lord Orion was the master of a small duchy at only nineteen years of age. The choice to give it all up had not been a popular one with his family; they felt releasing land and title, especially to *Ravantheos* whose wealth was already a thing of renown, was a dishonour to the name Devilsbridge. Of course, much had transpired since – Lord Devilsbridge had earned the rank of Impenetrable Shield, among the highest distinctions in the Order. It had allowed him to regain his previous titles upon retirement; his honour was tested and found inscrutable, and it was for this reason that Lord Ravantheos had invited him to the thirteenth seat on the Council of Morningmist upon its vacation after the previous House's destruction. Therefore, Orion's measured response surprised his friend Estedar not at all, when he delivered his speech.

"At this time, I prefer to keep my evidence private, as I build this case, potentially against not a solitary, but *dual* Houses of the Council, who I will prove *conspired* in the downfall of the former Thirteenth House before my appointment." This elicited more than a few whispers and hisses from the other Lords, but both Devilsbridge and Ravantheos took note of those who remained ominously quiet. Sometimes it was silence that spoke volumes, though exactly *what it meant* left an air of mystery. Orion had stepped back, apparently done speaking, content to be abrupt and to the point, unlike his previous castigations which roused the Council into furious arguments. Again, Estedar sighed heavily, shook his head while hiding a wry smile, and raised his hands to call for attention.

"Then, as Head of this Council, my decree: There shall be an open vote – Do we call for Lord Devilsbridge to resign his Seat? The members shall vote immediately, in the open, before I make my *next* proclamation. Those calling for Resignation, show the sign of the Closed Fist, those calling for Continuance, show the sign of an

Open Palm: vote now." Although shocked that Ravantheos would call for an open vote instantly, the Lords knew that his word was law within the Chambers, and summarily, there was a showing of hands within seconds. Neither Ravantheos nor Devilsbridge, of course, could vote. This kept the number of votes to eleven total; in this regard, there would always be a clear count for and against and it proved the impartiality of the Head. Estedar silently hoped his estimations about the vote would play into his plan, and they had. Upon count, there were five Fists calling for Resignation and six Palms for Continuance. More importantly, both he and Orion knew exactly where they stood with the other Lords, or at least, they knew who *openly* opposed the Devilsbridge criticism.

Orion raised a hand to speak after the shifting silence, as the eleven voting Lords cast glances back and forth at each other – it seemed the referendum had revealed to each of them something unspoken about their fellows. He watched with eagle eyes some of the glances between house representatives, seeing furrowed brows on some, thoughtful expressions on others, and unmistakable contempt on the rest. Breaking the palpable tension, Devilsbridge addressed Ravantheos, "You mentioned a further proclamation?" He was intrigued and more than a little apprehensive, unable to guess his friend's intentions for once; Estedar's face was grim, though Orion detected a brief, wry smirk as the Head turned his attention to the whole Council. The closely split vote afforded the Lord an opportunity he had previously lacked the proper excuse to enact. Now he closed in for the kill.

"Now that the vote is passed – *thank you, Gentlemen and Grandesses* – it is my decree that Devilsbridge shall have special dispensation regarding *compliance* with an internal investigation. Meaning, I expect each of the Houses to cooperate with any reasonable request made by Orion Devilsbridge and a single officer chosen from his House." Ravantheos cocked his head at his friend, whose face remained stoic, though his eyes gleamed at his friend's bold play, and intoned, "I expect you shall choose your eldest daughter, Y'Tasziah?" More than a few grim and nervous glances were tossed back and forth between the assembled parties at the mention of the notorious Occultist. The announcement had its intended effect – Y'Tasziah was without peer when it came to uncovering *dirty little secrets*. Even the honest Houses feared her powers.

Seeing the looks of valid concern and mouths about to open in protest, Lord Estedar raised a hand so that he could clarify, "This is insofar as Law would dictate you reveal public domain only – I do not expect confidential records of a *sensitive nature to your clients* be revealed." He gave a reassuring nod, specifically to the Grandesse of House Eres'Felant. His last addendum brought a look of relief to the middle-aged noblewoman's face, apparently diffusing her initial alarm at the proclamation. It was House Eres'Felant that specialized in investment security and archival storage of sensitive materials for the non-conciliatory nobles of Morningmist. Her entire fortune relied upon keeping secrets for others; it would have been a major breach of contract to force her primary company to reveal any of them. As a parting statement, Estedar added, "Since *none* of the Ruling Houses has *aught to hide*, I expect there will be no issue in acquiescing to this decree." The knife-edge of sarcasm, coupled with the finality of the statement left the Council speechless.

After a short pause amid the ensuing silence, and with a grim sigh, he again focused on his old friend, the words echoing in the stone chamber, "Devilsbridge – you have one hundred days, commencing tomorrow, to bring to the Council *concrete, indisputable and specific* evidence of *any* House involvement in the destruction of Zennitarr. If you fail to do so, the Council shall hold another vote regarding your Seat. Is this clear?" Lord Orion knelt before the assembly, fist to chest, head up, blazing eyes raised: the Knighthood could never leave the man. As an Order Knight would swear an oath of truth before his peers, he answered, "I pledge my sword, yes."

Y'Tasziah leaned against a plum tree, lost in these thoughts until she pushed herself off, resuming her previous pace with determination. What lay before her was the first in a chain of tasks crucial to exposing the perpetrators of the eradication of twenty-one nobles and countless innocent people in their employ. House Zennitarr had been a staunch ally and proponent of Devilsbridge long before its destruction, and it was imperative to Lord Orion that they root out the villains responsible. All this and more, Y'Tasziah's father had recounted to her in complete confidence only weeks prior. His tone had been solemn when he tasked his eldest daughter with missions specific to the uncovering of House involvement and collaboration in the destruction of House Zennitarr. It was with this in mind that she lowered her head silently and approached the gated archway that led to the streets of Morningmist. The elf's information would be a crucial first step.

Two heavily armoured guards snapped to attention at her approach; silvered pikes gleamed in the white-blue morning light. Y'Tasziah raised a hand and smiled wanly. "Anything to report?" She asked the question dismissively, not expecting the guards to have encountered anything significant. The older one let out a chuckle while the younger man at his side bristled at the informality and cocked his head sharply at his fellow while he spoke. "Yes, Milady. If it would please you, we shall relate the details immediately." The soldier saluted crisply and raised the visor of his plate-mail barbute. Y'Tasziah could tell the man was young, perhaps a fresh recruit, clean-shaven... *a little green.* The other, who had been in the employ of Devilsbridge for many years, she knew well. Sir Casmein Bhinshier bore a knowing smirk and winked at her.

Y'Tasziah was clearly amused at the strict protocol of the junior officer; Casmein had likely been training the pup in his duties and it was obvious that the boy needed to relax a little. The tension and rigidity he exuded, though certainly understandable in his position, was still humorous to the other two.

Y'Tasziah decided to play along; Casmein knew the lady well enough to know that she might help him break the youth in. House Devilsbridge treated every member in its employ as family. True, her father demanded the utmost discipline and respect in his House, but Y'Tasziah lacked Orion's degree of formality. She preferred being *playful*. She turned crisply to address the younger guard, who stood ramrod straight, waiting for her approval to begin his report. "Your name, soldier?" she barked, gazing directly into his striking, ice-blue eyes. Y'Tasziah shifted her stance, put a hand to her hips, and made sure to highlight her heaving bosom. He was certainly a good-looking young man, in his prime and full of the same desires as other men his age. *Time to turn up the heat,* she thought, internally taking pleasure in the soldier's sudden discomfort. He struggled to keep his gaze intent on her *face* as he spoke.

"Kilbrand Erasmus Teinwick, Milady. First Private of Devilsbridge House Guardsmen Corp Number Three. If it pleases you, we did have somewhat of an occurrence this morning, and it pertains directly to yourself, Lady Devilsbridge." He nodded slightly, politely, but Y'Tasziah noticed his eyes flutter down to her breasts for a solitary moment, though he had tried desperately to keep them level. At this, she crossed her arms tightly, pushing her chest out even further – Teinwick shifted his feet nervously. Y'Tasziah batted her long eyelashes provocatively at the lad. "Continue, *please,*" she emphasized, grinning disarmingly. The young man visibly gulped, and Y'Tasziah relished in the fact that it was likely due to his codpiece becoming suddenly and *uncomfortably* tight.

Trying unsuccessfully to retain his composure, young Kilbrand stammered, "Ah, ahem – an ill-dressed *knave* of a man strolled up to the gate by way of Thoroughfare Avenue 'bout an hour's past the break of dawn. Of course, at his approach, I challenged the man to state his business with House Devilsbridge, to which the ruffian spat upon the cobblestones and practically *grunted* his reply." Again, the young man nodded to accentuate his point, and again he could not control his eyes from drifting downward. They lingered almost imperceptibly upon the ample curvature of her breasts, and he pursed his lips. A bead of sweat made its way down his forehead, coming to rest in the finely groomed eyebrow above his right eye. The older captain drew his lips tight as well, but this was to keep himself from openly laughing at the obvious torment that Y'Tasziah was inflicting on the poor lad. *Probably going to need a cold shower after this shift ends*, he thought, and let out a chortle, forced to turn away so as not to completely lose control and spoil the game.

"And what did this... *vagabond* say?" Y'Tasziah continued, widening her marvelous, painted eyes, locking the lad in a serpent-like stare, "I am *intensely* curious, First Private Kilbrand Erasmus Teinwick of House Devilsbridge Guardsmen Corp Number Three," before adding in a sultry, conspiratory tone, "Was it perhaps something... *inappropriate* for a Lady's ears?" Her face turned eager, almost hungry, as if the thought aroused her and she bit her lower lip as further indication of her arousal at her *naughty thoughts*. She drew uncomfortably near the sweating youth, arching her neck, enticing him to whisper his reply into her waiting ear. "Tell me, were any *dirty* words uttered?"

"T-t'weren't... the words – nay, m-milady," came the stuttering, croaked reply. The stoic prince had suddenly turned into a toad. Kilbrand's face flushed scarlet, dampened with nervous sweat. His breathing became irregular; any semblance of composure went some place along with a rush of blood flooding areas forbidden.

Y'Tasziah took a step back from the struggling soldier; she decided he'd had enough purgatory for now, and looked to Casmein, who no longer hid a nefarious grin. The captain burst into laughter finally, and Y'Tasziah smiled warmly at the befuddled young man. "Be at ease, good Kilbrand, we've just been having good fun at your unfortunate expense. I know you're new, and you've made it abundantly clear you *do* take your duties seriously." She continued, motioning for Casmein to stop laughing, "Your cohort here knows me well; I am not one to stand on ceremony – please don't think of me as the untouchable Lady Devilsbridge, but call me Y'Tasziah and treat me as you would any other." She put a reassuring hand on his pauldron. "What *did* the man say?" she asked plainly this time.

Visibly calmer in seconds, Kilbrand heaved a deep sigh of relief, even smiled slightly. "Well, milady," he began, but corrected his formality, "...*Y'Tasziah*. Ahem he asked me to apologize to you on his behalf, named hisself as Quathlis Ethekeer or some-such, and slipped *this* to me through the gate." Teinwick pulled a sealed letter from his belt, and extended it to Y'Tasziah, who eyed the rolled document curiously for a moment before she took the paper and slid it under one of the straps in her garments. She sensed its enchantment immediately, though she did not mention the fact to either guard. *Better to keep that a secret*, she noted internally. She sensed that Casmein now had something to say, the veteran's countenance seemed serious now, so she bade him speak.

"The man bore a cloak and hood, so I demanded to see his face proper that I might describe him to you, should you ask; I thought it might be relevant to know his true appearance." It was clear that the seasoned captain had been paying attention; he *was* an experienced guardsman, and though the man did enjoy mirth at the expense of his subordinates, he certainly understood his duties. Casmein possessed an exacting attention for detail and the sort of common sense that was less-than-common these days. "When he drew back his hood, I recognized him as a pale elf instantly – angular features, pointed ears, almond eyes, and silver-gold hair. I've only seen a pair in my entire life, *including him*. He looked like he'd been through the wringer too; he couldn't have cleaned up long before – from a fight. Saw traces of blood on his cloak and neck. Under the cloak too, he wore a rapier – finest looking hilt I've seen in my life, bar none. I asked him what skirmish he'd been in..." Casmein smirked, as if recalling it amusedly, "He just gave me a wry smile and told me he'd dispatched a werewolf, and that he was about to face an even more ferocious beast, spun on his heel and that's the last we saw of him."

Therefore, Y'Tasziah mused, *the ravens have spoken true*, as she recalled the disturbing screeches from her nightmare with clarity now. The sorceress must have appeared overly pensive, because Casmein stopped chuckling and his expression became grave. "Y'Tasziah? It's not hogwash then, is it? A werewolf, truly here in Morningmist?" he seemed incredulous, but believing – it was uncharacteristic of the lady to furrow her brows and frown at such an outlandish claim. The captain glanced over at Kilbrand, who again looked nervous.

Y'Tasziah dismissed their concerns with a wave of her hand, "Perhaps. Nevertheless, it seems dealt with, thankfully, if anything this Aelyph'en speaks is true. I've yet to personally meet the man, though I am inclined to trust the source he used to contact me." She smirked mischievously – a silver-eyed raven always delivered the elf's previous missives: the creature was either a fey summoning of some sort, or it had been the elf himself in an assumed animal form. Regardless, when the bird spoke, it did so in fluent Mithrainian with the hint of an exotic accent, which led Y'Tasziah to guess the latter possibility. Now she was immensely curious to peruse the sealed letter – the elf's apology seemed to allude that he might be late or unable to attend their scheduled meeting, an unfortunate circumstance considering the critical urgency of her mission. She decided to read it immediately and slid the rolled parchment from her belt.

The seal was a waxen substance with silver strands infusing it, and Y'Tasziah could feel enchantment radiating from within the strands and the scroll itself. It was a precaution against the viewing or opening of the document by anyone but the individual for which it was intended – standard with sensitive material. She again gave the guards a disarming smile as she sauntered politely to the side and turned her back to them a moment. Both stepped away in respect of her privacy. A sigil of twin crescent moons was impressed in the wax seal. It looked noble, even royal – inspecting countless official House missives had trained her eyes to identify minute clues that proved authenticity and pedigree. Y'Tasziah removed her gloves and carefully pressed a thumb deep into the soft substance. The wax felt warm for a moment, and then dissipated into silvery mist, leaving the scroll ready to open. She unfurled the document and flowing letters of silver ink streamed along as her eyes scanned the single sheet, the words disappearing moments after reading them. However, the message itself was simple, if cryptic:

"Mistress Devilsbridge, I hope this letter finds you well. Unfortunately, a profoundly serious (and unforeseen) event has taken place, requiring me to slay the Ascended Lycan father of my half-orykan lover, and I must of course console her to this fact. Forgive my blunt brevity regarding this matter, and please trust that I hold your interests in the highest regard, however I must cancel our arranged meeting for today. Knowing that your needs are time sensitive, I have arranged for the subject of your particular interest to be in a certain place at a certain time, that you may ascertain for yourself the validity of my information. I think in seeing this individual; you will suddenly understand the implications of what I have to offer. At precisely noon today, look for a man of average height and build, hooded and dressed in drab garb,

who will seat himself alone at a table near the hearth of the tavern within the Gilded Hammer's Guild Hall. His appearance surely altered; I am certain that your sorcerous talents will easily bypass such rudimentary illusions. I caution you against immediately approaching this individual once you realize who he is – however, I feel that you may be able to track his movements until the time is more appropriate to make his direct acquaintance. I will attempt to make myself available tomorrow to discuss the implications and reveal to you everything that I promised to assist in your investigations.
–Regards, Qualthalas Ithrauss Aeth'Akir"

After the sorceress read the moon elf's flowing signature, the parchment itself became warm and melted away into nothingness, leaving not even a faint trace of the enchantment it held. *He's certainly skilled,* Y'Tasziah noted, and, with a curt nod to the two guards, bade them open the gate. She'd have to leave promptly to make it across the breadth of Morningmist to arrive at the Gilded Hammer for noon. It was through five districts she'd have to travel, two of which were less-than-savory and would require care to avoid trouble. Seeing her demeanor turn serious, Casmein promptly pulled the lever adjacent the portcullis, and the sound of a great chain issued from inside the stone pillars on either side. The gate rose at an even pace, but Kilbrand stepped forth instantly, stammering, "You have no escort, Lady...*ahem*, Y'Tasziah? Is it wise to roam the streets alone these days?"

Y'Tasziah's eyes flashed dangerously for a moment, but then she remembered the youth had no inkling of her actual power. Casmein grimaced; he saw the look cross the Occultist's face for a moment, and was quick to chastise the lad, moreso for his own sake. "Know your place is not to question the actions of a Devilsbridge. She's more than a match for ten armed escorts anyway. Mistress

Y'Tasziah can hold her own against her father's skill at arms – which, as you know, is *without parallel* in the city." He flashed a grin at Y'Tasziah as she marched purposefully through the gate, smiling warmly to the captain. Kilbrand turned to Casmein, still concerned, and uttered in hushed tones, "I saw her bear no arms, and her attire is… *less than protective*, shall we say?"

Y'Tasziah heard his comment, glanced back over her shoulder, and gave a reassuring wink. "I am *always* armed, First Private Kilbrand, though your unnecessary concern is… *touching*." With a flick of her wrist and a whisper, purple shadows burst forth from her outstretched arm. Before an eye could blink, an ornate scythe, emanating dark and ominous power, manifested in the grasp of Lady Y'Tasziah Camylla Devilsbridge. She spun it with practiced ease up, over and around her shoulder; it slid easily into the waiting palm of her other hand then dissolved into nothingness. With this, she made hastily for Thoroughfare Avenue and disappeared around the corner.

Lady Y'Tasziah Camylla Devilsbridge

Chapter 8

THE GRAVEWALKER

The thin crack in the brickwork behind the picture yielded no secrets initially. Both Qualthalas and Kaira had inspected it thoroughly, poking, prodding, and meddling with tools they had drawn from their various pouches and bags. At least it seemed they had some time – there had been no sign of pursuit, no ominous sounds; the building was vacant for all they knew. Kaira was tempted to just exit through the locked door they had entered from, risking an encounter in the alley with whatever dark being had attacked Qual. A level of annoyance had returned to the half-orykan woman whose patience failed her at the best of times, let alone when trapped in a musty, dark warehouse. She looked to Qualthalas as he carefully disassembled the frame surrounding the picture, hopeful it would reveal a key or secret that would allow them further into the grated cellar door they'd found tucked in the corner of the otherwise nondescript room.

"Let's forget this folly, Qual; if we dash out the door to the alleys we might surprise the assailant, if he's even still lurking there. It might be safe now for all we know," Kaira urged. She stalked about the room like a caged wildcat. Still intent on the poster frame – he'd cracked the seal and was now removing the glass pane – the elf shrugged at her and asked, "Where would the fun be in that? *Safety*, Kaira... do you really think? Tsk." Qualthalas' sly smirk had worked its way back onto his face, he cheerily popped apart the casing, and fingered the bent metal to see if it bore any markings or etchings in its interior. After a few seconds of groping the inner edges, he finally exclaimed, "Aha!" for he'd felt something scratched into one of the edges. He patted his pockets fervently, searching for a light, and then rolled his eyes at himself, released *Ithrin'Sael-I-Uiin* from its scabbard and plunged the blade a few inches into the stone floor.

Kaira stopped pacing, bemused by the busy elf as he tapped the rapier down a few more inches into the floor for good measure, wondering how the blade could be so *impossibly sharp*. Obviously, the nature of the sword was something Qual took for granted, but it wasn't any simple rapier that would sink into solid stone so easily. Kaira knew it was heavily enchanted and she'd seen more than a few magical weapons, but none except Mourning-Song was that strong. The arcing outline of twin silvery crescent moons, which extended from his cheeks to his temples – Qualthalas' runic facial tattoos – revealed themselves a moment as the elf quietly whispered, "*Alath-L'whiin.*" Both his face and the rapier glowed with a faint silvery radiance, enough to illuminate the room as if from starlight. The moon-markings receded into the elf's complexion, barely discernable, but the rapier held the conjuration, providing enough light for the elf to inspect the scratchings he'd uncovered.

"What does it say? Some cryptic riddle or..." Kaira secretly hoped it would reveal a hot breakfast and then a comfortable bed. Still emotionally and mentally drained from the morning's events, Kaira would have loved to trade this whole fiasco for blissful sleep. Qualthalas seemed too intent on the frame to notice her question; he was fixated on the marks, lips pursed as if trying desperately to glean the meaning of a subtle clue. She repeated, "Qual, what's it..." but he tersely cut her off.

"It is nothing," came the elf's flat reply. "It's a scratch I made when prying the damned thing apart." Uncharacteristically, the roguish moon elf flung the frame across the room in anger. It impacted the wall opposite him and bent horribly, making a nasty racket as it clattered to the floor. Kaira stepped back and out of the way as the glass pane sailed past next, shattering to pieces as it squarely hit the floor and made a huge mess that would be hard to avoid. Qual gripped the poster with both hands, tore it apart down its centre and cast both ripped sides to the ground. An unnatural rage, fueled by frustration and sorrow, filled Qualthalas entirely; it was unlike him to lose his composure this way, but the events prior had unhinged something in the moon elf that simmered beneath the veneer of carefree calm he always wore. His fingers were bleeding now; he'd cut himself while hurling the glass, but he did not notice the thin trickle until he brought fingertips to his temples, massaging in slow circles – a calming ritual his mother had taught him as a child. Blood dripped down onto Qual's cheek and the sudden wet feeling brought a semblance of reality back to him. The bard exhaled sharply, and then took in a slow, deep breath. He cast the unbidden thoughts of his mother into a deep recess in his mind.

Kaira shrunk back a little; she wasn't sure how to react to the little tirade the elf had just displayed. It was so completely contrary to Qualthalas' normal behavior; she began to wonder if he'd somehow been enspelled. *No*, she thought, *he's just as hurt as I am right now; it's the protective mask that's gone.* Qual's jaw was clenched, eyes closed tightly, and he seemed to be humming something in a rhythm as he rocked back and forth on his heels. His fingertips left the sides of his head, interlocking in a complex pattern as they met just in front of his stomach meditatively.

Deciding to leave the elf to his meditations a moment, Kaira strode over to the trap door in the far corner of the room, taking care to avoid the glass shards scattered across the breadth of the area. She crouched in front of the heavily barred grates atop a hardwood set of doors moored in the floor. It was the only other exit to the room and would lead to a deeper level of the building. She saw the few deep gouges Qualthalas had made earlier in the wooden surface before he'd given up in favor of inspecting the picture for clues. The trap door had proven impervious to the thrusts of Qual's rapier, which meant it bore potent magical protection, and might be dangerous to tamper with further until they could ascertain its function.

Kaira felt she should probably refrain from meddling with the trapdoor until Qualthalas regained his senses, but then the elf's previous words echoed in her ears, bringing an impish smile to her face. "Where would *the fun* be in that? Safety Kaira... *really*?" she muttered, poorly imitating Qual's accent. She reached out to grip the bars then flexed a few seconds before heaving upwards with every ounce of strength she had. She thought she felt the framework give a little, and furiously continued to apply as much upward force as she could. Although it deeply pained her to use her recent anguish, she focused on an image locked in her mind of her father's face, in his younger days before the curse, working in his smithy, pounding metal into shape and form. In her vision, he looked peaceful; Baergrenth smiled widely as he forged; he *lived* to work metal. Kaira growled and every muscle in her body seemed to ripple, the cords in her neck stuck out, her legs strained, and a furious fire spread through her nerves, waking an ancestral strength deep within.

A groan issued from the metal bars as they bent, yielding to her might, and abruptly they relented to the awe-inspiring force of orykan fury. The grate ripped apart; the next sound was a loud crunch as the whole iron grating flew into the ceiling. Debris from the impact showered down on Kaira, and she jerked to the side deftly as the bent bars rocketed back to the floor, cracking the stone underneath like a hammer of the Gods. Sweating from the exertion, Kaira went to one knee, and felt her elven companion's gentle hand rest upon her shoulder. Apparently, Qual's little temper tantrum was through. "Well, that's certainly *one* way of doing it," he stated, taking a low stance beside her on the cracked stone flooring. "Perhaps what we needed all along were more direct methods." He held up something that looked like a makeup compact, and with a flick of its clasp, revealed an acrid-smelling yellow pasty substance contained within.

"Do you plan on applying some rouge and charming the trapdoors open, Qual?" Kaira teased, "I'm not sure they're quite your type; cold, indifferent and difficult to spread apart." Qualthalas snorted at the remark and gave the perimeter of the doors, which were set too deep in the floor to see the hinges, a quick once-over. He then scooped some of the paste with a single digit and meticulously applied a thin line in a box shape surrounding the framework, making sure to clog the holes left in the floor after Kaira had ripped the grating out. The half-orykan barmaid pushed herself back a short distance and pinched her nose, disgusted by the acidic stench the creamy mixture was emanating. Qual drew a cloth from one of his pouches and took care to thoroughly wipe the substance from his finger, shut the clasp on the compact, and discarded the soiled handkerchief atop the wooden doors. He too crept back, fluttering his hands to wave the smell away, sat down beside Kaira, and watched.

For nearly a minute they dwelled in silence together, waiting until the pair observed little bubbles forming within the chemical, which was swiftly turning to a churning, frothy liquid. The bubbling intensified as the reaction took place, and Kaira watched in fascination as the stone itself began to seethe and ripple where the liquid contacted it. Without emanating any heat, the floor heaved and melted. Instead of disappearing into the cracks leading below, the stone gradually rose in thin sheets that grew upwards as crystals in a deep cavern would. The acidic smell disappeared, thankfully replaced with a dusty, earthen fragrance that reminded Kaira of freshly poured cement. Excited, she continued to watch while the entire trap door sunk a few centimeters as the housing of stone surrounding it yielded to the chemical change.

"I would think if one were to apply *this* makeup, he might develop a complexion problem," came Qualthalas' words; he too stared bemused by the spectacular reaction. Layers of stone had risen vertically at odd angles and miniature quartz shards dotted the structure, composing a rather interesting sculpture from the natural minerals in the flooring. He and Kaira could feel a slight shift underneath them as a narrow crack snaked out from one of the corners of the trap door, extending a metre or so towards the centre of the room.

Soon they will descend, Master, thought the night-clad, hooded figure nestled in the shadowy recess of the locked door through which his prey had entered the warehouse. He continued to observe the two, silently, as he had been for the past few minutes. Belts, buckles, and pouches containing tools and killing devices adorned the man's dark leather attire, all affixed tightly to avoid making the slightest whisper of noise. In his hand was a wickedly curved ebony dagger set with an equally black ruby at the base of the hilt. Not poised for attack or defense, the instrument emanated a stifling magic that deepened the shadows surrounding the assassin, made his footsteps whisper-quiet, and concealed the mental vibrations that all intelligent creatures exuded. He had stepped, intangible, directly through the surface of the door only a short time ago, to examine the progress of his quarry. It was he who had fired the darts into Qual's shoulder from a specially designed wrist-launcher, which he still wore, loaded with another trio of poisoned darts.

He bore a mirthless smile, ash-grey skin, fine features, and a lithe, muscular form. Every movement was deliberate and graceful as he crept unhurriedly towards the desk, his footsteps silent as heel followed toe with each step. Goggles that bore dark crystal lenses adorned his eyes, enhancing his already heightened vision to the point he could see with extreme clarity in the darkness. The Gravewalker inspected the deactivated runic floor inscription, saw every detail of the ripped poster cast to the ground, observed the pinpoint hole from Qual's rapier where it had pierced the tile earlier; nothing escaped his perception. He read the environment carefully, accurately represented the past events in his head while he simultaneously traced a complex set of gestures with his empty hand, soundlessly invoking a recollection spell. Ghostly images of Kaira and Qualthalas mimicked their earlier movements, and he watched the scene unmoved as the death-spiders descended, saw the burst of power as Qual's magic destroyed them, and committed the remaining details to memory before the simulacrum faded from his view. His next focus became the pair of figures ahead: his target.

Kaira and Qualthalas were still transfixed by the shifting framework of the trapdoor, unaware of their quasi-intangible visitor as he trod upon the shards of glass scattered all over the floor. Not a single sliver stirred at the contact of his steps, not a noise marked the grim approach of the figure, who halted only a scant few metres behind the elf and half-oryk. Amber triangles of light superimposed upon his vision after a moment of analysis, identified critical points and weaknesses; a small readout in the language of the indigo elves provided the Gravewalker with key information regarding racial vulnerabilities and strengths. It was an enhancement granted by an experimental fusion of divination magic and barely understood technology that his master had recently captured from the Magmic gnomes. The Soulharvester had unlocked what secrets he could and had put them to immediate use. Cazares was more than mildly impressed with the capabilities the arcane science provided.

The ashen elf exhaled calmly, his breath was rhythmic and controlled, timed with equally imperceptible heartbeats. He trained his wrist-launcher for a moment upon the elf, let it linger there with a twisted sneer, filled with temptation – then aimed at the neck of the woman. His enhanced vision revealed distance to target, showed him suggested trajectory and identified with pinpoint accuracy where his darts would strike. His arm lingered extended, unflinching discipline overriding the tension in his muscles as he kept perfect aim, though he stayed his attack. It was not quite time. Nor was it his intent to assault the pair, only to observe and encourage their progress into the labyrinth below. His instructions were clear: provide Qualthalas *motivation* to proceed at a steady pace: distract, inhibit escape, and provide a sense of urgency. Choice of method was his prerogative and, for now, Cazares simply chose to watch.

The floor shifted again, unsubtly this time, and Qual and Kaira staggered as the trap door succumbed to the destruction of the framework holding it, and it fell into the depths, making a resounding crash as it impacted stone below. The tile and brick-work beneath the two buckled and cracked in several places, threatening to shatter completely. Qual's compound had weakened the underlying structure enough that a substantial portion of the floor was facing imminent collapse. The dextrous moon elf grasped Kaira's wrist, instinctively pulling her to the opening, and gasped, "Jump down quickly and run – I'll be right behind you!" Kaira heeded his advice and leapt downward five or six metres to land upon a rocky cavern floor below, and then bolted forward as fast as her strong legs could carry her.

Glancing once over his shoulder, Qual swore he saw a blurred, dark form recede further into the shadows of the room but had no time to investigate as his footing gave way and the floor beneath him crumbled, sending the elf tumbling along with it. Bricks, mortar, rock, and tile came crashing down with him, and he tucked slightly, turning through the fall to land on his side, absorbing as much of the impact with his body and arms as he could. He was on his feet in moments; scanning ahead and seeing Kaira, he made for her as fast as he could, rolled to avoid a large piece of brickwork that narrowly missed his head, and scampered to safety as a greater portion of the room above buried the area behind him in a sea of debris.

Qualthalas started to cackle, unhinged, as a wave of relief collided with the realization that further danger loomed ahead. Qual's hands went to his knees to steady himself, and he exhaled sharply. When he looked up, he saw Kaira slumped against the rough reddish rock wall nearest her. One arm dangled at her side, and Qual saw blood streaming down it from a nasty gouge in her shoulder; it may have been dislocated in the fall. Concerned, the bard rushed to Kaira's aid, words of mending flowing from his lips instinctively. He caught her as she fainted forward into his arms. Qualthalas held his lover tightly as a warm glow radiated from the hand he had hooked under her armpit and grasped the wound firmly. The flow of crimson ceased, Kaira's shoulder popped as it set properly back into place and the flesh crept back slowly over the bloody wound. Watching intently as his spell repaired her body, the elf observed the intricate weaving of blood vessels, muscle, and sinew – it was as if some skilled artist was painting a masterpiece in three dimensions at the mere bidding of his touch.

With a profound sigh, Qualthalas cradled the woman in his lap. At first, he assumed blood loss had caused her to lose consciousness, it had been fortuitous that he had been swift enough to catch her. Listening to her breathing, Qual noted it was deep, slow, and rhythmic, almost peaceful. He brushed some of the tight auburn curls from her brow, noting a giddy smile on her face. *Has she been playing all this time*, he thought, but dismissed the notion once she began to babble incoherently in Orykan, her words a jumble of nonsense. Qualthalas, alarmed, inspected her from top to bottom, and then it became clear: three iridite darts protruded from her side, just above her right hip.

"Dureith-Sci'yan," Qualthalas swore in Moon Elvish, "Ethreil'as Niphrau-tu'sie Yeh-Qua Muirah-hess'h!" he challenged angrily to the darkness looming in the general direction of the room they had escaped. Clearly, this was the handiwork of the same assailant who somehow caught him unaware earlier, and the elf was infuriated that again this mysterious stalker had avoided detection. Qual laid Kaira down gently but hurriedly, unconcerned with the effects of the poison. He remembered the blissful slumber induced in him earlier and knew that this reprieve might benefit his lover; she certainly deserved an alleviation of the entire burden placed upon her.

Ithrin'Sael-I-Uiin sang as it flew from its scabbard to Qualthalas' hand, though to his surprise, the weapon displayed no reaction – no glowing runes, hum, or hiss marked the presence of danger. It was as if he was alone in the darkness. Though he could see well enough due to the innately keen vision of his race, Qualthalas couldn't get a good look back up through the collapsed floor, which loomed above some thirty paces away through the tunnel he'd run through. Again, calling on Mourning-Song's magical light, he intoned the words, "Alath-L'whiin," and the rapier responded with the familiar silvery glow of starlight. Qualthalas gripped the handle tighter and focused, the light intensified reactively, the area now awash with radiance.

Focusing his view on the opening they had dropped through, Qualthalas gritted his teeth and prepared defensively. He took a closed stance protectively in front of Kaira's sleeping form. The starlight from Ithrin'Sael-I-Uiin refused to penetrate an unnatural curtain of blackness that concealed everything from the edge of the collapsed floor into the remaining room beyond. The darkness countered his magical light, deepened, and snuffed out the illuminated area it touched with roiling inky fingers that reached out from the void. Runes along the length of Qual's brandished blade now sprung forth unexpectedly as a humanoid figure coalesced out of the thirsty shadows. He stood there atop the rubble left by the collapsed floor, across the remains of the corridor, and stared at the moon elf and half-oryk. Qualthalas narrowed his eyes, and a fierce hatred spread through his heart when the runes dancing along Mourning-Song turned a blue-silver hue – the indication of 'Homeland and Kin.' The withering darkness surrounding the Gravewalker, and the radiant silver glow of Qualthalas' crescent moon tattoos clashed in the stillness between the two estranged kinsmen. With a hissing voice that turned Qual's veins to ice, Cazares Seraszar Aeth'Akir spoke a single word in mock greeting as he politely inclined his head, "Cousin."

Chapter 9

ALL TURNS BLACK AND COLD

Stunned, Qualthalas appraised the black-clad figure before him, illuminated in the cool starlight of Mourning-Song; his jaw clenched from the shattering realizations forming in his mind. Though his unusual black crystal goggles obscured the villain's eyes, it was the countenance and demeanor the man wore that sparked Qualthalas' recognition. The way he stood, shoulders angled, head cocked curiously to the side, and the apathetic, flat voice momentarily returned Qual to his younger life upon the silver moon. Memories from his early adulthood flooded unbidden to his consciousness, a myriad of confirmed suspicions tumbled around with an equal measure of unanswered questions as Qualthalas spat the name out finally, "Cazares."

The Gravewalker inclined his head in acknowledgement, a slit of a smirk spread across his dry, black lips, then melted into a sneer of derision. It was clear that both elves remembered their shared youth with a marked lack of fondness. *Is that a look of regret or just unbridled anger, my dear cousin,* thought Cazares. He continued to stare intently at Qualthalas, relished in the emotional reaction his presence inflicted on the 'Crown Prince' of a people he had left behind over a century prior. The terrible eyes

Cazares possessed revealed heightened blood pressure, heartrate, and facial sweat – all the indications of extreme anger felt by the elflord before him. *Good, this means he will be brash and off-centre, easier to steer.* His cousin deserved some punishment on his supposed princely vacation on the surface of Antiqua; *the pompous ass has been lording his royalty and bedding every waif he's met until now.* Unlike Qualthalas, who had journeyed to the planet of his own volition, Cazares–a pariah to the Sillistrael'li – was forced to descend to Antiqua as the only moon elf (albeit one of mixed blood) ever exiled for the murder of one of his own.

Though they shared similarly royal blood and bore the same surname, the resemblance split sharply beyond their comparable upbringing and early life entitlements. The eldest brother of King Adamon, Archduke Balthrael Fer'is-Andruil Aeth'Akir, Qual's uncle, had sired three children: Maris-Eleine, Sabiasz, and lastly, *Cazares.* The first two children were both centuries older than their half-brother was, comparable in age to Qualthalas himself. Maris-Eleine, the eldest sister, was an accomplished astronomer under the tutelage of the masters of the Academy of Stellar Science, a prestigious institution in the Sillistrael'li kingdom. Sabiasz, the middle child and first son of the Archduke, was born a decade after Qualthalas, and the pair had attended the same studies in Enchantment and dueling. Soon after Sabiasz' birth however, a rare virus struck the Archduke's wife, and she died when the boy was a mere thirty years of age. It devastated their family and the kingdom at large; the death of a moon elf only came under uncommon circumstances like these.

After a year of silent mourning, the Archduke had resumed his courtly duties, which comprised of the planning and allocation of new districts as ancient Aelyph'en families grew, slowly taking up more space upon the silver moon. Balthrael's team of arcanists had developed a new procedure involving the drawing and replication of small portions of atmosphere and terrain from uninhabited areas of the planet below. By teleporting underground pockets of usable materials and precious air into the protective fields that maintained the moon's habitability, they could expand their spire-laden cities with minimal impact. Once they constructed the necessary provisions, the moon elves then cultivated oxygen-producing plant life, which stabilized the new districts before integration into the kingdom's infrastructure.

It was during one of these operations that, through what all considered a bizarre twist of fate, Balthrael had come to meet Cazares' mother, albeit as his prisoner. The Archduke had not been far from the team when sudden cries of terror, the sound of spellcraft, and the clash of metal erupted from the construction site nearby. The 'terreportation' brought several tonnes of solid granite, an unexpected carved section of polished obsidian, and a furious, battle-ready indigo elven *Deathwitch* into the midst of the camp. Disoriented and already paranoid, after centuries spent fleeing persecution in the long aftermath of civil war among her kind, the panicked blue-grey skinned woman lashed out violently at her supposed abductors.

Akhara Szord'Ryn had lain waste to an entire city block and stood poised to slay two of the spellcasters on the team before Balthrael himself challenged the potent Occultist in combat, proving the victor only narrowly. As she lay unconscious before him, deep ash-blue skin, and flowing raven hair in stark contrast to his pale tone and locks of silver-gold, the moon elven noble had raised his double-axe to perform the killing stroke, but he hesitated. Balthrael continued to watch as her chest raggedly rose and fell, limbs still twitching involuntarily from the electrical wave he had unleashed. Balthrael had been forced to use potent Elemental magic in the battle to incapacitate her. At length, heart still racing from battle and a rush of emotion, he shouldered his gleaming weapon, thoughts introspective as the elflord considered his actions, were their roles reversed. Knowing that spontaneous transportation into the midst of a *Ner'Eith-Sariss* metropolis would cause him to react in a similar fashion, Balthrael decided to grant the woman mercy. Commanding the gathering throng of soldiers to stand down and prepare a holding cell, he gently took Akhara into his arms and carried her away, all the while fixated on her beautiful exotic form.

Akhara endured imprisonment for nearly a year before Balthrael could successfully petition for her conditional release, after leveraging his considerable political clout to convince the other Royal families to entrust her into his care. He would bear responsibility for any crimes she may commit and agreed to close monitoring of her activities over the next decade. For those ten years, she was restricted to Balthrael's property, unless the Archduke himself accompanied her. Akhara was fitted with a special bracelet that continually relayed her position to the Arcanists of the Ivory Citadel, who scrutinized her every action. Returning Akhara to the underground labyrinthine cities of her people was out of the question; the inherent risks involved were simply too high. However, as an outcast, Akhara had no desire to go back to hiding in seclusion from the massive civil war her people endured. She accepted this set of shackles willingly over the prospect of capture, torture or *worse* at the hands of either side of the conflict.

Akhara's occultist coven of Deathwitches was branded an enemy of the traditionalist Church of the Black Circle, and they had scattered into seclusion as the clergy hunted them. The Darklord, bent on reforming the Underworld power structure, also sent his agents in search of the Deathwitches, and recruited or forced most into his army. As a former clansman and distant relative of Zhiniel, Akhara found herself harried numerous times by his search parties and knew that capture or death would be her eventual fate. Though the Darklord had decimated the clergy of the Temple of Ennetra, she would sooner remain alone than bend to another form of tyranny. The silver moon was an ideal escape.

During this time, Balthrael and Akhara had grown inseparable despite heavy resistance from his family, especially from Maris-Eleine and Sabiasz, who felt she was too swiftly replacing their mother. At first, the siblings both despised her, but after years of seeing their father's previous depression turning into happiness, they began to let her into their lives as well. Though she was far from a gentle woman, prone to her own suspicions and paranoias, Akhara showed a gradual understanding of the moon elves. She somehow broke herself of the assumption that males were inherently inferior, though it took many years to refer to any with terms of respect or admiration. She learned that the ingrained teachings of her society were something she could find personal growth in letting go of them.

Eventually, she approached Balthrael about the possibility of resuming her Occultist studies, and they found a few Aelyph'an sages who were willing and capable of teaching her further. Soon after, Akhara found herself relaxed enough to smile occasionally, and her spirit broke free of the shackles wrought by being a pawn to a wholly different society for all her previous life. She began to refer to Maris-Eleine as '*Kalath'I'Las*' which was a blending of Moon and Indigo elven language that meant 'Revered Daughter' and they often spent time together studying the strange parallels between astrology, astronomy, and occultism. Sabiasz, however, never fully accepted Akhara, though he begrudgingly gave his father consent to marry her officially after nearly a century upon the silver moon.

Though he genuinely loved his new wife, at the behest of King Adamon, Balthrael went alone one night to the massive tower of their father, Ithrauss. The two close siblings had a recent discussion about Balthrael's *Indigo Elven wife*, and the possibility of their union producing offspring. Adamon, with only the best interests of his brother and the kingdom in heart, had urged the Archduke to see their father, the most powerful Diviner ever known, to ascertain if there could be any complications resulting from the union. The Sanctus Orb was already prepared when Balthrael entered his father's tower: Ithrauss had known his son would approach him and thus performed the Rite of Prophesy that very night.

The reading proved troublesome. Though no physical reason existed to prevent the couple from pairing to produce a child – moon elven and indigo elven blood and anatomy were compatible – the sands painted a disturbing picture of strife, bloodshed, and betrayal. Initially, Balthrael assumed this meant his beloved was indeed a spy, but Ithrauss informed him otherwise. The sands spoke not of Akhara, whom the ancient sage had also become accustomed to, but of their offspring. Pointing to thin black and red veins within the sands, which twisted in a grand spiral, Ithrauss' face was compassionate when he explained the full meaning of the obscure patterns to his son.

"Unfortunately, my son, these speak of a spiraling descent," explained Ithrauss in somber tones, "into a pit of madness due in no small part to an outside plot which the child *will* succumb to." His face was marked with concern and empathy, and he sat, slightly exhausted, upon an antique high-backed chair, his hands clasped together within the sleeves of his robes. "Balthrael…" he continued, his voice strained, "I fear the events of this reading are… already set in motion. There is no arguing with prophesy, we can only make preparation, and hopefully, understand that which we cannot change. I know only that the child will inevitably fall to the seduction of darkness, yet there is always hope, and the chance for redemption: for *anyone*."

Balthrael's initial anguish diminished at those final words, though he did not fully grasp what Ithrauss meant when he said '...*already set in motion*.' If the prospective child would be bound to a dark fate, then he and his wife could simply resign themselves to the fact that the pair should refrain from bringing such a being into the world. Moon Elven birth rates were extremely low as it was, and there were effective methods of contraception available through the medical specialists of the Sillistrael'li. It would be a simple matter to ensure Akhara would not become pregnant. Ithrauss smiled a wistful smile, mixed with sadness and expectation; he could not help but unconsciously read his son's surface thoughts. To him, they were as loud as if Balthrael was shouting. Ithrauss softly explained with three simple words, "She already is."

The outcast's ensuing words broke the silence at length, pulling the pair back to the present. "It seems we both left something behind, up there, didn't we, *cousin*?" Cazares intoned every word with mocking sympathy as he continued, "Me – my compassion, and you – your *stones*." The half-indigo, half-moon elf gripped the air in front of his crotch, made a slicing motion, miming castration, and then dropped the invisible 'package' on the ground with a cruel snicker.

"You've never understood the meaning of, much less possessed a hint of compassion, *Caz-Ris'se*," Qual hissed the taunting nickname he had given his cousin – 'Snake-Tongue' in Moon Elvish – an insulting play on the name's proper pronunciation, which meant 'The Tongue of Wisdom'. Though Cazares had absolutely despised that biting insult as a youth, he registered nothing that indicated he cared any longer. In fact, he had lost interest in Qualthalas for a moment, adjusted his goggles, and purposefully revealed the dart-launcher strapped to his black glove. His other arm snaked down and across, reaching for something hidden behind his back.

In anticipation of a surprise attack, Qualthalas' empty hand traced a quick series of arcs in front of himself, ending with a slashing motion as he incanted, "*Uorin-Sar'inde.*" The air rippled as an invisible frontal hemisphere formed from solidified mana, a general protection against projectiles of most varieties – magical and physical. Qual's left foot swept back, extended, as simultaneously his right foot turned inward, knee bent to stabilize his weight. Ithrin'Sael-I-Uiin crossed his body, resting in a parrying position, still humming, silver-blue runes bathing the area in pale light.

Casually, Cazares produced a water skin, deliberately holding it high as he unstoppered it, took a drink, and stated, "You're jumpy. I was simply parched." Then, after another draw of the cool, clear liquid, the pariah wiped his lips, pointed nonchalantly at Qual's bared weapon, and flatly questioned, "What do you plan on doing with that *relic*? We both know I have nothing to fear from *The Mourning-Song* – your fabled rapier. That museum piece is incapable of piercing the flesh of kin, is it not? A rather ineffective item, given the circumstances..."

It was wholly true. The ensorcelled rapier's one weakness, a safety measure entwined within its various magicks, was that it could bring no harm to one of moon elven blood. Qual's grandfather, Ithrauss, had himself enacted the enchantment, using the most ancient blood of his ancestors, and wound a powerful Divination spell into the artifact's essence. Mourning-Song could detect even a hint of Sillistrael'li bloodline, which rendered its point and edges incapable of contact. Qualthalas had never considered bearing his sword against kin; truthfully, until now, he had forgotten about Cazares entirely, which angered him even further. He should have anticipated that his cousin, who had always been far too ambitious and cruel, would fall in with evil forces. It was not as if *Ithrin'Sael-I-Uiin* was the sole asset in Qual's considerable arsenal but acting without it would put him at a severe disadvantage against his kinsman. At length, he sheathed the blade, sighing.

"What is it that you want, Caz?" Qualthalas asked in a resigned tone, taking a more relaxed stance, though he was still wary of attack. After all, the bastard had knocked Kaira out, he was obviously up to no good, and Qual understood with certainty that his cousin's actions somehow twisted into the plot of the indigo elven Darklord. "You obviously aren't intending to kill me, or you'd have struck earlier while we were more vulnerable. Do you intend to deliver a message from your puppet master?" he provoked, attempting to incite Cazares into revealing information that might be helpful. He didn't expect much; his cousin had always been highly perceptive, and a superb liar who would surely see through the attempt, but it couldn't hurt to try. Qualthalas remembered with a pang of regret how he had goaded his cousin as a youth, though most times everyone observing considered it well deserved.

Following his birth, which had gone without incident, Cazares was welcomed into the Sillistrael'li society, as any new young lord would be. After Akhara had her first tender moments with the babe, nestled upon her breast, the soft skin contact solidifying the bond between mother and child, they swaddled Cazares in warm linens and silks. Balthrael beamed with the same joy he felt with each of his previous children, the foreboding prophesy momentarily forgotten amid the wonder of new life. He turned to the door. The Archduke emerged from the birthing chambers; his new son cradled lovingly in his arms as he presented the new Lord to the Royal Aeth'Akir Court. It was time for the declaration of name, which he practically cried out in a booming voice, "I present thee, Lord Cazares Seraszar Aeth'Akir!"

It was an auspicious event. The moon elven hospital was abuzz with medics, Sae'Ret-ii Clerists, all forms of magical and scientific specialties mingled freely, engaged in discussion with each other and the cheerful members of the new family. The facility was massive from a typical Sillistrael'li perspective: from its central tower, which formed the bulk of the structure, five lesser spires adjoined it with sweeping walkways and the space in between abounded with carefully curated gardens. Besides being beautiful to behold, the entire facility was a marvel of research and treatment for all ailments minor and major. Here, the Sillistrael'li studied and practiced herbalism and medical alchemy along with several forms of healing magic within the grand spires. It was also a place of meditation, introspection, and therapeutic relaxation. Moon elves regarded mental, spiritual, and social health as important as physical, realizing the whole of a being affected each of its other parts, and treated each with respect.

The entire Aeth'Akir royal family was in attendance, dressed in vibrant fine fabrics – silvers, golds, deep bronze tones, purples, reds, and royal blue hues danced around at the event. Qualthalas, a relative youth only a few hundred years of age, snickered and shifted his gaze towards an attractive maid standing nearby who glanced his way with an interested smile several times. He was clearly not interested in the new cousin. His father and uncle were practically fawning over the little towel-wrapped, wriggling infant, and Akhara hovered protectively nearby always. Qualthalas made a token appearance, regarded the babe with a casual eye, and swiftly wandered away after the platitudes of congratulation and well-wishing. Though babies were infrequent, and everyone seemed to make a big deal whenever one of the things came *squealing* into the world, they bored Qual. He found infinitely more interesting the appealing young girl from earlier, leaned against a marble pillar nearby, as she cast suggestive glances his way. With a charming smile, he sauntered over.

"Children don't really become interesting until they can at least speak," he mentioned to the maid, who smirked crisply, while she admired the handsome elven prince. The girl showed no interest in the ceremonious occasion either; she was here because her duties demanded it. Qualthalas whispered tantalizingly into her ear, "Though, I hear the procedure in making one is *much* more interesting," he chuckled and winked at the maid, who, in the blossoming of her womanhood, clearly felt the same, and the pair disappeared swiftly from the event to go experiment with each other in an unoccupied bedchamber of the facility.

The next time Qualthalas saw his young cousin was twelve years later, and he discovered the boy could *certainly* speak. It was at a festive ball, attended by lords, ladies, and common folk alike, and the child was wandering through groups of dancers, mimicking their movements, and loudly singing his own versions of the songs. Cazares came to an abrupt stop within arms' length of Qualthalas; both were, at first, oblivious to the identity of the other. Qualthalas wore an ornate mask adorned with the iridescent feathers of an exotic bird, and a brocaded shirt of golden silks. Cazares sported his favorite black tunic with dark blue stitching, the only thing he would wear to occasions such as this.

"*If'Leithe-An'a!*" the child shouted with a laugh, and pointed *rudely*, Qualthalas felt, at the mask, and proceeded to dance in a circle around the prince, cackling. The words were strange though, to Qualthalas – they were a mixed blend of Moon Elvish and something similar, but of a distinctly foreign dialect or accent. It meant 'Bird-Beast' or something of the like in Qual's estimation. Seeing the boy's deep blue-grey skin and upon reflection, he realized this must be the mixed-blood boy his uncle had sired a decade or so past. Qual attempted to brush the youth aside, and hissed at him, "*Tith'Qu'Augh-Nei*," which meant 'Half-Ling' in Moon Elvish, but the child scowled, his lip started to quiver, and he began to bawl. For, in his mother's tongue, the words were interpreted as 'Little Bastard.' Cazares swiped at Qualthalas angrily, merely grazed his hand with the slap, then trudged away to find Akhara and Balthrael who were entwined, waltzing nearby.

Qualthalas turned back to his date, whose eyes narrowed at the self-indulgent princeling. "That was extremely insensitive," she stated accusatively, clearly not impressed with Qualthalas' callous treatment of the boy. Qual tried to appease her, promised to apologize, and made his way to where his uncle and aunt knelt by Cazares at the far end of the dance floor. As his cousin approached, the boy flashed a devious grin that neither of his parents saw and pointed emphatically. The crafty youth proceeded to wail as if bitten by a snake. Akhara rose with a menacing glare, held back only by the gentle hand of Balthrael. The Archduke frowned and shook his head side to side at his nephew in disapproval, though he displayed no anger – children and young adults rarely got along well. A moon elven youth of two hundred years barely knew his place in the world, and Balthrael understood this. Judging by the flushed cheeks and furious red eyes she flashed, Akhara certainly did *not*.

Qualthalas' words of apology sputtered out; his usually glib tongue rebuked by her vengeant look. He knelt before his aunt, hanging his head dramatically, as if to emphasize his remorse and turned his eyes slowly upward. It was then he saw Cazares from behind Akhara's flowing skirts open his palm briefly and secretly, so only Qual could see the gold and sapphire ring he'd tucked away. With a devilish grin, the child promptly put the ring to his lips and swallowed, stuck his tongue out at his cousin, and resumed his whimpering. Qual's eyes bulged out as he stood and stared at his own outstretched fingers, now noticing the missing, expensive gemstone band!

Qual instantly regretted when the words, "Little thief!" came tumbling from his lips, eliciting from Akhara the sharpest slap he had *ever* felt (and there had been several up to this point in his life.) Many of the crowd turned to gape in shock as Qualthalas pitched over onto the marble ballroom floor, dazed by the backhand of his indigo elven aunt. The force with which she had slapped the prince shocked even Akhara, and she turned an apologetic look to her husband, who simply pursed his lips and clucked his tongue.

Qualthalas looked up to see Cazares' triumphant look as he stifled a gleeful laugh, and this was the first of many times he realized there was true *malice* in the eyes of the boy.

Qualthalas wondered if his cousin's eyes bore the same malevolent hostility possessed all those years past. To Qual's amazement, Cazares sat down and crossed his legs, carefully lifted the goggles up from his face, and rubbed the area where they had sat. His eyes were not *eyes* at all! They resembled nothing of the angry, deep maroon and red-flecked orbs Qualthalas recalled vividly from his youth. They had been replaced with a sheen of dark metallic reflection, and where the irises should have been, each eye sported a trio of red pinpoints of light – truly inorganic in form and function. Qualthalas' shock must have been apparent, because again his cousin smiled that nondescript, emotionless smirk as he stated, "One of the many gifts bestowed by *Master Szord'Ryn.*" The pinpoints of glowing crimson rotated to focus as regular pupils might; they dilated and expanded in a wholly mechanical way that disturbed Qualthalas to look at. Moon elven engineers had theoretical models of ocular replacements for rare occasions when their kin lost sight due to accident or disease, however they lacked the science to link the function to a patient's brain. Yet, here stood Cazares with what Qualthalas estimated were a working pair, bearing enhancements far beyond what he imagined possible.

"Marvelous, aren't they?" Cazares posed to his bewildered cousin, "With a simple adjustment, I can see that barrier you erected, you know." The black-clad elf paused; his head tilted slightly forward as if he was taking stock of Qualthalas. The red dots ceased their rotation and widened their spread as the beams intensified with a quiet, mechanical hum. "Your heartrate is high. Are you experiencing *fear*, dear cousin?" Cazares asked quizzically, as if he cared. He continued to analyze his estranged kinsman for signs of reaction, observing the detailed readouts imposed on his vision. It seemed the two were doomed to appraise each other relentlessly until one revealed something the other sought in this mental duel.

"I'd call it revulsion, actually," was Qualthalas' curt reply, but then with a touch of real empathy he asked, "What has he *done* to you, Caz? I know you've always sought power and favour, but this..." At the unexpected rebuke, Cazares bristled and straightened his night-blue runed cloak; it was apparent that something in Qual's words had agitated his kinsman, who slowly stood and crossed his arms, seeming pensive. He muttered under his breath, repeating the scathing word the prince had used, "Revulsion..." It described well how Cazares had viewed the entire Sillistrael'li society and evoked the painful memory that had catalyzed the path of vengeance leading to his exile.

The young Cazares spent most of that chill night gazing out the window of his bedroom, locked within the soaring tower of his family home for 'misbehaviour' during the day. *A fine gift indeed, Qualthalas,* came his bitter thoughts; hatred for his older cousin simmered deep within the black pit that was his heart. It had been his fiftieth birthday celebration, significant in Sillistrael'li society, viewed as a turning point when children entered early adolescence. Cazares scoffed at the notion – he had matured ten years prior, due to his *mixed* heritage. Loathing and utter *revulsion* for the kingdom of the moon elves seethed in the depths of his core and he gazed longingly at the courtyard far below. He tilted his upper body out the window, with a steel grip upon the sill.

Cazares recalled his cousin's smug, grandiose entrance to the event, practically *wearing* the young lady Su'Reisse Noviar-Ka'lias as his companion. His hated cousin *knew* that the pretty, innocent girl was the only female that Cazares had ever taken a liking to, and obviously, the cur had used his charms to seduce the girl just to spite him. At the sight of the two arm-in-arm, Cazares had stormed out of his own birthday celebration in a rage. He backhanded a priceless statuette on his way, which smashed upon the ground and caused his own mother to restrict him to his chambers. His maroon eyes clouded over as he remembered Qualthalas' triumphant smirk and his biting utterance, "Temper, temper, *Caz-Ris'se…*" while an infuriated Akhara escorted the youth away by his pointed ear.

The darkness in his room, held at bay only barely by the light of a single everburning candle, responded to his emotions–and the shadows deepened. Cazares took no note; it was an unconscious reaction; one he did not fully understand or even realize was abnormal or mystical. The grey-blue skinned youth sighed and pushed himself back, spun and went to his bed, rooted around under the mattress, found the concealed slit he had made, and reached inside for his prized possession. Cazares felt the smooth, cool blade first, then curled his fingers lightly around the leather-wrapped handle and brought forth the wickedly curved dagger from its hiding place. He had found the razor-edged blade with a black ruby set in its roundel tucked in a hidden compartment, along with several other interesting items secreted away in a small chest while snooping through his mother's chambers.

The mischievous juvenile possessed a natural aptitude for stealth, for getting into the special places forbidden to children; secrets seemed to call to him, and he followed their tantalizing whispers as a moth drawn to flame. Surprisingly, his propensity for skulking rarely got him into trouble; seldom was Cazares discovered in these moments. Any time someone did manage to interrupt his obsession, he found his lying explanations implicitly believed by the weak-willed moon elves. The youth had no inkling that his deceitful words carried innate arcane power. His was the deceptive voice of a Naga'Zhi: a serpentine race whose elders possessed beguiling powers that could bend any but those of the strongest will to their suggestions.

Cazares deftly rolled the blade over his palm, flipped it around and practiced several killing strikes he had learned in his blade tutelage classes. His instructor Azounis, a renowned weapon master of the Sal'Edor-ah family, was proficient in many styles of melee combat, and a capable tutor. Initially, he found Cazares' interest in the dagger and his queries about assassination techniques somewhat disturbing during their lessons, but, at the seemingly eager boy's behest, taught him what he knew. Lessons in stealth and practice in distancing and timing with a weapon with such a small reach were paramount, and again the boy took to them in earnest. Azounis had thought of bringing it up with the youth's father Balthrael, but Cazares had assured him that the lessons were for pure sport and knowledge alone. Strangely, the master completely believed what his pupil said, and dismissed the thought that there was something nefarious dwelling in the child.

A voice inside Cazares' dark mind whispered, "*Go to the window and show no fear – there is no harm in jumping.*" Unlike his own internal dialogue, this voice certainly manifested from an external source. Intrigued, he made his way to the window and looked down in a trancelike state. It was a clear twenty-metre drop to the courtyard below, but, somehow unafraid, Cazares mantled the frame of the window and leapt into the open air. The voice in his head spoke hurriedly as he sailed over the edge, "*Now focus, and slow your descent. It is in your blood to do so.*" As his momentum carried him out and he began to fall, Cazares did as the voice commanded, feeling an innate magic activate in his mind. The air around him thickened. Exultation coursed through the youth as he gradually controlled his descent to the ground below, and in seconds, his toes touched ground. He stood there, silent upon the stone of the courtyard and looked forward.

The next few minutes were a blur in Cazares' memory. The series of events leading to his incarceration felt surreal, as if he had been a visitor in his own body. He vaguely recalled slipping past several people wandering the city, as he made his way to the modest spire home of the lovely girl, Su'Reisse. He told the house servants he had a missive to deliver her, and she was summoned to the garden courtyard without further question. His recollection was a hazy dream, detached from his will. He had confronted Su'Reisse in the garden about her involvement with his hated cousin, remembered her hasty explanations that she didn't mean to cause him grief, that Qual was only a friend and would remain that way. He was sure she lied to protect herself and that *Slae-En'nua Sibar'Akas* Whore-Prince of hers, he shouted curses – and grew angrier every moment of the altercation.

The ruby knife was in his hand, though he had not drawn it; he extended it as if offering it to the girl. Then he uttered the fateful words that led to his trial and the order for his exile from the kingdom of the Sillistrael'li. In that moment, Cazares hated not only his cousin, but also Su'Reisse, the entire moon elven kingdom, *everyone* including himself and he wished it all dead: "You should plunge this knife into your heart, like you did to mine!" His last memory of the night, before collapsing next to her, catatonic, was of her glazed eyes when she took the dagger from his hand and did *exactly* as he had instructed. The curved blade slipped between her breasts and washed the ground in a pool of crimson. His only love, the one bright jewel that shone in a sea of hatred and resentment, flickered, and died – *and it was all Qualthalas' fault*. As Cazares snapped back to reality from his long internal reverie, he sneered coldly, whispering, "Now it's *your* turn to feel this loss, *cousin*."

The temperature plummeted in the whole cavern, and Qual noted the darkness surrounding his cousin deepened as wisps of shadow swirled in from all around him until the void obscured Cazares entirely. The same coldness crept up the back of his neck. Qualthalas suddenly spun and instinctively brought

Mourning-Song singing from its scabbard in defense. It whistled as the deft moon elf slashed in an arc behind him, while he maintained an awareness of the area his magical shield protected. The rapier met only empty air though, but another cold, dark void formed where Kaira lay, and Qualthalas screamed in abject terror as he realized the rest had been a clever ruse. "No!" he cried, rushing into the blackness with wild abandon. His twin-crescent facial runes flared brightly, its starlight a beacon tearing through the void, but to no avail – Kaira had vanished, and only frost lined the cavern floor in her absence.

Whether the whispered words echoed throughout the chamber, or in his mind, Qualthalas could not discern, but that same icy void gripped his soul as they rang in the shaken moon elf's consciousness, "We shall meet again soon enough, *dear cousin* – and don't fret – I will be taking good care of your companion..." With that, the darkness and cold receded, leaving Qualthalas alone in the rubble amid the rocky chamber. The elf crumpled to his knees, a feeling of utter defeat and worthlessness tore through him in waves, and he sobbed openly. Mourning-Song clattered to the floor, absent of any indication there was anyone or anything nearby to observe his anguish. All that remained was the black and cold in the chamber to accompany the black and cold in his heart.

Chapter 10

THE LETHAL FEATHER DUSTER

After a few minutes spent controlling his wracking sobs on the cold stone floor, Qual's sorrow transformed into fiery determination. A wilful fury boiled deep inside; one that had not stirred in decades. A forbidden spell taught to him during his intense subterfuge-training, one that he had locked away all knowledge of, sprang to his mind. Touching fingertips to his cheeks, where the silver moons still pulsed with determination, his lips formed syllables foreign to him. Another Qualthalas spoke for him now; he gently laid to rest the crushed thoughts and broken feelings somewhere in a deep recess of his soul.

The other voice emerged from his lips, questioning, "Where are we?" At first his words were wispy and ethereal but increased in force, awakened from a long, deep slumber. Qualthalas softly answered himself aloud, still detached from the other personality as it surfaced, "We've been led into a trap, and Kaira has been taken. Our peril is great... I did not invoke you consciously. It came... unbidden." A great internal debate arose in Qualthalas, one that defied the logic of thought or emotion. He felt his soul in a rift of unexplainable proportion, in which countless versions of his own mind struggled to gain a platform amidst a cacophony of their making. One powerful voice emerged; a unison of numerous shattered pieces of psyche formed an amalgam of thought and intent; as it spoke profoundly, the other voices quieted, stilled by its magnitude.

"We shall transform the *Crescent Moons* masque, Qualthalas," it echoed within his essence, a detached, yet aggregate entity composed within the Crucible of Souls. The unified voice continued, "...but beware the associated risks – take care to preserve the quintessence of your heart as you take on this new role. We believe you shall prevail." The silvery runes that shaped the twin crescent moons adorning his face initiated their transformation, melded, and shaped new structures beneath Qualthalas' skin. The runes embedded within took on a crimson hue as the masque adapted to the needs of the elven prince who bore their mark. Theirs was a language lost to antiquity; a gestalt of the fabric woven through time, thought and soul – a compositional matrix that, by virtue of his unique birthright, was Qual's to command. The risk however, to which the entity referred, was in losing his personality amid this vastness of consciousness and will. The Masque of Myriad Minds threatened to rend his existence apart as it separated portions of Qualthalas' persona and reconfigured them to fill the needs his difficult life required.

The twin moons took on a more angular appearance, reshaped into three pointed triangles above and below each of his eyes. "*Tho'n Ythe-Qu'eil*" Qualthalas spoke, his changed voice ringing with purpose, reverberating throughout the chamber, repeating in Mithrainian, "*the Scarlet Fury masque.*" His mindset was altered as well – gone were his heartache and dismay, replaced by a stoic, vengeant purpose. The moon elf's senses awakened sharply: he became hyper-aware, predatory, and animalistic. Qualthalas' canines extended slightly, his eyes reflected and amplified the ambient light until he could see perfectly into the shadows, and every muscle in his body tightened.

Lost in the raptorial instincts he now possessed, Qualthalas crouched like a cat, then leapt forth to test his newfound reflexive strength. From that stationary position, he surged clear across the chamber, twisted midair as his feet met the wall some six metres away at a height well over twice his own. He coiled for a moment, braced against the stone, then redirected his force, rebounding, he dove for the floor. As it rushed to meet him, he curled deftly, rolled several times, spun on his heels, and slid backwards another few metres to rest in a low stance. Sharp elemental words rang out as his hands knifed the air before him in twin slashes, forked lightning streaked out from his fingertips and obliterated a section of the very wall from which he had leapt. Adrenaline coursed through him, and shaking, he released a primal cry. Loose stones trembled and clattered about the chamber at the ringing, resonating echo of his voice.

Qualthalas struggled against the instinctive urges that pulled at his thoughts, swift to remember the words of warning issued prior. He slowed his breathing and commanded his body to relax the great tension building throughout; stifling that feral nature welling within him consumed a considerable portion of his willpower. This boiling fury must be held in check as he made his way through the subterranean lair before him. If the empowered bard allowed the masque to conquer his spirit, he would become lost to it, become dangerous in a way he could not abide. Qual internalized his gratitude for the gift, then peered through the darkness to analyze the fissures his lightning strikes had carved into the wall. The new, primal senses at his command had revealed a weakness; he had detected a tunnel beyond the cavern wall the instant his feet made contact. Only a few metres of stone separated this chamber from the next, and he exploited the rush of power to carve an opening where none had been apparent before. His way was clear, his mind determined, and with a fire coursing through his veins, Qualthalas cast a ringing vibration spell that shattered the fissures, creating a path large enough to charge through.

Qual checked himself after his initial strides towards the opening, forced his steps to slow, then sauntered through the large excavation in his typical fashion. It was a good sign; keeping to his nature meant he retained a measure of control and steeled his resolve. "Easy, Qual," the elf muttered to himself, grinning. Through the opening, his newly enhanced sight revealed a larger chamber, one that was partially hewn by hand or mechanical means toward the furthest and – if Qual's sense of direction remained accurate – south facing end. There were markings etched into a stone arch in that vicinity, though he was unable to discern if they were runes or carvings at this distance. He moved to advance further in... and froze. Relief washed through Qualthalas that he had not burst through as his original urge had dictated. The stealthy bard's foot paused scant centimetres above the floor; he felt something vibrating almost imperceptibly underneath. Experience told him it was the triggering mechanism beneath a pressure plate, and Qual took care to avoid the surface, sidestepping lightly like a cat.

He crouched low, and with bare hands felt at the rough granite next to the trap trigger. Now he could hear the humming from beneath, and considering what he now knew of his nemesis, Qualthalas surmised it was both magical and mechanical. Although the rogue in him was intensely curious about the advanced technology that his foe implemented, he resisted the compulsion to take apart the pressure plate to investigate further. More pressing was his desire to advance quickly; Kaira's life was in danger – or worse. He knew his enemies were masters of subversion and control. He dreaded harm coming to her and wanted to pursue Cazares to find the answers he sought. Surrounding the engraved arch, Qual sensed traces of the same magic his cousin had used to whisk his lover away. Wary of traps, the elf carefully picked his way across the floor, low to the ground, ears sharp for danger.

His suspicions were confirmed as he neared the centre of the room, where his keen eyes picked up holes in the floor which appeared to have been drilled by a precise instrument. Cleverly carved into the base of the chamber at odd angles that made them hard to discern from the natural contours of the floor, the miniscule shafts suggested a trap involving projectile spikes. He guessed dwarvish handiwork immediately, implying the Dun Dwarvish clans were in league with the Darklord necromancer. *Ingeniously constructed traps*, he thought, and avoided the obtuse angles of the holes, while he weaved a path through with delicate steps.

The familiar hum of Mourning-Song in its scabbard sounded off in alarm, and Qual bolted to the right as a large shape silently descended from the ceiling. Moments prior, there had been nothing – the elf had taken care to observe the ceiling for similar holes to the ones in the floor. Now, eight hairy legs, vastly larger than the vampiric swarm specimens, clicked as they met the chamber floor where he'd stood only a second earlier. Qualthalas recognized the cloying scent of brimstone, and saw the fading magical aura surrounding the creature, strong indications that it was conjured by a spell.

The monstrous spider, some two-and-a-half metres tall at the top of its hairy back, reared with a clicking screech and swiped at him with a chitinous, crimson leg. If Qual hadn't repositioned, the deadly arachnid would have dropped directly upon him with its vicious-looking barbed appendages. Qual remained mindful of its spinnerets; these creatures could web their targets from afar before closing with deadly mandibles. He took a moment to scan the chamber for emanations that might indicate if its summoner was nearby. Sensing no other presence, he unsheathed Mourning-Song and noted the pinkish runes crackling along its blade. *A summoned creature, fiend-bred,* he internalized, noting long, ebon, hornlike spines secreting a viscous fluid that dripped off its reddish exoskeleton. Qual uttered a quick protective incantation, *"Y'auth-Keh!"* and touched his breast above his heart. A field shimmered and flowed around him while he took a combative stance; the spell would protect him from poisons for a short duration in case the dripping fluid was toxic. He suspected heavily it was.

The giant thing, unabated, scampered towards him at alarming speed for a creature of its size, mandibles as large as his arms, and bone-white, snapped at him with a loud clacking noise. Qualthalas dived backward, wary of its poison-coated legs, and struck with Mourning-Song. Its attuned edge sliced into one of the spider's plated limbs, and tore a deep gash in the protective, chitinous armour. The wound practically spewed an ichor of brown that stunk of the abyss and hissed as it splattered the chamber floor. Everything about this abomination was caustic. He would have to be cautious even when wounding it. Perhaps he should rely upon his newfound powers to keep a distance. Qual backpedaled with blinding speed, easily outpaced the swift creature, and fired a series of icy shards, projecting the spell without use of vocal incantation. Mentally cast spells were weaker than their fully formed counterparts were, but it served the purpose of slowing the creature's movements while he plotted his next move.

The quick-thinking elf recalled the trap's position in the centre of the room where the spider struggled to free itself from the ice encasing three of its limbs. The monster screeched and flexed its gory mandibles, while its remaining five free legs pushed its body upwards. Qualthalas leapt towards the trap trigger. He heard a sharp *Crack! Crack! Crack!* As the spider freed itself and shook off the icy shards, it too, leapt in fury at its warm-blooded prey. Midair, the elf aimed his feet precisely at the epicentre of the mechanism under the stone. Qual proved the quicker. As he landed deftly upon the pressure plate, what must have been hundreds of spikes shot out from the small holes in the floor, into the exposed underbelly of the nasty arachnid. The thing released and ear-splitting shriek as volumes of the same brown ichor as before spewed out of countless wounds that covered the floor in a bubbling pool of acid. The massive convulsing creature crashed to the floor; its legs bent at odd angles as they twitched in a completely unnerving way. The thing feebly attempted to stand, but Qualthalas was already upon it, forced to trust the dwindling spell's protection as he savagely thrust Mourning-Song into the creature's body and head. He pincushioned the creature with vicious wrath before finally carving off several of its limbs in a single slashing strike.

Spittle flew forth as the furious elf roared at the creature dying before him and his sword arm vibrated from the rush of adrenaline coursing through his veins. Burning ichor coated Qualthalas from head to toe, but his body hardly registered pain from the oozing venom that sizzled on his flesh. His tattered cloak bore multiple holes from the dangerous substance; his armour and clothing sustained permanent damage from the countless droplets that spattered the elf. The Scarlet Fury Masque illuminated the spider's sizzling corpse with an ominous crimson glow, and Qual found he could not fight the burning rage building continually inside. Although suppressed, Qualthalas still carried thoughts of Kaira's capture by his jealous and murderous cousin, and he could not help himself from fearing the worst. Unhinged, the feral elf flew at the runed arch across the chamber, still coated in the destructive blood of the caustic creature, vapors exuding from most of his personage.

Slow it down, Qualthalas, he reminded himself. Still vibrating from the battle, the elf willed himself to control his breathing. It was a long internal battle before it finally settled into a rhythm of deep inhalation and exhalation, but then Qual began to take stock of his situation more rationally. The burning sensation of the spattering of acid all over him crept through his nerves with a considerable amount of pain. Involuntarily he winced and attempted to draw a recovery spell to mind. Acidic and caustic burns were extremely hard to heal even using magic, and the gouts of fluid that were covering most of his body had damaged a significant amount of his attire.

Qual rapidly discarded his cloak, which was in tatters now anyway, and loosened his belt. One of the attached pouches clattered to the floor, its contents spilled out of several holes burnt through it. Much of his gear was ruined, but he did retrieve a few vials and packets of components that remained undamaged. These, Qualthalas stowed in his special container, the one with the extradimensional space inside. Though the items would be harder to sort through, at least they were safe. The magic that bound the pocket of space inside had kept the pack protected, which was a blessing at least. Qual had heard chilling tales about items like this doing unexpected things when severely damaged. They had ranged from reports of the contents being forcibly ejected all over the immediate vicinity, to the items being sucked into a vortex, unrecoverable, and the wildest tale was a claim that the owner was pulled in as well, purportedly living his last few days trapped inside the space before, inevitably, the air ran out.

Qualthalas looked across the breadth of the room, into the fissures and cracks of the rock, and paid careful attention to the shadowy corners. Confident that nothing else imminently threatened him, he fully stripped all his clothes, armour and gear off. Naked and chilled, the cold in the hard stone tile of the floor sucked the heat from him. Qualthalas pulled a small scroll from his pack, unrolled it, and inspected the serpentine words that slithered along its surface. He concentrated hard; his thin eyebrows furrowed, and his eyes bore a hole through the page as the words unraveled before him and began to make sense. The summoning and conjuration of things was never a focus of his magical study, nor was he practiced in the casting of such complicated rituals. Hence, he had bought this scroll from an itinerant thaumaturge he happened upon in his many travels, early into his forays upon Antiqua; the woman was aging but attractive still, scarlet hair, wild eyes, and firm hips...

Out loud, Qual chortled at himself. *Ever the scoundrel, even at a time like this*, he reflected upon the fireside camp they shared for a fleeting time. Customary in his aimless wandering in that time, he flattered her with his words and flirted mercilessly. Even though they hadn't done anything unbecoming, the provocative elf certainly made the woman lustful through his charms; she had licked her lips and shared a tasty, peppered cider from her only mug with him by the campfire. She spoke little and listened to his outlandish tales intently. It had occurred to Qualthalas that she probably hadn't felt a man toss her down in her bedroll in some time and, for a while, he considered giving her the ride of her life that night. At length, and with a forlorn look, she sold him the scroll and a few others at a heavy discount and bid him *good night* with a wistful tone of finality. He shrugged; she must have possessed a shred of dignity that the roguish bard lacked, or perhaps she had a lover waiting for her in some musty tower deeper in the province.

Qualthalas was now grateful for her kindness and for parting with such a useful incantation. With the script fully deciphered in his mind, the moon elf slowly and carefully practiced the words of magic inscribed upon them, lest he make a mistake in the casting. Scrolls like this were handy in a pinch, especially since Qualthalas had no inherent knowledge of the primordial form of magic it contained. With intent now, he held the parchment up, took the tiny silver pin attached at its bottom, and pricked his right thumb. A single drop of blood came out; this he pressed into the scroll, activated the spell formula, and thereby bound its sorcery to himself. Aloud, he read the words inscribed within, softly but with purpose. "Ala-ca'ath Noduwaar Koi-iss'a Soh... Massa Kwei Onathath Tau," the phrase spilled out, foreign on his tongue. Scribed in a barbaric southeastern language, one he was only vaguely familiar with, Qualthalas felt the magical force flow through him and surrendered a portion of his own mana to empower the incantation. Theirs was a spiritual, shamanic language, symbolic of the forces of nature. By all rights, Qualthalas should not be able to cast a spell of this kind, but luckily the magic was encapsulated within the fabric of the scroll itself; all he had to do was provide his blood and mana as a catalyst and intone the words properly.

The cold and dark of the chamber abated as the parchment lit in flames, consumed by the energy it contained, and the whole area churned in a small circle surrounding the elf and his discarded gear. He stared in wonder as the tile on the floor, the stone of the roof, and the nearby wall transmogrified into a small room which surrounded and sheltered him. A door, just big enough to squeeze through, formed immediately in front of Qualthalas, followed by a one-way window – opaque from the outside, yet clear on the inside. A magical torch sprung from one of the inner walls, providing dim orange light to the dwelling, and his perception was boggled momentarily as the size of the interior grew. All around him, cracking and groaning sounds accompanied the remainder of the conjuration as it filled with the necessities of living. The central chamber of the little house sported a fireplace, a small table and comfortable chair, along with a black fur rug that seemed to grow out of the floor. Two more rooms were fashioned in this manner: a bedroom with a comfortable set of blankets atop a pillowy mattress, and a lavatory complete with a chamberpot that emptied itself, and best of all, a steaming hot bath.

Curious, he opened the door and peered outside. The house, from the exterior, appeared to be a single room, formed from the surroundings, only large enough for one individual to occupy. The presence of a window was concealed from the outside; it appeared only as a flat sheet of stone that seemed slightly out of place amid the rest of the rocky exterior. Branches and roots poked out at odd angles from the dwelling, sporting sharp barbs that would dissuade anyone – or any*thing* – from assailing the lair, and he noticed creeping vines twisting and tangling themselves around the entire perimeter, poised to snare any creature that dared approach.

"I certainly paid her too little," he muttered, truly in awe at the usefulness of the spell, "perhaps I should've given her that roll in the hay as a thank you." Qual chuckled again, and went back inside, still aching from the stinging wounds upon him. He made his way to the bath, sidestepped his clothing upon the floor as he crossed the central room, and slipped into the steaming waters. Instantly his skin was soothed, and he could smell roses and hibiscus in the clear, warm water as he slipped deeper into the tub. Qualthalas pushed his predicament away just long enough to relax and was surprised to see that the wounds from the acid were slowly mending as he laid back and sighed.

"Now what to do..." his words echoed his thoughts. It was clear that he was waltzing into a carefully laid trap. Kaira was in imminent danger, and even unprepared as he was, he had best not tarry too long. *However*, he admitted, *I'm no good to her if I'm in a shambles*. After a few minutes spent contemplating within the steaming bath, he decided that given his new powers from the runic tattoes, he'd have to trust in his instincts to pull through. He hadn't the luxury of time to formulate an elaborate plan, nor did he truly know what to expect once he continued onward. It was apparent he was being funneled somewhere, considering the obvious presence of the runed archway just a few metres from his temporary sanctuary. The portal existed by design, the only egress from this trapped room, and he supposed it *purposefully* emanated the teleportation magic his cousin employed implicitly for the benefit of leading him to it. Had it not been for Kaira's capture, he would have certainly turned back. *Not an option,* Qualthalas thought, steeling his determination, before he reluctantly slid out of the hot bath. There was a warm, fuzzy towel waiting upon a hook attached to the wall with which he dutifully dried himself. Inspecting his body to find no remaining sign of the burning wounds suffered, Qual discarded the fleecy fabric and went back to the main chamber.

The elf's disheveled clothing and gear still lay in shambles upon the floor. "What, no built-in maid and tailor? Tsk, tsk," he clucked his tongue with mock criticism. "Perhaps though..." the moon elf uttered, wondering about the capabilities of the magical water. Qualthalas decidedly gathered up his leather armour and a few of the better pieces of his clothing but left the heavily damaged cloak and pouches on the ground. He returned to the bath and unceremoniously plopped the items into the water and watched. He drew near to the tub and peered closely at his gear, then poked at it expectantly with a finger. Unfortunately, the waters did nothing to *repair* the damage, but at least it served to neutralize and wash away the caustic venom that had clung to every piece.

Well, it was worth a shot, he mused, and removed the pieces from the tub. It was all still salvageable and usable, albeit a little 'holey.' His armour was basically pristine; most of the burns were completely superficial, scorch marks upon the surface of the enchanted leather were the only evidence left from the altercation. He shook off the gear and returned to the blazing hearth, which crackled with all the warmth and none of the smoke of a real fire. His equipment dried quickly, and as it did, he rummaged through his pack, in search of some backup clothing. Qual laughed when his sensitive fingers felt a plethora of peacock feathers and the soft felt lining from one of his many stage ensembles. This would do perfectly.

Although they were all gaudy in the extreme, the tailored costumes he procured for his rigorous performances were designed for function and durability, hence they would suit his needs. *Well, he somberly noted, except for the hideous colours.* Qual wouldn't be hiding from anything dressed in this one, and he hoped the ruffled feather collar wouldn't impede his vision if combat ensued. At least the fur-lined interior would keep him warm, and the seams were ample enough not to restrict his movement. He found a simple cloth undershirt, and a pair of extra tight breeches, which he pulled on, sans undergarments. *What did the soldiers call it again?* "Commando," he laughed at the term, not really understanding the military connotation. It was a human figure of speech anyway; it didn't have to make sense. None of his situation held logic by any reckoning, so the peacock feather stage costume and tight pants served to complete the insanity. "All in." he repeated another saying, common in betting games of chance, for this was certainly a gambit at best and suicide at worst. He expected to be dead by the following dawn... if dawn even existed in this underground labyrinth.

After securing the remaining gear and donning his armour over the undershirt, Qual admired himself in a hand mirror he had plucked from his container. He looked fine, but a little incomplete. He rummaged further in the pack, finding his rouges and a few hair clasps, which he applied with practiced ease – adding blues and greens to his eyes and face to accentuate the peacock appearance as he did on stage, and intricately bound his hair in tight braids encircling his head. It was functional in that it kept his mane out of his face and eyes, yet he felt his quick handiwork to be stage worthy as well. Qualthalas decided that if he could retain a level of detached mirth and carry on as if he was acting in one of his displays, he might be able to stave off the burning rage and animalistic instincts barely suppressed thus far. It was a good plan, even though it wasn't a plan at all. *Sometimes, he thought, that's all I'm really doing. It's all just an improv show.* In a bold, emphatic voice, he shouted out as if to a large audience, "I am a lethal feather-duster!" and with this, he laughed and bowed low, amid the uproar and applause of the crowd. Satisfied with himself, he marched proudly out the door of the dwelling, led by delusions of grandeur, and made his way, *stage left* to the ominous, runed portal.

Chapter 11

FOLLOWED

It loomed in front of him, carved of granite and inlaid with obsidian runes that pulsated with unseen force at his approach; each ripple was a gentle drawing like water pulling back from a beachfront. Qualthalas, resplendent in his colourful garb, addressed the portal courteously, as he might an old friend. "Well then," he commented, leaning to inspect the first and lowest of the runes that ran along its surface, "what secrets do you hold, O mysterious gateway to the unknown?" The rogue's dextrous fingers traced lightly around the jagged symbols first, followed them upwards carefully to the top of the arch, and then back down the other side. The moon elf's heightened touch felt every rough ridge, every minute crack in the carved stone. A feeling of unease resonated through his nerves; in the portal, he sensed both ancient Arcanism and the all-too-familiar pervading danger the further into Zhiniel's web he delved. Anger flooded Qualthalas suddenly, sharpened by his instincts, and he bore a ferocious scowl, lips tight, brow furrowed in dark thoughts. The portal just stared back at him in thick silence, and Qualthalas' previous light heart became a burning fury again, bubbling forth from the well inside.

Qual tore at the impassive stone; a tiger's wrath in his hands –
his smooth, pale skin bled as he raked feral claws down the rough
granite and howled in impotent rage. The spiral of unbridled havoc
in his emotions wrestled with discipline and control. Though he
realized that reason was slowly escaping him, Qualthalas was lost
for a few more moments while he repeatedly battered the archway,
until he regained his sanity and ceased the pointless assault.

Out of sheer frustration and a touch of shame, the elf turned
away and crossed his arms; he had no idea how to activate such a
device, though with focus he now sensed the form of magic suffusing the impressive portal. The structure of the arch veritably
reeked of the Shadow Plane, affirming the idea that his bastard
cousin possessed the ability to pass through it. Knowing this, he
surmised that its activation employed an ethereal essence of some
sort. The runes, carved from obsidian, bore innate attunement to
both shadow and fire. Qualthalas' keen intellect began filling in
the missing pieces, his conscious mind was able to take control
again, and he focused on deep breathing as his thoughts raced
with theories on how to engage the archway before him. One
hand scrambled to retrieve something he desperately hoped was
still intact in his extradimensional container, while the other drew
forth Ithrin'Sael-I-Uiin from its silver-tipped sheath.

With the tip of the rapier held outstretched in his left hand,
Qual traced over each of the runes in turn, using only periph-
eral vision to guide him as he blindly concentrated on finding
the vial he needed from the crowded pouch. His fingers curled
around a smooth surface he hoped was the correct glass jar and
brought it forth to view. The subtle crease of a smile played upon
the elf's narrow lips, and he mouthed the thankful words, "Asinh-
Khet'a," to whatever entity directed his hand. A voice whispered
in his mind in response, "Thou'rt most welcome…" and though
Qualthalas dismissed it as an effect of his mental state, the soft

speech seemed distinct from his usual inner dialogue. Qual cast his musing aside before he gave it any more thought as he completed the rune tracing with Mourning-Song, effectively committing the pattern to memory. The elf excitedly unstopped the vial of viscous blackness, which churned and bubbled in its glass prison upon exposure to the air.

Taking care not to spill any of the stuff, Qualthalas turned the vial over, applying it to the base of his rapier near the hilt as he tilted it downward, allowing the strange mixture to flow slowly down to the tip. The curling blackness enveloped the blade, wrapping it in tendrils that spread like fingers, surrounding, and obscuring the gleaming metal. The globules reached out, pulsating, and undulating like dark tentacles of a squid, searching their environment with a supposed life of their own. Qual had always suspected that keeping… "*whatever it was,*" would eventually come in handy in his journey.

In his wanderlust during his earlier years upon the silvery moon that was his home, Qualthalas had trekked across the frozen tundra of the dark side of Sillis-Thal'as to a recent crater made by a small meteorite. He loved exploring beyond the beautiful but tedious cities of his people, journeying to discover new and unexplored areas of the moon. From a new vista, he could look up more clearly at the stars and see his home's counterpart, the ebon moon, *Es'Vaniss-Thal'as* looming like a black pearl in the sky. Clearly visible in its entirety from this vantage, the sister moon hovered higher above Antiqua than Sillis-Thal'as but due to its synchronous orbit, the dark moon was typically only visible from the great moon elven kingdom as a slit that hung deep on the horizon. Something about its sinister, shadowy appearance always felt like a veiled threat to Qualthalas, though the sages assured their people that it was uninhabitable and desolate. Who could know what secrets it held, or once held? Though he had never studied the topic academically, (there were far too many classes, such as Enchantment, where girls surrounded him) astrology had always intrigued the young elf. Perhaps when he was older, he would take up a course or two in the discipline.

Though unaccosted in his travels, there were still strange and terrible creatures that lurked beneath the frozen vegetation of the areas well beyond the nation's borders. Many of the encounters with these apparent horrors ended in bloodshed; Qualthalas suspected that warm food was scarce in this environment. Large wormlike creatures with giant ice-encrusted mandibles had attacked several of the expeditionary parties led by his uncle Balthrael in past forays. Although none of the elven forces suffered casualties in these attacks, the moon elven elders deemed return in great numbers unsafe, as the disturbance seemed to attract the creatures the more members present.

The air was nearly devoid of oxygen, so the creatures mostly stayed under the surface, where pockets of atmosphere stayed trapped, suffusing the crust of the moon with life while the above was mostly inhospitable. For the sake of comfort, Qualthalas adjusted the enchanted silver facemask that allowed him to venture this far out of the terraformed and safe city limits. If his father had only known what he was up to… there would be hells to pay. He smiled, maintaining his concentration upon the dweomer he had cast into his locked bedchambers; it was complex enough to respond to queries from outside and made noises at random to keep the appearance that the young prince still occupied his room. The magical effect also allowed him occasional observation through its focal point, and he could himself speak once or twice through it, though this sort of outside manipulation risked breaking the spell.

Approaching the ridge of the approximately thirty-metre-wide crater, Qual crept low and slow up to its edge and peered over. The elf had a clear vantage overlooking the mark where the celestial object had impacted, though he surmised it was extremely small and lacked the velocity to pierce the moon's surface in a dangerous way. The area remained bathed in an unnatural warmth, though the young elf was uncertain if the residual heat was an aftereffect of the meteorite's descent, or possibly, due to something it had released underneath. Occasional fissures of a mana-infused silvery lava (for lack of any better definition) burst through to the surface from impacts such as these. His people readily gathered the prized material when discovered, for it formed the basis of a critical natural resource for the Sillistrael'li kingdom. The substance maintained a warm temperature and held the pliability of soft clay. The moon elves' astute mages manipulated the strange material with various magics, making it harder or softer as needed, thicker or thinner through alchemy. Elven architects used the silvery compound to join stone or wooden objects; its use was almost limitless through only minute adjustments.

For a few minutes, Qualthalas settled into a low crouch atop the lip of the crater and remained still as he observed the area keenly. His eyes darted from the central impact site to the edges of the surrounding ring and back over his shoulder once or twice. Nothing changed. Deeming the environment safe enough to approach closely, Qual crept over the ridge and made his way with feather-light steps toward the centre of the depression where a blackened set of streaks in the terrain betrayed the meteorite's resting place. Coolly he noted some weaving, snakelike patterns in the exposed crunchy frozen vegetation usually hidden under the settled powder of the moon's surface. Likely, some of the strange worms had investigated the area after the object had hit, attracted by the sudden shock and subterranean vibrations.

Qualthalas traced their paths to a dark tunnel obscured in the shadow of the furthest ridge where the creatures must have broken through to investigate the crater. With gloved fingers, the elven prince traced the grooves made by the contracting and expanding muscles of the worms and found little moon dust in the muskeg. The striations looked relatively recent; he placed their exploration within the last few hours, but it appeared they had merely approached the centre, then doubled back to the far side of the crater and finally burrowed back down to safety. It was unlikely they would return, at least that was his hope. Careful steps brought Qual to the epicentre where he knelt to scrutinize the impact site in detail; scorch marks and burnt vegetation created a ring around a mounded-over central hole.

An inky black, roiling tar startled the elf as it bubbled up from the small cavity, its tendril-like fingers of blackness seemed to reach out with life, and he cautiously backed away, unsure of what he was looking at. His eyes detected no discernable heat from the substance – or creature – whatever it may be. Watching it in wonder for a while, he noticed it seemed to focus its form of writhing tentacles in his direction, searching as if they sensed his presence, though they lacked the mass to reach him with their slender tips.

Fingers shaking, Qualthalas drew forth a large jar and held it towards the thing to coax it inside. Slowly he moved the large phial closer, until the first few fingers reached inside and explored the interior space of the container. He continued to advance as more of the substance filled the jar, and when he reached the apparent source of the fluidic shadowy mass, it practically leapt into the receptacle with a sucking sound. Qual popped the stopper excitedly onto the jar and held it up for his silver-blue eyes to inspect. The substance or being – he was still unsure what to classify the thing as – churned and squirmed inside the glass, formed fingers again, which probed the top and sides of the jar until it became almost inert, seeming relaxed. He would have to decide later if he would bring his discovery to one of his arcane tutors for study or if he should keep it a secret and perform experiments on it himself. However, the uncomfortable prickling now coursing up the back of his neck broke the wonderment and excitement of the finding as Qualthalas sensed a silent observer nearby.

Turning his head slowly, almost nonchalantly, the young elf was certain he saw a figure duck down behind the same ridge he had come from. *Was I followed somehow*, his mind raced with worry, for surely, he would be in trouble for risking this adventure on his own. Making sure to conceal the jar, he slid the glass gently into the satchel strapped around his torso, clasped it shut and tightened the straps and hooks, leaving little chance it would tumble out. Qual turned on his knee and pretended to inspect the fissure for a few moments, suspecting the observer still lurked beyond the lip of the crater, just out of view.

As a precaution, the young elf loosened his shortsword in its scabbard, prepared to draw it swiftly in case it was not one of his kin but some as-yet undiscovered threat. He was sure the form had been bipedal, so unless this guest was something his people had never encountered, Qualthalas felt certain it implied trouble of a more reprimanding nature than a physical one. Nevertheless, the incognito prince remained cautious as he forged a path directly back up the ridge to his initial observation site. *Might as well face the music*, he thought grimly, but a wry smirk crept across his lips. Trouble was something the silver-tongued elf usually talked his way out of and, as heir-apparent to the throne of the kingdom, his punishment was typically a stern lecture about his lack of discretion and the importance of his own life.

When Qual neared the edge of the crater, as suspected, the mysterious figure revealed himself as he slowly stood, brushing sediment and powdery silt from flowing silvery robes. *"Oh, dre'zal-eithe,"* Qualthalas cursed under his breath, instantly recognizing the slightly stooped ancient sage that now stood, arms crossed beneath a stern face that peeked out from his hood. *Hello, Grandfather,* Qualthalas thought and winced visibly. At this age, the young prince had not yet developed the practiced nonchalance and deflecting nature he was so widely known for later in life. He stood there, lower jaw agape and unable to muster a glib excuse for his presence at the crash site, nor would he have tried against his ancient kinsman. Any moon elf who ever tried found that *Elde Ithrauss* could sense a lie about to exit one's lips before they even spoke it, so attuned was he to others' minds. In hushed tones, the older adults recounted the former King's role in previous ages, when the moon elves came into conflict with several of the races of Antiqua, long before their ascent to Sillis-Thal'as. Apparently, the Diviner could draw confessions and secrets from enemies by sheer force of will alone, performing interrogations often without even making his presence known. Ithrauss turned his glaring eyes upon the sweating elf and let his mischievous grandson bask in disapproval for several moments before betraying his sense of amusement by allowing a smirk to spread across his creased face. However, Ithrauss knew young Qualthalas felt abashed by his admonishing intent, and that was the effect he had desired. At length he spoke.

"I do not recall," came the slow, powerful voice from beneath the hood, pausing long for effect, "asking the *Crown Prince of the Akir'Aelyph-Ana'ii himself* to scout ahead for me. Pray, I must be *aged* to be forgetting such orders." Qualthalas balked at the statement, unsure if his grandfather was chastising him or leading him on. He took a step back slightly and turned in his knee, bowing in apology. Just as Qual started to stammer an explanation, his grandfather chuckled and cut off his swiftly prepared speech. "Save your words, Crescent-Moons," he scoffed, waving a hand dismissively at his young grandson, "I can smell *Phas'Ker-et* from a kilometre away." Qualthalas stifled a chuckle upon hearing the old man utter something so vulgar. Ithrauss continued, this time his voice was kind and conspiratory, "Besides... I am curious what you've found here, and discoveries are always better when shared, wouldn't you say?"

It had been fortuitous that his grandfather had come, and they shared an enjoyable time subsequently, investigating the crater fully together, uncovering the tiny hunk of meteorite thanks to the tools the old man had brought. They spoke casually and eventually Qualthalas had trusted Ithrauss with his own earlier discovery, revealing the jar of inky substance, which the venerable elf turned over and over in his hands, thoroughly intrigued. Later, after agreeing to hide the young elf's minor transgression, Ithrauss had brought the object back to his laboratory for further study, and revealed its nature to Qualthalas, allowing him to keep most of the fluidic compound. It had been revealed to be non-sentient, but an undiscovered essence that reacted to light and heat as a living thing might. Its origin was of another plane entirely, the *Enthril Al'Ouinn-Qa*, or 'Darkfire' dimension.

Losing himself in that memory helped Qualthalas maintain a measure of control amid the chaos of his emotions and instincts. He smiled when picturing his grandfather's face, his calm demeanor, and his subtle humour. In fact, the thought of Elde Ithrauss almost made him homesick, and he considered once this debacle he was embroiled in was resolved and Kaira was again safe in his arms, he might even risk taking her for a visit to his homeland. If he lived through it, that was. Peering along the length of the rapier, Qualthalas observed that the thick fluid had entirely coated the blade and was pulsating and undulating along the enchanted surface. He prepared to duplicate the runic pattern he had traced the weapon along earlier. Though unfamiliar with the intricacies of the indigo elven dialect, (his aunt and perhaps a handful of moon elven sages being his only exposure), it was similar enough to his own language, having developed ages long past from the same root tongue when their peoples were not so distinct. Qual was confident he could speak the phrase well enough, and with the dark material he possessed, postulated it might open the portal.

Qualthalas extended his rapier out to the first symbol, tracing it, eyes closed in concentration as he intoned the word with what he hoped was the proper inflection, "*Auneiss*," he began somewhat falteringly, but when he felt the portal hum and the dark substance coating his rapier begin to vibrate, his confidence was soon bolstered. He continued with a stronger voice and remembering his aunt's accent, spoke the second syllable accordingly, "*Fras't-ahn*." Again, the portal buzzed in acknowledgement, and Qualthalas opened his eyes to see the runes aglimmer with a violet hue, which intensified as he assertively proclaimed the rest of the words, the echoes resounding in the chamber.

Upon his utterance of the last of the etched syllables, the portal's before-inert interior emitted a sharp '*crack*' as a vortex of energy formed, swirling in violet and inky black. His rapier was gleaming, its fine edge now bare; the activation of the runes had consumed the coating of ichor-like substance from the Darkfire Plane, leaving Qual with only the empty jar in his pack as a memento. Mourning-Song responded to the portal's energy exactly as Qual had presumed it would – scintillating topaz lines cut a jagged path along the blade, indicating teleportive magic was at work within the device. Although expected, it served to confirm that this was indeed a portal of transportation and not a summoning device, which it could very well have been, considering the meaning of the phrase Qualthalas had just read. Roughly translated to the best of his knowledge, he repeated it in Mithrainian, "In Shadows we tread, to the Realm of the Dead." He laughed at the poetical nature of the verse, found it ironic that he would encounter magic like his own in the employ of his greatest foe. However, he surmised, the teleportation device may not have been manufactured by his nemesis, Zhiniel, nor even be of subterranean origin. It was far more likely the arcane aperture was 'appropriated' by the Darklord or his legions from any number of races the indigo elven necromancer had subjugated over what Qualthalas estimated as nearly a thousand years, maybe more, in his covert and nefarious campaign. With only conviction to guide him, Qualthalas boldly stepped through the rippling, crackling surface, and disappeared from the room.

Scant moments later, after the rushing sound of the elf's departure had faded, something stirred in the room. Curiously and silently, a figure emerged from behind the small sanctuary the elf had only minutes ago inhabited. Gleaming yellow eyes peered from under a hood of vines and branches that cascaded down its vaguely humanoid form like a robe, and it flowed through the dwelling as if melded in part to it. A regal crown of antlers adorned the creature's head and a quiet sound like a wind whispering through trees issued from a cavity beneath its hood. The misty ground enveloping the strange entity left a moist trail upon the floor as it swept toward the portal. A branch-like appendage formed and reached out, small twigs for fingers stretching forth to graze the surface of the still-active vortex, tentatively testing the magical energy swirling within.

Nearby, from a crack formed in the roof by the absorption caused by Qualthalas' shelter, an extremely oversized rat poked its nose out, whiskers bristling as it tested the air. It scampered down the roof with sharp grey claws and skittered to the tile floor below, still sniffing the air as if it smelled food. The creature made its way to the door of the dwelling and attempted to burrow under, scraping at the tile until it broke apart, then made short work of the stone and dirt underneath. Nose-first, the metre-long rat had almost squeezed the top half of its body inside when it suddenly shrieked in pain. Barbed and root-like vines encircled its torso and hind legs, the sharp thorns shredding its flesh as they pulled back, dragging the creature forcibly from its partial tunnel and onto the open floor. A wolf's howl echoed in the chamber as a second whip-like appendage shot out from the Primordial, curling around the squealing rat's neck. The wicked barbed coils tightened rapidly around the doomed creature and its eyes bulged out just before a popping sound came from its spine and the vermin went completely limp. The elongated arms of the fantastical thing retracted slowly, drawing the corpse up into its viny embrace, enveloping the dead rat entirely in moments. If Qualthalas had still been present, he would have surely retched from the sound of crunching and grinding as the entity consumed the dead rat within its vegetative form, and blood seeped out onto the floor, staining the tiles crimson.

After the horrid noises of its gruesome feeding subsided, the creature twitched and convulsed a few times, and the patches of moss growing on its branches glowed with a vaguely ruby hue as the creature absorbed the rat's blood. A crunching and jostling happened inside the strengthened Primordial; from deep within, something moved to the area that should be its head buried in the hood of vines. Within the shadowy recess, yellow teeth and ivory white bone erupted forth as the rat's skull and jaw became the new face of the entity. Its glowing citrine eyes reformed within the sockets of its new visage, and a macabre grin it bore, seeming to produce a ghoulish smile as its jaw hung at a crooked angle below its picked-clean skull.

"Ha-ooouh!" it howled in its semblance of mirth and satisfaction. After its long seclusion, the Primordial was eager in its strange way to explore this place, and to find the elven creature who had summoned it along with its shelter. It formed thoughts only of impulse and the basest of emotion, for it was more a force embodied than a living being. Conscious and willful, but not intelligent by any contemporary standards, it possessed only cunning, and instinct guided by its bizarre personality. Though bound to the powerful scroll Qualthalas had used, the strange being had not been created by its magic – it was in fact an ancient force that had been captured and contained by a powerful ritual.

This Primordial had formed millennia ago in the wildest of places, where carnivorous plants and ferocious animals hunted and fed upon one another ceaselessly. In this chaotic jungle, its life birthed from the savage miasma of predatory urge and entropic carnage that permeated the area; through this, the creature had forged its unique self-identity. A powerful Druzaic Master, who bound the entity within the scroll for emergency use, had imprinted its essence and matter along with the dwelling materials using a primal magic rarely practiced. Unfortunately, the master fell prey to a cabal of raider Warlocks, who had no idea the power the sealed parchment contained, as they picked it from his body along with his other belongings. The murderous arcanists had pawned off these spoils, in the various underground dens they frequented – for a tidy sum, sure, but the profits were soon gone indulging their wicked pleasures and vices.

After the dwelling established itself, the creature had re-formed along with it, and remained hidden outside, observing the elf with its gemstone eyes and surveying its wholly new surroundings. Parts of it were attuned to the underground, so it had a rudimentary understanding of the stone and earth that were everywhere around. It could sense living beings and had a predatory desire to hunt and consume smaller creatures for the essence that nourished its thirst. It was this instinct that motivated the entity to reach forth into the portal with viny hands, which it felt suddenly drawn into by a force beyond its understanding. The viny creature succumbed to the urge to press forth, and happily thrust the rest of its body into the vortex, disappearing in the same way the warm, fleshy elf had done minutes prior.

Chapter 12

UNDERPREPARED AND
OVERWHELMED

An overwhelming vertigo assailed Qualthalas as the portal's magic hurled him a tremendous distance into the bowels of the planet. The disorienting rush of the plummeting sensation made it impossible to gauge the actual depth as his entire composition passed through some nightmarish, alien dimension and ejected the elf from an arch identical to the one into which he had stepped. Its mirror surface rippled once, then became still. His enhanced senses in complete disarray, the hapless rogue stumbled out and struggled to retain his footing on the cavernous and irregular stone of the floor. Taking a knee quickly as the myriad distortions of perspective righted themselves akin to snapping rubber bands, Qualthalas barely held back the urge to retch. Blurred and watering, his keen almond eyes darted about as he steeled his grip upon Ithrin'Sael-I-Uiin; he barely understood what he was seeing.

Porous, volcanic stone formed strange sculptures all around, twisting and reaching up from the uneven ground to the shadows above. The chamber surrounding the portal was so vast that Qual was unable to see the ceiling with his sharpened vision, so high it loomed. The stiflingly hot and acrid air reeked of sulfur, suffused with ash particles. He suspected the chamber was deep enough to be in the vicinity of his enemy's very demesne, or in proximity to one of the subterranean cities of the Dun Dwarves or Magmic Gnomes. Through the stone, he could feel a rhythmic thrumming, like a heartbeat or... a forge perhaps. Hissing sounds escaped the cracks and fissures in the floor and walls of the chamber, coated in yellowish powder, which also dotted gnarled surfaces throughout the strange underground landscape. He could breathe, barely, but knowing that danger lurked in the form of toxic vapours so deep underground, he rummaged swiftly for a scarf and drew it over his lips and nose.

The ringing, steady clank of mailed boots marching with disciplined order in the distance added to the disquiet building inside the bewildered elf. That same rhythmic drumming of hard-soled feet swiftly closed on his position, so Qualthalas rushed to conceal himself behind a massive, convoluted outcropping of lava rock, slipping into a shadowed nook. From his vantage point, he could observe much of the rest of the chamber, which seemed to have innumerable exits scattered throughout its winding venue. It would be difficult for an invader to move forces through an entrance such as this, let alone navigate its twisting tunnels; certainly, the natural composition of the area held a tactical advantage considered by the necromancer.

The steps hastened and their echoes made it difficult to estimate their number or exact direction with certainty. Qual slowed his breathing and put a hand behind each of his sharp ears, making a quick tally in his head. He surmised there were roughly eight to ten pairs of feet, marching in an orderly fashion from perhaps thirty to forty metres somewhere ahead of his current position. These were soldiers, likely, judging by the cadence of their steps and the steady pace they employed. It appeared that the Soulharvester was sending him a grandiose welcoming party indeed!

Thinking quickly, Qualthalas slipped a steel flask from a clasp on his belt and twisted off the cap. Estimating the soldiers would arrive within minutes at most, the elf frantically raced about, steps hastened with the imbued strength of the *Scarlet Fury Masque*, spreading the contents of the bottle throughout the room. The liquid turned to a pungent vapor that permeated the area as it diffused, serving to mask his scent, and providing a mild toxin that opened its victims' minds to suggestion.

In the short moments he had, Qual formed a vague plan to separate his foes and pick them off as opportunity arose. Then, after thinning their numbers with ambush tactics, he would assault the mind of one of the last enemies remaining, subverting it through coercive magic to his service. He would choose whichever seemed the most brutish of the vanguard force to manipulate; in that case, he could use the enemy against its cohorts in the ensuing battle, and then afterwards glean whatever information he could from his subject's mind. It seemed a solidly laid plan... if a little rough around the edges. He knew in a situation he was underprepared for, it paid to improvise on a foundational idea of some sort. The thought reminded him of his years of training before departing Sillis-Thal'as, how swiftly his previously lackadaisical existence had changed.

About eighty years past, during his preparations to descend to the planet proper, among the young moon elf's focused studies were grim lessons of necessity. Not knowing what to expect precisely, he soon found the bulk of his study involved in the art of infiltration. At his grandfather's behest, the superiors of the Twisted Strings guild were to impart their extensive expertise in the field to the aid of the young prince. Ithrauss had contacted these key members in secret; Qualthalas had no intimation his grandfather retained command of the former Akir'Aelyph-Ana'ii Royal Intelligence Organization, under the guise of the Twisted Strings.

Their identities were secret, and the members of the organization were scattered throughout the moon elven kingdom, finally able to live out relatively normal, albeit mundane lives. Though their original purpose in identifying and eliminating security threats was of little use upon Sillis-Thal'as in its long period of peace, their skills remained honed despite years of relative inactivity.

Qualthalas had been shocked and surprised when he felt a strange sensation creep up his spine as he practised his fencing skills alone in the personal study hall afforded him by his father, the High King. The prince glanced about nervously, thinking that perhaps he was developing paranoid thoughts and trepidations about his upcoming mission. Unbeknownst to the young elf, the first of his grandfather's associates had come to teach his first hard lesson. Briefly resuming his parries and thrusts but having grown tired of swordplay, Qual sheathed the newly acquired Ithrin'Sael-I-Uiin with a long sigh. He glanced over at the various stations set up within the spacious hall, and reluctantly made his way to an assigned stack of books detailing the history of the planet. They included events and geography as well as established kingdom borders, though the information was somewhat dated, the archivists had done their utmost to include addendums derived from current observations they could make upon Antiqua proper. Beside the stacks of books, much to his chagrin, his grandfather had placed a portrait of the prince, commissioned years past. Qual hated the picture for some reason – the nose, the lips, they just weren't right somehow. He shook his head and moved on past it, ready to study something new to allay his boredom and agitation when, without warning, all lighting in the room went out, leaving Qual in utter darkness.

Unsure of what could possibly be happening; Qualthalas called out and found his voice stifled somehow. The room lacked any natural echo whatsoever, his voice just felt hollow and faded promptly after leaving his lips. *Something is very wrong*, he thought, crouching low and reaching for the table directly in front of him as his keen almond eyes adjusted to the blackness. Dismissing the lighting failure as an effect from some sort of magical disturbance was an easy assumption to make, however the silence that surrounded him was wholly unnatural. He could sense the work of concealment magic in it, and his mind raced with possibilities. *Are we under attack?* He dismissed the idea quickly – so deep in the city, it was unthinkable that an intruder could have made it this far without the Diviners and his grandfather knowing instantly. *No, perhaps an experiment really has gone awry*, he postulated. Since Qual's station dwelled in the heart of the Arcane Academies district, numerous spires of magical study surrounded him, and odd occurrences such as this were not unheard of. However, Qualthalas could not shake the pervading sense that someone had purposefully caused these effects directly and was close-by.

Qual felt a humming at his hip. Curious, he unsheathed *Ithrin'Sael-I-Uiin* to see silver-blue runes creeping along the blade, illuminating his area… and unfortunately revealing his position. A voice came from directly behind, quiet and threatening in the stillness, "Young Prince, you'll have to be far more perceptive and swifter to act if you plan on infiltrating the human kingdoms…" the whisper disappeared, sucked up by the stifling atmosphere. Qual spun and fully unsheathed his rapier, which continued to glow dimly; in its light, he caught a momentary glance at the figure before him. As the man sidestepped behind a bookcase, Qual was shocked to see it was no elf, but a Neph'al – a human – clad in loose silken garb tied at the waist, wrists, and ankles by tight sashes. In addition, more disturbing to him were the pair of blades in the man's hands – short and straight, notched at the tip; the metal was blacked out so as not to reflect light. *It was an assassin!* His mind reeled at the thought; for the first time, the Crown Prince felt the possibility of the importance of his life to the kingdom under his father's rule. How could a human bypass so many defenses as to penetrate this deep into the city? Moreover, if his grandfather was unaware of the man's presence, what obscure power did he wield?

Again, came the quiet voice, which now seemed to speak to his mind, and upon hearing it again, Qualthalas felt a vague recognition, like he should somehow know the young-looking Neph'al man. "Qual, you should be focusing on your enemy, not upon your musings." The peculiar man spoke casually, using the prince's nickname as if he too knew Qualthalas; it was more than a bit unnerving, but the voice was correct. The time for wondering was not at hand – he should focus on escaping and alerting his grandfather, or anyone for that matter, of the blatant security breach. A sharp kick to the back of his knee sent the elf to the floor, and though Qualthalas scrambled to bring his rapier around to defend himself, the young man was blindingly fast. Both exotic short swords cut at the elf's midsection, just barely touching, slicing through his doublet enough to draw blood but leaving only superficial wounds. The fine-featured blonde man took a defensive step back suddenly, smirking, "If I'd employed poison, you'd be a dead elf in moments."

The individual's movements were fluid and graceful; with practiced ease he shifted to a low back stance, one sword held high, arcing over his head towards Qual, the other low and across his midsection, guarding. Considered an advanced study in the elven kingdom, double-sword techniques took years to master; guessing by his facial features, which were surprisingly unhidden by hood or mask, the man appeared in his early twenties, if he was indeed a human. It shouldn't be possible to have attained the skill level he displayed in those years unless he had received training from infancy. The voice in his head spoke again as the man wore a wan smile, answering his thoughts, "Either that or you've been squandering your last two-hundred and eighty-nine years, *Crescent-Moons*."

Qualthalas balked at the statement. Rising cautiously, he wondered how in the hells this man knew so much about him. Mourning-Song hummed rhythmically, and now its hue and runes were continually altering their pattern as if confused by the individual presented before it. Something about this strange assailant was extremely out of place. He could not be simply what he appeared, and though Qual had lost the sense that his life was in danger, (for the man was right, he could surely have killed Qualthalas if he had wished) the enigma he presented was prevalent in Qual's mind.

"If you must know," the man spoke aloud this time, "I am here... *somewhat* at your grandfather's behest... and I wanted to test your skills myself." The man shifted and advanced menacingly as he completed his speech, "Without trying to sound condescending or harsh, you have a lot to learn, young elf. You are underprepared for what lies before you." As if to prove the point, with an impossibly fast set of thrusts from both blades, Qualthalas found himself unarmed, Mourning-Song sailed silently across the floor only to come to a skittering stop about four metres away. The clattering of metal on stone faded just like the voice preceding. Qualthalas narrowed his eyes and again surveyed the man, who had stepped back and sheathed his blades in a single motion, carrying them upon his back. In particular, he studied the eyes, deep blue with flecks of silver, pools of wisdom and intelligence unparalleled held within; the man was certainly older than his physical form alluded.

"In that, you *are* correct." The human wore a wan, conspirational look upon his face as he answered the elf's very thoughts, "I am not what I seem, Qualthalas Ithrauss Aeth'Akir, it is only in Time that you will learn my secret." It was possibly the most cryptic statement Qual heard uttered thus far in his life. But his 'instructor' gave him no pause to consider it, for he had already advanced on silent feet and as Qualthalas rolled towards his rapier, the man again moved faster, kicking it further into the room, laughing. The amused sound dissipated into nothingness; it was as if the aura surrounding the exasperating man muted every local vibration. Frustrated, Qual spat out, "What is this lesson supposed to teach me, *Rai'an-A-t'ari*?" Although his tone was irate, the young elf referred to the man as 'Respected Master' out of regard for his skill and if he was indeed here at Elde Ithrauss' request, Qualthalas owed him that courtesy.

Smirking coolly, the man relaxed his stance and pointed at the rapier. "Foremost, as I said, I wanted to see your skill for myself..." a little smirk, not unlike Qual's own characteristic mischievous sneer, played upon the man's young face as he arched an eyebrow. He looked so familiar in that moment that the Crown Prince furrowed his brow, trying to recall if he had met the man somewhere and had forgotten. Unabated, the Respected Master continued, disturbing Qualthalas' musings, "Secondly though," he paused to emphasize his gravity, "I am here to instruct you on the bonding rituals for *Ithrin'Sael-I-Uiin*." The man's penetrating eyes scrutinized the elf for a reaction, knowing full well his declaration would produce a significant one. Though the blade itself was famous, the origin and details of the creation of Mourning-Song were closely guarded secrets of the Akir'Aelyph-Ana'ii dynasty; it was a moon elven relic nearly as old as Qual's grandfather.

Indeed, the almond-shaped sky-silver eyes of the elf narrowed at the claim. *What is he playing at?* Qualthalas wondered. Archived in detail, it was well-documented that the blade was crafted millennia ago in the Midnight Forge and presented to her Majesty, Leixanth Tsair-Cian'na Aeth'Akir; his twice-great-grandmother, upon her inauguration as High Queen of the Sillistrael'li. The artifact's ongoing empowerment involved magic of the highest magnitude from among various disciplines. Arcanists, Elementalists, Sages and Thaumaturges had woven runes both offensive and defensive in function into the blade every century since its creation, coinciding with the rare dual-lunar eclipse when the dark moon overshadowed the silver one.

Qualthalas had been required to study Ithrin'Sael-I-Uiin extensively in his Enchantment school, both theoretically and practically for years before receiving permission to touch it. Further, the very retrieval of Mourning-Song from its encasement was an event of high import. High King Adamon had to summon both his brother, Balthrael, and his father, Ithrauss, to accompany him to the heavily guarded sanctuary where it slept in a matrix of specially formed sapphire. How could this outsider – this *human* – claim to possess the ability to unlock for Qualthalas the inner workings of…

Impatiently and with a tense frown, the man uttered a command word, "*E'threiss.*" Utterly against logic, *Ithrin'Sael-I-Uiin* materialized in the human's still-outstretched hand, and its runes danced with starlight that cut through the darkness. "Elves may have enchanted and possessed the blade, true – but have you ever uncovered knowledge of *who it was* that forged it?" The man tapped the tip of the foil upon the ground and the stiff silence surrounding Rai'an-A-t'ari abated instantly. Another verse of magic he spoke, lyrical and sibilant, "*Tharas-Selen'ar Iss-Sho'ikan Varisse.*" Mourning-Song emitted an audible ringing pulsation that intensified enough to feel it reverberate, shaking the floor of the study hall. Its runes leapt from the surface of the blade to swirl and orbit the man himself, glowing in the deepest indigo as they transformed into a script that Qualthalas had never encountered. Presenting it solemnly to the elf, hilt-first, the Respected Master stated simply, "There. It is now unfettered: my gift to you."

Though speechless and dumbfounded, Qualthalas reached for the handle with a shaking hand and closed his fingers tightly around

Ithrin'Sael-I-Uiin. Simultaneously, the man let go of the blade and utterly vanished, just as Ithrauss and two heavily armoured guards burst through the doors to the study, looks of alarm upon all three of their faces. The pair of gleaming plate-clad warriors fanned out, longblades at the ready, looking to Ithrauss for orders. His eyes scanning the room fervently for the intruder but only seeing his grandson, thankfully unharmed, Ithrauss held a palm up to the guards, silently signalling them to stay at the ready.

The old elf called out to Qualthalas, who stood, mouth agape; Mourning-Song was still glowing with the deep blue light, and its runes were only slowly reforming upon the metal of the blade, shifting back to their usual dormant pattern. As they settled, the Crown Prince could hear an incomprehensible melody of pure musical tones that radiated throughout his consciousness; it registered as a voice of acceptance, albeit in a way alien to normal understanding. Ithrauss noted this invisibly while making his way to Qualthalas, suspecting what had happened. He registered not even a hint of a smile or knowledge of what had transpired, for he was unable to augur any of the previous occurrences within the study hall; it was only assumption and estimation that he possessed. That and he verily wanted to gauge what Qualthalas would tell him of the event if his suspicions were correct. Ithrauss knew there existed only one being who could fully unlock the blade, but would his grandson tell him the truth of the meeting? He was intensely curious but hid his intentions skillfully as he laid a hand on Qual's shoulder, shaking his grandson gently from the overwhelming reverie.

Ithrauss urged Qualthalas, in a soft voice, to answer, "What occurred in here, grandson?" as he made a sweeping gesture about the room, "Everything seemed normal at first, but then I noticed a permeating silence surrounding the study hall." He scrutinized every facial expression that the young, shaken elf went through in those next few seconds. They ran the gamut of emotion – confusion, suspicion, anger, bewilderment and then... *calculation*. Ithrauss held his approval from showing. *Good*, he thought, *this means he might know when not to speak for once, even if it seems right at the time.* Ithrauss raised an eyebrow; making it clear to Qualthalas that he expected a detailed explanation forthcoming.

Qualthalas sighed, and an air of false arrogance and exultation replaced the abject look of confusion. The lie that left his lips was impressive (the young elf almost believed himself) and again Ithrauss had to hold back from revealing that he could see right through it, as Qual glibly stated, "After extensive study, I have prevailed in unlocking the blade's potential." He looked to Ithrauss, expecting the old man to mock him for lying so brazenly, but to his surprise, Ithrauss wore a convincing expression of shock, and even leaned in as if to hear him say it again. Unabated, the young elf continued as if speaking to a suddenly hushed audience, "The area was bathed in silence and darkness for a few minutes as, I believe, Ithrin'Sael-I-Uiin *communicated* with me – there was a feeling of bonding, and then it glowed a deep blue and dissipated the effects." His grandfather hung on his words, astonished, but a look of pride and acceptance beamed on his countenance.

Qualthalas made a grandiose flourish with the rapier, which was now gleaming its customary starlight, the runes having regained their place fully upon the blade. His grandfather appeared impressed, inhaled sharply, and congratulated his grandson by clapping him on the shoulders. Ithrauss held the young elf there a second, locking Qualthalas in his eyes as he delved into his subconscious. Though the lad did his best to believe his own falsehood, his budding mind was no match for the old elf's cunning as the ancient one studied the events as they truly played out. He memorized the details quickly as he scanned his grandson's recent thoughts and withdrew mentally before Qualthalas was at all aware of the psionic probe. Once his grandson received full training and his birthright, mental intrusions such as this would prove virtually impossible.

After the endowment of the Masque of Myriad Minds, even I won't be able to touch his psyche, thought Ithrauss. For a moment, he turned his lips down in a slight frown; such burdens would his grandson be forced to shoulder, in the name of national security. Perhaps even the fate of their entire world hung on Qualthalas who, though capable, was certainly underprepared, as the Respected Master had implied. Ithrauss was resolved to use every resource in his considerable arsenal to ensure the success of the mission, and the overall safety of his grandson. His frown soon turned to a reassuring smile as he again patted Qualthalas on the back, and turned to leave, signalling to the soldiers that all was secure. The old moon elf paused at the doorway and with a characteristic wink, (one that Qualthalas himself would adopt as a habit) Ithrauss gave one parting remark. "I *should* tell you more of the secret origin of Ithrin'Sael-I-Uiin, young protégé... I may have neglected to pass on some critical knowledge I possess on the *unusual* circumstances of its creation. Come to me in seven days once you've completed more of your training."

With that purposeful last comment, Ithrauss let himself out of the hall, and finally allowed a deep laugh to burst forth from his lips. He'd have to brush the youth up on his tactical deceit skills if he were to infiltrate the human kingdoms below. The ancient sage had allowed his grandson only seven years to prepare for his descent to Antiqua, which in the long-lived terms of elves was not a long time. He knew, though, that a great deal could change upon the planet in those scant few years, with the determined pace of the ambitious races that dwelled upon the surface... and, more importantly, the Underworld below. The thought again brought a frown to the elder's countenance, for he had recently detected disturbing emanations deep within Antiqua's crust. There were many interferences to his scrying attempts, most of them natural – the buried technology of past civilizations and mysterious crystalline structures that seemed to house intelligence being the primary sources. However, there was something else: he suspected their subterranean cousins, the indigo elves, thwarted most of his auguries into key locations using purposeful negation fields. Someone was hiding something down there, and Ithrauss speculated that soon enough, Qualthalas (wittingly or unwittingly) would find the source.

After his laughter abated, Ithrauss dismissed the two soldiers still standing at the ready. "I've no need for an *entourage*, my friends. Report back to Adamon that all is well with the prince's studies and that the momentary anomaly was merely due to his success in attuning to Ithrin'Sael-I-Uiin, nothing more." The soldiers both crisply saluted and strode with a steady pace in the direction of the magnificent multi-spired palace that housed the royal Aeth'Akir family. Ithrauss shook his head. He had matters to attend forthright and wanted no accompaniment in his tower, least of all whilst conversing with the individuals he needed to contact regarding *improved otherplanar security*. He was mildly annoyed that this interloper had evaded his detection; the words of the bearer of the Sanctus Orb echoed in his ears, repeating their cryptic warning.

"*The Boy Who Would Be God cannot...*" the eyes of the Ma'jai still pierced his mind at the recollection, "*do not let him make my mistakes...*" Ithrauss knew the intruder to be the Boy to which the Ma'Jai had referred. The last phrase was what worried him more though, even though he did not understand their portent, "Your grandson... their lives are entwined..." and Ithrauss feared that this initial introduction could spell danger for Qualthalas. He wanted to prevent further encounters, for though the vague statements shrouded the specifics of the mystery, the expression upon the countenance of the Ma'Jai left little to interpret. Their interaction meant trouble of a sort that could pose interference in the fabric of reality, and this meddling individual, even if he meant no immediate harm, certainly had an agenda of his own. With those dark thoughts, Ithrauss startled as he felt a raucous, unhinged laughter erupt around him, though there was no real sound to it. It was detached, as if the impression of a barely contained insanity located somewhere parallel in time found his concerns *terribly amusing.*

Ithrauss responded aloud, "If I cannot dissuade you from your interactions with my grandson, then might I at least suggest extreme caution? I know not exactly what or who you are, but surely you must understand that interfering with temporal fabric is potentially catastrophic." The impression he sensed permeating the area seemed to recede as if in great consideration, and oddly, Ithrauss felt assured that the safety of Antiqua was of utmost importance to the incomprehensible being. He wondered if it was a God of some sort, perhaps it was even beyond the ancient Gods that had purportedly created the intelligent beings of the world. Again, came the impression of laughter, this time tinged with cynicism and wistful sadness as it faded into the void.

"I am sure I would find your story most intriguing." Ithrauss called out into the nothingness, unsure if the presence lingered or was even still listening. Lacking any further indication prompted the sage to focus on more visceral tasks at hand. He soon had to meet with his agents, the officers within the Twisted Strings, to give further instructions and direction on Qualthalas' lessons in the coming years. It now appeared they would have to work extensively on sharpening the young prince's resistance to influences from outside sources.

Ithrauss started to make his way along the sleek marble pathway to his tower but felt an aching tiredness throughout his frame. He sighed at the vagaries of age and snapped his fingers twice as he weaved an arcane pattern in the air, thrusting his hands skyward then, sweeping them to both sides as he fanned his fingers out. The air itself rippled and whipped up fine, chalky dust that swirled around the spellcaster as he was borne upwards by his incantation. He flew then, rapidly, straight to the highest veranda that encircled the laboratory near the very summit of his grand spire, alighting softly on the cool surface. Ithrauss dismissed the spell with a wave; he needed to conserve his magical energy in the coming days as he prepared the special inks and infusions he required.

Several hundred years had passed since Ithrauss had bestowed upon any individual the potent investiture of the Masque of Myriad Minds, which he was preparing to inscribe in Qualthalas. It was a delicate procedure; even moreso than casting the extremely powerful magic required, it was also a surgery that demanded the constant attention of several Sae'Ret-ii Clerists. Layers of skin were both stripped, then healed, while exotic inks were meticulously grafted into the exposed flesh, throughout the painstaking operation. His thoughts on the work ahead, Ithrauss thundered into his laboratory and began organizing the disarray with intent.

In the meantime, still shaken from all the confusing implications, Qualthalas absently rummaged through stacks of books, glancing from time to time at Ithrin'Sael-I-Uiin, which lay in its scabbard, propped against a chair. Qualthalas didn't want to admit it, but the events that had just transpired shook him, and he was almost *afraid* of the relic. The questions dancing around in his head were staggering, and he could not concentrate to save his life. He paused as he flipped through a book entitled, *The Royal Kingdom of Queen Bethaziel Sia-Satana Auniel of Huromithra,* one that looked both important and intriguing... he would have to come back to it when he was not so distracted. Some of the details were surprisingly racy. However, he was in no mood for political intrigue now.

Sighing, he set the volume aside and approached Mourning-Song. It hummed gently at his touch, and he felt the soft silken wrap of its meticulously crafted hilt in his fingers as he gingerly curled his hand around it. Something felt tangibly different; the rapier responded to his grip and felt feather light as he raised it and swished it around in a series of deft cuts. It practically sang through the air, pulsing with its own energy – the tension in his mind vanished and Qualthalas began to sing a melody of enchanted music that the blade seemed to amplify naturally. The spell-song was of soothing, of longing for purpose, of banishing doubt. The elven prince smiled and continued to practice, all the while speaking with the artifact as if it were alive... and perhaps it truly was.

Over the course of the next seven years, Qualthalas buried himself in the intense, focused tutelage of his grandfather's agents. Each surprised him, both in sheer physical prowess and with the vast knowledge they were so keen on imparting to him, and he drank it all in as if possessed of a fire inside that finally burned with a desire for *something more*. The moon elven prince had been imprinted with the Masque of Myriad Minds, and though the memory of the operation had been wiped from his psyche, the Sae'Ret-ii Clerists had all noted how easily performed the procedure was. Apparently, the royal Aeth'Akir line was predisposed to magical grafting; never had a patient recovered so quickly from the horribly invasive surgical and magical work. After the week-long procedure, where Qualthalas endured stages of sedation and consciousness alike, and submitted to almost torturous tests and mental manipulations, he had come out unscathed.

When he first looked in a mirror, and saw the twin, silvery crescent-moons, which were his namesake emblazoned across his face, he felt they uniquely suited him, and beamed at the honour of possessing such a powerful tattoo. Many other subjects who had undergone the procedure took years of counseling and adjustment to the powers of the Masque, but Qualthalas embraced it, and the use of the Masque became the focal point of months of his study. The High King had even commented, upon visits to his son while he studied, that Qualthalas had matured vastly, and was impressed at both his newfound determination and the sheer advancement in so many disciplines he had attained in such short time. When he finally departed for Antiqua, all present to wish him off were confident that he was truly ready. Qual had stepped through that starlight-infused portal, secure in the knowledge that he could succeed at anything the world below would throw at him, and even smiled and winked at the crowd as he bid his people a tearful goodbye.

However, his experiences upon learning the actualities of the world destroyed those naive expectations, he reflected, *so different it is now.* He mused only briefly, coming back in thought to the grim reality that lay before him. Enemies were fast approaching, he was in peril far beyond his anticipation, and the fate of more than just Kaira, whom he was so dreadfully worried over, loomed over him. Qualthalas was in the worst of predicaments, out of his element, and deep in the territory of an enemy who knew no equal. Mourning-Song hummed in response to his forbidding thoughts, glowing in purple as night-black runes crept along the surface of its blade. The footsteps grew nearer, and Qual was sure they would enter the chamber in mere seconds. "Here we go," he whispered, tucked away in the shadowy recess again, "I hope you're ready."

Qualthalas inhaled slowly, exhaled evenly, letting his heartrate slow, that he could better control the feral instincts raging inside. He had found a measure of control in the inferno; it was a calmness bolstered by his determination, and the magic residing deep within Ithrin'Sael-I-Uiin that thus far kept him sane amid the growing darkness. He waited in anticipation of the steady mailed boots, which must have been primarily from indigo elven soldiers, as indicated by the runic markings on his blade. There was a strange sizzling sound then, and Qualthalas was puzzled because it had come from behind his position, where nothing should have been able to approach. Twisting his head sharply to look behind, the elf barely stifled a look of surprise and swore aloud.

It was the portal. Re-activated and crackling in the same fashion as when he had stepped through; more foes must have followed him and waited for the right moment to launch a pincer strike. Now, the elf was amid an even more elaborate ambush tactic than he could adequately prepare for. Qualthalas sensed the soldiers had indeed entered the chamber from two entrances far ahead and to his right; they were still a fair distance from his position, but after a few steps in, the heavy stamping stopped abruptly, and all was horribly, gravely silent.

Qual's *Least Favorite* Rendition of Himself

Chapter 13

IN STRANGE COMPANY

Thankfully, there was no one present to see the abject look of terror etched into Qualthalas' face as the first of many creeping vines crawled out along the cavern floor, reaching out from within the crackling portal's surface. He inhaled sharply, but stifled a cry of surprise, willing himself to remain calm and take stock of the strange situation. Several more of the root-like appendages made their way forth, feeling about in a way that disturbed the elf immensely. The primordial emerged fully and its horrifying rat-skull face grinned with a crooked smile. The macabre thing released a wail of excitement. To Qualthalas it appeared like something out of a twisted nightmare, hideous to behold. Worse yet, the soldiers had noticed the noisy disturbance now, and one called out in an icy-stern voice, "Fael'threiss emynh-tau noth-terrar coveir'sa baelyi'qua!"

Qualthalas struggled to translate the harsh indigo elven speech in his head from what little he knew, and its similarities to his own dialect. Though he knew his understanding was imperfect, the intent of the words was something like, "Reveal yourself, intruder, our master demands you before him, willingly or as a corpse!" He briefly considered walking out into the open and surrendering, but the clicks of several crossbows and the unmistakable sound of unsheathed blades had him doubting the 'willing' part of the claim. He breathed slowly and timed his calm inhalations and exhalations with the rhythm of his heart. It was difficult to resist the welling panic as he silently watched the cackling, bestial thing as it swept forward into the chamber. Qualthalas could not help but imagine the creature tearing him to shreds with the wicked barbs dotting its whip-like vines.

A light crunching sound of the heel of a boot dragging across a loose pebble alerted the elf to the advance of his enemies. The steps became softer, more careful as they inched around a magmic formation nearer his position than he had hoped, but Qualthalas could pick out the movements easily with his enhanced senses. Silently backing out of his alcove, he whispered, "*Visan'a*," and Ithrin'Sael-I-Uiin ceased vibrating; its runes dimmed, barely visible. *Subtlety is my ally*, he thought, inching his way around the far side of the igneous outcropping. Qual's eyes darted back to the plantlike creature. The thing was creeping in the opposite direction, for which the elf was thankful; perhaps it would provide distraction for some of his foes. He edged slowly and warily along the porous rock, taking more care in his steps than the soldier who loomed ahead.

The back of one indigo elf, clad in scaled umbral armour made an easy first target as Qualthalas planted a hand firmly over the mouth and slid his rapier between his foe's breastplate and girdle. It drove straight through; the tip protruded from just under the shoulder, likely piercing his enemy through the heart. What should have been a scream was only a light gasp from the lips of the mortally wounded soldier. Qual felt blood trickle out of his enemy's mouth and nose as it issued a dying gurgle. He must have penetrated a lung as well. Laying the soldier down quietly, Qualthalas registered shock at finally seeing his enemy's visage through the open-faced helm it wore. Soft, supple, and deep blue skin, fair features and arched eyebrows – it was a female!

Qual's mind reeled from the impossibility of what lay before him. Unless the numerous treatises on indigo elven culture were horribly inaccurate, theirs was a uniformly matriarchal society. Though certain males of the subspecies retained minor titles and positions of power, it was solely at the behest of their superiors. These superiors were invariably women of authority: matrons of entire families, Templars of Ennetra and Daemon-Callers, to name only a few. A female serving as a soldier underling to a male necromancer was unthinkable, or so everything Qualthalas had researched had stated.

He had no inkling of the massive civil war waged centuries prior; in fact, none but the subterranean races knew anything of indigo elven affairs. They had receded into legend since ceasing their campaigns upon the surface world; hundreds of years past, leaders of all parties signed several contracts between their society and the empires of Mithras and Huromithra. Both sides had agreed to noncontact. The underground citadels of the Sovereign Syndicates would be safe from incursions from the great Neph'al nations if they agreed to stop their guerilla-like raids upon human settlements.

The implications that Qualthalas considered from this knowledge were grim, cementing his opinion that Zhiniel was a force sorely underestimated. The ignorance of his threat could spell the downfall of entire empires when he would invariably decide to break the treaties and assault the surface. This revelation could be monumental, it was imperative that he escape. Qual's thoughts turned dark. Though he would lay down his life to save Kaira, he might have to force himself to decide for the good of the entirety of Antiqua. New hatred for his cousin, who had thrown in with a tyrant the likes of which the world was unprepared for, boiled inside Qualthalas, along with abhorrence for the necromancer himself.

Only saved by sheer reflex, Qualthalas deflected a heavy crossbow bolt aimed for his head, Ithrin'Sael-I-Uiin singing through the air to intercept the deadly projectile. The assailant, this time a male he noted, was perched upon a three-metre-high outcropping of solid granite, swearing, and loading another bolt into the device. Before Qual could counterattack, the soldier barked something out loudly to alert the rest of his companions and retreated into the shadows. There was a great commotion from various locations spread throughout the chamber. However, another noise, shrill and terrifying erupted soon after, from the furthest reaches of the cavernous room nearest the portal. A scream of intense pain and terror, followed by a chilling predatory wail preceded two loud thumps and a heavy crunch from a body hitting stone. The legion footsteps of the trained soldiers, which had been directly approaching, suddenly halted as the opposing group waited to ascertain what had newly developed.

The primordial bore down on its prey, leaping upon the soldier who was unable to move; his spine had shattered from the sheer force with which the creature had hurled him. The indigo elf feebly held his mace up in self-defence, which the viny, cowled creature ripped from his hands with several tendrils and then it proceeded to tear apart the soldier's platemail armour. It could sense the blood and flesh underneath the metal shell of its victim and emitted a joyous shriek as it wrapped barbed roots around the screaming elf's midsection. The vines shredded the tender flesh, muscle, and the bones of the ribcage, digging through to find the still-beating heart, which it drew forth with sickening ease. The horror of the last second of life played upon the stricken face of the soldier before he succumbed to the release of death. The primordial devoured the organ greedily; two indigo elves were approaching in silence, watching with revulsion as it slurped and gurgled, crimson streaming into its form. There was a vast amount of blood all around the creature now, amid their companion's innards and several shattered bones. Even to the hardened military force, the sight was jarring.

They receded into shadow and retreated to the far end of the chamber from which they had come. The tactical decision was not a hard call to make. Nothing of the like had they before encountered, and not knowing the capabilities of the creature nor its origin was a severe detriment to any organized assault. The commander's opinion was that it was likely a cohort or servant of their enemy, the moon elf named *Qethe'lis* in their native tongue. He was purportedly a magical adept and a skilled manipulator, so in his estimation, caution was advised. The group prepared several concoctions stored in clay spheres laden with explosives that would lay shrapnel and smoke in a small area and the commander signalled silently to his troops to move in on both flanks.

Knowing that the creature was busy feasting, judging by the cackling noises and delighted caterwauling coming from it, Qualthalas took the opportunity to search his first victim, hoping to find something that might have a tie back to the Darklord. On her belt, carefully stored in a cushioned pouch were two clay orbs, possibly grenades of some sort. The elf quickly unclasped the entire pouch and attached it to his own belt. The body held very little else of immediate use, besides a pair of well-crafted daggers, which he left in her sheathes, the discarded short blade that lay beside her, and a pair of ornately fashioned earrings. Unable to spare another moment, he pocketed the earrings for later inspection – perhaps they were magical or sentimental; he might be able to glean more from them later. Presently, he decided to move from his position, following the outer wall of the chamber carefully with light footsteps.

The pair of soldiers that approached from Qual's side of the chamber was surprised to see him leaning against the wall in plain sight and looked from the elf to each other suspiciously. One raised a double-crossbow loaded with cross-pointed obsidian bolts, meant to penetrate armour, and embed themselves. They looked closely at the pale, blue-tinged skin, and silvery hair of the elf, seeing the crimson diamonds tattooed upon his face. Those features all matched the given description; however, the intruder sported a gaudy, green-feathered surcoat, and a painted face, along with an eclectic assortment of mismatched garb. The second soldier, armed with a light spear and throwing dagger, laughed mockingly at his opponent, and moved in. The one with the crossbow issued a few words, "En'yth Awei-lex'ei, phar'ess," which asked less-than-politely for Qualthalas to lay down his weapon and surrender.

The advancing indigo elf bit his lip, still eyeing his target warily, having the sense that something was amiss about the strange interloper. The moon elf had not moved even slightly when con-fronted, he just relaxed there against the wall with his rapier casu-ally in hand, pointed at the floor. A subtle crunching noise to the right of both soldiers had them startled as the two simultaneously spied the very same elf creeping through the shadows as he tried to sneak his way past. Turning, the one with the crossbow loosed both bolts even as the other threw his dagger at the cunning oppo-nent who they realized had been employing illusions to mask his true location. When all the projectiles flew harmlessly through their target, the soldiers realized their mistake, but not before the real Qualthalas, who had indeed been leaning against the wall the whole time, rushed forward.

Bringing Mourning-Song down in a swift arc, he batted aside the closer opponent's spear then took advantage of the opening to thrust twice into his knee. When the surprised indigo elf pitched forward, Qual's next piercing stab found its way past a slight gap in the armour between shoulder and neck, killing the soldier instantly. As the crossbow-toting enemy attempted to drop two more bolts into the wicked weapon, Qual pitched one of the readied clay orbs at the soldier's face. It shattered easily upon striking the metal helm, exploded, and sent shrapnel through his opponent's soft flesh, which elicited a pained shriek as the crossbow clattered to the floor. Blinding smoke surrounded the enemy, but this did not hinder Qualthalas in the slightest as he sprung forth, first landing a solid kick to the armored midsection, then following with a swift set of singing strikes from Ithrin'Sael-I-Uiin.

Injured and in severe pain, the soldier stumbled backwards and lost his footing, crumpling to the rough cavern floor while desperately reaching for his backup weapon. He found it and slashed blindly forth with a hooked knife, anticipating his enemy had closed the gap swiftly. Qual however, had played cautiously, whispering the last words of a binding transmutation spell. His fist turned upwards, he spread his fingers wide, and then made a grasping motion. Crunching and twisting, the porous rock beneath the soldier responded with identical movements as it reached up to encase the struggling, panicked indigo elf in a crushing stone grip. Qualthalas relaxed his hand and pulled down; likewise, the stone sunk half a metre, and the grinning moon elf completely released the incantation just shy of squishing his captive like a grape between his fingers. It would have been effortless to slay the indigo elf using this magic, but better it might be to keep a severely injured enemy alive, before enacting his plan to control one of the others. The soldier was immobilized by the cage of rock, heavily wounded but not dying. Qualthalas counted that as an asset, and moved along the wall further to the back of the cave to inspect from where his enemy had come.

Inspecting the flooring, he found it exceedingly difficult to discern the group's tracks. Although his vision was keen as an eagle, this was where the indigo elves held an advantage in their subterranean environment. Through thousands of years of adaptation, their subrace had developed the ability to see heat emanations, which served them both in hunting and in defense. Had Qualthalas been blessed with this form of thermal vision, he may have been able to pick out the fading warmth from the softer-soled boots, but alas, he did not hold this in his pack of tricks. He continued cautiously to the rear of the cavern in search of an exit.

The stone at the furthest reaches of the expansive area differed from the volcanic rock found in other parts of the cave. Formed of much smoother granite, it did not appear as if hewn by hand; it was still natural in appearance, but what vexed Qualthalas was that it seemed solid across the entirety of the back of the cavern. He was certain they had come from this very spot though, which indicated they had either used magic to gain entry or that possibly there was a secret entrance hidden in the wall. Frowning, Qualthalas weighed his options. He could either perform a search of the wall or continue his hit-and-run tactics against the remaining forces. The exit would have to wait, he decided. Egress from the cavern would likely require a key of some sort, which he would only acquire if he could best the entire squad and take his time to search and interrogate one of them.

Meanwhile, a group of three soldiers had taken up positions behind pillars surrounding a large opening in the middle of the chamber, where their commander stood at its centre, invisible. The indigo elf possessed a sharp mind, one honed by Zhiniel's lieutenants through relentless training regimens and arcane study. They waited silently in ambush positions, each ready with a shrapnel-bomb and their personal choice of melee weapon. Commander Drath'ivein Taras-kha'a stood silent, four-flanged halberd across his shoulders prepared to mutilate the cursed moon elf or the viny horror if either enemy approached. He concentrated on an outcropping to his right and a subtle illusionary noise made the sounds of scraping boots and crumbling stone. In three other nearby locations, he enacted the same sort of lure; he kept the noises subtle enough to be believable, yet just loud enough for his attentive foe to hear. Angered by the slippery moon elf's guerilla assaults, he hoped to draw Qualthalas out into the open, and considered ignoring the order to keep his quarry alive.

When the moon elf sauntered directly into the open chamber in front of him, dropping the corpse of the nearest of his squad to the floor, the commander smiled in admiration. Qual's rapier was glowing crimson and dripping blood, which he flicked off casually as he advanced. Theirs was a brutal society and the elf's actions were uncharacteristic of most of the mercy-filled surface dwellers he had encountered. Qualthalas squarely approached his position, stopping just out of the polearm's reach, and cocked his head to the side quizzically, staring straight at the indigo elf. Wary, the remaining two subordinates still hidden behind the magmic pillars held their clay bombs at the ready, suspicious of a trick.

Though incapable of detecting heat emanations like his subterranean cousins, Qual could easily defeat invisibility through his own spellcraft. Minutes prior, it occurred to him that his opponents may be employing illusions, and so prepared numerous perceptive enhancements with magic. He had sensed each of the commander's admittedly skilled illusions as they formed, and the auditory auras of the spells converted in his vision to pings of blue-silver globes. The commander himself was fully visible to Qualthalas, outlined in an amber glow, which made it effortless to address him directly.

"I am graciously prepared to accept your surrender," the impudent costumed elf offered with a slight bow to the commander, speaking in moon elvish. The commander's predictable laugh followed the bold request, and knowing that his opponent could somehow see him, the obsidian plate-clad warrior leveled his halberd at Qualthalas. Though he held an accent that suddenly reminded Qualthalas of his aunt Akhara, the indigo elf replied in fluent Sillistrael'li, "Feathered jester, I would sooner carve your head from your shoulders, were it permitted, than yield." Qualthalas tilted his head and smiled wanly in acknowledgement of the slight. He knew how ridiculous he looked, but the commander had given up valuable information without knowing it. That Zhiniel's officers received instruction in moon elvish was a valuable piece of knowledge, but of more use was knowing that their orders were to bring him in alive. Though he had no inclination as to how, Qualthalas knew that he was somehow valuable to the necromancer, which meant there might be advantage in negotiation.

"I've a counteroffer," proposed Drath'ivein, pointing to the floor, "lay your magnificent rapier at my feet then let my soldiers bind you and call off your viny companion." Shaking his head, Qualthalas meant to retort, but his attention went suddenly to one of the soldier's movements. The indigo elf had slowly drawn back his hand and was about to pitch one of the shrapnel bombs, however that was as far as the move went.

A whip-like sound startled everyone as the razor vines of the Primordial terror encircled the soldier's outstretched arm. He turned and screamed, tried to pull his arm back violently against the terrible strength of the entity, to no avail. With a whooping howl the creature unleashed several more vines, which encircled its prey's knees, neck and other hand, dragging the kicking soldier to the ground with a heavy crunch. More cackling ensued from the hooded figure's deathly rat-skull face as it toyed with the struggling elf, turning him around repeatedly while wrapping even more tendrils around his limbs. It looked up with its glowing yellow eyes and lifted its victim completely off the floor, holding it forth in macabre presentation to the stunned onlookers. There were moments of tense silence where none of the elves reacted, simply transfixed by the surreal, alien thing before them.

The barbed vines tightened, then with a gleeful, "A-ooouh!" the Primordial shook violently as its coiled grips began to spin around each of the encircled limbs of the now-screaming soldier. The lacerating barbs chewed through flesh and bone before they severed each of the twitching elf's appendages, including his head, releasing a bloody fountain throughout the chamber. Everyone panicked, except for the creature who seemed ultimately pleased with its display. The commander's only remaining subordinate pitched his incendiary orb in the creature's vicinity and took to heel in the opposite direction. The piercing shards did little harm to the entity's shifting form, though the smoke seemed to annoy the Primordial, who hissed and waved its limbs about to disperse the cloud.

Qualthalas was next to act. Emitting a low whistle, he shifted back a step and with a verse of magic, erected a barrier composed of force that he hoped would delay the creature's pursuit. Tactically thinking, he made sure to interpose the shimmering field behind the indigo elf captain as well, trapping him next to the writhing Primordial. He saluted the commander crisply with his rapier and bolted after the subordinate who had panicked and ran. Finally, the commander braced himself and brought the massive halberd forth to face the disturbing entity. The thing was busy gathering up the broken pieces of the elf he had torn apart, drawing each into its viny form as it had done with its previous victims. The commander grimaced at the loathsome creature as it efficiently consumed his subordinate, crunching and rearranging the various parts deep inside. It cast a few broken pieces of armour out of its form and fixed its terrible glowing citrine eyes upon the next prey who stood there aghast. In its sight, the Primordial could now see the commander emanating hues of red and amber; it had absorbed enough indigo elves to assimilate their natural thermal vision. A jittering cackle erupted from the rat-skull face again as the creature swept forward like a blanket of deathly clawing vines.

Qualthalas easily caught the fleeing indigo elf midway through the cavern. Already shaken, the panicked soldier would be the perfect candidate for his domination spell. Sensing the moon elf about to overtake him, the soldier spun and threw a dagger, which Qual batted away expertly and beamed his roguish grin. Certain that the subterranean elf had ample time to breathe in the concoction spread about earlier; Qualthalas skidded to a halt and intoned the arcane words of his enchantment. The moon elf locked psyches with the shaken soldier, gripping his mind easily and commanding it to recede under his telepathic influence. "You are now mine," he commanded, and the opposing elf swayed as he succumbed to the overwhelming psychic assault. Soon though, the indigo elf stood erect albeit with a glazed look in his eyes and nodded solemnly at his new master. Knowing the enemy was fully under his dominion, Qualthalas asked, "How many of you were there when you entered the cavern?" He hoped to get a clear idea of how many remained. The soldier, in a daze, replied, "Nine."

Qualthalas did a quick tally in his head as he considered what had transpired thus far. The creature had dismembered two of his enemies; Qualthalas had killed three, trapped one in stone, and charmed the one in front of him. That left only the commander and the crossbow-toting sneak that had retreated after alerting the rest of the group to his presence. He felt the odds were now heavily in his favour, though it was unclear what the viny entity's intentions were. Qualthalas had a sense that it meant him no harm personally. Thus far, it had only killed his enemies and he detected residual magic from the summoning scroll upon the entity. He marveled at the unique yet macabre nature of the thing; perhaps he could form an alliance of sorts with the creature after settling the problem of the remaining troops.

As commander, Drath'ivein had sworn to bring the lone moon elf into custody alive, and to this end, had entrusted his second-in-command, Neinir'iss, with the special rod that allowed entrance and egress from the enclosed chamber. He was surprised to see his subordinate perched high above, readying his special double-crossbow for a strike at the sinister vine-covered horror while making rapid hand signs, awaiting his orders. The captain of the dwindling indigo elven force steeled himself as the creature's viny whips slithered in a mass towards him, serpentine and deadly. As numerous roots reared up at him, the commander swept his mighty halberd in an arc and released a spell of thaumaturgy. The polearm simultaneously erupted into flames, cleaving through the thin tendrils and lighting many of the root structures supporting them on fire. The Primordial shrieked in obvious pain and withdrew its roots; however, it cleverly swept them behind its main body to rest in a pool of blood, which the tubers soaked up as a tree might absorb water. It cackled and shook its branches with renewed strength then surged forth with an ear-splitting howl of challenge.

Neinir'iss exhaled and loosed the two specially prepared bolts from his crossbow, which whistled sharply and buried themselves in the thick mass of the Primordial. It cast a hooded glance at the attacker, perched high within a recess of igneous rock, and hissed. The ambusher smiled as the bolts inside the creature exploded and a sticky, pungent tar spewed out, filling much of its nebulous form, coating the creature in the substance. With the Primordial's advance severely impaired, the commander took the opportunity to slash through the initial mass of vines reaching for him. He side-stepped quickly as a trio of heavier appendages sought to grasp his legs and backed away, out of their reach. Cracking sounds issued from inside the Primordial, who was now struggling significantly; the tar concoction was hardening and fusing the mass of mobile vines together. Drath'ivein spun around fully, drew his weapon high and used the momentum to deliver a staggering blow straight to the creature's hood-like face. A shriek of fury erupted from the depths of the Primordial as the rat skull shattered, sending pieces of bone flying about the chamber. The citrine eyes remained in their place though, and they burned with hatred, within the now-hollow cavity of branches and antlers that made up its head.

Qualthalas, with his dominated lackey in tow, watched the events unfold from behind one of the pillars surrounding the central chamber. He carefully debated on intervening in the fight, the odds of which had suddenly swung in favour of the two indigo elves working in concert against the furious and wailing thing. The commander continued to harass the nearly immobilized creature with blows from his halberd, keeping its attention trained on him as his stealthy companion readied another pair of bolts that erupted into flame once engaged in the firing mechanism. This could spell real trouble for the Primordial. Qualthalas recognized the alchemical ichor coating the hideous thing; it was useful for fusing doorframes, locks and the like. Once solidified, the substance became highly volatile. If the soldier perched above loosed one of those flaming bolts into the central mass congealed inside the flailing entity, it would violently explode.

Judging his options, Qualthalas decided to make the critical choice to aid the Primordial. He issued an order to his thrall, "Go to your commander and pull him away from the viny thing; he is in danger and your duty is to protect him at all costs." These reasonably termed suggestions left little chance of the subject breaking the spell. If he had forced the soldier to attack his commander, his will may have been strong enough to resist. Dutifully, the indigo elf rushed out and grappled with his superior, who shouted angrily at the unexpected interference. Meanwhile, Qualthalas jogged around the backside of the igneous pillar and began an incantation as swiftly as he could. The crossbowman raised his weapon and pulled the trigger.

The next moments were a confusing blur as the chain of events played out. Distracted by his subordinate who had apparently lost his senses, the commander easily overpowered the weaker soldier and turned his halberd upon him. Numerous shattering noises issued from the Primordial's vines as it cleverly collapsed inward then expanded, which freed it from much of the hardened compound, and two large tendrils shot towards Drath'ivein. The flaming bolts discharged and streaked towards the Primordial, however midway in flight they disappeared through a small vortex as Qualthalas incanted the last verse of his spell with perfect timing. The commander cleaved through the knee of his former cohort and again spun with the momentum of the halberd, ready to deliver a decapitating downward stroke upon the betrayer. Halfway through the maneuver, an array of heavy vines jerked back on his feet and another set of tendrils tore the polearm from his grip. Drath'ivein crashed to the floor, kicking against the vines as they deftly tore apart his greaves and dragged him toward the predatory horror. Up high, Neinir'iss could barely open his mouth in shock before his own flaming bolts struck him in the back of the head after exiting from the return portal Qualthalas had strategically positioned. He fell off his perch with both projectiles embedded in his skull, dead before he summarily hit the floor below.

The Primordial, still pulling a struggling Drath'ivein closer to its waiting mass, turned its empty cowl to Qualthalas. Only the glowing citrines remained hovering therein, the strange gemstones that acted as the creature's eyes pulsed with blazing life as it emitted a warbling sort of noise. It reminded the elf of a songbird's chittering call, and its head was cocked in such a way that

Qualthalas surmised it was trying to ask something of him. The commander tried to hack his way free of the barbed vines with an axe he had pulled from his belt, spewing curses and insults in his dark tongue just as tendrils encircled the weapon, his hand, and his mouth. The cooing sound continued to issue from the Primordial, and Qualthalas stepped back warily as the creature ceased dragging Drath'ivein in and instead raised its prey high only to hurl the indigo elf at Qual's feet in a heap.

Is it... offering him to me as a prize or in thanks, Qualthalas mused, as the defeated commander struggled to regain his breath and stand. The creature still held the wounded elf tightly around the mouth and decided to help by hauling Drath'ivein roughly to his feet. Blood streamed down upon the commander's armour from numerous lacerations on his face, particularly from his torn cheeks as the creature loosened its grip. It had almost taken his jaw off. Its root-like vines had an incredible combined strength, as evidenced by the ease in which it threw around the fully armoured soldiers. Qualthalas inspected the indigo elf who barely stood before him, saw hatred burning in his eyes, which he leveled directly at the moon elf. He spat a mixture of blood and bile at Qual's feet and simply said, "Get on with it." With a defiant glare at the Primordial, he added, "At least spare me death from that *thing*."

In the meantime, the domination Qualthalas had exerted over his subordinate had dissipated, not surprisingly, considering that the soldier had lost his leg from the knee down at the hands of his own commander. Blood soaked the floor surrounding the fallen elf, attracting the creature's attention suddenly. Having given Qualthalas its prize in the form of the commander, the Primordial's gleeful cry erupted again, feral, and wolf-like, as it wrapped its coils around the dying soldier. The indigo elf was mercifully delirious from blood loss and already close to death, so, when the creature dragged him in, his last seconds of life barely registered anyway. Both Qualthalas and the commander grimaced as the terrible entity fed. That they had both observed the process before did nothing to alleviate the churning in Qualthalas' and the commander's stomachs. The moon elf regarded the disgusted, stern visage of the hardened battle captain. Seeing no possibility of subverting the strong-willed indigo elf warrior and knowing he already had a prisoner to interrogate, Qualthalas' face turned grim, and he nodded with a measure of respect at Drath'ivein. The fallen commander closed his eyes and whispered his final words as the moon elf raised his blade, "Inir'yll Tze'qannis Nelei-T'kva'a." *Death is no release from service.* The whistling noise of Ithrin'Sael-I-Uiin cleaving through the stifling air was the last living memory the commander experienced.

Chapter 14

NATURE AND NECROMANCY

After dispatching the indigo elven captain, Qualthalas backed to the nearest pillar while the Primordial finished its sickening feast, though he forced himself to observe the grim process of consumption to gain a better understanding of the strange being before attempting communication. He doubted the apparent force of nature was capable of true speech, but it possessed a certain cunning will, albeit an alien intellect. He noted the regenerating branches and vines upon the creature's draining of its victim's blood and saw several bones and some sinew newly woven into the creature's nebulous structure. It carried several attributes of the more deadly beings of Nature's kingdom. Its creeping vines were thorned wickedly and seemed to act like appendages. The creature's root structure absorbed blood and rejuvenated its form. It certainly possessed the predatory instinct of an apex killer, a wild and ravenous spirit inhabiting an evolving body to suit its needs. The term, "Primordial Amalgam" sprang to mind; Qualthalas had studied a masterful tome entitled, "A Question of Origin," extensively, which detailed comprehensively the creation and proliferation of the various classes of life known to inhabit Antiqua. The dryad matron he consulted regarding the curse of lycanthropy was also Primordial; she was a tree-spirit charged with the protection and care of the Natural Order. This being, however, seemed to be possessed of a different purpose. This parasitic devourer fed off sentient beings indiscriminately, as if embodying the will of the hunt itself.

The creature had finished feasting thankfully, however now it focused its yellow gemstone eyes on Qualthalas and it made a rasping noise deep inside. Although wary, the elf made no defensive preparations, lest the creature sense it as hostility. He sheathed Mourning-Song deliberately; masking the vibrant chartreuse runes etched upon its blade and raised his hands as he might to a wild animal. A set of its tendril-like vines crawled along the cavern floor towards Qualthalas, who remained vigilant and noncombative. When they neared him, he struggled against the urge to flee, but again the creature made its curious warbling noise as the vines reached up and formed a semblance of fingertips, matching the shape of his own hands. The Primordial cawed next, like a raven, then followed with the cry of a raptorial bird-of-prey, and its tendrils pointed to the elf's neck.

Realizing it might recognize the vibrant plumes of his costume as belonging to a peacock, Qualthalas chuckled and relaxed. It was trying to greet him in its peculiar way. Slowly he reached up and unclasped the feathered collar then held it out for the creature to inspect. The vines carefully reached out and entwined the garment with minute feelers that probed the fabric, leather and feathers that made up his costume piece. It made a shrill squawking noise; accurately reproducing the call of a peacock then cackled and snarled before making a piercing shriek that Qualthalas realized was the sound that same bird would make when dying. The creature returned the neckpiece to the elf and withdrew the vines back into its main body.

Seeing it meant him no immediate harm, Qualthalas took a step closer to inspect the creature more fully. Its form of vines and

branches twisted in a spiral and condensed, and its viny appendages suddenly formed again, full of the sharp thorny barbs. It
issued what Qual interpreted as a warning growl, a low rumble
like a wolf with its hackles up. This made Qualthalas pause, but he
did not back away, instead he held his palms forth and spoke, "Do
you understand speech?" He used the Mithrainian tongue, since it
was the most spoken language in the lands above, but the creature
only tilted its hooded visage to regard him with yellow gemstone
eyes which glittered in their cowl.

It ceased its guttural moan and its tendrils rose into the air and
branched out, but these looked quite different from the attacking vines
displayed earlier. They sported fronds that resembled blood-red fern
leaves bearing countless powdery yellow spots. Alarmed, Qualthalas
backed up a step unconsciously, unsure of what the Primordial was
doing. The previously stifling atmosphere of the subterranean cavern
suddenly filled with a sweet, fragrant scent that the elf did not recognize. Then he noticed the countless, minute spores floating in a cloud
that surrounded him. For a moment, he panicked, until he could hear
a wispy voice like rushing wind speaking to him in his thoughts.

"Whissssper ssspeak…" came the strange psychic emanation
which seemed to exude from the spores themselves, which must
have been connected to the Primordial in some inherent way
that allowed it to translate its base ideas. Qualthalas stilled his
mind and opened up slightly; it was a technique his grandfather
had taught him that allowed a level of protection from mental
assault while still enabling communication. The great moon elven
archives catalogued several encounters with psionic beings, and
his grandfather was himself a master of telepathy. His first mental
projection was a question wrapped into a single word, "Origin?"
Qualthalas posed the question with images of trees, swamps, and
beasts of nature, in the hopes the creature would understand what
he was asking. From where did it hail?

"Mmm..." it intoned aloud as if debating how to answer the query. At length, its thoughts formed as two words, clear in the elf's head, "Savage Jungle." Images of the most lush and chaotic forest of strange trees and vines flashed through Qualthalas' mind. Carnivorous yet captivatingly beautiful plants and predatory animal species the likes of which the elf had never seen before – tore, ripped, and consumed each other in this feral landscape. Lightning raged as deluges of rain gripped the place, then it turned sunny and radiant in his vision, finally becoming a twilight realm; it was the most surreal place Qualthalas had seen. He wondered if it existed upon Antiqua physically at all, or whether it might be a spiritual plane, unrecorded in the annals of the great archive. The Primordial responded to Qual's thoughts with an amused cackle, "Real." More images flooded the elf's thoughts, this time of the entity's experiences within the wild land as it struggled to survive – killing, feasting, and assimilating its prey. He saw a bright streak as a large comet descended and obliterated a vast swath of forest and the exposed, bleak terrain beyond the jungle.

Recognition of the event sparked in Qualthalas suddenly: upon the Mazatanian continent, the archives detailed the largest celestial disturbance in recorded history. The event was thousands of years in the past and had transformed the massive wilderness into a twisted landscape of sulfurous volcanic mountains as the resulting impact shifted the tectonic plates underneath. The civilized races abandoned Mazatan's entire northern portion in the aftermath of the destruction; Oryk, Gaub'Blynh, and Neph'al populations migrated to Huromithra by sea, fleeing the pyroclastic ash and the poisonous radiation that permeated the area. Qualthalas mentally noted that an expedition to the place might be in order, that is, if there was a world left after the Darklord enacted his nefarious plan.

That last thought ripped Qualthalas' perception back into the sulfurous cavern, where the creature seemed to nod its viny countenance. He felt that it could sense the disturbance of the nec-romancer's fortress close-by; the Primordial snarled in acknowl-edgement as it projected another thought fragment, "deathly miasma below." A few fleeting images and an impression of disgust emanated from the creature: it had fought numerous skeletons and zombified monsters in vaguely similar caverns some time in its past. Further, Qualthalas could sense a hatred of unlife that stirred within the Primordial as it left a parting thought, "Abominations." Qualthalas nodded and brandished Mourning-Song with a sweep-ing cut, "I too abhor these things. Let us find out more, together?" He motioned for the Primordial to accompany him and made his way to the end of the chamber where the hapless indigo elf still struggled, wounded, and trapped in clutches of stone.

The soldier's ashen skin turned even paler as Qualthalas approached with the horrible viny thing in tow. Knowing the terror the thing impressed upon his foes, the moon elf wore a merciless smile as he knelt close to the soldier, the tip of his rapier pressed precariously above the indigo elf's heart. "My companion here is positively *famished*," Qualthalas began, while thorny tendrils slithered into the cage, "so now you have a choice." The creature played its part masterfully; vines crept around the soldier, alter-nately removing pieces of his armour and lightly wrapping around each of his struggling limbs. The enemy jerked his face back as a set of the barbed roots caressed his cheek, drawing a thin line of blood that was swiftly absorbed by the creature's hungry tubers. The Primordial snickered and its form shook and rattled. Another of its appendages crept out slowly and produced a picked-clean skull, which it held out towards the cage mockingly.

Sadistic but unquestionably effective, mused Qualthalas as the soldier visibly shuddered and fought to turn away, though he finally loosened his tongue, "Neinir'iss possesses the only key. If he fled as ordered, then we are all trapped here." Qualthalas narrowed his eyes at the imprisoned enemy, retorting, "Trapped until more of your cohorts arrive, you mean. Which one was Neinir'iss?" He let the tip of Mourning-Song dig into the soldier's flesh, which sizzled and flashed brilliantly. The indigo elf winced. Accustomed to hours of pitch-blackness or levels of very dim light, the race had grown sensitive to sudden bright flashes of radiance. Ithrin'Sael-I-Uiin hummed and strobed with dazzling beams now attuned to the enemy presented before it. Seeing the soldier bite his tongue, he laughed mercilessly, "Well, if I had to guess, I would say it was the crossbowman." Qual stuck two fingers out and pointed them to the rear of his head. "The one who mistakenly buried two bolts into the back of his own skull." At this, the indigo elf seemed to gain a measure of his courage, and he spat towards Qualthalas. Annoyed, the moon elf stood, turned his back and sheathed Mourning-Song. "Dinner," he called out to the Primordial as he sauntered back toward the central chamber to search the downed crossbowman for the key to the hidden exit.

Although he wore a metaphorical mask of cold indifference, once he reached the pillars surrounding the central chamber, upon hearing the screams behind him suddenly go quiet, Qualthalas retched. It felt good to expel the meager contents of his stomach, and he chuckled amidst the heaving of his midsection as he spit mostly bile upon the cavern floor. A flood of unbidden tears streamed down his face, making a mess of his stage makeup. He felt an absolute clown and let out a hooting laugh, unhinged and terrible. His emotions were a blur, alternating between despair and feral rage as his true feelings fought with the conflicting urges and compassion-suppressing power of the Scarlet Fury Masque. Fortunately, for the tormented elf, someone could feel his anguish – someone who cared. Sensing the spiral of imbalance threatening to cripple the overwhelmed crown prince, there came a voice that existed both within and without Qualthalas; that spoke a single word, "Balance." It rippled through him, cascaded through the entire area and it existed as a singular command that was unequivocally sublime.

The word sang to Qualthalas, evoking memories of the most stirring chords of music; it was a piece of the universal rhyme that weaved the intricate fabric of time, reality and being together. He did not know it, but the exquisite, feminine vocalization belonged to a Muse. In fact, she embodied the voice of the Cosmos itself for she was a Celestial entity of the highest magnitude, the Goddess, Eternal Melody. Although Qualthalas was not of her creation, she watched over the chaotic life of the crown prince of the moon elves often, from her solitary aerie in Haevona. Her divine will coursed through him, empowering his most profound bardic magic, the morning stars that made up her empyrean crown radiated through Ithrin'Sael-I-Uiin as it illuminated the darkness, and her compassion now kept the Masque of Myriad Minds from driving Qualthalas to the brink of madness.

The Muse had a certain affection for warrior-poets that stemmed from her aeons spent in the presence of another Celestial; she felt his absence profoundly, even though it was at her bidding he had departed. The spirit of Love and War had matters, in her opinion, far more important than doting on her; though it brought him severe heartache to leave, he obeyed the Queen of his Heart implicitly. Of an angelic order known only to the Gods themselves, it was the duty of Spirit Fierce as a Divine Executive known as the *D'nakh-Kao'kab* – Dawnstar – to attend the judgment trials for Celestials accused of insurrection against the Divine Order. His own infamous disciple, in the form of El'ucypher the Mourning Star, was imprisoned and awaiting such a hearing. As such, feeling him so distant from her, the Eternal Melody felt a compulsion to act on his behalf in aiding Qualthalas.

The beleaguered elf sighed heavily and gathered a semblance of self-control once again. The sound of the sacred word had vanished, but its spiritual energy resonated within, guiding him unconsciously on his path. He approached the fallen corpse of the enemy, the crossbowman, and looked down upon the dead indigo elf with a merciful eye. In other circumstances, perhaps they could have been comrades. The man had a life, one that Qualthalas had taken in battle, and he suddenly remembered his views on killing. *"Only as necessary, never from malice, and always with reluctance,"* were the words he had once used. He had not felt reluctance when he created the portal that led the soldier's bolts into the back of his own skull. Now though, he gently turned the body over and looked in the man's wide-open eyes, seeing only lifeless darkness. *Do not regret the past, look only forward,* came the internal voice of the Masque. Something had changed in its configuration; Qualthalas no longer felt the feral instincts or marked lack of compassion it had originally instilled.

Confused, Qual rummaged through his pack, searching for his silver mirror, and inspected himself in its reflective surface. The Scarlet Fury Masque was vanished, replaced with his customary Crescent-Moons, the silent silver twins adorning his face and gently illuminating him in starlight. He caught himself smiling slightly in the mirror, feeling a little more in order. His makeup was still a steaming mess, and he had some vomit on his boot, but emotionally he felt much more stable. Perhaps the Crimson Fury Masque had been an error in judgment, for though it gave him unbridled killing power, the humanity loss it instilled weighed on his conscience. Qualthalas was glad to rid himself of it, and though perplexed at the cause of its change, he did not question the fortune. The mirror returned to its place in his pack, and he drew a flask of precious, clear water, which he put to his lips and drank from greedily. He splashed some of the cool liquid on his hands and briskly rubbed down his face, clearing off the smudged make-up and invigorating himself in the process. As an afterthought, he poured a little on his soiled boot.

Upon returning his focus to the task before him, the elf knelt and pressed the eyelids of his slain foe closed. "I'm sorry you followed a megalomaniac. Perhaps in death you shall find a measure of peace," he whispered to the corpse. Remembering the final words of the squad's commander, he doubted his own prayer. A necromancer had unnatural ways of forcing slain minions into further service; *a two-for-one deal that is hardly fair*, he thought grimly. Qualthalas contemplated burning the corpses, but he knew it would be for naught; Zhiniel was powerful enough to rip their souls out of the nether with but a trace of their essence. Reanimated corpses were enough of an abomination, but the prospect of facing these enemies as incorporeal undead was far more terrifying. His fingers already working deftly to search through the dead elf's belongings, Qualthalas smirked when they closed around an onyx rod engraved with golden script.

"Ae'iss-ah No-hru Sussan'ti-ah Fal-Ab'ralthar," he chanted in the Calthreic dialect. Forced to study its precise script every day for an entire year under one of his strictest tutors, Qualthalas mastered the planar language with rote discipline. Its origin was upon the Plane of Axiom: a place of utter calculation, with strict laws and numerology governing its strange automaton denizens. The native magic of the dimension was invaluable in categorization and itemization of the properties intrinsic to any object or substance. Qualthalas was innately sensitive to magical emanations, especially so when it came to enchanted items. After casting the spell, the sensation of the object's purpose became clear. He could ascertain how the thing activated simply by running his fingers upon its smooth surface. The runes etched into the onyx were in the Daemonic script, which was unsurprising. He knew that the indigo elves traditionally made pacts with the denizens of the Abyssal Planes; it made him wonder that the rod might be useful elsewhere.

Studying the jagged words took some time. He concentrated intently on the letters until the lingering magic of his incantation deciphered them into something he could comprehend. The spell worked to automate certain mental processes, so when he now read the entire script, it was as if he was fluent in the Daemonic tongue; Qualthalas was confident that he could use the rod properly. Now, he just had to find the exact location in which to insert it.

Returning to find the Primordial finally finished its feast, Qualthalas reached out on the mental plane, finding it pleasantly easier to converse, thanks to the effects of the spell. "I suppose you are bound to accompany me... what *shall* I call you?" He meant the last phrase to be an inner dialogue; however, the creature bristled its viny form and turned to him with an inquisitive noise that sounded like a hooting owl. Qualthalas raised an eyebrow upon seeing the strange thing's new face: it was sporting the skull of the former caged prisoner, which peered out from the cowl with the citrine eyes glimmering in its sockets. The moon elf swallowed hard. "Does your kind take names?" he rephrased; pointing at himself he stated, "I am Qualthalas." This appeared to spark some recognition within the Primordial. It excitedly chittered and extended numerous appendages, then let out a roar that shook the cavern.

The moon elf's mind was flooded with images of constant predatory carnage, again within the confines of that savage jungle where the feral creatures and venomous plants preyed upon anything weaker than they were, in a seemingly endless cycle of life and death. It was certainly a unique microcosm; again, Qualthalas vowed to explore the place one day. Pangs of hunger next wracked the elf's psyche, and he felt the constant need for his vines to suck up blood, absorbing the memories and capabilities of numerous other beings. The sensation ended abruptly, and the Primordial gazed upon him expectantly, as if waiting for his approval. Since the creature had no innate language besides instinct, it dawned on Qualthalas to give it a name in his own tongue; he had the perfect designation in mind. "It would seem you are now dubbed the *Neihwe'un* – the Feasting Vines." Upon hearing the elf utter its new name, the viny horror erupted into cackling fits; this seemed a definite sign of accord, and the name certainly suited its function.

Qualthalas still held apprehension at the thought of the creature as a companion, but it subsided slightly after giving the wild being a name. Still sensing the lingering vestiges of the primal magic of the summoning scroll upon the Neihwe'un, the moon elf's curiosity got the better of him. "You do not attack me, though you have shown no reservation in consuming most anything else in your sight." He followed the statement with the simplest question, "Why?"

The Primordial projected what Qual surmised were its last moments before being constrained within the scroll he had used. Caught somehow unawares as it fed off a great stag, where it had gotten the magnificent crown of antlers it wore, Qualthalas viewed through the creature's bizarre eyesight the form of a wizened, gnarled man intoning syllables he did not understand. He could feel his vines becoming weak, enveloped by a primal magic more powerful than his own, and finally succumbing to a numbing sensation as he shrunk into a compact place. The feeling of claustrophobia overwhelmed him through the creature's memory of the event, and he felt bound, compelled to obey an urge to merge forms with raw matter of earth and stone. Then, as the confusing visions ended, came the unexplainable feeling of meshing into specially prepared parchment of yew pulp – then simply oblivion. Given what he now knew of the creature's past, Qualthalas estimated that the creature had slumbered inside the scroll for well over a thousand years before the timely utilization of the spell that released the Primordial, along with the dwelling, back onto the physical plane.

These revelations of the Feasting Vines' origin and subsequent capture brought a valid concern to Qualthalas, so he felt it necessary to ask, "You are compelled to obey and protect the sanctuary's summoner then?" To this, the vines writhed and twisted, and the moon elf felt pangs of both acknowledgement and bitter resentment. He paused before conveying his next thought, for he was truly unsure of what the answer might portend. In a small, stoppered vial, he held yet the ashes of the scroll; it was enough to manipulate the spell effect, and he had saved it for reference, but there might be a risky use for the remains. Grinning nervously, Qualthalas approached the creature and held up the vial, and if a tangled mass of vines, bones and detritus could wince, it did so visibly. However, surprise registered in his thoughts as he queried, "What do you think would happen, Neihwe'un, if I were to unbind you from the compulsion this holds over you?"

There was an uncomfortably long, tense pause where neither individual spoke, nor moved, and the sulfurous air was all that shifted between the two as they surveyed each other, physically and mentally. Qual cocked his head to the side, unsure what the silence meant, but perhaps the innate psychic nature of the creature allowed it to consider the answer in telepathic solitude. A ripple of thought surged forth, abruptly causing the elf to take a few shaky steps backward as a wicked cackle issued from the creature, and visions of the possibilities flooded Qual's mind. He saw himself immediately wrapped in vines and sucked into the creature's mass in the first, then he saw the creature simply depart for whereabouts unknown, but it was the last vision that gave the elf a measure of hope. In it, the Primordial, with its curious nature, remained by the elf's side, protected him from several enemies, content to feast and enjoy Qualthalas' company. It had existed primarily in solitude through its early years of development and needed the perspective of a living companion to give its experience in life a different breadth than it had previously known.

. Qualthalas chuckled and wanly smiled at the creature and projected his own thoughts, both as a warning, and as an indication that should the creature attack, he would not go so quietly. His vision, which the creature seemed to receive lightheartedly, was of the elflord summoning a sheet of flaming wind, which burnt the creature to ashes, which he scooped into the same vial he was still holding up. Eerily, the Primordial issued an accurate duplication of Qual's chuckle, perfect to pitch and tone. The two were immeasurably nervous when the elf pulled the stopper, incanted several arcane words, and let the ashes scatter.

The Neihwe'un curled up into a spiral and flattened to the floor; this was a different shape than it had ever taken, as the spell unwound, and it felt freedom for the first time in a millennium. Although certain he was safe, (actually, he was not at all convinced, but Qual liked to lie to himself from time to time) the moon elf did unsheathe Mourning-Song as a precaution, watching the runes carefully. They shifted to a vibrant cyan; the rapier hummed but did not issue the hissing sound that Qual dreaded would occur and it scintillated as the creature rose from the floor of the cavern. The Primordial stood fully two metres erect, most of its form flowing around it like a writhing, viny robe, and its two appendages formed in the shape of shorter arms than its killing whips had been. In turn, the arms constructed skeletal fingers from several bones it had amalgamated, in a semblance of three-clawed hands, which it flexed as if testing its new grip. The face was the last piece to reform, with the skull of one of the indigo elves brought forth, its yellow gemstone eyes glowing eerily from behind the eyeless sockets. As he surveyed the creature, Qualthalas thought, "You are truly unlike anything I have ever seen before, my primordial friend."

"As are you, Aelyph'en," it intoned mentally, "for all creatures before you have been my prey." The creature stretched its lower half along the ground, shrinking its stature to just above Qual's height and gathering the remaining bones nearby. Its surface roiled as tiny roots wound around them, creating a makeshift armour plating surrounding its central mass, "Protection for battle below, where danger lurks. The smell of tainted nature and undeath permeates beneath us. It is large... vast." Qualthalas noted its vocabulary had improved considerably; even though he knew that its spore-based psionic communication method was interpreting the creature's strange thought patterns, it was apparent that the Primordial projected ideas with increased complexity. He surmised it had absorbed some of the indigo elves' advanced intellect. The potential of such a being was considerable, though he wondered if it retained things like emotional disposition and propensity for cruelty. He certainly hoped not. Consuming his enemies might turn the Primordial against him eventually if that were the case.

"If I speak aloud, will it be a problem?" asked the moon elf apologetically, "Mental communication I find taxing and perhaps it may help you develop your voice, which seems to have sprung from nowhere." Qualthalas sheathed Ithrin'Sael-I-Uiin, and its humming subsided. In answer, from within the writhing form of the Primordial came at first a deep vibration, which then lessened in pitch as the creature adjusted sinews and hollow pieces of wood to produce a wispy, haunting voice. The sound was akin to sharp winds passing through swamp reeds; Qualthalas felt it suited the creature. It spoke, "As you choose, Aelyph'en Qualthalas, but only in times of peace. When we fight, we use the whisper-speak, yes?" The creature made a valid point. Silent communication was invaluable in battle. "I concur," Qualthalas replied cordially as he turned towards the rear of the cavern, "let us make haste, I have the key to our exit from this sulfurous place, and I am anxious to find this 'tainted' area you speak of."

Together, the two moved to the back wall of the cavern, Qualthalas walked briskly, the creature flowed like a manta ray along a sea floor. Qualthalas produced the onyx rod and spoke the words etched into its smooth, jet-black surface: the wall in front of them shifted to form an opening large enough for five men abreast to pass through. *For troop movement, to be certain,* Qualthalas thought grimly, as he and the creature passed through the newly formed exit into a passage hewn from granite. The atmosphere in this place was refreshingly less stifling than the sulfurous staging area full of fallen foes. The wall reformed moments later and left the pair in dimly lit gloom to survey the new area, leaving the dead to rest behind.

Zhiniel smiled coolly as he treaded silently among his fallen vanguard, scrutinizing the remains of the corpses the Primordial had consumed. He reached down to scoop up a few grisly, bloody parts and softly chanted sinister words of necromancy, "Caul'est-enn Elich-baras no-kotaris s'aa." At his unholy command, several bits of once-living flesh and bone scrambled from their resting places to form a monstrosity of undeath that he shaped into a large construct. His keen mind fashioned a disgusting four-armed thing from the pieces left of the subordinate troops; to him it was a macabre piece of art that he crafted from their discarded remains – another tool at his disposal. The deathly golem rose high, and where cavities remained in its structure, a sickly green-grey material fused the disparate components together. Animus was the term: the plasmatic substance drawn from the Plane of Death by his sheer will. Necromancy was a difficult discipline for the most seasoned of arcanists, but for Zhiniel, who had studied its myriad forms for thousands of years – it was like breathing. The mindless thing acknowledged its master with a low groan that gurgled from its wholly misshapen, daemonic head, which Zhiniel had formed into a minotaurean semblance. Appropriate, since his quarry now approached a labyrinth of his ingenious design.

Deftly, the necromancer's fingers weaved an intricate pattern in the air as he concentrated on the giant abomination of bone and sinew. Silver runes spread in a circle surrounding the thing, which intensified for a split-second, then vanished along with the construct, leaving Zhiniel alone again in the stifling air. He traversed the cavern in search of the fallen captain, Drath'ivein, and the sabotage agent, Neinir'iss. The duo had performed admirably, considering the unexpected element in the form of the Primordial; an asset far beyond the scope of what Qualthalas should have possessed. Although it vexed him, Zhiniel relished in surprises; already his calculating mind was adjusting numerous plans to execute. Contingencies in the hundreds formed from the new variable, which he was swift to consider capturing for dissection and utilization within his experimentation chambers.

Even though the creature's assistance had impeded his immediate plans to lure Qualthalas into the labyrinth, wounded and more severely detrimented by a protracted battle with his legions, the advent of studying this unique and rare specimen excited Zhiniel's intellect. While he observed the battle casually through the scrying crystal as it unfolded, he had analyzed the creature intently when it appeared. He knew of the existence of Primordials: in fact, he came into conflict with several of subterranean origin over his many years and possessed a few living ones for study. This creature, however, was fundamentally different from the variety Zhiniel encountered, and its ability to absorb not only matter, but reason and experience intrigued the necromancer. Already the vast intellect of the Soulharvester worked upon machinations, concocting various schemes involving the use of such a creature. He would either subjugate or imprison it as he had the others, or perhaps turn it against Qualthalas. He left the train of thought to his subconscious for the moment; the intact corpses of the captain and the crossbowman now lay at his feet.

"You have served me well," were Zhiniel's impassionate words. The necromancer inclined his head to scrutinize the pair's wounds with the trained forensic eyes of a chirurgeon. Drath'ivein had died from a single, well-placed rapier thrust to the heart, evidenced by the precise hole left in his breastplate. The moon elf's swordsmanship was expert, he noted. Looking to Neinir'iss, he smiled at Qualthalas' clever use of the minute portal that caused the crossbowman's bolts to pierce the back of his own skull. Though rudimentary, his adversary's tactics were well thought and effective. Training in ambush and subterfuge were evident in the moon elf's ruthless assault on Zhiniel's vanguard forces. Nevertheless, Zhiniel had expected that the clever elf would overcome his initial troops. If the Darklord had intended on destroying Qualthalas, he simply would have slain the whelp outright with a single stroke of his war-flail, *Soulflayer*. The moon elf, or more aptly, the connection to his kingdom on Sillis-Thal'as was too precious a prize for Zhiniel to discard during his bid for world domination. Killing Qualthalas would only bring the momentary satisfaction of snuffing out life, which the indigo elven fiend so enjoyed, however, having the Crown Prince of the Akir'Aelyph-Ana'ii dynasty under his control would prove exalting. Domination of the silver moon represented a link in the chain he would wrap around Antiqua, as every living soul therein bent to his will. After taking Sillis-Thal'as, he would delve the secrets of the ebon moon; beyond were countless other systems within his grasp.

The tyrant closed his narrow, cruel eyes in focus, while he composed the blasphemous formula for a greater necromantic ritual. These two, he would bestow with the power of undeath far surpassing the deathly golem's construction. First, he knelt low and pressed a mailed hand down upon the face of Drath'ivein and incanted the infernal spell that would tear the captain's soul from the nether of oblivion. He felt raw power surge through him from the Death Realm, like incalculably cold shards of ice that flowed through his veins. He enjoyed the pain; it brought a sharp focus to the necromancer as he uttered the binding phrase to the spirit which lingered nearby, "Ast-Araeis'kaa Qoth-Mataz Orelivas'Nie Locana-Towail'des Ephrenix Novir'h."

The body, cold upon the igneous rock floor, stiffened as its muscles contracted. Zhiniel observed the spirit descend upon its formerly living form as a ghostly wraith, its wispy nothingness merged with the dead flesh, and the corpse convulsed. A gout of blood erupted from the puncture-wound in its chest as the heart beat a solitary time before it became still and lifeless again. Countless times the necromancer observed this behaviour in reanimated minions, although rote by now, the process still fascinated him. Although the body was a dead shell now, no longer able to grow muscle or repair itself of injury, it could no longer feel pain either. The Animus that now bound the dead spirit enhanced the corpse with the powers of the grave. Zhiniel evilly smiled.

Drath'ivein strained to squint his eyelids, blinked once, then twice, and let out a garbled phrase. The Darklord waited patiently for his loyal soldier to become accustomed to the new state of being. It was a confounding process for a dead soul to regain motor control of a body that no longer functioned on the same principles it had in life. Animus replaced the chemical interactions of a living brain with a network linked to the will of its former personality. Instead of the brain interpreting a being's intent and sending instructions via nerve pathways and electrical impulses, the spiritual force of the once-living soul now directly controlled the body by sheer magnitude of will. At length, Drath'ivein found his voice, raspy and hollow, "The moon elf was formidable, and that *thing* he commanded..." Zhiniel cut him off, "I am aware. You performed your duty well, Drath'ivein."

Zhiniel turned his head purposefully towards the corpse of Neinir'iss and inquired, "Was his service adequate to warrant a new state of unlife such as I accorded yourself?" The Darklord paused to allow the captain a moment to compose his words. He idly traced lines in the air, and a spectral hand manifested, plucking the pair of bolts from the back of the crossbowman's lifeless skull, making a shucking noise as they tore free. Drath'ivein raised his head, beginning to acclimate to the cold numbness of the undead body he now *inhabited* and nodded, his words slow and deliberate, "His service was exemplary, Master Szord'Ryn. However, Neinir'iss failed to comply with my order to retreat with the onyx rod, instead coming to my aid against the moon elf. I imagine the quarry escaped into the labyrinth with the... vine-creature." His physical form involuntarily shuddered at the memory.

"It is well, *O'Saniss-thal.*" Zhiniel intoned the final word with a hint of praise, the captain's promotion surprised Drath'ivein; O'Saniss-thal were regarded as elite commanders in the ranks of the Darklord's vast subterranean empire. He often reserved such a battle promotion for intelligent undead and the worthiest of his living cohorts. It was a rite of passage to follow service in life with a higher calling in death. At times, Zhiniel would perform a ceremony for such servants, killing them by his own magic and returning them to the world infused with the gift of death. Though by all appearances, Neinir'iss was guilty of disobeying a direct order, Zhiniel revealed his plot now to the newly awakened Revenant, "He did exactly as I instructed. I always intended the moon elf to take the rod and believe himself clever in defeating your force. He will gain entry to my fortress, and then..." Zhiniel paused, and a wicked smile crept across his face, "then he will know true despair."

Drath'ivein's ash-grey, dead face registered no shock at this prospect. All who served knew the machinations of the Soulharvester involved deep plots and manipulation both on the outside world and within his legions. He knew no enemy he had not vanquished, subjugated, or turned completely to his unbending will; this elven prince would be no different. His lunar kingdom would summarily follow. In the twisting tunnels of Zhiniel's dark mind, already written were the words upon the page, he had but to take the steps leading to them.

Zhiniel produced a nearly opaque, midnight-blue sapphire from somewhere hidden away in his intricately woven chainmail robes, along with a strange device which hummed as he fit the gemstone into a socket within the twisted metal framework. He pointed to the exquisitely crafted double-crossbow that lay pristine upon the rock beside Neinir'iss' pallid, cold hands. "Bring it to me," the necromancer commanded, and Drath'ivein immediately did as ordered. He shuffled forth slowly, bent down and plucked the weapon from its resting place, then presented it to his master. Zhiniel affixed the unholy reliquary to the crossbow; the metal contraption, complete with the embedded sapphire, fused instantly to the structure of the deadly implement.

The captain could no longer feel the physical sensations of pain or cold, nor anything else for that matter, but his spirit coursed with a numbness as blue fires leapt from the crossbow, fading quickly into the aether. Severe agony followed by an equally torturous death would have met a mortal as life evaporated from their body due to the devils-fire; only a charred, desiccated husk would remain. Drath'ivein merely shuddered in his unliving shell, his blighted soul protected against the essence-draining flame. The entire crossbow remained gleaming with a ghostly blue light; Drath'ivein released his grip as it became spectral and remained suspended in the air before him. His eyes, now crimson in undeath and gleaming unnaturally, noticed the astral disturbance surrounding his companion's corpse. At first appearing as swirling wisps of shadow, he watched as Neinir'iss' blood evaporated under his skin, becoming ethereal as it flowed out in a stream that led directly into the crystal apparatus, now part of the weapon itself.

Invisible, even to the commander's deathly gaze, but tangible on some desecrated spiritual plane, shreds of Neinir'iss swirled around the floating crossbow, inextricably drawn to the gemstone that pulsed as it captured his soul. Zhiniel openly laughed in his sinister, mocking way as his powerful magic cheated the Lord of Death. He could feel the wrathful aura of the God of the Dead all about him and relished in its impotence against his necromantic might. Drath'ivein regarded his master, literally with new eyes, as he realized beyond the keen intellect and insurmountable will he possessed, the extent of Zhiniel's arcane supremacy. It was possible – likely – his master could be the most powerful wielder of magic on Antiqua.

Appearing as it did in life, though ghostly and disconnected from this plane, the hand of Neinir'iss manifested, closing tightly around the handle of his prized weapon, now the container of his essence. The rest of his shadowy image followed, trailing off into nothingness near where his feet should be. Though the ground beneath the apparition was warm from the molten lava deep below, it began to steam as the chill aura surrounding the wraith's form radiated its unnatural cold. Soon the igneous stone frosted over, and Neinir'iss moved silently towards his commander. He opened inky eyes upon the world anew and spoke in a whisper; even his new voice was a shade of its former self. "This is... different than I expected..." he turned then to regard Zhiniel, who stood straight, admiring his work with glinting eyes.

The Soulharvester laid a hand upon the ethereal shoulder of the crossbowman as if it were made of solid matter still, and his gauntlet frosted slightly at the touch. He could feel the penetrating cold emanating from his soldier, though it bothered him little. The necromancer was nigh impervious to the effects common to the undead; he had built up tolerances through study of his half-fiendish lineage, bolstered these innate characteristics with spells and infusions of both magical and technological nature. The freezing touch of his spectral assassin could kill, once focused through study and practice; he would surely unleash this new terror upon the gnomish kingdoms soon after the Void-Wraithes honed his abilities. Now, the power just wicked off his flesh, uncomfortable only slightly as his body adjusted swiftly to the aura.

"Different, Neinir'iss – what is it you expected of this gift I have granted?" Zhiniel seemed perturbed at the apparition's earlier comment; his tone demanded the subordinate qualify his words immediately. Neinir'iss hissed like a snake; it was a wicked form of laughter to hear, like water hitting the coals of a fire. "Darklord, no, I am far from displeased. Elated, freed from physical form – no, Master – this is *deliciously perfect.*" The spectre swept low in a humble bow before his overlord, his words sincere. Neinir'iss had suffered from a rare nervous disease in life; it made his muscles ache when he moved quickly. Born to a Syndicate household, the likelihood of the 'crippled male' surviving long was slim. It was probable his fate would be death upon one of Ennetra's sacrificial altars, his essence devoured by the daemonic entity that styled itself a Goddess.

Zhiniel's entire campaign changed that: he saw potential in the young indigo elf harnessing power from his pain and had liberated the youth along with several other orphans after eradicating the Akah'so-Qun'aa Syndicate in a raid upon their nearby fortress, outside the main city of D'zurien-To'th. When Zhiniel had charged into the chamber that housed the defective members of the clan, he saw a squalor that disgusted him. There was no pity in his mind, only a burning rage upon finding such useful things locked away in a cell, their potential wasted by the foolish adherence to Ennetra's teachings. His skeletal soldiers swarmed the room, and Neinir'iss recalled staring at them defiantly, expecting his skull would be shattered soon by one of the maces they wielded. However, they set about removing shackles from the children and servants and when he met the gaze of the Darklord; he crept forth to stand before the imposing figure with a measure of pride. He pledged his fealty immediately, before even Zhiniel demanded it, which garnered him the master's approval. It was not a groveling plea for life, which the necromancer sorely hated hearing; in the youth's words were a litany against being counted as invalid. Now, in his undead form, he was further from crippled and useless than ever. He was empowered.

The three left the chamber soon after, through a circle of darkness that Zhiniel conjured effortlessly, bound for the citadel where they would learn to harness the new power afforded them by the master. The frost covering the floor melted and steamed after several minutes, dissipating into the sulfurous air of the cavern, and all was still.

Chapter 15

PATH OF THE DREADHEART

Deep in the annals of Antiqua stirred the machines and complex thaumaturgical apparatus of Zhiniel Al-Nistir Szord'Ryn – the *Darklord, Harvester of Souls*, the *Willbreaker*, and *Fiend-Born*: his titles were as numerous as his dark machinations. The necromancer's citadel, a massive ebon spire of pure, glass-smooth obsidian at the epicentre of the expansive central cavern of the indigo elven city D'zurien-To'th, thrummed and reverberated like its heartbeat, crackling black energy coursing out from it through the metropolis. Four gigantic cornerstones, which served to support the roof of the cavern, surrounded the towering structure; they were also the conduits of energy harnessed from dissimilar sources. Animus from the Plane of Death flowed through columns of night-blue runes upon one, while a second, lined in blood red and jagged symbols, exuded a miasma of desecration from Apocrypha, the hellish plane of the Archdevils. The third, shedding a subdued but golden light from vertical shafts etched its entire length, drew pure sunlight from countless hidden receptors upon the surface of the planet, while the fourth tore the very essence of life from Zhiniel's many prisoners.

Within the spire, itself, buried in a maze of halls and antechambers, were Zhiniel's personal laboratories, study rooms, grand libraries, storage facilities for captured technology, and the resting chambers for himself and his dark concubine, Zaeliar'a. Several of the *Dreadheart's* missions took her to far-off places in search of mysterious relics, such as the tablet she recently secured. As his second-in-command, the imposing woman frequently made journeys to *persuade* the neighboring denizens of the inhabited underworld kingdom – in the indigo elven tongue known as *Bazrin-Dal'ateir* – to pledge fealty to her master. Soulthorne traveled nearly as much as she remained within the fortress at Zhiniel's side. This day however, Zaeliar'a languished upon silken, crimson sheets in her personal chambers as she mentally prepared for her next assignment. She lay naked, stretched her full length upon her stomach, toned and tight muscles flexed as she traced a fingertip along the razor edge of her claymore, which hung from the corner of her four-post bed. Extending her tongue, she licked the exquisite blood that trickled from her finger as her equally deep red eyes flicked up the moment Zhiniel entered the chamber.

His customary adamant stare nearly softened a moment as he gazed at her lithe body, eyes roaming the length of her beauty before locking upon her face. He swept gracefully across the room toward her, the chains of his robe a whisper as he approached, and the Darklord knelt in front of her, face-to-face. Zhiniel ran a strong but slender hand through the scarlet strands of Zaeliar'a's long hair, which she wore down this day. To an outsider the gesture would have seemed intimate, romantic even, but the affection they held for each other was from a different source: that of a mutual respect for the other's power and ambition. They did lay together, often. Both enjoyed the carnal act of sex for the endorphins it produced, the physical exertion required by both parties, and perhaps for the excitement of the play for domination. In this arena alone would

Zhiniel permit another to be his equal, and Zaeliar'a he deemed the only worthy combatant to face him.

Both their eyes played with lust for an instant; Soulthorne even dared touch her bloody finger to his lips, painting them with a line of red. Zhiniel's wicked frown betrayed nothing of his emotions, if there were any, as he kissed her and stood, bidding her to rise. He turned and swept his arm widely, and in the air formed a vision: that of a pale-skinned elf and his viny, primordial companion surveying carefully the labyrinth both now wandered, trapped. Zaeliar'a knelt upon the bed, hands deep between her knees, rubbing the tight muscles as she examined the image. "The little princeling is getting closer. Though..." she mused, "should the denizens of the maze take him, what then?" She asked the question idly, unconcerned – for she knew her liege had likely a dozen plans in such an event.

Zhiniel said nothing, merely motioned crisply to the side with two fingers, pulling the image away, to reveal another projection; an ancient, robed elf of the same race as the previous one paced a summoning chamber, surrounded by cohorts of varying origin. They seemed to be in great debate, consulting each other heatedly. It was difficult to ascertain the subject, given the silence of the illusory image, however both indigo elves were proficient in lip-reading, and as such, they deduced the talk regarded national defense. Zhiniel smiled callously as he explained the significance.

"The ancient one is Ithrauss, Qualthalas' grandfather, and master of the Twisted Strings. You will recall your brief encounter with their agent aboveground, yes?" He chuckled, and his lips creased tightly. The organization's members were powerful and influential experts in the fields of subterfuge and information gathering. Soulthorne had managed to corner and silence one of these agents with a measure of difficulty, a testament to their prowess. Zhiniel leaned against one of the sturdy ironwood posts of the bed and looked over his shoulder at Soulthorne expectantly. Zaeliar'a nodded, turned, and pulled herself near the edge of the bed, then waited for the Darklord to continue. "He is concerned for his grandson... so *touching.*" His mocking tone brought a cruel smile to the elven woman's lips; she knelt at his side while he absently ran his fingers through her hair again. Zhiniel explained further, "The elder's scrying spell abruptly ended when the prince passed through the obsidian portal, but of course, this means the old one's organization is aware of our presence and general location." In the vision, the wizened moon elf turned his head sharply, suddenly on alert, and his piercing blue eyes stared straight through the illusion, directly at Zhiniel, who bowed slightly. With a swift wave of his hand, the projection vanished. Zhiniel recognized the Diviner's hurried gestures, and though he wanted his cousins upon the silver moon to glimpse the future ruler of the entire world, it was not an appropriate time to have the old man spying on the Darklord through his own devices. "The sage is certainly crafty; he remained busy, though most of his brethren have been rendered docile from an abundance of peace."

Slender, blue-grey hands worked their way from the tightly corded muscles of Zaeliar'a's neck down to her smooth, bare shoulders, relieving the tension with the expert touch of a skilled masseur. Though thousands of years had passed since his early life as an indentured slave to a ravenous priestess of the Black Circle, Zhiniel kept his expertise with reflexology honed. The practice enhanced the dexterity and strength of his fingers and complemented the daily spellcasting exercises he performed rigorously. Zaeliar'a was one of the few indigo elves who knew some of his past, though Zhiniel held no shame for it, nor did he keep it a guarded secret. He occasionally used the fact as a coercion tactic, gaining the respect of liberated former servants and slaves as he falsely built a rapport with them through commonality. In truth, his slavery to the Circle was an artfully crafted ruse: though fully indigo elf in all appearances, Zhiniel was a diabolically engineered creature; his rise to power was no accident of circumstance.

The science that the Archdevils employed in his creation was beyond anything native to Antiqua in the present time, concocted before the advent of the Neph'al seeding upon the planet. Zhiniel's sire, who bore a name unfathomable in any mortal tongue, was bound to a parallel dimension – by divine contract, *forbidden* to enter the cosmos of this reality. The calculating Infernal readily accepted this restriction, issued by immortal Celestial Godlings, in exchange for the right to retain the powers it had seized from their masters. Their attempts to destroy the Archdevil proved ineffective time after time, and only through the selfless act of sacrifice by the highest of the Celestial Order, had his incarceration even been possible. The Angelic beings originally thought their wording ironclad, inescapable and complete. When the Archdevil pressed his palm into the symbolic papyrus of the contract without hesitation, and sealed the order with his profane blood, they knew a mistake must have been made.

Time is irrelevant to a true immortal, and anachronisms were this devil's specialty. Contingencies of a complexity as intricate as an entire universe were enacted the instant it placed its fingers upon the scroll. Soulbound within a theoretical reality, contained in the most advanced supercomputer constructed by divine hands themselves, the entity laughed triumphantly. Within the supposed prison of this artificial world, the Archdevil's engrams subtly and instantly altered history. The singularity surrounding the machine was filled at a speed that even the crushing gravity of a collapsed star's black hole could not match. Thus, the progenitor of Antiqua it became, infinite expansion into the past beyond the conceptual beginning of time, forged a future bound by a single thread: the present. The Archdevil had only to twist its manipulating hands to draw time through the hourglass, and as each moment passed, all its creation grew.

Zhiniel knew his destiny. With every calculated move, the thread of the present drew closer to his assured domination of Antiqua, and to ascension. Even as he laid Zaeliar'a back upon the bed, working his way through the muscles of her ribcage, her breasts, and her tight stomach, his mind continued to explore possibilities and formulate intricate schemes. The multiplicity of his thoughts detracted nothing from his focus, for his will was omnipresent, grounded in learning from the past, living in the present, and shaping the future. She could see it in his devilish eyes, indomitable. This look of intensity never left his face, even in the rare times he slept beside her. She turned onto her belly, he worked through the entirety of her back, and she felt unnatural power flowing through him suddenly, a tingling sensation neither cold nor hot.

"In addition to your other preparations, you will remind our gnomish friend of the terms of our contract." Zhiniel stated as he finished the massage, hands working down her powerful thighs to her smooth calves and finally her feet, and she turned over again, rejuvenated by his ministrations and the vibrant life force absorbed. She simply nodded in acknowledgement; her journey through the fortress would take her past the experimentation chamber allotted to the gnomish scientist and his assistants, so a quick detour would pose no delay.

"Your infusion as you massaged me – it was energy from the Fae Realm?" Zaeliar'a inquired of him, more as a statement than question for she knew the answer. As he explained the details of her assignment, she pulled her naked form to the side of the bed, while he parted his robes, hands still gripping her feet tightly, massaging them while he pressed himself into her. She arched her back and brought him in tight to her, flexing her legs with his thrusts.

Their lovemaking was strangely efficient; the two enjoyed the act immensely, yet still they focused on the mission parameters the whole time, interweaving conversation and pleasure seamlessly. If one dared call the sentiment they shared love, it was a strange love indeed.

Once finished, the two rose from the bed in unison, completely bare of garments; Zhiniel had cast his robes aside after the first minute of their escapades. The chamber air was warm and comfortable; masterfully crafted tubes carried heated water throughout critical areas of the spire. Briefly, they glanced at each other, and nodded crisply as the pair made their way to a specially designed chamber of naturally hewn stone, where a stream of clear water flowed upon porous rocks, enchanted such that they remained blistering hot. In the steaming sauna, they sat silently, sharing comfortable quietness and the warmth of the soothing and cleansing mists. After several minutes of this luxury, Zhiniel was the first to stand and take his leave, gathering a towel and drying himself off efficiently before donning his lightweight chainmail robes, giving his consort a final glance as he closed the chamber door behind him.

Zaeliar'a lingered much longer in the steam, allowing herself to relax fully, knowing her duties would soon bring tension, fury, and likely, combat. Her lips parted and she licked them in anticipation. Zaeliar'a loved battle, and enjoyed killing as much as she enjoyed sex, perhaps more. To her, slaughter was as much an art form as music was to a musician; she composed with her body and sang the lyrics with her blade. The battlefield was her canvas, and the blood of her enemies, her paint. The dance, when complete, gave her a fleeting sense of fulfillment: the power that fear and death provided was a sweet nectar she drank often, and with purpose. It quenched the thirst within her; one that was never fully slaked, only temporarily satisfied. Her tensions, physical, mental, and sexual now relieved, Soulthorne removed herself from the sauna, and tread with a steady pace on bare feet back into her quarters. She felt light and strong as the Fae energy suffusing her granted a euphoric state of heightened consciousness.

The enchanted world of the Fae, saturated with a vibrant, intoxicating energy was her eventual destination this day. Though one might mistakenly assume its beautiful denizens as peaceful and harmless, Zaeliar'a knew certainly how dangerous and devious they truly were. Veils of secrecy, ancient pacts and diabolic sorceries were all within the purview of faeries; the lords and ladies of their four courts held insurmountable influence over several mortal realms. Diplomatic relations between the Soulharvester and both the summer and spring courts of the Fae had utterly failed, as Zhiniel's assumption had been before entering their otherworldly empires. These two regimes held close ties to the mighty Celestial Hierarchy, and both had prior knowledge of his campaign for total domination of Antiqua, which in their estimation put their kingdoms at risk. The fall court preferred a more neutral stance, neither opposing nor supporting the Darklord in his bid for supremacy. This was also his expectation, for Zhiniel knew their monarch to be a shrewd tactician, one who would wait for an assured victory before forging an alliance with any other power. Only the vile 'Tyrant-King' of the winter court had readily entered into agreement with Zhiniel, bargaining for the right to pass into the frigid wastelands of the northern kingdoms to recapture the royal fugitives who had escaped his grasp by fleeing to the mortal realm. In return, the Lord of Frost swore in blood that he would bring the other three Fae Lords into agreement, by sheer force, if necessary, into amenable contract with the Soul Harvester. He cared nothing for Antiqua or its people, nor did he have any desire to rule any part of it, but a burning lust for the blood of his brother consumed him, and the desire to tear the beating heart of the only rightful challenge to his rule, absolute.

The mission before her was no delicate charade of diplomacy for it was the spring court, often viewed as the most docile of the four, which she prepared this day to assault. Capturing several of the nobles of the League of Rain would send a message to the higher lords and ladies of the spring court, perhaps inciting their ire, but certainly leaving no doubt regarding the zeal of the Soulharvester. She would spread her favorite weapon – terror – throughout the territory, slaying with impunity any fae bold or foolish enough to oppose her as she swept through their lands. Then, accompanied by no other forces, she would lay in wait for the assured retaliation from the elite vanguard of Eostré, the Blossom Queen. Singlehandedly Soulthorne would vanquish and cage these powerful faeries, bringing them triumphantly to the demesne of her Darklord, where they would be tortured, subjugated, or subverted into service in whatever way Zhiniel saw fit.

Zaeliar'a walked to an archway connecting the bedchamber to her personal armoury and placed her right hand upon a clear glass panel built into a fixture on its surface. The apparatus hummed as a warmth spread through her fingers while a thin beam of blue light made its way from the bottom of her palm to her fingertips. Although the device made no indication of its function, the blend of technology and magic allowed access to only the unique life signatures of her and Zhiniel alone. Rays of various types of destructive magic would obliterate any other being that attempted entry as they passed through. She stepped under the arch into a hewn granite chamber adorned with vertical bands of hammered lead, silver, and copper. A series of tubes housed in the ceiling bathed the chamber in a dim, violet light as Zaeliar'a's pace took her to an intricate gnomish-designed contraption at the centre of the room. Upon a carved dais sat the skeletal device, comprised of straps and mechanical clamps attached to steel rods, each holding a piece of her armour. She had commissioned, or rather *ordered* its construction to aid in the donning of her crimson and gold inlaid platemail suit. Hydraulic cylinders supported the heavier pieces such as the breastplate and greaves, while jointed armatures held the smaller components, positioned to connect each piece to her body as efficiently as possible. The process would have taken her thirty minutes to affix the armour normally, even with the extensive practice she possessed; with the assistance of the exoskeleton, she needed only five to be fully equipped.

Zaeliar'a stood at its centre and proceeded, moving the rods, clamps, and arms into place, attaching the treated leather straps, buckles and loops in a specific order as the layered armour covered her head to foot in impregnable metal. Although extremely heavy and thick in the places where she stood to take the most damage, the interlocking parts of the armour provided for effective mobility in combat thanks to enhancements both magical and technological. The stoutest oryk would have staggered under the weight of the platemail, but Soulthorne possessed physical strength far exceeding what her lithe and muscular form would suggest. She strode about as if clothed in silk, her movements unimpeded even as she slipped her feet into the final two pieces of the armour: her plated boots. Presently her head remained unprotected, however, an open-faced helm would snap into place in an instant at her command, along with a semicircular neck guard concealed in her gorget.

Next, she looked to the shield clinging to a stand, along with a selection of single-handed weapons: axes, broadswords, and short spears, all of which she trained in extensively. She preferred the destructive might of her two-handed claymore, which still hung from the corner post of her bed, so she ignored the weaponry and moved to the benches and shelves of specialized gear. Many of the devices spread neatly before her would impair, maim, or slay their targets, each designed with a specific and nefarious purpose. She selected a belt with several throwing discs attached, wicked razors that exploded with a blinding light, capable of both killing and causing disorder in her enemies. Onto this belt, she next attached a shock-resistant case containing three vials of Imps' Fog, each of which could cover a sizable area in thick, poisonous vapour that numbed the mind while wracking the body with spasms and nausea. Her final selection from among all the implements was a small globe of meteoric iron designed to explode into slivers of the metal most baneful to the Fae. This she would reserve for a deadly foe; it would shred through their typically weaker armour and imbed into their flesh, burning and causing excruciating pain. Satisfied, the Dreadheart left the room filled with deadly tools of battle, making her way back through the arch, across the bedchamber to her mirrored dresser, removed her gauntlets and casually pinned her long red hair up in her typical fashion.

Shutting the door crisply behind her, Zaeliar'a stared down the long hallway lit by miniature braziers hanging from steel hooks along its length. The dim amber light they provided was comfortable and warm, staving off the slight chill that crept through her flesh. Conscious of the sensation, Soulthorne adopted a brisk pace, willing her heart to pump faster as she approached one of the spire's exits. The heavy metal-shod doors led to a balcony of sorts where several dark-clad crossbowmen stood at attention when she arrived. Spanning the great chasm surrounding the central spire, a massive suspension bridge loomed before her, swaying gently in the darkness ahead. Zaeliar'a licked her lips in anticipation of the first destination on her itinerary. She was thirsty thanks to the earlier exertion, even suffused as she was with the vibrant energy the Darklord habitually drained from his captured Archfey.

Recently, a few had died in their cells. Weak yet defiant, the crafty prisoners had pooled their power into the strongest of the group and rather than use it to affect escape, she instead unleashed a spell that obliterated most of her kin. The proud Fae noble would rather send her companions to oblivion than have them suffer as cattle. Zhiniel himself had attended the matter scant minutes after the report of the incident by the *Chainmaster*, a sadistic Dun Dwarf whose occupation as a torturer and slave-keeper prior had found him terrific opportunity within the Darklord's legion. The tan-skinned Fae lady stood tall with a triumphant glare at the indigo elf as he approached, expecting him to meet her with rage. Instead, the Soulharvester wore an expression of approval as he opened her containment cell and surveyed the blackened soot that sat in piles surrounding her, once her friends and compatriots.

"This is an impressive display of defiance, Lady Pelein, as befits your noble lineage. I commend you." Zhiniel tilted his head slightly as was the Fae custom of admiration. The lady's voluminous golden eyes narrowed, her expression, shocked. This was the first she had seen her captor up close, she expected someone who fit the image from her frequent nightmares during her imprisonment, not this oddly cordial and strangely attractive elf that stood before her. However, when he extended a hand to her cheek, she instinctively recoiled, and that was when Lady Pelein's heart turned to ice, for she saw a wicked smile upon the Soulharvester's face and knew she was doomed.

Zhiniel's demeanor transformed into malice as he lunged forward, gripped her tightly by the golden hair, and wrenched the lady mercilessly from her cell into the centre of the prison chamber. Pelein struggled vainly, but his touch weakened her upon contact, and a scream erupted from her lips in despair. The few remaining Fae locked in cold iron chains wallowed in misery in their confinement, watching with horror as the Darklord tore off her already ripped and soiled garments, casting her naked onto the stone floor. A circle of black runes carefully carved into the stonework erupted with a sinister purple light and the faerie felt all strength leave her body; she crumpled to a heap and wept as her end drew assuredly near.

The Chainmaster wrung his hands in anticipation, thinking the Darklord would allow him to torture her, however when he approached the weakly squirming woman, Zhiniel cast a dark stare that withered the cruel dwarf. The dun-skinned slaver backed away deferentially as his master turned to the terrified prisoners in their cages and flatly stated, "Defiance, while admirable, is unwelcome in all those who choose to oppose my dominion." Zhiniel's attention shifted back to the faerie barely able to move beneath his feet, and he incanted a spell that awakened the runes surrounding her. They leapt from the stone, transmuted into vibrant chains of seething energy that wrapped themselves around the trapped Fae. Lady Pelein tried to scream as she writhed in agony; the necromantic bands tightened around her neck and limbs, they lacerated her flesh with a cold, aching pain. Zhiniel knelt close and locked eyes with the dying woman, and with acid words, spelled out his earlier decree to her people, "You may bow willingly, give to me what I ask and find prosperity in service, or you may have all that you value taken and find yourselves bound in chains beneath my heel. I give you *only* the power of choice: the freedom of will to seize this world in my name… or know the darkness of death at my hands." With finality, Zhiniel placed his palm upon her forehead and watched the last vestiges of life depart the once-proud Lady Pelein. Her terrified, tear-stained eyes lost all light as he stole the essence of her soul.

"Dispose of this *husk*," came the parting command of the Soulharvester as he silently left the prison. He cast only a single dispassionate look at the few remaining, broken Fae held tightly in chains. His dark message received, he expected no more trouble from the prisoners; he did not care for their loss, either. There would be more of their kind soon enough. Zhiniel ignored the prickling sensation of the vibrant life-force now coursing through his body. He made his way to the chamber of his dark mistress, knowing the gift of its power would alleviate the insatiable thirst she possessed.

It had, briefly. Zaeliar'a had only twice dined on the pure force of the Fae, and each occasion left a lingering urge for more of its sickeningly sweet essence. It reminded Soulthorne of the rush she felt when ingesting honey for the first time: the overpowering taste of sugar and... *something else* that was simultaneously intoxicating and nauseating. She postulated that the reason the Fae lived in planar seclusion might dwell in the fact that they were made of living vibrancy. Several creatures sustained themselves by draining life, drinking blood, or by feasting on other sentient life for this singular reason; such things rejuvenated them, and the Fae were a prime example of delicacy.

Soulthorne dismissed these thoughts and crossed the vast, swaying bridge that led to a massive balcony overlooking the metropolis below. The Dreadheart had not once looked down during the brisk march across. The sight, so far below, often pleased Zaeliar'a, but this day, she preferred solid ground to take in the view. Between the otherworldly energy coursing through her veins and the swaying of the bridge, she felt nauseated to the point of vertigo, but now that Soulthorne stood upon more steady footing, she turned to see the myriad lights and bustle of the gigantic city that filled the entirety of a kilometres-wide cavern.

The scope of the metropolis, which housed hundreds of thousands of indigo elves, undead beings, devils and a multitude of other races, was in an understatement: monumental. Zaeliar'a marveled at the view before her, but it was what she could *not* see that made the city so vast. For, the visible parts, which covered the floor, walls, and roof of the titanic cavern, were only a fraction of the metropolis' composition. It expanded from the central spire outward in all directions, a mass of architecture including tunnels, vertical shafts housing elevators, enormous chambers, twisting corridors dotted with secret rooms of varying purpose; the list was as expansive as the city. Highly disciplined soldiers, devious and lethal traps, and the powerful living dead that served Zhiniel meticulously guarded the entrances and exits to other occupied areas of the underworld. The city lay buried so far beneath the crust of Antiqua that no direct physical passage to the surface existed; the only means of entry were the obsidian teleportals like the one their moon elven guest surreptitiously stole his way through hours before.

Soulthorne took it all in; the enhanced awareness of the Fae energy within her afforded new sensory experiences as she lingered minutes upon the railing of the balcony, alone. She recalled with clarity the words Zhiniel had whispered in her ear weeks prior, when the pair took in the same view upon the same balcony, "This is all ours." The statement shocked her then, and the memory of it even now had her reeling. 'Ours' was not a word the Soulharvester ever used in describing a possession. It was the first time she, or anyone still existing for that matter, heard that solitary word escape his lips. The thought of its implication made her heart race for a few seconds, though she knew not why. The chill of her skin broke the reverie, and without another moment's pause, Zaeliar'a turned on her heel and marched straight past a regiment of skeletal guardians, who saluted in a mechanical, programmed way as she passed. Up a flight of ebon stairs wide enough for a score of soldiers to march abreast, the sound of her plate boots made a sharp clacking noise with every step, she traveled upwards to the first destination on her list. Seven stone doors, carved intricately with Dun Dwarvish script, loomed before her, the entrance to Math'Kalon Dendril: *The Hall of Hell's Hammers.*

Seven of the cruellest and most diabolic of the Dun Dwarvish clans pledged fealty to the Flayer of Webs: their title for the motif upon the Soulharvester's banner served as the name by which they called its master. Clever and self-serving were these seven traitorous Thanes, their names accompanied by rounds of spitting and muttered curses when spoken by their kin. Honour, as a principle, was paramount to every dwarven subculture, both subterranean and surface dwelling. It was also something the Hell's Hammers sorely lacked. When these dissidents absconded from the Gaer Boltac-Keirn, an association of ninety underworld dwelling clans of Dun Dwarves, they left behind a path of destruction, blood, and corpses in their wake. The seven renegade clans, upon arrival in D'zurien-To'th, declared themselves the Hell's Hammers and each appointed (through several battles to the gruesome death) a leader, bestowed the title of Thane. Their infamy would spread throughout Bazrin-Dal'ateir as murderers and marauders under the orders of the Soulharvester; neither their enemies nor their former kin were exempt from their savagery.

Straight into the Assembly of Thanes came the echoing, heavy footsteps of the Dreadheart as she stormed past the swiftly lowered weapons of the dwarven host guards. Though the Hell's Hammers were aptly described as insane, they were far from stupid or suicidal, save for one, who made the fatal mistake of calling out, "Zasmakari ontegaal-neth!" which was Dun Dwarvish for "The Devil's Concubine." Two unfortunate facts sealed the lone fool's fate.

The first was that the purpose of Soulthorne's visit was to remind the Thanes, *unequivocally*, from whom their orders came. Recently, the Hell's Hammers had executed a series of pillaging forays on their own accord, slaughtered a few bands of indigo elf traditionalists: loyal followers of Ennetra who lay holed up in makeshift, hidden refuges. The dwarven mercenaries had taken liberty on the goods found, several of which were religious relics of the Daemon-Queen: items that held interest to Zhiniel. In addition, they subjected the survivors to horrors that only the depraved could imagine. Some, they still held as slaves, locked away in their own private torture halls. None of these things were theirs to take, and the Soulharvester would not abide disobedience, least of all from the self-appointed Dwarven Thanes. He had graciously accepted the rogue faction into his legion, rather than crush them along with their defiant kin who still vehemently opposed his dominion over Bazrin-Dal'ateir.

The second fact, and the one which swiftly and neatly separated his head from his torso, was that Zaeliar'a fluently spoke the Dun Dwarvish language. Her tolerance for insult was non-existent. Hence, he became the first example; disrespect towards the highest-ranking member of the Darklord's army was his death sentence. Soulthorne's right arm snapped to the Claymore resting upon her back. At her touch, the clasps fused to her armour released the weapon, and it veritably sang as she closed the distance to the open-mouthed, grey-skinned dwarf with a single stride. His hand barely made it to the axe on his belt by the time her giant sword swung with blinding speed in a sweeping arc, severing his head, complete with the stunned look upon his face. It hit the carpeted floor with a smack just before his body toppled next to it. A few of the crazier berserkers nearby drew weapons at the spectacle, and Zaeliar'a widened her stance and stared each of them down. Her red eyes flashed as if aflame, her blade bathed in the blood of their fallen brother. Soulthorne licked her lips in anticipation, her greatsword dragged purposefully along the floor, cut through the bloody carpet, and made a foreboding, grating noise as she strode forth.

The three Thanes present for the whole debacle sat up in their elaborately carved granite thrones, intrigued. Gruenvald the Bastard-King, Ruegor the Merciless, and Maugbanz Three-Fingers (each grandiosely self-titled) wondered if the rumours of the brutal might of the Dreadheart held any weight, and thus, they simply watched as well over ten psychotic, armed-to-the-teeth, and famously vicious Reavers descended upon the lone indigo elven warrior-woman. Honour should have dictated they face her in singular combat, but the group moved around to flank the heavily armoured she-devil. A few of them cackled with a mixture of drunken glee and bloodlust as they circled her, most of them held expertly crafted, paired war-axes – dwarven weaponsmiths were renowned for the sharpness of their implements of death and killing was a sport to these grim people. The more seasoned – and *sober* – of the group hung back to gauge the strength of the opponent who stood coolly in their midst, apparently unfazed at being outnumbered ten-to-one.

Two moved to attack in unison; the crazed dwarves rushed wildly at Soulthorne with axe swings aimed at her knees to carve through what they surmised was a weak point in her impressive platemail. With supernatural speed, later murmured about by the survivors, Zaeliar'a sidestepped and turned such that the first axe blow clanked resoundingly off the heavy part of her greaves, leaving not a scratch upon its crimson, enamelled exterior. The move sent that dwarf sprawling past, and with a singular motion, she deflected the other dwarf's expert strike with the edge of her claymore. As her sword rose from the ground, she turned on a heel and spun, the arcing motion carried the blade upward to an apex, and it hung a second, gleaming above her head. The stumbling dwarf had scarcely brought the second axe across his body when her ebony claymore descended, neatly found the gap in between his breastplate and shoulder, and twisted downward. It penetrated the armour like paper, and continued through the Reaver's heart, the opposite lung, and protruded from just above his left hip. Soulthorne's heavy metal boot-heel made a pulp of the other dwarf's face as she continued her spin, executing a sidekick with a martial finesse that would leave a fighting-monk envious. His skull cracked open from the sheer force of the blow, and he was dead before his body crashed into the ruined carpet.

Zaeliar'a's unrelenting assault continued as she leapt to the offensive, to the shock of the remaining assailants. With her blade still buried in their twitching companion, Soulthorne watched more of the berserkers charge at her as if in slow motion. In the few seconds it had taken her to kill the first pair, they had barely managed to close a few metres distance, so blinding was her ferocity. Her blade made a shucking sound, exited the first dead dwarf back up the same way it entered him, and spattered the ceiling with a wet, red torrent. Again, she leapt, as quickly as a mountain cat, turned the carving edge of deathly steel sideways and cleft two more shocked berserkers in twain. Unabated, the obsidian blade tore apart mithril armour and ripped through ribcages, scattering broken shards of bone and bloody chainmail across the floor. A spiked steel chain snaked out from behind Soulthorne and wrapped itself around her left arm; a wizened older Dun Dwarf hoped to slow her attacks enough for one of his horror-stricken companions to land a well-timed blow. Jerked off his feet by her impossible strength, the chain wrapped tightly in his fist snapped taut, as the Dreadheart yanked him towards her. The grizzled berserker knew with certainty that he rushed to meet death in the form of this impressive woman. She caught his throat mid-flight; the force almost snapped the dwarf's neck as her stone grip terminated his movement, and she suspended him with a single arm a full metre off the ground.

Taller than the dwarf by nearly half a metre, yet only half his girth, Zaeliar'a must have weighed about the same as the stocky berserker, even considering her heavy armour. Yet, she held him in a single vice-like hand as if he was a paperweight. He stared directly into her crimson eyes, admired her fine features a moment, and nodded at her in admiration. The ominous eyes that locked onto his glowed with supernatural intensity, and the dwarf's formerly approving look turned to pure *dread*. Her pretty lips parted to reveal sharply pointed fangs, just before they sunk deeply into his neck. A sudden, palpable chill in the room emanated from Soulthorne while she stood there and drained the life force of the sputtering veteran, in front of all his remaining comrades. The runes engraved in her claymore, previously invisible, gradually filled with a throbbing power that cast scarlet light upon the already bloody scene. She discarded the desiccated corpse unceremoniously down at her feet, wiped her lips, and tilted her head. Weapons clanked to the chamber floor and the remaining Dun Dwarves unanimously bent a knee, the Dreadheart's reputation made ironclad to the ruthless Hell's Hammers, spelled out in their own blood.

Maugbanz, the eldest and perhaps most shrewd of the three Thanes still sitting languorous in their lofty thrones, stood, and clapped as he weighed his forthcoming words carefully. "Quite a show the lady Soulthorne has entertained us with, eh boys?" He motioned emphatically at the carnage all about the grand hall and the other two simply nodded grimly. They could feel the tension throughout the air, met with the smoldering glare of the vampiric general of their liege as she strode confidently straight to the stone steps leading to the seven thrones. Maugbanz turned to his companions, the look on his face urging them to speak. Ruegor shifted, remaining uncharacteristically silent, scowling at his shamed men – the ones still alive anyway. His berserkers had humiliated him, and although his blood too burned with the desire for chaos and battle, the fools should have known better than to attack the Dreadheart. Consequences were not something they understood, but he certainly *did*. Gruenvald, however, got up from his seat and took a step forward, his tough, calloused hand resting on the pommel of the broadsword worn at his side.

Before he spoke though, Zaeliar'a issued a warning, her blade pointed straight at the Dun Dwarf's throat, "Choose your words carefully, Bastard-King. The Darklord would gladly appoint your seven corpses as the new Thanes of the Hell's Hammers." Ruegor and Maugbanz both grimaced as she withered each of them in turn with her cold stare, eyes shining menacingly. Gruenvald cleared his throat and took his hand off his sword, and simply nodded, sitting back down on the stone as he straightened his hammered gold crown. "Then let me say *this*, Lady: perhaps tis we who should listen first whilst *ye* speak?" He glanced to his two companions, who followed his lead, in turn sitting and nodding their approval of the Thane's strategy. Ruegor finally broke his silence at that point, smiling a near-toothless grin sure to charm the lass as he asked, "Aye, Lady Dreadheart, if t'was merely a *drink* ye cared to share with us, we'd have opened the casks of *freshly-acquired* blood-wine!" His guffaw rang through the hall to deflect the baleful tone of the conversation.

Soulthorne saw clear through the feeble attempt to lighten her mood, drawing back her lips to bare her fangs in a sinister snarl. "That is the heart of this matter," she growled as she buried the tip of her giant blade in the granite floor between them. A large crack snaked out from the point of impact, which would remain a permanent reminder of her visit. "Were you *instructed* to lay assault upon the hidden cloisters of Ennetra?" She arched one of her fine eyebrows and leaned in, inviting their answer. With only silence forthcoming, she turned suddenly to Ruegor, whose smile vanished as she continued the rebuke. Pulling her blade from the floor, she returned it to its place on her back and ascended the steps, footfalls echoing in the deathly quiet of the chamber. Towering in front of the red-bearded dwarf, she whispered softly enough that the other Thanes had to strain their ears to hear. "The dead follow orders *implicitly*. Would you care to join their ranks?"

That scarcely veiled threat lingered in the thoughts of the three Thanes evermore, and the rest of the short conversation afterwards bore assurances from all seven that the Hell's Hammers would never again stray from their commands. When Zaeliar'a finally left the great hall, satisfied her message was thoroughly ingrained, she heard Maugbanz whisper, "Seems we've made a deal with a greater devil than we." She smiled in assent, for the murderous and bloodthirsty Dun Dwarves, feared unanimously by their enemies, were mere pawns in Zhiniel's schemes.

The comment about devils carried an odd irony, Zaeliar'a mused, for her next destination lay within the sulfurous demesne of the Infernals: *actual* devilspawn, who also served in the Soulharvester's legion. The specially prepared chamber leading to the devils of Apocrypha lay ahead through twisted tunnels of igneous rock, deep below the city proper. The gates to the various levels of the Hells emanated strong magical auras, masked in part by natural geothermal phenomena throughout the area. Zhiniel had taken careful measures himself, utilizing concealing magic upon rare materials to further hamper any attempts by the surface to detect their presence. She passed several guards, hidden away in cleverly carved alcoves along the stretch of seemingly endless corridor. Any unlikely intruders who managed to pass through these fissures would find hinderance by sulfurous vapors and the uneven composition of the flooring. They would also find themselves blocked inside nigh-impenetrable mana barriers, which would render their forces vulnerable to flanking attacks from Zhiniel's camouflaged soldiers. Although, as a vampire, she had no biological need to breathe, Zaeliar'a rarely stopped cycling air through her lungs. The long-practiced habit served to conceal her true nature. She decidedly ceased the expanding and contracting; the noxious fumes could not harm her physically, but their repugnant stench was unbearable to the heightened senses she possessed.

Vampire physiology was a confusing blend of anatomical modifications and magical changes from exposure to the negative force of Animus from the Death Plane. The infusion of energy, typically from a vast ingestion of the powerful blood of an elder vampire, was a painful process; it carried the characteristics of both a terrible disease and a diabolic curse. The traditional ritual involved the master vampire draining, then replacing the subject's blood, much like the fairy tales described. Many did not survive the ordeal as the will fought to survive bodily death, and the process drove several fledglings mentally insane or disjointed from the self. These became simple, subservient thralls: the broken spawn of their creators.

Zaeliar'a's transition had been doubly terrible, yet carefully planned and monitored by Zhiniel himself. Using medical technology developed from resources found in a buried facility from some previous civilization, the Darklord employed a team of specialists and his own magic to perform a meticulous transfusion of the *vitae* into her body. Her unliving progenitor, promised by Zhiniel an entire necropolis upon the dark moon once he conquered it, was the eldest surviving Vampire Queen, Caligastia Voxparl, currently residing in her Blood Palace, deeper still within the city. Zaeliar'a would pay her blood-mother a visit before the end of her long journey, but first there were the devil lords to attend.

Finished navigating through the maze of deeply descending corridors, Zaeliar'a came to a halt before an ornate set of double doors, black as pitch and carved with the wicked language of the Infernals. Some called it the Nameless Tongue, others the Writ of Darkness; to Soulthorne, it was just a set of sigils like any other, and with a crisp, loud voice, she called out the harsh syllables required to gain entry. Few mortal scholars dared to speak the Infernal language aloud; doing so was tantamount to allowing dark forces entry to one's soul, for their speech consisted of bargains, promises of corruption, and a convoluted series of axioms beyond the ken of comprehension. If Antiqua itself was ancient, the temporally displaced realm of the devils was far beyond reckoning; some Archdevils purportedly slept for millennia, locked in dreams of scheming and conquest. Conceivably, his inception by the master of all devilkind was the driving force behind the complex intellect of Zhiniel himself. The words reminded Soulthorne of the Darklord, terribly efficient, yet complicated in structure: effective in practice. The doors swung open before her, and she strode through them into a curtain of inky mist, which enveloped her body in a chilling pain that burned like frostbite. The simultaneous sensations of fiery immolation and freezing coldness wreaked havoc on tactile sensation, hinting at the nature of the plane itself. The pain subsided only moments after she stepped through, yet it left a lingering memory: a feeling of eternal entrapment in the dichotomy of exothermic and endothermic scale.

Zaeliar'a shook the feeling off, as she did every visit, and marveled at the stark architecture that expanded before her eyes. A dim, yet pervading orange-red luminance bathed the wicked spires and bladelike edges of the structures of the Infernals' demesne, its shadows alive and hungry as if they too calculated with intelligence alien to rational thought. The concept of the layers of Hell that mortals carried paled to their actuality, and the unlucky souls who survived to recount the experience often described it as "more terrible and diabolically beautiful than you can imagine." Moreover, in truth, it was. Rivers of blood, their shores littered with stained ivory bones, flowed throughout the bleak landscape, bridges of sinew and rotten flesh connected minute landmasses upon which emerged the habitations of the devils themselves. Crimson, black and orange towers filled with inverted curves that could sever flesh like carving knives, each adorned with the same jagged runes of their apocalyptic tongue populated the land in a bizarre hierarchy of power. Some rose in the distance, towering over the others like blasphemous monuments to their creators; some littered with burnt tomes of fallen religions, others with the melted armaments of destroyed Celestials. All were horrors to behold, as individual nightmares put on display, categorically defying all that was righteous in existence.

Movement in the demi-plane was an exercise in sheer will. With enough mental fortitude, and the correct focus, the environment itself could propel an individual at vast speeds along its landscape in any direction. Control was key. Zaeliar'a concentrated on her objective: a solitary and uniformly ebony obelisk that, unlike the other buildings, hovered in the ash-choked sky, boasting the sheer power of its master. She felt a rippling sensation as she leapt, then flew to its base high above the masses below. Vulturous horned devils with leathery wings, wicked smiles, and lashing tails acknowledged the vampire general upon approach as she rushed past them, intent on her goal. They knew she served Zhiniel, the bastard son of their exiled, yet undisputed ruler; assaulting her would be contractually foolish. Yet, powerful as she was, had they not recognized the Dreadheart as their ally, hordes of devils would have ripped her to shreds and affixed the remains to their domiciles as a trophy. Upon reaching the seemingly impregnable obelisk, Zaeliar'a felt her form drawn through, absorbed by its mirror surface, and then ejected into its nebulous core. The interior was devoid of light, yet something stirred at her disturbance, a diabolical psyche permeated the structure, and she knew she was not alone.

A voice, deep and penetrating, formed of a malignant will resounded through the unseen surroundings, echoing her thoughts, "We visit the magnificent hall to behold the wonders of our subjugation." Indeed, that was her mission here. Soulthorne's duty involved observing and reporting on the devils' experiments upon select members of the surface races deemed strong enough to merit this unique form of domination. The voice issued a command, "Of darkness, make light," and the chamber pulsed with the same muted amber hue as the outside sky, subtly painting her surroundings. From another hidden dimension entangled within the material folds of the hellscape, the contents of the room materialized. Cylindrical vats of crystal lined the interior walls of the structure, suspended from anchors high above by glowing liquid chains. In an agonizingly slow circle, each rotated such that the subjects within, enveloped by a hazy, translucent ichor, were displayed in full. Each of the scores of them was a member of a different surface race, paragons of their species, interred for extensive anatomical study. Receptors of a charcoal-coloured sinew attached to various points of sensory input on the subjects' bodies, writhed within the chemical confines, both extracting and inputting information, which they relayed to and from the Archdevil's central archive.

Though the devil itself remained unseen, its pervading presence could be felt everywhere in the structure. Zaeliar'a surmised either the entity simply deigned to conceal itself to her, or that the entirety of the obelisk *was* the Archdevil itself. A feeling of maniacal self-importance washed through her as the chamber shook with hideous, hissing laughter. When it subsided, the malevolent aura returned, and the devil spoke again in its rich, seductive voice, "The visitor has guessed the nature of her host correctly. All she must do is speak our *Truename* if she wishes an audience in full." Soulthorne, accustomed to the devious manipulations of such beings, laughed incredulously at the bold offer, but refused flatly. "It is not my desire to entreat your highness for such purpose. Show me now the most promising subject and I shall leave with my report." There was a sense of dismay in the air, but also the intimation that her choice held wisdom. It was impossible to tell if the structure itself shifted or if it pulled her somehow, but Zaeliar'a found herself before one of the giant crystal cylinders, though she took not a single step forth. From within the viscous substance that bubbled inside the vat, motes of amber light intensified and the creature within became clearly visible.

To her surprise, Zaeliar'a saw that the creature was neither a Neph'al as she expected, nor any of the stronger, more civilized races of Antiqua, but a female gaub, of the Wellick variety, judging by her stark white skin and blue hair. The Gaub'Wellick, like most of their cunning racial cousins, roamed in nomadic fashion across the Mithrainian and Huromithran continents, and Soulthorne became curious about the details of the creature's capture and internment. The voice responded and the crystal prison turned opaque, displaying images upon its exterior, pulled from the diminutive creature's memories to supplement what it said. "This one consorted with a sorceress, found attraction to her power and beauty; desirous were her thoughts." The image somehow carried emotional content and other sensory information, relayed the gaub's enrapture with a human woman who was certainly attractive: long, dark hair with red at the tips, dressed fashionably with a comely figure. Her dark eyes, which the creature felt were marvelous, held a mysterious power in them that suddenly aroused Soulthorne emotionally and sexually as she experienced the stored response of the gaub.

"Intoxicating, sweet taste..." the entity observed. Zaeliar'a felt the devil's aura shift to a lustful, rapturous delight that infected her with a needful wetness and her thighs shuddered involuntarily. Her skin bristled at the sensation of a tongue lightly dragging upward from her inner thigh, closing in on her crotch. Instinctively, she thrust her fist at the invisible force and was shocked when she contacted something, though the physical sensation dissipated as her hand impacted it. Fury replaced the borrowed feeling of lust within her, and Soulthorne reached for her claymore, but found all action slowed, her limbs weak. The pure force of the Archdevil pulled her to the ground; though she struggled, within the obelisk the command of the Archdevil rendered even her mighty will impotent.

"But a plaything, are we, in the confines of the master's embrace." Unseen hands, clawed and horrible, pawed at her skin as if she were naked, began touching her back, her thighs, and her breasts. They forced her into a prone posture on all fours, pushed her head down, and arched her back into her favorite position as if her deepest desires were known. Panic registered, along with a strange exhilaration that came with vulnerability, but both emotions she controlled, and slowed her breathing. Never had Zaeliar'a felt a will utterly suppress her own, this dominating psyche so oppressive… save for one alone. Aloud, the Dreadheart calmly iterated, "Your intrusion upon me is unwelcome, Neirchezaphet the Baleful." The force withdrew some, taken aback at the intonation of its Truename, which the vampire elf should not rightly have known.

The form of the soot-black-skinned, bewitchingly attractive Archdevil coalesced from the matter of the obelisk, rising as if from a dark pool. It was naked and possessed a perfectly structured humanoid body, but with sharp clawed hands, leathery wings and horns that curved skyward, all tipped in an acidic green colour. It bore a bemused smile now, disarmingly pleasant with a mere hint of malice glinting in its glassy ebon eyes. Zaeliar'a still could not stand; it was as if the gravity of the room weighed her beyond even her supernatural strength, and she challenged the Archdevil with her gaze, defiant and with unbridled fury still smoldering. The creature approached, knelt beside her, and dragged one of its cruel nails down her spine. A line of blood ran along its course, between the rosy cheeks of her heart-shaped backside, then trickled down her leg. Again, though her armour still covered her from head-to-toe in impenetrable metal, the devil somehow circumvented the magical protection as easily as it would the air.

Neirchezaphet laughed cruelly, but anger flashed in its eyes in seeing a complete lack of fear in its prone and helpless victim. Still, it whispered threateningly in her ear, "You will be so very difficult to *break*, little plaything." The Archdevil's face split in the semblance of a smile, to reveal wicked rows of curved, shark-like teeth while it continued, "So much more delicious for us, is this." With that, it gathered up Zaeliar'a's scarlet hair in its claws and pulled sharply, forced her attention as it circled behind her slowly. "We are tantalized by the pains and pleasures of the flesh, yes?" The devil pulled her backside in – dangerously close – as it let go of her hair to stroke its talons up her thighs with a solid grip before making its declaration. "We shall undertake the entry we so wickedly want, torture and passion inside each other, my plaything." Soulthorne steeled her mind and braced herself for the inevitable to begin.

Just as Zaeliar'a felt the fleshy tip of something brush up against her, the Archdevil's entire body and the obelisk itself shook violently, and both pitched to the side. With a resounding crack that shattered several of the crystal cylinders and washed the floor in their vile contents, the obelisk itself ruptured. A gaping fissure snaked from top to bottom, crackling with deep indigo lightning that forked throughout the chamber like the hands of a giant; it rent the entire structure nearly in two. Abruptly freed of the overpowering influence of the Archdevil, who she heard issue a horrifying screech of agony, Zaeliar'a spun on her knees and swept herself backwards, then skipped up onto her feet. Before her, Neirchezaphet lay sprawled, shuddering and clutching the side of its face, which bore an oozing crack identical to the damage inflicted upon its obelisk. A familiar voice boomed from outside the opening torn in the structure, "Gaze upon your demise, Archdevil Neirchezaphet Achromasorvante. Know my *wrath unchained."*

Both Soulthorne and the sundered Archdevil turned eyes to the gaping fissure in the obelisk to witness Zhiniel the Soulharvester hovering in the ashen sky. His chainmail robes twisted about him wildly and crackled with the same energy used to rip apart the obelisk. His long, ivory hair whipped about chaotically, his eyes and countenance filled beyond comprehension with an unhinged rage. He was terrifying to behold for even Zaeliar'a; she had never seen a display of utter anger erupt from the Darklord, nor this unlocked power he now held. Soulflayer, his magical nine-headed flail, gripped tightly in his outstretched hand, practically leapt forth as Zhiniel rocketed through the giant crack in the obelisk and it snapped straight out, sheared both the devil's legs, and spattered the chamber with green vitriolic acid. The blow to the devil was mirrored by the obelisk; its lower quarter hewn from the centre fell to the ground below and obliterated a lesser devil's abode into smoldering ruin. Rivers of blood flew skyward from its horrible impact and rained upon half a kilometre of terrain. The crater surrounding the sheared piece of Neirchezaphet's obelisk soon filled with the rivers' blood, and later became known as The Lake of Wrath's Judgment. The shard in its centre became another ambitious devil's palace.

Still mid-air, Zhiniel twisted and brought the mighty flail down on the Archdevil's back, flayed its skin to shreds of green and black. His hand, drawn back for another swing shook with fury, but Zhiniel stayed his rage a moment, and lighted upon the now cracked and oozing floor of the chamber. Soulthorne took a step towards the Darklord and laid her gauntleted hand upon his shoulder. To her amazement, his own hand met hers there for an instant, just long enough to understand his unspoken words, then he knelt and laid the same hand roughly upon Neirchezaphet's forehead, gripping its skull between the mighty horns. "Did you take me for a fool, *Beznagh'ovas-torah?*" he hissed, pushing the devil's head sharply to the floor. Zhiniel turned a cheek to Zaeliar'a then issued the closest utterance to an apology he would ever make; another first, "Your peril was merely a ruse to draw out this traitor, but I had not estimated it would attempt what it did." The Archdevil struggled to squirm out from under the Soulharvester's unflinching grasp, but found its strength sapped by the same gravitic power it once wielded. Zhiniel glowered cruelly at Neirchezaphet before he continued.

"You should have never broken the compact we signed, *former* Archdevil Achromasorvante. Your position, nay, your very existence is hereby revoked. Zaeliar'a – raise your blade." The mighty, once-unassailable devil now forced to grovel under the crushing weight of its own power, tried to bargain for its life. "You cannot destroy me!" it shouted, "The obelisk will fall without my influence, all your precious experiments and both of you will die with it!" Zhiniel laughed at the pitiful being, and commanded Soulthorne, "Separate this deplorable creature's head from its body. Its power, I grant you."

Dutifully, Zaeliar'a executed the Archdevil with a single downward stroke, her claymore drove through its shuddering body straight into the substance of the obelisk, which merely rippled at its former master's demise. A gravitic power swept through her, along with countless formulae and a portion of its keen intellect as she absorbed its infernal essence. Zhiniel held the link: a contract, beyond the Archdevil's vast knowledge, allowed the Soulharvester absolute dominion over any Infernal bound by his progenitor's agreements. Neirchezaphet had sorely underestimated Zhiniel's importance within his anachronistic creator's infinite plans. None but the Unspeakable One possessed the authority to strip an Archdevil of its soul completely. Through law and contract, power passed between the hands of devils like mortals traded in currency. Positions changed and influence was won through manipulation and trickery, however a devil's utter destruction was a thing of near impossibility. None were foolish enough to bargain away the last shred of their essence. Even if a devil's physical form were obliterated, the Unspeakable One's Celestial contract would return the creature in its basest form to the Hellplane to regenerate slowly, as it served and dealt yet again to rise in the infinite hierarchy. A handful of Celestials, the Lords of the Nether Planes, and a few other creatures in existence wielded the power to smite a devil such that it truly died.

Neirchezaphet's oozing corpse lay on the floor, irrefutable proof that Zhiniel held such authority. He looked to Zaeliar'a, and then offered a slight nod to the centre of the chamber, where now stood a new Archdevil, eager to take the place of the former master. Although the Darklord allowed her to keep much of the devil's essence, he knew the entirety of it would overwhelm Zaeliar'a, and shunted portions of it into himself and into maintaining the integrity of the obelisk. The final portion he invested in Trigobakevicsz, the Archdevil who waited earnestly to continue where the fallen had failed. Zhiniel addressed the new overseer, "Grind these horns into dust. Some use may as well be made of the former master, display it as a reminder of failure to me, and the penalty for incurring my wrath." The Archdevil bowed obediently and set to the task with delight. It was not the hedonistic sort, more akin to a scientist than the torturer and debaucher before it. Already familiar with the control scheme of the laboratory, it scurried about, resembling a devilish rat with three long, barbed tails and horns like whiskers that sprouted from its face.

"Carry on with your mission, unabated, my Dreadheart. I have matters to attend." With this abrupt statement, Zhiniel vanished, leaving Zaeliar'a to finish the observations with Trigobakevicsz, who accommodated every inquiry implicitly and with a degree of respect uncharacteristic for its kind. The devil explained the processes fully, revealing that all the test subjects were in a state of waking dream, their desires and deepest secrets slowly drawn out through a simulation, recorded, and catalogued in the central archive. In turn, this process opened the creatures up to subtle manipulation and offered true insight into the workings of their minds. The great and complex machines, woven into the structure of the obelisk, calculated the data gathered from sinewy nodes attached to each subject. It generated a probability matrix used to coerce others of their various species; more information gathered equated to higher probabilities. Much of the technical explanation escaped Zaeliar'a, however the usefulness and basic function of the experiment was clear. If the Darklord could enrapture enough of the populace by way of these programming tanks, he could effectively eliminate resistance to his dominion.

She cordially thanked the new master of the obelisk, and made to leave through the giant crack, which she observed slowly sealing itself. However, the Archdevil motioned for her to follow it deeper into the facility. Warily, she walked beside as it explained in a raspy voice, "The facility has exits direct to D'zurien-To'th, Lady Dreadheart. Approach this panel and touch *here.*" It motioned to a flat disc, horizontally suspended amid a misty cloud that swirled with the same bleak amber light of the infernal sky outside. Still hesitant, Zaeliar'a eyed the devil cautiously. It cocked its head and cackled in understanding. "This one is unlike the unwise master before it. Neither deception nor assault will you find from it. A half-devil, like your *friend*, am I. Loyal is this one to the liberator." The creature's tone in referring to Zhiniel struck Soulthorne as reverent. She placed her hand upon the disc and its colour changed at once to a violet hue. She felt its attunement to several locations within the metropolis, one of which was in the immediate vicinity of the *Caez'Iss Do'thren-sa'a* – the Grounds of the Living Dead, her next destination. Zaeliar'a narrowed her focus upon this location in Dzurien-To'th, the device emitted a bell-like tone, and she seamlessly appeared before the familiar bony gates, glad to put the hell plane behind her.

Zaeliar'a welcomed the musty, crypt-like smell that hung in the air surrounding the gigantic compound, which served to house thousands upon thousands of corporeal undead. She appeared only a few metres from the gates comprised of pure Animus and the giant, carved ribcage of an Elder Drakhan, slain in service to the Darklord centuries ago. Reaching a height of seven metres, the necromantic gates stretched from the floor of the cavern to the ceiling, blocking entry to the barrows and crypts beyond its imposing structure. The sentience of the long-dead dragon stirred in its bones as Zaeliar'a approached, and the macabre barrier emitted a cold, malignant aura. When it recognized the Darklord's general, the gates swung open, and spoke in a voice ancient and terrible, "Enter, mistress Soulthorne."

The scent of decay and rot wafted through the already stifling air. Zaeliar'a strode through the entrance with purpose, and marched past twin regiments of chainmail armoured skeletal soldiers who stood at attention in tight formation to each side of the gate. The Drakhanic bones creaked and moaned moments after her entry, shut themselves tightly and knit back together, once more barring entry to the compound. None of the decaying troops stirred in the slightest as she marched past, their skeletal visages only peered out vacantly from behind steel visors. However, as Zaeliar'a reached the end of the impressive columns of animated dead, a cold presence approached in the form of a dark-clad knight covered in platemail nearly as heavy as hers. His skull-shaped barbute, along with the silver runed bastard sword, and tower shield, bearing the crest of the nine-headed flail, identified the knight clearly.

Sandros, Grand Marshall of the Blighted Knights stood before Zaeliar'a, saluted crisply, and turned to introduce his new squire, freshly made undead by the Soulharvester himself. Also clad in dark platemail, custom-crafted in similar design to the ancient death knight mentor's own, the Revenant spoke in a grating voice, introducing himself, "Drath'ivein, Mistress Dreadheart." The commander, his halberd sweeping to the ground in front of him as he knelt low, iterated, "it is an honour to be in your presence." After the disgraceful treatment at the hands of the former Archdevil earlier, the respect Zaeliar'a now received was familiar and welcome. She bid him rise and returned his liege's salute, then accompanied the two undead soldiers along the ebon brickwork avenue ahead.

The spacious, carved-out cavern served to separate the undead within from the rest of the city (some had voracious, uncontrollable appetites and would not discern between citizens and sustenance). Rows of stone-etched mausoleums, each with stairs leading down to the entombed dead below, provided a barracks of sorts for legions of mindless minions. These served as the ground troops of Zhiniel's army – corpses in various states purely animated by the force of Animus, able to follow simple instructions but lacking self-directing will. The only instinct of such creatures was to kill living beings if encountered, due to the negative energy aspect of the Animus force from the Plane of Death. Life, to the eyes of these undead constructs, registered visually like the smell of blood registers to a shark's ultrasensitive sense of scent. Horrific stories told of undead hordes slaying entire villages indiscriminately were not without basis in truth. However, unless damaged extensively, their bodies required extraordinarily little sustenance to maintain their states of animation. As the foot soldiers of an entire undead military, they proved extremely effective against living targets that lacked a way to combat them effectively. These numbered in the hundreds of thousands, collected over millennia by the Soulharvester who exhumed the graveyards of countless unaware surface-dwellers to add to his stocks. Zhiniel held a disdain for most of the warlike races above: for their propensity to kill each other endlessly, justified by reasons too tired to consider valid. However, the pointless bloodshed certainly provided him an unending supply of troops.

Evenly spaced amid the hundreds of these tombs were large, pyramid shaped necropolises that functioned as the quarters for even more dangerous varieties of corporeal undead. These were the more powerful, self-willed undead who retained most of the characteristics they held in life. Several were cunning, intelligent, and experienced, minds encoded through the Animus, encased in resilient dead bodies, directed purely by the force of will and sense of self they possessed in life. Though the populace of the kingdoms above sat locked in terror of the unthinking dead, it was these, and others even more terrible that should have kept them awake at night. Although their numbers were far fewer, creatures such as vampires, revenants, death knights, mummy lords and ghouls were vastly more capable than mindless zombies and skeletons. Some of the powerful members of this type of undead possessed the ability to issue verbal and even mental commands to the lesser ones. These stood as the lieutenants of the undead army, and as such, their capability in battle was far more devastating.

The death knight regarded Soulthorne carefully, seeming pensive. Somehow, he expressed his emotions through the enclosed helm, just the way he subtly angled his head at her made Zaeliar'a pause and ask, "What is it, Sandros?" The two knew each other, for a time intimately, in what seemed like their former lives, before the Darklord had liberated either of them. Both were lowly slaves of the same Syndicate family, Sandros a guard captain, albeit a low ranking one, and Zaeliar'a a handmaid to a highborn indigo elven Bloodwytch. The link between them: Sandros was one of the witch's many husbands, and Zaeliar'a the perpetrator of her eventual demise. The spark between them fleeting, neither still held the same affection, regarding each other now as peers, but the respect remained. Once more, the knight stiffened, and Soulthorne insisted, "Speak your thoughts, Grand Marshall." It was a command this time, one he dared not refuse.

"It is not mine to question the wisdom of our Darklord." Sandros started, the statement alarmed Zaeliar'a – for surely, the death knight meant to pose a question of significance. His cold presence became colder still, his demeanor pensive, as if carefully weighing his forthcoming words. Zaeliar'a prodded, "But?" Sandros stopped in his tracks, motioning ahead, down the winding path that led to the only anomaly in the entire compound filled with countless walking corpses. "I will put it plainly. Why station a laboratory, the head of whom as you know is a *living* gnome, in the very epicentre of death itself?" He swept a hand wide, to accentuate the point, and made a fist, his gauntlets produced a grating sound as plate and chain gnashed together. "Daily, I must listen to the complaints of this prisoner, and bring the creature special foods and supplies from remote locations; I am not a governess! My time is wasted on such things."

Zaeliar'a relaxed and heaved out a sigh. "Sandros, your objection is noted, and admittedly correct. All will be made clear shortly, for you have touched on the purpose of my visit. I will not say more, but you will accompany me into the research chamber and do as I command." She clapped his pauldron crisply, icy to her touch, though it did not bother her in the slightest, and without further pause, continued down the hall. The pair of dead men followed in tow. Now the knight and his squire were intensely curious. The Dreadheart's usual visit consisted of checking the equipment and debriefing the diminutive scientist, whose name no one could pronounce, 'gnome' usually sufficed, or sometimes 'Galf' which was a shortened version of his long-winded name. Either something was amiss, or the Soulharvester wanted to ensure the captured servant stayed in line. Abruptly, Zaeliar'a took a sharp turn down one of the many side passages in the hall, much before the entry to the heavily guarded lab.

"Lady, I am certain you are aware this is not the path we must take." The death knight and revenant both increased paces to catch up with their vampiric general as she strode confidently past several doors to the end of the hall: a bare wall with only an empty torch sconce adorning it. She turned a half circle to face the pair, but her stare went past them to the corridor's entry, checking for any observers. Seeing none, her hand grasped the sconce, which fought her for a moment before it twisted to the side. Only then did Sandros and Drath'ivein notice the floor near the wall possessed a semicircular groove, neatly concealed in its architecture, and the wall itself turned full circle with them upon it. The hidden room beyond was pitch black, though all three possessed eyes that could penetrate any darkness; they saw clearly that this was a secret observation chamber, filled with crystal mirrors for viewing several key locations in the compound.

Dim light flickered from the monitors, revealing scenes of prisoners held within an arrangement of cells and belonging to both surface and underworld races. From the middle of the chamber, they could view any of the displays, each categorized by district, contents, and cell numbers. Soulthorne drew her escorts' attention to one image: that of a huddled group of magmic gnomes. The group therein seemed in good spirits; their cell, though still a prison behind locked bars, contained bedding upon comfortable cots, a semi-private lavatory, tables, and chairs. "*These*," Soulthorne explained, "are the family and cohorts of your Candremig Arcostronophix Galflagwindel." She sauntered to the display and felt along its backside for something. There was a *click* as she removed the small screen from its housing and handed it directly to Drath'ivein, while providing Sandros a conspiratory nod. "Obedience is expected of all within the legion. It is time to remind our gnomish Maguscientist of his duty."

Zaeliar'a made to exit the chamber, heading to the same sconce used for entry, however, something caught her eye upon another screen; something interesting was playing out, and her curiosity got the better of her. She gazed intently at the image of a group of prisoners that she recognized. They were recent test subjects for some of the newer enhancements engineered by Zhiniel and a powerful undead spellcaster, a wizard who had locked his very soul into a phylactery. This diabolic form of willful undead was termed a lich; few arcanists existed who held the knowledge to enact the spells and preparations required, and fewer still succeeded in the transformation. This associate of the Soulharvester hailed from the Fae Realm, a Lord within the Winter Court by the name of Duke Axelay DeVentis, the only Fae ever to attain lichdom.

Although he appeared as a middle-aged, extremely attractive man with very angular features, stark white eyes and long, braided hair, Zaeliar'a knew it was a cleverly crafted illusion. The duke's natural appearance, though similar, betrayed his undead nature with its deathly pallor and withered skin; the Fae worked hard to keep his true form a secret. Even the practitioners of magic within the Winter Court forbade the process of lichdom; the negative plane energy clashed with the intensely positive force of their own extradimensional world. A lich's presence posed an actual danger to security in that the negative aura they projected could tear a hole in the fabric that separated the Fae Realm from the material planes. Zaeliar'a watched intently as the robed figure in the image funneled the group consisting of two humans, a wild elf, and a rarity in the form of a Minotaur through a portal she knew led into a labyrinth of ingenious design. According to Zhiniel, the prying moon elf and his strange Primordial companion would soon be stumbling around the very same maze into which Axelay released these prisoners. It would have interested her to watch their progress, to see if the roguish elf and Primordial would have to fight and kill them, or if they might best the strange pair. However, the matter here was urgent, and she had another two stops to make before departing the citadel, so she pried her eyes from the screen and led her undead companions back through the hall.

Before she entered the laboratory, Zaeliar'a halted a few paces shy of the door, and faced Sandros directly. "Remove the helm," she ordered stiffly. The death knight balked at the request, shaking his head negatively. "I have not removed it in nearly a decade, I…" he started, but Soulthorne cut his protest short, "Do as I command, and follow me inside." She stared at him while he raised his mailed fists to the clasps holding the front and back halves of the barbute together. With a twist and a metallic rasp, they separated, and the knight carefully drew the pieces apart and slid them off. Only a skull, eyes aflame with yellow-orange balefire and wispy grey hair that clung to the decaying scalp greeted her view. Both Drath'ivein and Zaeliar'a nodded in approval, though horrific, the knight's appearance was also majestic somehow. Soulthorne removed a plate gauntlet, extended her hand, and touched his cheekbone reassuringly, "This is you." With that, she refastened her plate glove, turned on a heel, and unlocked the heavy leaden door with a touch of her palm to the panel glowing at its side.

Zaeliar'a roughly shoved the door open to see the diminutive form of the gnomish Maguscientist madly organizing a complex set of apparatus across the room, his back turned to her. His shrill, annoyed voice called out over his shoulder, "Interruptions are *not* welcome. Whatever it is, go away and bother me later – or better yet *never.*" Clinking and sizzling sounds issued from the station he hurriedly worked at, adjusting dials on one complex machine, tapping another with rods of varying material, and plugging in cables to yet another. Not once did Galflagwindel glance at the interlopers who were disturbing his experiments, they were inconsequential to his work, and thus merited none of his attention. Only when her thudding boots approached, and she laid a heavy metal gauntlet on his shoulder did the magmic gnome turn to face Soulthorne. When he finally saw who it was that dared interrupt his proceedings, his face turned ash-white and his rude earlier demeanor vanished, replaced with utter *dread*.

"The... you... I had no inclination of a visit... Mistress Dreadheart." The gnome backpedaled suddenly from her touch, fear apparent upon his wrinkled and soot-smeared face. He crashed back into a bench, so hasty was his retreat from the indigo elven woman who murdered several of his colleagues in their *Arcanasium Scientia* and seized his family, his friends and his life's work. She was the one who delivered the Darklord's horrible ultimatum upon his hidden enclave built surrounding the magma chamber of an active volcano several months now past. Unwisely he paid no heed to the warning, and Candremig utterly rued the day she returned with more of the blasted *Imithrignarar Postimisgravosi* (*deep blue interloping Aelyph'en matriarchal dominators of the deeper underworld*, in the technical gnomish nomenclature) and changed his isolated life forever. Mercilessly she and her indigo elven troops maimed and slayed the experienced but non-combative spellcasters he employed, their defenses against her assault pitiful and ineffective. His daily nightmares of the assault and capture would likely plague the poor gnome until the end of his life, which now he feared might halt abruptly under her sword. Zaeliar'a's glowing red eyes, which now bore straight into his soul haunted his thoughts constantly, the only reprieve was in the absorption of his work.

Fangs peeking out from behind her scowl made the gnome cringe as he struggled to right himself from the earlier tumble.

Candremig fumbled with something in his hand, nearly dropping the item to the floor before jamming the slim device into one of his deep apron pockets. His hands and brow dripped with sweat, he had discarded the usual thick gloves he wore, and the goggles perched atop his forehead constantly threatened to slide off amid the chaos of his fervent experimentation. Soulthorne glanced back at the silent pair of undead men behind her, and then fixed those terrible eyes back upon the gnome. Candremig visibly winced when he noticed her attention focus on his apron as she inquired, "What is that device? I do not recognize it." Her crimson eyes were narrowed in suspicion and the wheedling gnome hastily stammered, "It's a prototype casing for the tablet your... *our* master requested." He instantly produced the device, careful not to reveal its counterpart tucked into the same pocket, holding it up with shaking hands for the vampire woman to inspect.

"You s... s... see? It is a mere housing now but," the gnome finally gained a sliver of composure as he prepared to boast about his latest development, "the latest design shows promise in that its resistance to the requisite electrical energy required to..." Soulthorne cut him short with a single word, "*Uninterested.*" She plunked the inert shell back into the gnome's hands and he shoved it into his apron, careful not to disturb the other, more advanced – and activated – tablet he had recently cloned from the original. Candremig Arcostronophix Galflagwindel, for all his eccentricity and bluster, was a scientific genius. Upon initial study of the delicate and extremely advanced computational device the Soulharvester charged him with unlocking the secrets of, he estimated it would take several months to decipher the primeval language coding it contained. Zhiniel fixed death-filled eyes upon the gnome and gave him exactly two months to complete a working prototype. He had finished it in a week, and copied the encrypted information contained on the ancient tablet in the hopes he might find a way to secret it out of the fortress, praying each night to Wekinishabanzat, the gnomish patron Goddess of Discovery that such an opportunity might arise.

From what he could glean from its internal database, the information contained within the innocuous, rectangular piece of silicon and blended aluminum frame, he knew with terror that once Zhiniel could utilize its secrets, the Darklord's lofty goal of world domination would be in his grasp. His tests revealed it was a relic of the Third Cycle, and certainly not of Antiquan origin. Though produced by human hands, they were not Neph'al or any known human race prior or since. Nevertheless, the signature he detected certainly indicated humans of some alien origin built the device and provided it to ancient civilizations as a means for scientific advancement. The very structure of matter and manipulation of raw energy were only two of the subjects explained in detail, the prospect of which excited and terrified the scientist equally. However, Candremig possessed enough wisdom to know that any purely scientific advancement could be – and certainly *would* be – weaponized by those who desired power. He accepted the fact that Zhiniel would uncover its secrets eventually, whether the gnome refused or acquiesced mattered little. The Darklord would simply slay and replace the gnome or devote enough of his personal time to tear its unimaginably powerful technology out and unleash it upon Antiqua. At least he could delay the inevitable, and possibly provide resistance to the Darklord's domination if only he could relay his findings to an ally upon the surface.

It was of inestimable luck that the Darklord had no such luxury to study the object himself, and that the item somehow defied the logic of his Infernal cohorts. Whoever encoded the information took great pains to render it impossible for the devils to manipulate the device, even remotely. The first ones to attempt analysis of the artifact immediately fell into fits, stricken with a debilitating affliction that paralyzed their otherwise ingenious minds with something akin to an unsolvable riddle that drove them mad. Those affected repeated paradoxical phrases and incanted unintelligible formulae continually thereafter and summarily ended up quarantined. Candremig felt not an iota of pity for these creatures, his race having a long and bitter history with devilkind, whose initial forays into Antiqua had encroached upon the magmic gnomes' habitations, their summoning portals appearing within the lava vents of the volcanoes they surrounded.

Still lost in thought, the hapless gnome barely registered the menacing glare from Zaeliar'a as she repeated herself, hand straying to the claymore upon her back, "I *demand* to know your progress on a working translation as *promised* to the Darklord!" The threat finally snapped him back to the grim reality of three powerful undead creatures who would love nothing more than to tear him and everything else he loved apart. Startled, he replied, "Give me four more days, five at most, and I will deliver him a working copy." Zaeliar'a's hand remained perched on the pommel of her giant sword, the gleaming weapon Candremig remembered carving through one of his most promising research students, and she motioned for Drath'ivein to step forth. Guessing her intent, the revenant strode up and presented the crystal screen from the observation room, which flickered to life with the image of the holding cell that contained the only remaining members of the gnome's research team, and his family. He shook with momentary anger at the implication, but reiterated, "Five days at most. I cannot rush this labour due to the delicate..." Once more Soulthorne cut off his impending long-winded speech, "I shall return in *four* days, and unless the Soulharvester is satisfied with your findings..." her voice trailed off and the gnome gulped heavily at the dire implication. Zaeliar'a's eyes went evocatively from the gnome to Sandros, the death knight's bony visage clear for the gnome to see, eye sockets burning with the amber flames of hellfire. Her final words, after the three left, forced the gnome to vomit several times before he controlled his abject terror and revulsion, redoubling his efforts to build a new model of the ancient tablet that might hamper Zhiniel without arousing suspicion of tampering. Echoing repeatedly in his mind were her last icy words to him, "Sandros will consume your cohorts and family, agonizingly, while Drath'ivein holds your *paeth-sar'iss* eyes open to stare as each of them die screaming. Then..." she stared deep into the horrified gnome's face as she mouthed the last words he never again wanted to hear, "they will all assist as you work more *efficiently*, in their fresh undead bodies – tirelessly, until your work is finally complete."

After Sandros and Drath'ivein departed to resume training and preparing some newly acquired skeletal soldiers, Zaeliar'a tread slowly through the rows of crypts, making her way to the lift that would carry her to her next objective. A massive excavation spanning an entire section of cavern, freshly carved, bustled with undead workers commanded by barrow-wights. These unliving supervisors directed the mindless and tireless monstrosities with picks and shovels as they cleared room to house more of their kind. The hunched, long-armed silhouettes of ghasts shambled about in the distance, carrying large loads of stone in wheelbarrows to conveyor belts leading to other areas of the city. The efficiency of a tireless undead horde that needed no pay, nor much in the way of sustenance lent much to the speed in which the Darklord's stronghold expanded. The metropolis of D'zurien-To'th, if one included the outlying districts and remote territories under Zhiniel's sway, dwarfed the largest of Neph'al cities in living population alone, rivaled entire kingdoms if one included the undead.

Zaeliar'a moved amidst the walking corpses taking care to avoid the poisonous aura surrounding the ghasts, though it could do her little harm, the stench remained clinging to any it touched.

Past giant support pillars of granite impregnated with metal rods and enchanted for durability, weaving her way in and about tents erected for planning and engineering committees, Soulthorne at last reached the far side of the chamber, and the lift that would carry her away from this area to the next. The chamber was so high she could scarcely see the ceiling, and twenty balconies each attached to districts that domiciled residents or contained training halls, laboratories, and arcane schools. Though his methods were unwavering and brutal, Zhiniel Al-Nistir Szord'Ryn, now the undisputed sovereign of the indigo elves and their increasing list of allies, had brought prosperity and advancement to all serving under his rule. Soulthorne mused that if the surface-worlders understood that the benefits of submission to his grand designs far outweighed the price he requested, they might hold a tighter grip on their own fates. *Gods, Entities and Celestials each claim the souls of their followers; most giving little in return except the promise of power or salvation, but why not seize it here and now, instead of in some undetermined afterlife?*

The lift ascended ponderously, though smoothly as Zaeliar'a paced its length, waiting for her stop at the ninth level floor. She gazed out over the expansive cavern of the undead and a sense of surety washed through her in the knowledge that victory was soon at hand. No force above could hope to stand before the Soulharvester's might, and most would bend knees and sign treaties after the initial tide of their army proved the scope of his ambition. Only one troubling thought invaded her subconscious; she could not push away the sense that her master, to whom she willingly pledged everything, might care for her. The idea swirled in her mind, pleasant in many ways, yet she desired not to be a liability in his unwavering resolve. His orders threw her into danger with every mission, every responsibility she undertook carried risk, and since his assault upon the Archdevil, she wondered if he might be putting too much weight on her value. Her cheeks flushed suddenly, and Soulthorne pushed the idea away, her destination now at hand as the lift slowed and came to rest on the ninth balcony.

The gigantic terrace curved along the inner wall of the cavern below, at regular intervals, guard stations occupied by crossbowmen, archers and spellcasters, overlooked the expanse underneath. Met with swift salutes as she passed each of them, Soulthorne approached the middle of the terrace and stopped, looking to her left where the wall was dotted with alcoves. Most held statues, depictions of warriors, Gods, devils and the like, except for one, larger than the rest, which lay bare. She strode directly into the large opening and casually walked through the apparent wall, an illusion that led her into a simple, unfurnished square room carved entirely of jade and inlaid with a golden set of eight trigrams upon the floor. At the centre of the engraving, invisible to mortal eyes but glowing in her vampiric vision, lay the symbol of Shadowed Souls.

Zaeliar'a lingered silently in the room for several minutes, leaning against the cool jade wall nearest the entry. It was calm and serene, devoid of sound, and the power contained in the stone infused her with uncharacteristic tranquility. Her mind stilled, she prepared to tread the complicated pattern required to pass through the trigrams into the splinter dimension linked to the Plane of Death. Here dwelled the ancient incorporeal undead spirits, elder, wise, and enigmatic. These powerful advisors she sought for the knowledge they held in extraplanar matters; before her journey into the Fae Realm, Zhiniel deemed their sage counsel a necessity. The eight sets of three sigils would instantly disjoin and disperse every aspect of any being, living or dead, if any error occurred in the precise activation of its pattern. Committed to memory, Zaeliar'a moved through the twenty-four steps gracefully, performing an intricate, combative dance, her steps lightly carrying her from one trigram to the next. Upon completion, she set foot on the central power rune and the chamber melted away in front of her eyes, as everything she perceived became one with shadows.

Materially, nothing changed, merely her essence was opened to the reality that lay locked in the chamber itself; the specially infused jade operated like a prism refracting light, and Soulthorne, mind, body, will and self, perceived the pocket dimension of the Plane of Death as it expanded all around her. Negative energy coursed through everything, suffused her undead spirit with vitality conversely to the way it could snuff out living essences like a candle. Everywhere in the nebulous dimension, the shadows of undead beings – spectres, wraiths, ghosts, and other immaterial things – appeared as glowing wisps, many vaguely human, and others wholly otherworldly in form. The background was an opaque curtain of blended ghostly light and strange shadows, forming structures like inverted obelisks and pyramids. Others were hexagonal, several prisms hung at odd angles in what could only be loosely termed as the sky. Motes of negative energy spiraled about each structure, passing between each, transferring knowledge and information between the powerful denizens of the plane. Her attention focused on a diamond prism that hovered almost directly above her, and Zaeliar'a had to concentrate against the disorientation she felt inside this plane to which she did not entirely belong.

A calling of ethereal voices beckoned from within the diamond structure above. It seemed near now, though neither she nor the prism had moved closer together. The laws of the Plane of Death relied upon magnitude; spiritually speaking, both her own mass and that of her destination increased significantly, hence she drew nearer. Increasingly she felt her own weight and that of the abode of the Shadow Lords increase until it was there within her reach, and she laid a hand upon its surface to be absorbed within its facets. From the epicentre of the structure, the eight Lords of Shadow each appeared to occupy one of the diamond's facets, all of them fixing their intense inky eyes upon her. In unison they spoke.

"To the everbright realm of *Fassimirlterethuramoria* shall sojourn the Dreadheart – mistress of the darkest of fiends. Night sky made light, weeping tears of earth and bone, shall they know despair in her wake." Always the eight Lords spoke in poetic metaphors; their wisdom predated physical existence, so ancient they were. Her understanding of their speech was testament to the unrelenting perseverance of Zhiniel in unlocking the deeper mysteries of the Omniverse. The twenty-four trigrams crafted by the Darklord himself translated their speech into a pattern that a mind could comprehend without hurtling beyond the brink of madness. Over the course of one thousand nine hundred years, Zhiniel poured through forbidden scriptures, consulted with multitudes of profane spirits, and consorted with aberrations ripped from other dimensions to assemble the inversion chamber that would allow him access to the Realm of the God of the Dead. There he found the Eight bound in their diamond prison and offered them the ultimate prize that eluded their eons-old grasp and the perpetrator of their incarceration: the unliving soul of Death itself.

Unbelievably, they bowed in deference to the Soulharvester: it was a solitary event of surprise for Zhiniel. Expecting his claim, so arrogant and assumptive, to be flatly rejected, even ridiculed by these spirits whose power far exceeded his own (at the time), the young necromancer was momentarily taken aback by their manifested cry of assent. The entities perceived the chain of time's rote and linear progression in a very alien way, far divergent from conventional thought. His progenitor had laid the foundation for his claim, both in the future and the past, which culminated in that present moment, and fulfilled a contract, singularly desired by the Shadow Lords above all other things.

Zaeliar'a entreated the Eight to continue, however, they silenced themselves, forcing her to be content with the riddle already posed. She knew nothing further would they impart, and their will demanded she meditate on the two sentences they deigned to bestow. Soulthorne found herself regaining her sight, laying upon the smooth flooring of jade, seemingly ejected from the Death Plane. Confusion wracked her vampiric mind as an aftereffect of visiting the very source of her undead power; slowly she realized she must have been unconscious for several hours before waking there upon the cool surface of the chamber. Many things though were clear in her mind, as if in her unremembered dreams she learned lessons absorbed from the spirits' enigmatic speech. Rising, Zaeliar'a departed the chamber and followed her own footsteps, for a time watching herself from a detached perspective before her being came back into balance and she again saw through her own eyes. She must visit the Vampire Queen.

On she traveled through winding tunnels, endless sets of doors and archways, past guardians both dead and alive, in a trance-like daze. The clack of her boots on smooth tile roused her from the dreamy state, and startled, Zaeliar'a turned her eyes upward to the raised drawbridge of the Blood Palace. The keep was without denial, the most lavishly appointed building in the entire metropolis. Surrounded by a functional, but redundant moat supplied water by twin falls cascading from natural fissures carved in the likeness of gaping maws, the keep stood solitary at the centre of a vast, worked stone cavern. In the depths of the moat swam deadly breeds of aquatic life: sightless eels, barracudas, and water serpents fed daily by the Queen's servants, literally so by those who displeased her in the slightest. Extravagant statues filled the tile pathways of the courtyard, lit by equally decadent hammered bronze and copper pillars, each adorned with four hanging lanterns of magical flame. Marble benches appeared to invite groups of visiting ladies and lords to conversation amid frameworks of hanging vines and vibrant plant life. The surroundings evoked a sense of liveliness and activity, and the palace itself was a magnificent example of Fifth Cycle Neph'al architecture, resplendent with curving spires, hooked parapets and hammered bronze and copper roofing, shaped and lit in similar fashion to the outside pillars.

Zaeliar'a knew it was nothing but a self-indulgent façade. *Where are the courtiers and the entertainment, my Queen?* She scoffed at the thought. The relationship with her progenitor little resembled that of a mother and daughter. The Blood Queen was cruel and hedonistic, infamously so in her homeland on the far western continent of Ral-Qariin, which Soulthorne considered a sand-filled wasteland, insufferably hot and dry, filled with puffed-up, garishly dressed nobles who squandered their wealth and held their people under their thumbs. Though the Darklord chose the vampiress not for her ways, rather her ancient, powerful blood, Zaeliar'a wished now that another – *any other* – had bestowed her the gift of immortality. Conversing with the incredibly narcissistic woman made her skin crawl. She dined upon only the finest specimens of life simply to keep her complexion smooth and tight; she wore the most garish and revealing outfits and bragged about the hideous expense just to ensure everyone was aware of her wealth. Her fortunes sat in massive vaults, serving no greater purpose than to fan an ego larger than the blazing blue sun. To Zaeliar'a, who felt this hoarding of resources truly despicable, it was another reason to hate the Queen.

Staring at the twin gargoyles perched high above, glaring with disdainful looks upon the courtyard, Soulthorne called out, "Shall I climb the ramparts, then? Or will you condescend to lower the drawbridge for *Her Majesty's* progeny?" She practically spat the title out like bile in her throat. One of the gargoyles blinked, laboriously, as if the disturbance woke it from a cheerful dream.

The figure's natural skin had the appearance of rough sandstone, sculpted in traditional fashion with great Drakhanic wings, a hooked owl's beak, slim musculature, and clawed nails. "Nalathor," came its dry, butler-sounding voice as it then let out a wide yawn of boredom before continuing. "My *name* is *Nalathor*, and the lady shall refer to me by it, and then she will say *please*." Just the way it spoke its own name urged Soulthorne to alight upon the ramparts and cram her sword all the way down the horrible thing's throat. Her reply was unaccommodating.

"Her Excellency will attend me in her court *immediately*, gargoyle. I have not the time to waste in parley with her servants, and if I must tarry in the mission entrusted to me by our Darklord, siege engines will accompany my return. Nothing would *please* me more than an excuse to lay waste to these walls, towers, and *you* I might add, dear *Nalathor*." Her eyes were blazing, but she added with a dry smirk, "Notice that I used your *name* and said *please*?" The gargoyle looked to its companion, and the pair of stony sentries gripped the mechanisms at their feet, swiftly lowering the drawbridge and raising the portcullis behind it. Once the lip of the polished amaranth hardwood bridge descended within a few feet of the tile courtyard, Zaeliar'a leapt across, stormed through the opening, and into the grand foyer. Both gargoyles sneered, returning to their apathetic, languid ruminations.

The opulent palace exterior, only exceeded by its exorbitant interior, sprawled out before Zaeliar'a, who regarded it all with disgust. Though, it was her dislike for its host that coloured her perspective. Lavish, thick carpets threaded with silver and gold littered the halls, upon which sat polished furniture, commissioned from famous surface world craftsmen. Not a speck of dust lay atop any of the marble and quartz busts of history's most influential rulers; the Queen boasted to her few guests that her collection dwarfed that of any other monarch. She aptly recounted their distinguished histories, threatening to shorten the lifespan of those forced to listen. Caligastia's three maids, appearing in their early womanhood, were triplets, wore matching uniforms, and were forced to fashion their hairstyles to such exacting detail that they remained indistinguishable from one another. She even demanded they attend vocal coaching regularly, to ensure each carried the same pitch and tone, especially when conversing or singing to any company the Queen had in attendance. The sisters possessed truly lovely voices and were among the properties most jealously prized by Caligastia. The cruel vampiress took intense pleasure in recounting how she had turned the three performers into pristine examples of vampiric perfection, and then unleashed them after the transformation – unable to control their new thirst for blood – upon their remaining siblings and parents. Even among the merciless denizens of the underworld, her tales of piti-less and sadistic acts were regarded with revulsion.

Staring at Zaeliar'a, resembling three ornately dressed dolls, the triplets – Luarene, Taelyssa, and Chereille descended the wide curved stairway leading down from their chambers. Their outfits, tailored to accentuate the lithe, perfect figures of the three, resembled what Soulthorne imagined as the ensemble of a harlot attempting to cater to the fetishes of a wealthy pervert. Their pert breasts pushed together and thrust upward, nestled between pink ruffles, and puffed sleeves in the fashion of a traditional maid. Each wore an identical pleated skirt, cut much too high, such that when any of them leaned even slightly, the view from their posterior revealed silk panties nestled in between soft folds of pink flesh. Another debauchery the Blood Queen partook of frequently that Zaeliar'a despised; the Queen delighted in dressing her chambermaids in this seductive fashion for the pleasure of her more depraved guests. She watched in voyeuristic ecstasy while any or all the three catered to the sexual fantasies of the guests, in any of the many chambers devoted to this form of entertainment. On the occasions the Blood Queen joined in the revelry, screams and moans echoed into the courtyard outside, so wicked were her ministrations. Though in appearance they were young and fresh, the triplets were now approaching three hundred years of age, and, accustomed to this way of life, seemed quite content with their lot. Often the most succulent of thirsts were quenched during and following their times of rapture.

Soulthorne regarded the three with contempt as they surrounded her, gleaming eyes taking in every contour of her face and body underneath the shell of steel she wore. Taelyssa, the brazen one of the three, laid a hand upon her chestpiece, cupping the metal over her breasts in an admiring fashion. She withdrew the hand swiftly as Zaeliar'a moved to bat her away, giggling, "You have the perfect breasts of an elf-maid, Lady Dreadheart. Do allow me the pleasure of seeing them some occasion?" This one enjoyed courting danger, and she knew Soulthorne would gladly decapitate her, but trusted in the influence of her blood-mother to keep her safe. Zaeliar'a replied icily, "One day, I may grant your wish. However, it will be your *last* day." The other two attempted to take her by the elbows, but the malicious look caused Luarene and Chereille to reconsider, and the three simply led her back up the stairs. Across the balcony and into an antechamber they glided together, flitting around Zaeliar'a, annoyingly touching her hair and arms, but then they spread out and became still. Caligastia Voxparl, the Blood Queen lay sprawled evocatively upon a lounging-chair, looking up with ancient, intense eyes that bored straight into Soulthorne, and she spoke, "Greetings, blood-daughter."

The Queen was barely dressed in only a blue camisole, which hung off her slender frame as a bare arm reached below and cupped the pale cheek of a young, freshly drained surface elven man, whose sightless eyes stared blankly skyward. Pinpricks, where her teeth penetrated the victim, dotted the corpse, spots of slowly drying blood upon each. "We took our time, Flindreas and I… but a mere appetizer was this boy." Caligastia rose and drifted forth, down the few steps of her raised dais to light upon the lavish carpet and stood in front of Zaeliar'a, wearing a feigned expression of pensive thought. "I do not suppose, my *dear* progeny, that you have graced my palace for the purpose of a fresh infusion?" Soulthorne understood where the question would lead the conversation, but decided to play the Queen's game, answering her, "In fact, blood-mother, I am, but – to your pleasure – I will take it in the *traditional* way." Zaeliar'a caught a moment of suspicion cross Caligastia's mind as her eyes narrowed imperceptibly, but then the Blood Queen smiled warmly, deceivingly with an abundance of excitement. She took Zaeliar'a's hands in her own with an affection that felt sincere, and she positively gushed, "Really? You mean to *partake* of me, to put those plush lips to my wrist and satisfy your thirst… or perhaps my neck, my breasts…" Enraptured with the thought, Caligastia drew aside the laced camisole to reveal her naked thigh and garmentless crotch, engorged from her recent feeding and the sensual thoughts passing through her. She ran a hand up her smooth inner thigh and immoderately touched herself, whispering, "You may feed from here as well, I'm swelling just imagining your lips playing upon…" So disarmed in her lascivious imagination, the Queen could not foresee what Zaeliar'a had planned from the start, and the newfound power of the Archdevil welled up as she made her play.

The sheer magnitude of gravity at the command of Soulthorne rocketed Caligastia to the marble floor, pinning her, helpless and unable to move. On her throat, faster than even the ancient Queen's eyes could perceive, Zaeliar'a descended and sunk fangs in, deep and vicious. So startled at the unexpected draining of her lifeblood, the vampire Queen only moaned in euphoria and mildly struggled against the iron grip of her blood-daughter. The three vampire handmaids just gawked at the sight, frozen, unsure if they should interfere or remain cautiously distant. Taelyssa approached first but was met with the same crushing weight that cast her matron to the ground and crumpled to the floor in similar fashion. Her two sisters' cries earned them both the same fate, but served to rouse the Queen from her entrancement, and she weakly attempted to interpose an arm between Soulthorne and herself. Zaeliar'a pulled back only for a second, wickedly laughing as she closed a deathlike grip on Caligastia's wrist, forcing her arm back roughly behind her head, further exposing her neck, which now gushed blood upon the already soaked carpet.

Greedily, Soulthorne drank from the gaping wound left by her teeth, sucked up her progenitor's potent vital energy, distilled in her blood by the Animus that bound all vampires to their source of immortality. Knowing this was a display of dominance, the Queen relinquished to the attack, with her free hand she pulled down her camisole, tearing it and exposing her heaving breasts. "Please," she whimpered faintly, pleading as her arm fell to her side, already too weak to move further. When Zaeliar'a grasped both her breasts and bit into each of them in turn, Caligastia found just enough strength to arch her back, and let out several shallow gasps of pain and delight. Barely audible now, her voice cracking, she begged, "More," and with the last vestiges of strength in her, reached to the frills of the camisole and pulled it up, over her belly. Still sucking on, and playing with the Queen's breasts, Zaeliar'a slipped off her gauntlets and reached down to spread Caligastia's legs wide. She caressed the vampiress softly, tenderly, running hands up her thighs, massaging her and bringing the Blood Queen to a writhing climax with her fingers. The area, so engorged, drew the remaining vitae to the pulsing flesh of her groin, and finally, Zaeliar'a withdrew and released the triplets from the force holding them.

"Come – feast," she bid the three, and her deadly, beautiful crimson eyes became impossible to resist as Zaeliar'a issued a dominating call, so infused she was with their dying dame's essence. Uncharacteristically, Chereille heeded the calling first of her siblings and, in a release of the pent-up rage of her family's forced murder at her own hands, buried her fangs into the artery of Caligastia's inner thigh. The other two followed only moments after, tearing into their sundered blood-mother with unrepressed thirst, draining her blood with slurping lips until finally, all three were sated and the Queen lay near Death. Caligastia knew with certainty that this was her final moment, that this planned treachery by her most prestigious blood-daughter would bring her to final torpor, from which she would never awake. Ever the egocentric, vain, and narcissistic Queen, Caligastia's last words escaped between ragged, passionate breaths, "My daughter, Zaeliar'a... I was promised... a Necropolis upon the Ebon Moon."

Cupping a hand behind her neck, Zaeliar'a stared deep into the fading light in the Blood Queen's eyes, and assured her, "And you shall have it, dear Caligastia, as promised." A solitary, bloody tear crawled down the vampiress' cheek as she finished her statement, "It will serve as a monument to your reign, a glorious tomb to be remembered by eternally." Caligastia's eyes closed, and she was no more.

Standing and wiping the blood from her face with the back of her hand, Zaeliar'a gathered up and donned her gauntlets, and regarded the speechless sisters with a reassuring look. Until a vampire fledgling's maker dies, they know no freedom from the utter domination exerted by their progenitor's Animus upon them. Zaeliar'a was exempt from Caligastia's influence; Zhiniel employed elements of his own life force in her vampiric transformation and had trivialized the hold that the Blood Queen should have possessed over her. The triplets, however, now completely free to think and act as their own will directed wandered around the vestibule as if lost. Soulthorne understood their confusion would soon fade, so she commanded the three, "Take up the blood-mother, and bring her shell to the crypt below, inter her within the royal sarcophagus and await the coming of the Darklord. There you shall witness the rites of her passing and inherit everything she once owned." They stared at her for minutes as if the idea was incomprehensible, until finally, the vacant looks left their eyes, and understanding crept in. As she made her way out, they followed, and the Dreadheart paused to regard them with a measure of affection, declaring, "The Blood Palace is now yours. Serve our master wisely, and never forget the gift of freedom his order bestowed." With those final words, she turned and walked away, leaving the triplets to their task.

It was neither regret nor mourning she felt, but Zaeliar'a held a peculiar feeling after taking Caligastia's life. It was, in a word, wholesome, as if the act released some tormenting cloud hanging over her, and even the courtyard possessed an aura less foreboding than usual. The gargoyles stirred not in the slightest as she departed and the drawbridge remained down, the portcullis wide open and inviting. Soulthorne sauntered amid the pillars and statues of the gardens, taking in the beauty of the atmosphere somehow unlocked by the former Queen's demise before making her way to the mouth of the expansive cavern. The conclusion of her journey neared.

Several interconnected chambers and tunnels passed by her on the final stretch of this long sojourn, the culmination of what felt like a complex series of trials. She felt tested and tried, but these ordeals were over, and left Zaeliar'a with a sense of victory and exultation towards what was to come. Zhiniel, in his personal study, marveled at the woman she had become – through his meticulous machinations and no small feats of her own will, his general, his *Dreadheart* instilled in the darkest recess of his heart a sense of gratification. An impossible light in the eternal night of his soul, Zhiniel mused that perhaps this weakness he felt when he stared at Zaeliar'a through the obsidian mirror may become a strength he once failed to grasp in significance. As she strode to the portal that would take her into the Fae Realm, the Soulharvester felt a pang of longing, and smiled at the sweet pain it caused, somehow understanding a concept before foreign to his vast knowledge. When she passed from his scrying view into the dimension of Eternal Spring, Zhiniel at last dismissed the image and mouthed the words, "Tread forth into your destiny, my..." leaving the final words unsaid, simply from not knowing what they should be.

Soulthorne the Dreadheart, Zaeliar'a Szord'Ryn

Chapter 16

MURDEROUS VINES AND
MOON ELF BONDING

"I must remember to complain about the poor atmosphere," Qualthalas mumbled, though in truth, the area ahead seemed pleasant compared to the sulfurous cavern and ugly reception behind them. The spacious triangular chamber they were now surveying seemed purposed for troop staging; of this, the elf was certain. Benches, half-provisioned weapon racks bearing all manner of killing implements of indigo elven design, tables, chairs and… *hmm, casks*, Qual mused, filled one half of the room. The other room was curiously bare, and Qualthalas kept his distance, noting that its peculiar arrangement of tiles bore a striking resemblance to the hideous trapped room containing the obsidian portal he'd found which had led him into this whole mess. *Found*, he thought to himself bitterly, *the Darklord presented it to me and funneled me this whole way. He may as well have led me by hand.*

The Primordial, Neihwe'un, advanced cautiously into the chamber and spread feelers about the room, roving over and around the manufactured objects, sliding under chairs, running along the cracks in the flooring. Its appendages crawled up walls, inspected the magically lit sconces that dotted the chamber, but finding nothing unusual, the vines retracted, and it let out a dejected, "Hoo-ooh." When it moved, wraithlike to the opposite part of the room, Qualthalas called out in warning, "Hold, my viny friend. Let us leave that side for now, I fear it unsafe." Neihwe'un took a moment of pause, then attempted to scoff at the elf's level of prudence, but the noise it produced came out a windy hiss, enough to rattle the nerves of a stout soul. Qual just chuckled though, as he fingered the top of one of the wooden casks from which the unmistakable fragrance of alcohol drifted. Conveniently, a viny tendril wrapped around an obsidian dagger tapped his arm and presented the weapon, handle-side out, to him.

"Ingenious." Qualthalas grabbed the knife and pried off the lid of the barrel, and sure enough, the cask contained some dark and pungent liquid that reminded the elf of whisky. He snapped up a plain ceramic cup from one of the nearby tables and dipped in. Then, he considered something, and looked to Neihwe'un, who wore what the elf surmised was an expression of curiosity. A low chitter escaped the creature. Qual chuckled, "Well, I suppose you're old enough. It is drink, to warm the spirits – Gods know we could use some of that before our inevitable and horrible deaths at the hands of the Darklord." He tipped the cup back and took a healthy draw of the alcohol and his eyes widened at the glorious taste. The amber draft veritably slid down his throat and delighted his tongue with a mild sweetness and bubbly sensation that tickled his mouth. "Perhaps we should let the indigo elves take over the world. Their liquor is divine." Qualthalas filled another cup as his entire body warmed and tingled; he felt energized from the brew and wondered at the drink's distillation process and from what marvelous plant it came. Then, he noticed several shoots buried in the cask. Laughing despite entrapment by a devious enemy, about to walk into even deeper peril, Qualthalas was glad suddenly for the company of his strange friend.

"Moderation, my comrade," he intoned, even as another full cup made its way to his lips. A pang of hunger rippled through the elf's stomach, reminding him that he had not eaten in a full day. He pulled the vines out of the barrel, much to the annoyance of the Primordial, who, in the meantime, had sprouted several muddy reddish mushrooms upon its form. Qualthalas busied himself, smelling and fingering several crates stacked neatly upon each other. These were much easier to open, though he found the contents wrapped in a thin, translucent material he was unfamiliar with, possibly a new development for preservation. Pulling at the material, finding it extremely stretchable and pliant, Qual reached into the tool pouch sewn into the back of his doublet, full of spares, but functional. He found a little combination flat file and knife, and then tore into the wrapping. Inside were loaves of baked waybread of some sort, layered with meat strips, thick breading, and chunks of a fleshy plant – perhaps mushrooms. This seemed like a soldier's rations, but feeling adventurous after trying their liquor, and terribly famished, Qualthalas tore off a hunk and bit in. He voraciously devoured the entire loaf, snapped up four more and stuffed them in one of his remaining sacks attached at his hip.

The elf turned to offer some to the Neihwe'un but considered the Primordial's recent feedings and its completely different physiology; he decided to finish it instead. He noticed then that his companion's form seemed smaller in stature, slightly more humanoid. Though it still wore its mantle of vines like a cape, it somehow condensed its body mass so that it stood just over Qualthalas' height. Its appendages flowed out from under the mantle, complete with shoulders, elbows, and the strange three-fingered bone-and-branch hands. The creature swaggered dangerously close to the tile floor opposite, so Qualthalas decided, fed and full of drink, he would join it and see if the pair could deduce an exit.

"You appear sated now, Aelyph'en." It spoke clearly in its windy voice, its lower feeler-vines crawled to the edge of the floor where the tiles began. "I still sense the great disturbance far below, in a vast cavern beyond something which I do not know a word for." Qualthalas marveled at its sudden command of verbiage. The scintillating topaz eyes now held a shrewd glint, as if infused with increased capacity for logic and reasoning. "The tunnels below are cut out of stone, they move, and shift with a strange energy that suffuses the place. It is..." puzzled, the Neihwe'un paused, its feelers buried in cracks in the stonework shuddering, "...meant to confuse and mislead. Other beings move through the adjoining hallways and rooms; there is blood and conflict." Recognition flared in the gemstone eyes as the Primordial found the unfamiliar word it searched for, "Labyrinth."

Qualthalas grimaced at the implication. He guessed the Darklord's intent in leading him to such a place. It would be a series of tests, then, and an unwelcome delay to rescuing Kaira. Though he had not forgotten her plight, the elf pushed it necessarily to the back of his mind, so the distraction of his worry could not impede his progress. His composure failed briefly, and his fist clenched in anger. Cazares would die by his hand if he harmed Kaira, of this Qualthalas was determined, yet he was far more afraid of her fate if the Darklord himself had some scheme involving the girl. She would become a bargaining chip, a pawn in his schemes: the Darklord certainly knew Kaira's value to him, the Aeth'Akir Crown Prince. Thinking in his nemesis' terms, larger than before, as a megalomaniac might, a cold realization dawned on Qualthalas: *he does not want me at all; he wants the silver moon itself.* "Of course, I have been such an idiot, the prize is as plain as day," he said aloud, as he paced the room with gritted teeth. Qualthalas drew in several deep breaths to calm the storm inside and relaxed. Fear was his foe. The elf let the dread wash away, and then faced the silent Primordial again. "How do we get down there?"

Neihwe'un issued a sound like lilting pipes: a *chuckle.* "Aelyph'en Qualthalas, have you returned from your thoughts?" Qual frowned, hoping the creature was not developing a condescending wisdom that he would find annoying: the elf found admonition got on his nerves, especially when it was true. The creature ignored the look and carefully bunched up a series of vines that crept forth and encircled a large tile in the centre of the bare portion of the room in front of the pair. "This covers the path forward, or more accurately, *downward*. Be wary, Aelyph'en – beneath the tiles, an emanation."

Qualthalas probed the first squares on the floor carefully using a pair of 'picks on sticks' that he unfolded to a metre in length, scratching and prying at the grout cementing them in place. Unyielding, he tapped next on the tiles themselves, testing for pressure sensitivity, and unconvinced they posed no threat, the elf nevertheless stepped gingerly on the one in front of him. Nothing adverse happened. Mourning-Song began to hum though, and Qual unsheathed the rapier, inspecting the runes, lit up in a dim yellow, he incanted a spell, *"Phel'i-mas Lian'tri Ar-kovah"* Gratifyingly, the eight tiles surrounding the large one lit up in the same yellow hue, indicating they somehow held significance to the puzzle. There must be stairs underneath, leading into the maze. The sequence remained a mystery. Neihwe'un swept forth abruptly, past the elf, and cackled as eight tendrils formed and hammered each tile in a swift pattern. "Memory of our feasted friends," it explained as the central tile sunk a few centimetres and slid into a hidden recess, revealing as Qualthalas expected, a set of stone steps that descended into the depths.

"Do you see anything more from their minds?" Qual inquired, reflexively glancing around the chamber they were soon to leave. He kept Mourning-Song unsheathed, its customary starlight glow aided his keen eyesight as he peered down the stairs to inspect the flat surfaces for irregularities, switches, or anything else of use. Neihwe'un hung back as the elf descended a couple of the steps, further compacted its form to fit into the narrow stairwell, and finally replied, "They feared the place below, though they circumvented the path through. The black key you possess they used to pass through unharmed, but there are chilling cries deeper in the maze, and death abounds."

With that heartening endorsement, Qualthalas lightly tread several more steps down, keeping Ithrin'Sael-I-Uiin before him with its soft glow guiding his way. After minutes of travel down seemingly endless steps, the elf grew suspicious; sensing that magic of some sort was afoot. He stopped and turned to look back over his shoulder, past the Feasting Vines, and found it quite odd that he could still see illumination above that matched the chamber they just left. Following his train of thought, the Neihwe'un confirmed his suspicions, "Our movement is hindered by magic, yes; the passage below remains far beneath us, the room is still only a short distance above." Vexed, Qualthalas slashed the smooth hewn granite wall beside him and continued as if unabated. After descending another twelve steps, he cursed in moon elvish, "Isset'sie A'bhaek!" There, on his immediate right was the mark in the wall.

"A trick of the dark-dwellers?" the Neihwe'un questioned; apparently, it had no recollection of such a thing from its absorbed memories. Qualthalas nodded, already rummaging through his belongings in search of the onyx rod he had looted earlier. He turned it over several times, remembering the script and read the words again, holding the key up to the wall, but nothing happened. Descending a few more steps, again the elf intoned the words of activation, and again there was no result. Frustrated, he tapped the device upon the steps, and he smiled at the sharp click heard, feeling a subtle shifting in the stairs. Qual looked up to the Primordial with a triumphant, wide grin that disappeared as the steps gave way, rotating suddenly at a downward angle. The Neihwe'un hissed as both it and Qualthalas abruptly slid down what was now a slide, but its reactions were swift. Vines shot back up the tunnel and latched onto the opening in the tiles above, anchoring it in place. The elf reached out as he plummeted and several barbed shoots rocketed out and curled around his wrists, cutting into them, but halting his descent several metres below.

Saved for the moment, the elf smiled wanly at his companion, got a better grip on the terrible vines, wrapping several around the thicker part of his sleeves and he exclaimed, "Nice catch!" Soon though, their fortunes turned sour as they both heard the definitive sound of the tile above slowly sliding back into place. More vines shot out of the Neihwe'un, tangling, and grasping at the edges of the moving stone plate, clashing with the device, trying to hold it open. Qualthalas slipped a little on the smooth footing, and his feet gave way such that he dangled and fell a short distance, thudding onto his chest, which unfortunately pulled the Primordial downwards. It screeched in its primal voice, struggling and scrambling with a mass of tendrils clawing at the plate, which seemed to be winning the duel of might. Whatever force it employed was powerful enough that it was shearing off smaller branches and feelers; soon it would snap shut entirely.

Qualthalas swore several times as he stretched his legs to the sides to brace against the walls, but they were simply too short to span the width of the passage. The bard knew a spell that could slow his descent, but a conundrum presented itself: he needed both hands free to perform the gestures required to enact it. Meanwhile, above, the Neihwe'un fought a losing battle against the unstoppable gearwork driving the tile. With several of its viny appendages already severed, the creature was in immediate danger of losing the rest. Thick sap, the colour of blood, oozed down the flat surface of the chute. In a desperate attempt to lessen the elf's inevitable fall, the creature wailed and stretched its form, the main bodily mass unwound, and it lost several bones and sinewy parts in the process. The Neihwe'un's form extended by several metres into a lengthy vine rope to lower the squirming elf as far as it could manage while it retained a tenuous grip on the plate above.

Qual shouted, "Drop me now, I think I can see the bottom!" He still faced a twenty metre drop, judging by the light just peeking out below. If he was swift enough to cast the spell just as he let go, it would slow his descent enough... he *hoped*. The Primordial groaned and stretched as far as its appendages would allow, then uncurled the vines from his Aelyph'en cohort. The Neihwe'un pushed hard against the slick walls, floor, and ceiling, to brace itself before the last of its tendrils above sheared in half. Qualthalas' hands moved like lightning as he fell, and he stumbled with the spell's wording slightly as he slid on his backside down the chute. Qual closed his eyes and envisioned a spiked pit or the mouth of some underworld horror awaiting him below, tucked and rolled as he flew out of the chute onto an equally smooth stone floor. Jarred from the impact at the bottom, he skidded and twisted to see, with horrid fascination, a gigantic crescent of razor-sharp steel above. It rocketed down from the roof of the chamber, intent on cleaving him in two as he slid directly under its path.

Ithrin'Sael-I-Uiin flew from scabbard to hand, as the sweating elf interposed the rapier diagonally above his head. The huge blade above struck Mourning-Song, and slid the length of its indestructible blade, forcing Qual narrowly past its killing edge. Luckily, all he lost was a coattail trailing behind as he skidded along the floor. His heart thrummed in his chest as if it would leap out and explode. Laughing, the pale elf reeled sideways, then regained his footing and looked to the opening in the wall. Shorn pieces of bark and branch skittered out onto the floor. The huge axe-blade climbed back up to the ceiling on stout chains and a loud clack-clack-clack sounded while the lethal trap rearmed itself. As he shouted in warning, Qual dashed to the aid of the Neihwe'un, but thanks to its malleable, nebulous form, the creature merely crept out the opening in a heap, tangled but intact.

The pair remained in the supposedly safe corner of the expansive hewn stone chamber while the Primordial crackled and snarled, pulling itself back into its familiar mantle-like shape. Bones, sticks, sinews and bits of bark and armour swirled and twisted throughout the creature, and in a few minutes, it seemed whole again. "Takeiss..." it hissed in the indigo elven language, aloud, presumably something from a stolen memory, which sounded like an exclamation of relief. Qualthalas laughed, reeling from the sudden rush and repeated the Neihwe'un's phrase, "*Takeiss* indeed!"

The scoundrel in Qual, who delved several similarly trapped musty dungeons and crypts in his early years on Antiqua, surveyed the room with discerning eyes. The height of the chamber seemed uniform at roughly five metres; it was rectangular in shape, about twenty metres on the shorter side by thirty on the longer one. However, the roguish elf noted five deep alcoves cut into the furthest wall, to the north, if his sense of direction was still accurate. He somehow retained the presence of mind throughout the whole trek to keep note of each turn taken in case he somehow survived to return with reinforcements. The only other items of note in the otherwise bare room were five steel braziers hanging from wicked-looking barbed chains anchored in the roof by thick metal collars. *That is not ominous at all*, thought Qualthalas; *you are really going for the nefarious villain décor this time, my indigo elven nemesis.*

The elf had enough presence of mind to point out the trap in the roof to his viny companion, warning it to avoid the floor surrounding the area. Thinking clearly despite the alcohol still infusing his system, he cautiously tiptoed along the middle of the room, eyes to the ceiling, scanning for similar openings. Now that he was closer to the centre of the chamber, he spotted several of the two-metre long, narrow enclosures that betrayed the presence of more of the roof-blades. Qual looked closer at the floor under-neath one of the devices, kneeling, and being careful not to get near where the blade would fall. The stonework of the floor was nearly immaculate, only the faint hint of a slit revealed the spot into which an activated trap would descend. The maker was careful in the construction; such a recess would prevent the huge axe from striking the floor, preventing damage to either. From the heavy design of the wide, curved blade that he had the opportu-nity to view much too close, and the pinion design of the braziers he noted earlier, Qualthalas recognized dwarven craftsmanship. *Dun Dwarves*, he surmised, *so Zhiniel did manage to rally some of the clans to his banner.*

Qualthalas added the information to his mental notes about his foe. The list was becoming lengthy, and Qual silently dreaded the surveillance upon the Darklord's stronghold. *It is time to do some damage*, he thought, wanting to examine the trap struc-ture further. Knowing the destructive strength of his Primordial friend, Qualthalas detailed his plan. "I shall activate the trap, and a massive blade will drop from the ceiling above," he said, point-ing to the slit in the ceiling. The Neihwe'un nodded its cloaked head, and the skull tilted upward; its eyes scintillated briefly, and its appendages snaked out in the familiar killing vine form. "Yes, perfect. Once you see the chains which fasten the axe into the roof, I want you to rip them apart." Qualthalas deftly tapped Mourning-Song, *snick-snick*, with two piercing jabs directly into the flooring under the trap. Nothing happened.

Pressure plates, maybe, he thought, so the elf danced about the surrounding tiles, stepping hard upon each yet there was still no effect. "Do I need to dance a jig for you?" he called out, wonder-ing exactly how to activate the device, amused at the situation. It was not often someone *wanted* a potential execution by a giant axe blade. "I might have to dash under it. Be prepared." Vines flexed and extended to both sides of the Primordial, and a sizzling hiss issued from the cowl in assent. Qualthalas drew in a sharp breath, skipped a few steps, and slid along the flooring under the trap however, something quite unexpected occurred. As swift as he was, the manacle that shot up out of the floor surprised the moon elf, and he could not pull his foot away in time before it clapped around and cinched itself shut. *Clack* came the ominous sound from the ceiling as the slit opened and Qualthalas envisioned himself hopping on one leg through the rest of the Labyrinth as the heavy blade descended.

Reacting to the peril his companion now faced, the Neihwe'un spun, and a torrent of vines whipped through the air with such speed there was a whistling sound as they wrapped tightly around both chains. "*Kraagh!*" it snarled, and the entirety of its main body slammed to the floor for leverage as the tendrils yanked with such force, they ripped the whole of the trap – pinion, chains, *and* blade – out of its mooring in the ceiling and flung it across the room. The axe came so close to severing his leg, Qual let out an anticipatory shriek but then cheered when he saw it go sailing several metres, clanking and rattling as the entire device bounced along the floor and impacted the far wall. It shattered and left a gaping crack in the stone where the blade struck before coming to a rest in pieces scattered about the floor.

Qual was already at work on the rivets that sealed the manacle around his ankle with a heavy punch and tiny hammer; he popped the rivets out and freed himself. The Primordial rose back up and took its humanoid shape, snickering again beneath its cowled face. "It seems I owe you a leg, my friend." Qualthalas beamed at the creature, but then quickly added, "Not *literally*; please do not develop any funny ideas." Its eyes sparkled as twin tendrils crept along the floor towards the elf's foot, writhing dangerously nearby. Alarmed, Qual raised Mourning-Song and pointed the tip at the nearest of the barbed vines, and the Neihwe'un crackled with hideous laughter at its twisted joke. *Humour now*, Qualthalas mused, *that is certainly a good developmental sign.*

The roguish bard sheathed his rapier, chuckled and padded over to the mess of chains, bolts, and other metal parts that once made up the axe trap. He squinted at the crack in the wall, hoping it might reveal another chamber behind, but the wall must have been extremely thick, or there was simply nothing beyond it. Next, he looked over all the bits of chain and other components strewn everywhere. Well-made, but standard fare, as traps were concerned. Lastly, he laid fingers on the huge axe-blade itself, noticing now a strange pad on the flat topside of the killing device. What he found most peculiar on close inspection, was the tangled batch of thin metal wire poking out of a rubber grommet at its centre. Curious what purpose it could serve; the elf pulled out a few picks and gingerly prepared to pry the grommet loose from the metal pad surrounding it.

Something deep inside spoke out in a warning tone, "Careful not to touch the wiring. You'll get a jolt." The voice was unmistakably his own but separate from his thoughts. *Am I developing a personality problem from the trauma or the masque?* Qualthalas laughed at himself despite his genuine concerns. His mind was playing tricks on him again, he was sure, but regardless he made sure to heed the warning, just in case. The rubber piece was nearly free when the Primordial made a shrill noise behind him, and his hand slipped. The pick barely touched a single bare strand of wire as Qualthalas glanced over his shoulder, but it was enough for an arc of lightning to blast the poor elf onto his back. His right arm smoldered and bore scorch marks its entire length, but there was strangely no pain at all, as Qual twitched in shock upon the chamber floor. For a few moments, he could not breathe, and everything looked dark until his sight returned simultaneously with searing jets of agony throughout his body.

Qualthalas fought the wracking convulsions, willing his muscles to calm themselves while trying to ignore the intense pain rocketing through him and he finally started to breathe again. For a full minute, everything seemed to tense up and the elf curled into a ball, unable to move. While incapacitated, he looked to the Neihwe'un, whose tendrils drew back threateningly, and it hissed at something ahead. The creature was intent upon something on the ceiling towards the centre of the chamber near the spot it ripped the trap apart. Qualthalas could make out several small forms skittering along the roof, more Gods-damned spiders!

It could have been due to the sudden electrocution, but the elf, weakly propping himself up against the wall, thought he saw a metallic glint on each of the tiny things now spewing out of the hole above. Meanwhile, the Neihwe'un emitted a deep resounding, predatory cry as it lashed out at the nearest things crawling forth. Tendrils curled around one of the spiders and with precision tore the creature apart; each of the smaller shoots gripped a leg and splayed apart, sending its limbs flying and dropping the body to the floor. Qualthalas was sure now these were automatons and not living (or undead) creatures, he heard the unmistakable sound of metallic bits tinkling all over the tile below. If he could only move to assist the Primordial, who was now wildly battering and swinging at scores of the things that were now leaping down in droves, Qualthalas needed to examine these things in detail.

The Neihwe'un seemed to be having difficulty fighting the swarm; the minute metal monstrosities had penetrated its outer structure and were infesting its core. Now Qual could clearly make out the pincers and tail-stingers these dark, silvery things possessed; they were not spiders at all but resembled little metal scorpions. These things were shredding vines with their claws and mandibles, and stinging the Neihwe'un incessantly, which individually might cause superficial damage, but their sheer numbers were clearly overwhelming his companion. *Time to repay the favour*, Qualthalas thought, gritting his teeth against the continued pain and convulsions still wracking his body. He stood on sheer will alone and drew Ithrin'Sael-I-Uiin.

Qualthalas discovered sheer will alone to be insufficient to allow him to cast magic; his fingers twitched involuntarily, and his lips formed garbled syllables, even rudimentary healing was impossible for the moment. Although the viny terror performed admirably thus far in its confrontation with the steady stream of attacking mechanical scorpions, it was clearly ill suited against the diminutive creatures, compounded by the fact that several were causing damage internally. On occasion, the Neihwe'un compacted part of its main body, crushing and summarily ejecting a few of the automatons, but more just managed to work their way inside, and now the floor looked like a crazy nest with all its bits strewn about. Qualthalas needed something specific to combat the steel scorpions, and he needed it now.

An exceedingly difficult spell came to Qual's mind; it would have been perfect if he could muster the concentration to cast it. Considering the impossibility under the circumstances, the bard wisely called upon the intellect within his mighty rapier instead. "*Na'nesth-uil ka-tauph'a phi'a-qu'es-maniin*," the elf issued mentally, and briefly touched his fingers to the twin crescents adorning his face. They lit with starlight, and the runes upon Ithrin'Sael-I-Uiin responded in kind, the area bathed in its familiar silver-blue glow. Rarely did Qualthalas awaken the soul encapsulated within the blade from its slumber; his reasons were twofold. Primarily, he did not wish to disturb the rest of an entity who once battled tirelessly against a tide of darkness that swept the cosmos. Of a more practical concern: using it in this way rendered many of Mourning-Song's other capabilities inert for hours afterward.

Thy peril be great, Prince of the Sillistrael'li, the voice of the blade awakened hummed in Qualthalas' consciousness, *how might the Soul of Conviction assist thee?* Slumped with his back to the wall, Qualthalas attempted to maintain the utmost civility as he replied, "I am wounded, shocked by a lightning-charged device, and our companion is in peril – besieged by steel scorpions, we quest through a labyrinth for the Darklord's lair…" The moon elf's voice trailed off, he was wasting time iterating the heap of trouble he was in, and it spoiled his mood to hear himself speak it aloud. Mourning-Song rang with a baritone laughter as it replied, *'tis a typical day in the life of the Rogue, Vagabond and Ne'er-do-well then.* Still, as it spoke, Qualthalas felt the rapier scan his mind briefly but thoroughly, memories of Kaira flashed by, and the elf choked. He felt a wistful kindness emanate from the enchanted weapon, whose tone changed suddenly to concern, *thy love be in peril, and it grieves thee deeply, O child of prophesy. Let us not tarry: I know thy will.*

The spell formula locked in Qual's still-hazy mind came forth abruptly, pulled from his consciousness while Ithrin'Sael-I-Uiin leapt from the elf's hand to hover before him. It danced and flashed with scintillating colour as the tip of the blade carved the arcane formula of the spell into the air. Mourning-Song slashed the syllables to life and recited the incantation with its ancient voice. "*Threil'a Vermei'qu-a'a Sonia-Phae'sui Ato-Ka'Phenia!*" Boldly, the artifact presented itself, hovered before the horde of mechanical vermin, and the air rippled as it unleashed devastating sorcery at the height of its magnitude. Qualthalas had to shield his eyes from the sudden blast of heat and orange light as the ensuing wave of force targeted each of the metal creatures and reduced them to bubbling heaps of melted slag. The Neihwe'un shrieked and ripped out the creatures formerly infesting its insides; it hurled their misshapen, melted chunks about the chamber.

The assault abated, Ithrin'Sael-I-Uiin returned to its master's hand, dimming; its runes ebbed with a subdued power as it readied for deactivation, to recharge and return the soul to its slumber within. However, before the mystical markings faded entirely, the voice spoke once again, in comfort. *I have power yet, Son of Adamon – may thy wounds heal swiftly.* As the burns and twitching in Qualthalas' limbs faded, so did the blade's magnificent soul, into its extraplanar home. Ithrin'Sael-I-Uiin mustered a few parting words, *trust in thyself, my friend, and good luck in your journey...* With that, the runes faded to darkness and the rapier slept, rendered mundane for the time being.

Qualthalas reverently sheathed Ithrin'Sael-I-Uiin and touched its pommel to his forehead, relieved that the immediate peril was at an end. He resolved to quicken his pace; the rapier brought to the forefront of his mind the danger still posed to Kaira; he would waste no more time before rescuing her so they could at least watch the end of the world together. As the Neihwe'un inspected the melted remains of the scorpions nearby, now that they were cool enough to touch, it discarded one and swept along the floor, careful to avoid another of the axe-blade traps. Once the Primordial reached the north most wall, its vines latched onto something upon the floor, then wheeled around and drifted back to meet the elf, who busied himself tightening his gloves and sorting his gear. Qual looked up and grinned wanly, "Now we're tied, in the life-saving department, Neihwe'un. I certainly hope we do not have to keep a tally by the time this mess is concluded!" Seeing the creature had something to offer him, the rogue, intrigued, held a palm out. The viny terror deposited an intact specimen of one of the mechanical scorpions into Qual's hand; it had managed to crush only the head during its violent battle.

"Some knowledge you may glean, Aelyph'en. I sense your desire to find the corruption below and your friend." The Neihwe'un rattled and shook the last misshapen hunk of metal from its form, where it broke into two pieces on the cold stone floor. Qual nodded and inspected the scorpion closely, intrigued by its intricate, lifelike design. Although the thing was comprised completely of metallic parts, its anatomy was an accurate representation of the creature it mimicked. "Yes, friend, I do think this will be useful," he stowed the creature in the last satchel he possessed and said, "but as you said, I wish to move along. Let us next inspect the alcoves; I am certain they are the key to egress." With that, Qualthalas sauntered to the closest of the indentations in the wall, and his companion followed, ready for anything.

Chapter 17

MISS TELAISS'AVIR WUTH-RENAIS MAKES A MOST SHOCKING DISCOVERY

Y'Tasziah moved at an even pace along the well-maintained concrete path that comprised most of the long walkway of Thoroughfare Avenue, which wound lazily through the Nobles' Quarter where Devilsbridge Manor lay nestled behind walls of brick and stone. She could have easily saved time by using her magic to jump short distances through its early morning shadows, flitting through the Plane of Eternal Twilight, however she opted to save her mana in case a dire need arose later in her travels. Considering all she had gleaned from the mysterious moon elf's missive, the individual she would soon observe was either deadly or a marked man, and either way, even observing him might stir trouble. There was also the matter of her route, which would surely take her past the docks, which currently harbored a cutter belonging to the Black Flag – the most notorious of the independent fleets. Most of these groups of privateers were glorified pirates and marauders, however the Black Flag Armada was feared unilaterally. Formed from exiled and wealthy nobles, assassins, and powerful renegade magic-users united by the freedom from authority that the Typhon Seaboard offered, the company rarely moored its ships at major ports, unless doing so involved a contract whose reward greatly outweighed the risk.

Pausing to contemplate the possibility of the Black Flag's presence being wound up in the current intrigue with the Houses, Y'Tasziah rested a hip against a pillar housing a blend of regional flowers and enjoyed their scent. At length, she deemed it unimportant to her current objective, but one that might warrant a detailed and likely covert investigation before the ship departed. A passerby, notably a nobleman from House Muirimar, gave a cordial nod of recognition of Lady Devilsbridge, and he stopped his brisk march to converse briefly. "Milady," the suit-coated man began, with a slight bend of the knee, "I suppose your early morn's journey precludes investigative duties. Not of Muirimar, I hope?" He smirked, with the hint of a concerned frown that creased his moustached jowls. Y'Tasziah smiled disarmingly, with practiced ease. Her mere presence put several nobles on edge in countless interactions: she'd learned to lessen the impact of her stature through fakery and wit. Devilsbridge considered Muirimar among the more scrupulous of the Thirteen Houses and though none, not even Ravantheos, were above suspicion, they had proven as mild supporters in the past.

She pushed herself off the floral street decoration, and with a dainty curtsey, replied simply, "No, not of House Muirimar." The gentleman appeared relieved. Though her statement left little room for further conversation, he tarried however, and seemed unsure of himself. Curious now, she inquired, "Does something vex thee, so early in the day – and such a beautiful one at that – perhaps whatever weighs on your mind is of relevance?" Y'Tasziah widened her eyes and blinked with open innocence; her ability to express sincere facial expression was unparalleled. Several acting lessons from noteworthy tutor Escautt Swann, an accomplished thespian, known for his acclaimed book, "How to Not Act," allowed Y'Tasziah to convey sincerity by reliving past events that mirrored the emotion she wanted to portray. Mastering that simple concept supplied her proficiency in deceptions that could even defeat certain magical honesty tests: she truly *felt* the way she was acting; the emotions in the moment were not a lie, even if her words following *were*.

Withdrawing pensively, the noble straightened his coat tails and repeated her question, "Does something vex me? No, Lady Devilsbridge, I wouldn't go so far as to say *that*." Y'Tasziah sensed the impending '*but*' forthcoming and gave a wan smile as the noble continued, "But, I cannot help feeling like I've been *watched* of late – and not by you or your House, if you take my meaning." He leaned in close, to speak in a hushed whisper, "It is not something that worries me, it is some… *thing*." His emphasis on the last word hung in the still morning air, and Y'Tasziah could appreciate his sentiment, for she too could sense a pervading presence that simply *did not belong* in Morningmist. However, wanting to reassure the nervous gentleman, she only replied, with a touch of concern balanced with comfort, "I am sure, master Etraedes Muirimar, that it is just a passing humor that will vanish soon. Did not the dark moon, Es'Vaniss-Thal'as, eclipse the Silver Moon recently? Surely the distemper is from the lunar events, methinks."

There was truth in the explanation, even a partial eclipse of either moon caused odd and sometimes outright bizarre disturbances in the natural flow of the planet's magical and mundane energies alike. Y'Tasziah suspected this, coupled with the myriad of political intrigues and problems plaguing the city were at fault for most people's uneasy feelings recently. However, she was certain equally that Neph'al instincts, known for sensitivity to otherworldly forces, were picking up on some… *thing*, as the man stated. She planned to consult the Enigma in three days' time regarding the matter; there was a greater celestial occurrence destined that night, and the opportunity for augury into mystical undercurrents. The pair laughed it off and finished the conversation with the usual blather of nobles – talk of trade, local gossips, and unimportant foreign affairs – both dismissed themselves to other duties and parted ways.

Y'Tasziah mused that if a *Nonatt* (meaning *non-attuned* to the magically initiated) could sense the underlying magical disturbances that, to her practically reeked of the planes, then whatever their portent; it could bode terribly ill for Morningmist. She picked up her pace, plotting numerous routes through the gigantic metropolis, knowing that extended interruptions might cause her to miss her appointed observation timing. The Gilded Hammer lay in the Sumbercolme District, so named for one of the original Houses of Morningmist whose influence at the time attracted several prominent artisan consortiums and adventuring guilds. Adorned then with banners and colours that represented the finest of Neph'al and many other races' combined craftsmen, the large territory touted unique architecture, much of which survived today. However, unlike those golden years of prosperity and growth, the district, as too many others had, seemed to decline steadily, measured in both wealth and security.

She was not so worried for her own safety; her ability to defend herself against ruffians using magic and physical combat was not in question. It was the *delay* they could represent, and the interruption to her mission by the consequential reports a noblewoman of her stature would endure by the ineptitude and inefficiency of the contracted guardsmen that chilled Y'Tasziah. She hoped to avoid conflict entirely, slip into the Gilded Hammer, and find the person she sought – then get the hells back to Devilsbridge Manor. She had several options for detour and opted to make for the gate leading to the Marble Maidens district: it was surely a longer route, but a much more secure path that would likely save valuable time in the end. Furthermore, if she felt she could spare a few minutes, a colleague of hers resided and studied in one of the sprawling arcane universities; he may have some insight for her. In addition, she had intended to thank him for a very spontaneous and pleasurable night they recently shared, but the morning after, her duties forced her quiet departure before he awoke.

Upon her approach to the wide, stonework arches that joined Thoroughfare to the Marble Maidens, she recognized the guard-captain. Formerly contracted to House Devilsbridge, the soldier, Asanna Kovaczi, offered Y'Tasziah a snap salute and smiled through her open-faced helm. Seeing that Lady Devilsbridge moved with a purposeful stride, she nodded to her subordinate and swiftly waved the noble sorceress through, not wanting to impede her with the usual questions and checks. Y'Tasziah passed through, slowing only to mouth the words, "Thank you," to Kovaczi, who mouthed back, "You owe me," though both knew it was only a jest. Hurrying through and taking a wide path between white stone fountains to her immediate left, Y'Tasziah made her way down into the valley area leading to the libraries and universities of the Scholars' Quarter.

The light misting as she passed between the spraying fountain jets cooled and refreshed Y'Tasziah as she enjoyed the light breeze and midmorning sun. Wanting to gauge her timing, she looked to the bright blue-white blazing sphere and marveled, considering the sheer size of such a celestial object. Although it seemed every school of astronomy and stellar magic wanted to argue about its actual mass and distance, Y'Tasziah preferred to look at the object from a less scientific view. It was immeasurably huge, so many times larger than Antiqua, which she did understand was large, as planets go. She dwelled a few minutes in the rainbow haze and took the opportunity to sip from her silver canteen of cold raspberry teawater, before stoppering it and continuing. She had about two-and-a-half hours to make her long trek through the city to Sumbercolme and the Gilded Hammer, so if she intended on a short visit to her colleague, she would have to hurry.

Once she had followed the large path deep into the valley, the fountains and pots of flowers and light pillars gave way to dormitories and enclaves – the Scholars' Quarter as it was aptly termed. This expansive area just beyond Morningmist's Marble Maidens District still served as a shining beacon of enlightenment within all the Neph'al Kingdoms of Mithras. Libraries, both public and House-affiliated could be found in varying sizes every few blocks, or so it seemed. Arcane and scientific universities that ranged in scope and specialty were surrounded by dormitories and individual domiciles that housed its students, visitors, professors, and guests. All thirteen houses maintained a presence here in the city, and their inhabitants and employees seemed the least concerned about *political affairs* (apart from political educators and students, of course) and more with the *pursuit* of knowledge.

However, not so much a *scholar* of the arcane and occult, and much more one of its *practitioners*, Y'Tasziah still appreciated almost every aspect of the place, and thoroughly enjoyed the times her duties brought her here. Of course, she could have any tome or thesis from within the area hand-delivered to her House's mansion; it was equally often she made the trek and spent days holed up in the Devilsbridge Arcanasium. It was nearly as comfortable as her own home, richly appointed, and often much more serene. On occasion, she spent the time in relative solitude within its chambers, which boasted fine equipment, fully stocked larders, (which she, herself ordered supplies for, so it had fresh fish, fruit, and bottles of fine wine) and most importantly, *a secret basement*.

A longing suddenly tugged at Y'Tasziah, but she pushed it aside and doubled her pace, at length deciding to visit her friend upon her eventual return in three days, when she must consult the Enigma. "I've delayed the apology for a week and a half already, he'll understand if I'm uncommunicative another few days, and besides – he could always approach me if his need *arose.*" She chortled at her clever pun and wound through an efficient, yet still-scenic route that avoided the younger wizard's dormitory to dissuade herself from having an impulsive change of mind. Scholars, predominantly Neph'al from both Mithras and Huromithra, intermingled and debated with a higher ratio of the world's other civilized races than any other District. She enjoyed the variety of life here; though Devilsbridge employed and trained their House members based upon merit without regard to origin, even they were primarily Neph'al, simply because the qualified applicants outnumbered other races.

Y'Tasziah worried this trend might never change. It was one of the problems her father pleaded the Council to address; cultural, political, and economic reasons practically begged the city to encourage more varied heritage within its walls. This was one of the few topics that Orion received majority approvals for in Council movements; only three Houses opposed citizenship scouting among non-Neph'al races, and they were careful to cite logical reasons, lest they suffer accusations of racial bias. However, Devilsbridge knew – all the other Houses knew – that it was no coincidence these same three Houses only possessed a handful of other races in their ranks, typically in the lowest possible positions with the least pay.

Two of these were Lord Orion's primary suspects in the Zennitarr Eradication, though he expressed his doubt regarding a direct connection between their xenophobia and the plot. In fact, Devilsbridge could not claim to fathom the old Houses' reasoning in avoiding nonhumans – in times past, Morningmist boasted the highest racial diversity of any major city upon Mithras. Neph'al humans of various origin certainly had their specialties, and possessed an ambition coupled with innately acute intellect that held them at the forefront of innovation. However, each other race could boast their own specialists, geniuses, and sages – even the less civilized yet non-hostile people of Antiqua held power and unique offerings that could make the city flourish.

Orion, and perhaps even moreso Y'Tasziah, imagined the days of yore brought back to Morningmist, heralding a new dawn akin to the founding times. In those early founding decades, Dwarven metallurgists proffered their expertise, creating the first steamworks facility, which still stood at the centre of the metropolis' industrial district, *Athra-Gatumag*, meaning Heart-Forge in the Stone Dwarvish dialect. The dwarven ingenuity and craftsmanship were only the beginnings of multicultural advancements in the already sprawling city. Other races – Aelyph'en of all varieties (including Indigo elven fugitives), the Gaub Nomads, Gnomish, Taurean Cen'it and Mino, Oryk, several less commonly seen races, and once even, a mighty Celestial – all contributed to the growth and development of Morningmist. This golden era of true progress earned the metropolis its eventual capital city status, brought the original Houses to its fair democratic Council to administrate, and it was then it truly deserved the lofty title, 'The Shining Jewel' of Mithrainian Civilization.

The reverie, as Y'Tasziah walked, ended upon the abrupt realization that her path had unconsciously taken her past the Arches of Typhon – which led to the Starwind Seaport District, which could have allowed her a glimpse at the Black Flag ship on her way to Sumbercolme. That route had been her preferred path, rather than continuing through the outlying streets of the Scholars' Quarter to the Athra-Gatumag with its maze of piping and confusing arrangement of engineering facilities. Though both the port and the industrial Districts both adjoined Sumbercolme, each held potential obstacles to her journey. If she wheeled and backtracked, she estimated she still had ample time to make her way through Starwind Seaport to inspect the ship, and apart from drunken sailors and possible vagabonds there was only a slim chance for any physical obstruction. Conversely, if she decided to continue onward to Athra-Gatumag, the potential for rerouting and detour remained high. The engineering and construction that constantly existed in the technical district often dissuaded her from passing through, even though on a perfect day it boasted the most direct path to Sumbercolme.

Knowing the likelihood of major delay if she chose to forge ahead to Athra-Gatumag, even though that posed less risk of assault, Y'Tasziah opted to turn back to the Arches of Typhon. Seeing the Black Flag cutter moored there might afford her a rare chance to glimpse some of its crew, it would be an asset if she could make a contact in their ranks; at worst, she would attain a familiarity with the physical appearance of the ship. This might allow her to later scry upon or at least track its movement once it left port. Conversely, the worst-case scenario in the industrial District would be a closure of entry to Sumbercolme directly; if that occurred, she would have to detour through *two* far-less-savory Districts than the port to reach her destination.

Lady Devilsbridge only took pause to adjust and tighten the straps adorning her garments, specifically those securing her coinpurse and the dagger on her belt. She certainly did not want to deal with a pickpocket or cutpurse, because the city's law still frowned upon lethal force, and then there were the reports to file afterwards... Thinking logically, she laced a few more strings in her bodice to conceal the bursting cleavage she had used upon poor Kilbrand earlier in the day. Although she did love flaunting her alluring body, the prospect of undue attention it might attract from sailors and unsavory elements left Y'Tasziah less than aroused. She glanced down. Upon seeing a mere hint of breast peeking out from the tight leather, she resigned herself to satisfaction and wheeled around back in the direction of the Arches leading to Starwind.

The guardsmen – if one dared bestow the title upon the pair of half-drunk wastrels – were far less accommodating than her acquaintance at the entry to the Marble Maidens. The first, presumably the one in charge, smelled of cheap spirits and the smoke from an illicit herb still clung to him underneath a generous spritzing of cologne that reminded Y'Tasziah of bleach. Maybe it *was* bleach. No amount of washing would ever be enough; Y'Tasziah wanted to forget the man afterwards, but if she needed to remember, she had only to recall the myriad of unpleasant aromas the 'guard' exuded in the late morning heat. He approached with glassy eyes and a vacant stare until he spied her ample breasts, even tied in a less-revealing fashion than earlier. Perhaps it was a form of penance for tormenting Kilbrand earlier, she mused sarcastically, and thought aloud, *"thanks be to the Gods for that!"*

"Eh, wassat, missus 'noblady?'" the guard questioned, the slurred blending of 'noble' and 'lady' rolled so *charmingly* off his cracked lips, and he approached far too close for Y'Tasziah's liking. He was well within reach of her Soulbound Scythe; she knew this because she'd instantly imagined carving the pig in twain with it just so she could carry on and distance herself from his reek. Y'Tasziah steeled herself for the inevitable conversation, and with a sincere apology to swine everywhere for equating this man to them, she stared him down like an adder would stare down a mouse. His companion backed away upon seeing the scathing glare; apparently, he possessed a shred of dignity or the common sense that, unfortunately, his superior did not. Unabated and oblivious to her shriveling gaze, the stinking man began his requisite line of questioning.

"T'wut, we owe the pleasure, missus..." he paused, expecting her to report her name and reason for visiting the docks. This was standard procedure, but, suddenly afire with annoyance, Y'Tasziah dared to step closer and turned her shoulder to the side to ensure the filthy 'captain' could see the crest of House Devilsbridge emblazoned there upon her sleeve. Reacting to his squinty examination, she iterated through pursed lips, "*Devilsbridge*. And my affairs here are, *without a doubt*, none of your business whatsoever, you *sot*, and sorry excuse for a guard." This time, Y'Tasziah did not have to act at all – this waste of an individual raised her *real ire* – it disgusted her that the city would employ such an insulting example as one of its guards, in any district, under any circumstances. It solidified her resolve to complete her mission, root out the corruption in Morningmist and set the city back on a path to greater prosperity.

The guard staggered back at her blunt rebuke. Y'Tasziah spat directly at his feet to accentuate the point. She warned him with a tone of finality, "Stand aside now or face wrath itself." Her Soulscythe burst forth from its netherspace origin, surrounded with billowing purple and black energy, and she leveled it, tip-down, scant centimetres from the guard's crooked nose. Y'Tasziah suspected the man's unfortunate companion would have to put up with yet another unsavory smell after he backpedaled and bowed his head, allowing her to pass without another word.

She stormed through the gateway and made a direct beeline for the impressive rows of docks that surrounded Starwind Bay, from which the district earned its name. Morningmist, as Capital of Mithras, boasted the second-largest seaport in the world, surpassed only by that of the Isle of Eregaphia, which lay amid the Sea of Churnarl far to the West. It was impossible to compete with an entire island altogether circumscribed by a gigantic lattice of multilevel docks. The fresh, humid sea air wafted several pleasant aromas, which Y'Tasziah took in readily, relieved to put the scent and importantly the dismal aura of Guard Captain Garbage far behind her.

The sun neared its apex, however, measured by Antiqua's rotational cycle of thirty-seven hours, consisting of one hundred minutes each subdivided into one hundred seconds of time, (relative to your planetary conventions, dear reader) Y'Tasziah gauged she had ample time for scouting. She could easily survey the dock where the Black Flag ship moored, swiftly make way for Sumbercolme and be at the Gilded Hammer with time to spare. She might even be able to enjoy a few glasses of wine before the arrival of this individual that the Aelyph'en, Qualthalas, had arranged for her to spy upon and unravel the illusions surrounding him or her.

Spotting the Black Flag vessel immediately – its sail a dead giveaway amid the bright colours and emblazoned emblems of every other ship in the bay – Y'Tasziah practically jogged to the long dock where it sat moored. Sporting the square, all-black flag of its namesake company, the cutter-class ship took her breath the closer she got to it. This was an engineering marvel, worthy of calling itself a sculpture, so magnificent the vessel was in both technical design and aesthetic consideration. Flowing silver letters imprinted with enameled mithril flake shone upon its port bow: *Rain Dancer* was the ship's name, one that Y'Tasziah approved of immediately. It occurred to her the implication of it being a cutter-class specifically; massive ships such as galleons often transported this class of ship and sent them to port either because the port could not dock the larger vessel or... because the fleet needed to scout. Even mighty and feared as the Black Flag were, Y'Tasziah doubted any plot to assault the capital – this was their way of keeping the large ship out of view while a small crew performed illegal activity in the city, then could flee quickly afterwards.

She smiled, thinking it similar in a way to her own role within House Devilsbridge.

Y'Tasziah had to tear her eyes from the Drakhanic carvings adorning the ship's railings – sea dragons amid roiling tsunamis fought with trident-bearing merfolk... she squinted and saw real pearls of black, white, and rare reds inset in the eyes of the beings. She scanned the above deck of the vessel, but there was no sign of sailor or captain at all. Again, she inspected the ship itself and became lost in its absolute splendour. The figurehead, she noticed now, was that of an ebony half-woman, half-wolven creature – if the sculptor meant the carving to be a werewolf, she was certainly the most noble, regal looking one Y'Tasziah could imagine. Hardly appearing as a slavering beast, this creature looked serene, like she danced upon the waves that propelled her, reaching out towards the horizon.

Sensing the slightest movement from the ship's crow's nest, Y'Tasziah raised her eyes to see another pair meeting her own gaze. A dark, olive-skinned, sandy haired youth of perhaps fifteen or sixteen years of age squinted down at her, and the boy stood up to analyze her from head to toes and back. After his appraisal, sea-green eyes locked onto Y'Tasziah with a mixed look of approval and boldness before the boy registered a curt nod in her direction. He acted as a seasoned sailor might, and Lady Devilsbridge fanned herself like a courtier while he continued to stare. This one would make a handsome and dashing devil of a man later in life, she knew with certainty. She feared for the lasses who would become enamoured with the lad as he regaled tales of his adventurous exploits at sea, and then took the swooning maidens to bed before departing from port the following morn, waving, and promising to return as they cried upon the docks.

Memorizing the boy's face and attire – feisty and rebellious with loose, billowing sleeves, unbuttoned collared shirt, black breeches and long, black boots, (he stood like a pirate, one leg upon the rail of the crow's nest as he watched her go), Y'Tasziah dared a wave and a sultry wink. She faked a few more flighty glances back at the young sailor, noting further details each time: the scimitar at his side, adorned with a crow's foot emblem, a simple silver chain around his neck, and a curious scar on his forearm. *Probably from a branding removal,* she deduced. The boy was either an escaped criminal or former slave from Ral-Qariin, which explained his olive, tanned skin, but not his fair hair – mayhap he was a bastard offspring of some noble, cast off into a life of crime and intrigue. Her imagination filled in a lot of assumptive details, but Y'Tasziah liked to make up such stories for those she never expected to meet again. It made them more memorable, and easier to perform scrying spells and auguries upon from afar.

The *Rain Dancer* itself, she longingly gazed the length of from bow to stern several times, out of a real need to supply accuracy in her eventual report to her father, and out of an equal desire just to marvel at it once more before it would leave port. Sometimes the sea would tug at her as she looked to its horizons, wondering often what such a life would entail. In truth, sailing was likely a lot less romantic than it seemed, yet Y'Tasziah dreamed of days at a time upon the rough waves of the Typhon Ocean. She fantasized attacks from bizarre and giant sea monsters, lust, and love from port to port, duelling… she sighed, as a conflicting malcontent grew inside her breast. Would her duties forever keep her from these adventures she so craved? Sure, she had excitement aplenty in her unofficial duties, which did pull her from the confines of House Devilsbridge and Morningmist itself on occasion, but she pined for a *real* adventure. She wanted something akin to the books she scoured over as a little girl, with knights and Queens and wild forests filled with all manner of dangerous beasts, to fight in crypts with vampiric horrors and search through trap-filled ruins full of ancient relics.

A sharp whistle directly ahead startled Y'Tasziah into snapping her eyes forward while she skidded to a halt only a metre from an ebon-skinned woman in her path: the apparent source of the warning. With the most crooked of smiles, the green-and-black clad lady looked amusedly over the sorceress and simply said, "Watch your step." To Y'Tasziah, it felt like a veiled threat wrapped in the trappings of advice, but as she narrowed her eyes and opened her mouth to retort, she bit her tongue. The unmistakable resemblance between the woman and the figurehead of the magnificent Black Flag cutter was no coincidence. This must be the ship's Captain. The dark-skinned privateer crossed her arms, pushed her chest out, her breasts heaved up within the loosely laced stitched leather doublet she wore, and she cracked her calloused knuckles for emphasis. She kicked a loose stone to the side and spread her feet wide in clear indication that she would not budge an inch before the Noblewoman apologized. Y'Tasziah liked the woman instantly, even though the assumption that she was a pushover annoyed the hells out of her.

Nevertheless, the potent sorceress hid her ire beneath a look of sheer, aghast terror at her own terrible disregard for her absent-mindedness (moreso she regretted losing focus and letting the seafarer surprise her). Dipping as a court-bred Grandesse might, in deference to a social error, Y'Tasziah swiftly formed an elegant-sounding apology, "Allow my sincerest apologies, mistress. I am unaccustomed to this area entirely, I'll have you know, and all the sights and sounds of the sea had me lost inside myself." That, again, was not entirely a lie, though when she batted her long lashes at the amused corsair who stood like a barricade still, the woman's eyes flashed with a sneer of disbelief. A rough and uncouth snort, however, was the only indication of a reply that the Rain Dancer's captain displayed. Y'Tasziah wondered if the impassive woman saw through her act, or if this was about to become a shakedown

– there would be a threat and request for undue payment for the insult if that was the case.

A gull overhead let out its shrill screech, and the captain smirked, finally speaking again in her firm, dusky voice, "Oh, I could see *that*. The step you need to watch is of a more *metaphorical* nature, my dear Lady." Her eyes finally moved from Y'Tasziah to her ship and back, and a wide, toothy, and dangerous grin flashed upon the dashing woman. "*Littlecrow* reported you gawking at my vessel, 'a little too long and slow to be the passing, romantic interest of a House Noble', he said, and I'd like to know," finally she moved, but only to lean in slightly. "What the Hells do you want, Devilsbridge *spy*?" One of the captain's hands strayed down to her hip. She tapped her fingers expectantly upon the pommels of adjacent twin longknives loose in their sheaths on her belt.

Contrary to her previous act of innocence and deference, Y'Tasziah dropped all pretense of the charade and relaxed. She let out a calm snicker, light and mirthful – she liked this pirate of a woman more every second. Instead of attempting further deception, Y'Tasziah decided to come clean, and expected that the Captain of the Rain Dancer might appreciate her sudden candor. "Fair enough; I should really have known better than to think I'd fool a seasoned *privateer*." At this the captain's shark-like grin disappeared, replaced with a slightly more respectful look upon the striking corsair's face, which Y'Tasziah noticed was smooth and tight, placing her in perhaps her mid-thirties, possibly early forties; she couldn't have been a captain long, but something underneath that exterior suggested that, like the sorceress herself, appearances were deceiving.

"I suppose, by weight of my Conciliatory House rank, I could demand a ship inspection." Y'Tasziah stated, gambling on maintaining a razor's edge in this parley with the Black Flag Captain. The ebon woman's eyes again narrowed dangerously at

BOTH SIDES OF THE BLADE

the remark, and she moved from her open stance to put a single boot before herself. Y'Tasziah noted the telltale nicks and stains upon the velvety green, indicating they had seen their fair share of confrontations. This time it was Y'Tasziah who stood like stone, unblinking and motionless, if only to prove they stood on equal footing, on the ground between them and in the battlefield of will. But, unabated and seasoned in keeping any opponent off-guard, the Lady of House Devilsbridge adjusted her demeanor and qualified the off-hand remark, "However, I have no vested interest in disrupting what is *obviously* nothing more than shore-leave for yourself and your fine crew." The sorceress again remained casual, unconcerned, and ultimately relaxed. She desired no overt confrontation with the Black Flag: in fact, Y'Tasziah sensed an opportunity and intended to capitalize on it – and quickly – if she wanted to make it to the Gilded Hammer in time.

"In truth," the sorceress continued, biting her lip as if considering whether to confide in a total stranger, "I am on a mission of great import to the city, and possibly Antiqua at large and I must not tarry." At this, the captain tilted her cheek in skepticism, and that is when Y'Tasziah moved in for the verbal equivalent of a killing blow, placing a hand upon the woman's shoulder and leaning close to whisper, "React like I've just told you the most idiotic thing, and then stay close – we are being watched closely right now." On cue, the captain batted the hand off her shoulder and let out a piercing guffaw, full of incredulous joviality, after which she barked out a loud reply, "Lady Devilsbridge! That was *one night* of pleasure! You surely cannot expect I will stay at port *three more days* just to satisfy your flighty whims!"

Y'Tasziah flushed with a slight amount of real embarrassment at the unexpected ad-lib accusation but understood the captain's intent. She pouted with indignation as she pleaded, "Two then, I pray thee, please, I..." tears flowed down the sorceress' bronzed cheek as she implored, "I need but *one more night with you*, before you are gone again for months! Tomorrow at least, allow me another audience in your quarters." Staring straight into the captain's eyes, who regarded her with mixed admiration and chagrin, Y'Tasziah ran her tongue provocatively along her bottom lip and bit it, which elicited the hint of a blush on the woman's dark cheek. The captain ran both hands up the Noblewoman's shoulders and drew them to her breast and kissed Y'Tasziah full on the lips. The sorceress snatched the folded black card tucked into the captain's cleavage and palmed it, then slipped the object into her belt pouch covertly. They shared a meaningful look, then both stepped away and gave longing, parting glances as each made their way to their respective duties.

Smiling and skipping along to maintain the charade, thoroughly impressed with herself at securing an impromptu audience with a bonafide Black Flag corsair captain, Y'Tasziah glanced around the bustling port. She intended to keep her eyes up and her movement brisk, weaving her way purposefully past dockworkers, sailors, and all manner of individuals, smiling gaily at the ones who either whistled or catcalled, practically dancing her way to the far side of the district. Though it played into her overly boisterous charade at the time, Y'Tasziah scrutinized her surroundings, considering it a real possibility that prying eyes could be following her. Several Houses, some of them bearing deadly intent, surely employed agents in a similar fashion to relay her movements to their superiors; intelligence and counterintelligence both necessary in reaction to the investigative decree of Ravantheos.

Deciding that speed and prudence warranted the use of her magic, Y'Tasziah the House Agent took charge, and though she kept the flighty air about her, the sorceress looked analytically to the stalls lining the dockside berm. Occupied by hundreds of customers and merchants, peddling and trading wares from both the city and the various imports managed by brokers employed by non-Mithrainian fleets, the Starwind Exchange experienced peak sales this time of day. The sheer volume of people and the shadowy outcroppings of colourful fabric overhangs played to Y'Tasziah's advantage – she might be able to lose herself amid them a moment, if she could only find a suitable set of shadows...

There, she thought, spying a single unoccupied stall – one she frequented which served cold and cooked, the most delightful fresh fish, with an apology note attached indicating it was undergoing maintenance and with a clever apology stating, "We will be 'hooked' up soon! 'Catch' you tomorrow!" Y'Tasziah laughed openly at the stupid jest but made a beeline for the throng of customers milling around the adjacent tent-like stall, intermingling with the wine-tasting patrons thereabouts. Any experienced operative would swiftly realize her intent and move in at once before she gained the advantage of slipping through the busy crowd in hopes of losing the tail. While she was curious to know if any counteragents were shadowing her, Y'Tasziah found it imperative to disappear and get to the Gilded Hammer – and soon. A glance to the Clocktower high above, which she neglected during the earlier events, indicated she had only a scant twenty minutes until the appointed noontime arrangement.

Two incantations sprang into the sorceress' mind. The first spell served to mask her physical appearance; though it did little to defeat more advanced detection methods, it would prove useful if the agent was already on the ground. Y'Tasziah extensively used the second spell in combat, and it had become a specialty of hers for avoiding melee against fierce or brutal opponents, or to close the gap on unsuspecting long-range fighters like archers and fellow spellcasters. Both she learned through the tutelage of the Enigma, and both employed the Gloaming Tongue of shadow magic, though the combative spell taxed her reserves of *mana* – the inner force that fueled a spellcaster's evocations of the mysterious and arcane. The length she had to jump, using the *Shadowshift* incantation, affected the drain on her personal power, and the destination she had chosen beforehand was near the limits of distance she could cover. Nevertheless, she now felt it imperative, and since she hoped to avoid any confrontation from here on in, Y'Tasziah resolved on the plan already formulated.

Once lost in the swarm of slight to moderately tipsy patrons of the wine-tasting she was ruefully missing, Y'Tasziah knelt low to adjust her bootstraps and enacted the first of her Occult spells, sibilant words escaping her lips, "*Celasillae Thurais-Sa.*" No one seemed to notice the difference at all when a taller, elegantly dressed platinum blonde half-elven woman stood in her place, adjusted her frilled afternoon dress, and took a tall glass of wine from one of the tray-bearing maidens at the event. Well, Y'Tasziah thought craftily, it seems I managed to find a way to taste some wine after all, and it's quite good. She bought a bottle from the vendor with coin and slipped it into her pack, before casually sliding over to the sign set up on the fresh fish vendor's stall. Y'Tasziah slipped in behind the stand and silently called upon her inner reserves of power, visualizing the dark alcove she spotted earlier, three levels above where she now stood. With only a light inky wisp of smoke that dissipated in seconds, she vanished instantly from the shadows to appear within the archway, sauntering out casually, as if coming out from a powder break, and turned sharply to her right, heading straight to the gates of Sumbercolme.

She lied her way past the guardsmen – proper soldiers these, who only noted her assumed name, appearance, and purpose for visit, promptly and efficiently, and urged her to be wary of individuals who seemed to follow her or get too close. Miss Telaiss'avir Wuth-renais, blushing of course at the care and concern the handsome trio displayed, thanked them profusely and promised to watch out, swaying her hips gracefully as she strolled down the avenue. The sky was slowly clouding over, covering everything in a somber muted grey-blue tone, and when the air filled with a light, refreshing misty rain, the lady summoned a light pink and eggshell-blue parasol to match her frilled dress, dangling it over her shoulder.

She did take care to avoid close contact with any individuals who seemed the ruffian type, though these were thankfully few. She imagined a solid swipe from her 'parasol' would solve any threat – it glowed with enchantment, masked slightly by her disguise spell, but though it lacked its usual length and deadly killing edge, even the blunt impact of her Soulscythe would lay a man down easily. How embarrassing that would be! If Y'Tasziah's pressing mission did not loom so imminently over her, she would have suffered the ensuing paperwork, just to see the official report state that a 'Miss Telaiss'avir Wuth-renais' felled a hardened criminal with her umbrella. At the thought, Y'Tasziah could not restrain the loud snort as she heaved with a belly laugh, eliciting a few rude stares from a pack of snotty little lasses who were gossiping at a set of benches nearby. She shifted her grip on the parasol, still smirking, and with a sideways glance extended both her index and ring finger at the pretentious girls, who all gasped in shock at the overt, obscene gesture. Apparently, Miss Wuth-renais lacked the couth of the established nobility; Y'Tasziah laughed aloud again, thinking she could get along with this half-elven maiden – if she had existed.

Only a few minutes remained until midday, but luckily, the Gilded Hammer's guildhall lay in a compound only a short distance ahead, and Y'Tasziah could already see its gates from her position. Access to the yard and meeting area that served as a guild-owned tavern for members and potential clients held no restrictions for entry, save that non-guild persons surrender any weapons until their departure, for obvious reasons. The Gilded Hammer held some prestige as an independent contractor who employed only adventurers of notable reputation, and its services regarded as top-quality in effectiveness, honour, and discretion. House Devilsbridge contracted to the group from time to time, and a few members of the House and the Guild alike found membership by way of the other. To say they were affiliated would be a stretch of terms, but the two organizations certainly got along in the city of intrigues.

Approaching the gates, Miss Telaiss'avir Wuth-renais fanned herself and patted her freckled, damp face and bare forearms with a handkerchief, monogrammed with a fancy "T.W." as she closed and hung the parasol from a loop at the back of her dress. The covered entry afforded shelter from the misty rainfall, and several flagged recruitment tents and information tables were set up surrounding the open portcullis leading into the small courtyard and meeting hall. A cheery, Sandscarred Half-Aelyph'en girl with dyed, curly pinkish hair that stood in stark contrast to her tanned skin, greeted Miss Wuth-renais, and commented on her lovely dress in an exuberant tone. Y'Tasziah spent little time on tarrying, simply explaining that she wanted to see the meeting hall for an initial impression before deciding if they were the 'right fit' for a minor commission she required. The girl, who may have been close to Y'Tasziah's age for all she knew – elven genetics and maturity mystified her – directed her down the simple gravel pathway leading to the obvious building, which read 'Gilded Hammer Guild Hall'. Simple, effective, direct – Y'Tasziah could respect that, even if it was an odd arrangement of similar words.

As she entered the establishment, she found it bustling with life and conversation. People of so many different origins – Dwarvish, Aelyph'en, Gnomish, several Oryk and Half-Oryk, even a group of sapphire skinned and rarely-seen Crystallines, all equipped in contrasting armours and gear types denoting their various specialties, clustered together among the tables and booths and – *the bar*. Since Miss Wuth-renais' only purpose in visiting was to scout its appropriateness for her venture, surely the bar existed as an equally appropriate vantage point from which to gain a feel for the place. She took to a comfortable and well-worn stool, leaning an arm casually atop the equally patronized bar top, while smoothing the ruffles of the dress and crossing her legs in a ladylike fashion. Y'Tasziah might have enticed some lass or lad by uncrossing them to briefly reveal her intricate laced and paneled undergarments, but not Miss Wuth-renais, no, that might be less appropriate. She smiled when the barkeep, a stocky human woman in her late fifties, with sandy greying hair and soaked hands, sauntered up, and with a friendly tone asked, "What'll be thy pleasure miss? Ye thirsty?"

Trying not to sound overly exuberant (or like a lush), Miss Wuth-renais inquired, "Umm... perhaps you can recommend a decent wine, just a small glass, if you please." The bartendress nodded and slid a bottle of imported wine off the middle shelf behind her, poured a small amount into a fluted glass and handed it to the newcomer. Y'Tasziah took it, swirled, and sipped at it with a sniff, and decided she liked the wine, and nodded back, so the bartendress poured a full glass and said, "First is on the house. Enjoy." The woman behind the counter moved to serve another patron, which suited Y'Tasziah perfectly. Her attention snapped to the heavy, cloying presence of powerful illusion magic at work. The aura moved down the stairwell, presumably from the inn rooms above, which were reserved for members of the guild. Y'Tasziah saw a man of average height and build, disheveled in worn, hooded robes, descend and take a seat, as described in the letter, near the fireplace in the corner: *alone*.

No question about it, thought Y'Tasziah, *that's the man*. Since she possessed a dual-natured, otherworldly vision granted by her studies and bolstered by the soul-binding contract with the Enigma, the sorceress knew an illusion masked this individual's appearance, just like her own spell. However, unlike her quasi-real enchantment, which masked and slightly altered tactile elements, such as her height, her elven ear tips, and the shape of her Soulscythe, the illusion surrounding this man was sheer phantasm. The robe was an actual robe; no aura or wavering lines in her vision indicated it to be anything but a simple (and terribly stitched) common robe. However, underneath, where the man appeared to be wearing only simple clothing, she saw elements of Enchantment, meaning he wore magical armour or protective amulets or the like. In addition, the dweomer upon his face, which he kept hidden, concealed under the hood, and careful not to reveal more than to nod at the waitress taking his order – when she caught the slightest sight of his flesh, Y'Tasziah saw it for what it was. If she had cast a spell of detection at the man, even one designed to sense illusions, it might have failed outright, or alerted him of the attempt. The magnitude of deceptive magic impressed the sorceress, and so incredibly lucky for her, and for his protection at large, she may be the only individual in Morningmist who could see through it.

The only obstacle to learning his identity would be in obtaining a full view of his countenance, because ironically, she could not pierce mundane solid objects with her sight. His plain, brown-black worn robe itself would be the challenge. Hiding her inspection of him by gazing longingly at the warm fireplace gave her a brilliant idea. Miss Telaiss'avir Wuth-renais might be a little awkward at times, especially with a few imbibed glasses of wine, and she was certainly prone to chills, Y'Tasziah decided for her alter ego. Rubbing her hands on the bare, smooth skin of her legs, she stood from the barstool and took up her nearly empty wineglass to saunter nearer the fire to warm up. The tavern was by no means chilly, but once Miss Wuth-renais' hands got cold, she needed to enjoy the radiant heat of a fire to get her circulation back into her fingertips. (She suffered a terrible frostbite when she was lost once as a child, and her poor aching hands *just never fully recovered*, the poor lass.)

Upon her approach, the man seemed to bristle and turned away slightly, though he hid the nervous action by putting his feet up on the chair in front of him, leaning back into his own as if taking a rest. *He's been in hiding a while, most likely*, Y'Tasziah noted. It was a good move, and the sort of action that would not arouse suspicion at all, under most circumstances. The mannerisms displayed likely counted him as a fugitive and not a hardened criminal – the movements were far too passive for a true outlaw. So, another piece of the puzzle set itself into place, but who was he, and how could he be important to her investigation? She had to see his face; the excitement and her innate impatience almost got the better of her, tempting the sorceress just to pull back *that damned hood*, but she remembered the Aelyph'en man's warning about approach, so she resisted. Instead, she bided a bit of time by extending her fingers towards the fire, letting its crackling glow warm the non-existent chill of Miss Wuth-renais until, satisfied, she clapped them for good measure.

Of course, Miss Wuth-renais was here to inspect the place a little more thoroughly, so, dwindling wine still in hand, she went to the window in front of the man and laid a hand on the glass before her. All it would take was a slight turn and she would see his reflection clearly. Such a subtle positioning revealed his face perfectly as intended, and upon seeing whom the man truly was, conversely set off an extraordinarily complex chain of events. When Y'Tasziah forgot the glass of wine and it dropped to the floor to shatter with only a few drops left, when she simply ignored it and walked straight to the tavern door, white-faced as if she had seen a ghost, there was no acting at all involved. The pardons, shocked looks and subsequent shrugs of the few patrons who noticed and offered their assistance were ignored. A few snickered at the lady as she left, thinking her stricken with embarrassment. Y'Tasziah headed straight to the open portcullis, walked through it without even a sideways glance, a goodbye, or any words at all, and continued a silent and direct walk back to Devilsbridge Manor, undisturbed, except by flights of screeching ravens passing overhead.

Chapter 18

THE SEVENTH CYCLE
COMES TO AN END

What greeted Qualthalas in the alcoves was not at all what he expected, though upon reflection of the nature of his nemesis, was also unsurprising. Concealed deeper within each of the alcoves were five ornate sarcophagi, adorned with precious metals and intricately tooled to depict what the elf assumed were the inhabitants as they appeared in life. From his intense, yet brief study of the history of Ral-Qariin, a faraway continent to the west of Mithras, Qualthalas recognized these as the tombs of royalty. Judging by the exquisite craftsmanship, they may even be past emperors and empresses, which, from an archaeological standpoint fascinated his inquisitive, knowledge-thirsty nature. Conversely, the understanding that the Darklord claimed ownership of these relics, coupled by the prominent display in such a fashion, held within simple alcoves tucked neatly away in a trap-filled labyrinth, disturbed the moon elf on many levels.

Viny tendrils caressed the features of the first of the group, in the far-left recess. Qualthalas inspected her also, in a less intimate way. Her regal, yet extremely cruel expression coupled with the necklace of large ivory teeth spoke to the elf poignantly, and he recalled a few passages regarding Empress Litha Tassandri Nivicius, the *Mistress of Crocodiles*. "...the bones and flesh of one hundred and seventy-seven devoted servants, slaves and companions she lovingly fed to her divine pets upon the completion of the sand-bridge which joined her palace to the temple of the azure sun..." The text went on to paint a gory picture of the Empress' obsession with her reptiles, whom she treated with far greater respect and admiration than her citizens. In public ceremonies, she and her crocodiles feasted upon the people of her kingdom regularly. Her followers possessed such fanaticism for their liege that waiting lists had to be fashioned for countless supplicants wishing to sacrifice themselves to her grisly practice. The tales were so chilling that Qualthalas had stopped reading of her exploits one day, deposited the book unceremoniously into a trash receptacle, and did not think of it once since. *Besides, when would he need knowledge of such ancient and macabre history, really?*

Now, Qualthalas regretted not reading the horrible book further, for it could have contained some clue to the puzzle that stood before him in the form of the five stoic two-metre-tall tombs, convinced they were the key to further progress. He moved briefly to each of the sarcophagi in sequence, noting important features and recalling what he could from the limited scope of his studies. The Neihwe'un seemed obsessed still with the first, having wrapped several tendrils around every contour of the gold and iridite figure. The Primordial was warbling to the statue in similar fashion to when the elf first encountered it, birdlike and excited. Qualthalas decided to leave his companion to its strange fascination and cautiously traversed the chamber to inspect the five braziers prominent in the main area of the chamber. The identical numbers – five sarcophagi to five braziers – could not be a coincidence, and Qualthalas held enough experience with cryptic puzzles found in obscure ruins to know a solution must present itself. It was all about correlation.

Yet another problem cropped up, this time in the form of the ancient script upon the plaques attached to each of the braziers. The deciphering spell Qualthalas utilized to read the Daemonic writings prior had long since faded. Though he recognized a few of the characters as Neph'al in origin, the words themselves were so far removed from modern languages that he could not fathom their meaning. Qual supposed another casting might be in order, but perhaps there were other clues he could glean from the patterns and carvings that banded each metal bowl suspended before him. Logic dictated that each brazier, whose purpose was to burn things, would require a suitable offering. Each oblation should represent something symbolic, attuned to one of the five rulers: *but what could they be?* He might have to inspect the sarcophagi again, though, regarding the first, he immediately recalled the crocodile tooth necklace of Empress Litha; perhaps the jewelry was somehow removable. The keys might not prove as difficult to ascertain as he initially assumed, so the elf hurriedly skipped back to the alcoves for another look.

Qualthalas returned to find the Neihwe'un had unwound itself from the empress and now regarded each of the remaining sarcophagi from a distance; it reminded Qualthalas of an aficionado of fine art critiquing a set of paintings. "My friend, I must ask – what is your fascination with these tombs?" the elf inquired, frowning as he inspected the creature with an arched eyebrow. The familiar hooded visage turned eerily upon the shoulders of the Primordial, underneath its citrine eyes prominently hung the necklace Qual had postulated would help unlock the puzzle. The rogue's eyes shone at the sight, but before he could open his mouth, the Neihwe'un uttered a chilling statement, "The dead do not sleep well in these tombs, Aelyph'en – the minds inside are at unrest, awake and full of vehemence." Without moving its visage, the ropy tendrils snaked out to the second of the tombs, curling around a scepter carved into its surface.

Qualthalas reeled from the implication: judging by the era these supposed dead monarchs occupied in history, most pre-dated even his grandfather's rule over the Aeth'Akir court. The ancient Empress of Crocodiles reigned for centuries over an entire continent, dating as far back as the earliest times of Ithrauss' *great-grandmother's* rule. Contemplating that the sarcophagus contained not a desiccated husk and bones of a vicious tyrant, but instead housed a sixty-thousand-year-old undead creature was… unthinkable. If these terrible Mummy Lords were to be unleashed upon the world, their combined power alone could topple entire kingdoms. Qualthalas stood stunned, mouth agape as he slowly allowed this realization and the ensuing inferences to settle in his disturbed mind. Zhiniel *displayed* these things as a show of power; this was surely a message – one that was becoming clearer to the moon elven prince with each piece of evidence he uncovered. The Darklord was prepared, methodical, and possessed assets far beyond any single surface race kingdom, beyond several in fact. The elf now worried what he might find when he did finally reach the city below.

Qual turned his attention back to the Primordial, who worked the tiniest tubers and shoots of its limbs into unperceivable crev-ices surrounding the scepter worked into the sarcophagus, then, with an unwinding motion like removing a screw from wood; it spun the rod up and out of its owner's grasp. *A small victory, these two objects were,* thought Qualthalas hollowly. Thinking again of Kaira, held by his traitorous cousin and in the clutches of the Darklord, Qualthalas purposefully replaced his trepida-tions with renewed purpose. He commended the Neihwe'un on its skilled performance, "Excellent work my viny companion, what of the other three? Have you ascertained how to remove any other objects?" Seeing minute feelers already probing the cracks and crevices of the remaining sarcophagi, the moon elf felt reassured they would overcome this challenge quickly. As the Primordial worked, it let out a grunt like a boar, apparently struggling with something heavy attached to the third crypt.

"Indeed, Aelyph'en, I have. What did you learn of the five hanging pots? Do they hold significance?" There was an abrupt cracking sound as the viny terror freed a large canopic jar from the third tomb, but seeing his companion freeze movement, Qual stiffened. "What is it? What happened?" he asked, concerned. Thinking swiftly, the elf thumbed Mourning-Song partway out of its scabbard, but then chastised himself – the blade could sense nothing in its current state. It might be several hours until the runes once again pulsed with life. The jar tumbled out of the alcove, luckily intact, but much to the elven bard's chagrin, its removal left a great fissure in the sarcophagus. When the Neihwe'un silently drew back its limb, shaking, Qualthalas saw blackened, rotten, and withered vegetation where it had once been supple and vibrant.

"Back!" the elf warned hastily, putting a hand to his lips and nose, which he knew would do no good; it was more of a reflex. The Neihwe'un flowed backwards, dragging the wounded limb along with it, motor control over the viny tendril apparently lost. Seeing the blackness creeping slowly up the appendage, knowing the necrotizing effect of exposure to this form of undeath, Qualthalas drew Ithrin'Sael-I-Uiin fully. Though the blade exuded no magical power, its material and craftsmanship were unparalleled; its gleaming edge could still cut through nearly anything. "Brace for it," the moon elf warned the Primordial, who hissed and shook in wracking pain. The creature understood Qual's intent and flattened out the limb as much as it could while the rapier descended and severed the bundle of barbed vines in one hacking chop. Green-yellow sap oozed out of the cut-off parts, turned black and congealed in seconds. "Hrrgh... pain," came the creature's deep, windy voice, but it held up the still-attached part of its appendage for Qualthalas to inspect. Thankfully, the sap flowing out of it stayed vibrant in colour, crystallized, and sealed the amputated ends.

"We are lucky, but we must take care now around that one. Stopping that crack immediately is imperative, lest the miasma spread – or worse." Qualthalas wondered at the creature's regenerative capabilities and nodded to the stump limb, "Will it eventually regrow?" Though in pain still, the skull within the viny hood formed a rictus grin, "I have survived much worse, Aelyph'en Qualthalas, the feasting will nourish the body." The moon elf had an epiphany suddenly, nearly forgetting the lingering danger of the exposed necromantic energy seeping from the sarcophagus, for a moment. "I have what is likely a terrible idea, my friend," Qual proclaimed, his lips creased in a wan smile of mischief, "however, let us first deal with the problem at hand."

From his numerous studies of infiltration, Qualthalas found it imperative to learn spells of a concealing nature, among them, thaumaturgies for the purpose of covering his tracks. As mundane as these sounded, some of the most useful incantations were also the simplest: a spell that could clean up blood and footprints was invaluable for removing evidence of his presence. A shattered vase in the noble's private chambers could be disastrous; hence, spells to repair and reassemble broken objects were also among the bard's repertoires. Qual gave the floor near the sarcophagus a cursory glance and noted with a smug grin several bits of gold and iridite lay there – enough to ensure the spell functioned.

The elf retreated a safe distance and performed the simple gestures and incantation, stretched his palm out to the fissure, now visibly seeping out a vile, inky cloud of death. The small pieces of casket laying about levitated and found their places in the cracked sarcophagus: neatly, but not completely sealing the little fissure. *Annoying*, thought Qual, but his mind worked swiftly on a solution, though it would be a dangerous one. He possessed a chemical compound that, when mixed, produced a short burst of intense heat. It would surely melt the soft gold and completely plug the remaining openings; however, to place it, he would have to get his hands uncomfortably close to the death mist. Ithrin'Sael-I-Uiin possessed the ability to render the necrotizing cloud inert for a few seconds; again, Qualthalas rued the necessity to awaken its soul in their defense earlier, "*but...*", he whispered, "what's the fun in anything being easy or safe?"

Searching through his secret pouch seemed a habit lately; the last few times he possessed the foresight to organize the rolls of vials it contained as he fumbled through them. This time, he found the one he needed promptly and made a resolution to be more diligent about managing his gear in the future. "If there is to *be* a future," he muttered, then shaking his head, caught himself falling into a melancholic mood, and began to whistle a bardic melody as he worked a putty around in his fingers. The Neihwe'un reached out with a slender chute, but Qual waved it away, "The risk is mine this time, friend. I'll be careful." The elf smiled; he had an ace or two still up his sleeve. Once the stiff putty rapidly became malleable, the smirking rogue twisted his arms and shook his shirt crisply. Two picks with tiny suction cups at the end dropped from his coatsleeves into his palm and he scooped up the putty between them. It was turning to a goopy mess fast, so Qualthalas moved swiftly, and plunged the matter into the cracks taking care to keep his hands away from the mist. Just in time, the elf averted his almond eyes as the reaction occurred, glowing red-hot with a sudden flash, fusing the soft metal of the sarcophagus tightly shut. The rubbery suction cups melted from the heat, and his two picks were now a permanent fixture on the carved tomb.

Qualthalas turned to his companion and smiled, then strode up to gather up the strands of its wounded appendage in one hand, Mourning-Song in the other. The Primordial balked at the sight of the razor weapon, but the bard chuckled and reassured the creature, "As I stated earlier, this is likely the worst idea I've had in a long time, but I think I still owe you a debt." Neihwe'un cocked its disturbing face, and the vines of its hood writhed around like snakes, not sure what to expect from the unpredictable Aelyph'en. Qual felt its psychic trepidation permeate the area; it had nervously released a few spores when he brought forth the rapier.

The showman in him returned, Qualthalas drew up his sleeve like a magician and lay the flat side of Ithrin'Sael-I-Uiin across the pale flesh of his outstretched arm. Without another word, and unlike the parlour tricks of the common street-mage, he twisted the edge and dragged it across his forearm. Even though the cut was gentle, it was deep, and his lifeblood streamed out as the elf winced in sharp pain – the tiny slit from the weapon felt like the sting of a papercut. "Drink now!" he spoke through gritted teeth, stomping the floor in pain several times, as the Primordial wrapped its little blood-sucking taproots around the wound and drew in the moon elf's blood. Intelligently Qualthalas sang a brief healing melody (the wound was superficial; Qual knew just where to cut to make it bleed profusely without endangering himself) and as the magical energy knit and sutured his flesh, it suffused the Neihwe'un as well.

His own red vitae coursed through the creature, and supplemented by the life-restoring spell, the Primordial's appendage regenerated expeditiously. Qualthalas watched with both professional and personal curiosity as the vegetation sprouted leaves and new tubers. Then, a marvel occurred as the Neihwe'un grew a rare blossom of icy blue tinged with crimson at the tips – lunar orchids, the kind his mother favored in her courtyard garden… The elf tried to avert his eyes as it moved him to weep. He could not think of her right now. Wiping away the tears, he vowed to tread those beautiful gardens with her for an entire week, once he prevented the disaster facing the world. Perhaps she would speak to him, maybe even sing one of her beautiful dirges; though the intense sadness they instilled could paralyze a man, they were so hauntingly sublime. He loved them the most.

Qualthalas avoided speaking of his mother to anyone – even Kaira knew to avoid the topic for the brooding sullenness it instilled in the Crown Prince. It was from her that he inherited the passion for verse and poetry, performance, and song. He touched the glowing silver crescents upon his face reverently, they made him remember her brightest moments and forget her darkest ones. The Elflord forced himself to dismiss her from his thoughts, his eyes became mirrors, his face lost expression completely for a moment, and his mind became tranquil. He looked away from the healed vines of the Neihwe'un unconsciously as the pair resumed the removal of the key items from the sarcophagi and took extreme care to avoid other mishaps.

Once they secured all five objects – necklace, scepter, canopic jar, serpent feather, and claw-ring – the two returned to the braziers across the room to determine *where* which object went. Qualthalas' trained eye picked out two certainties with ease: he recognized the giant winged serpent representative of the Valley of the Four Winds, its ruler commanded flights of the mighty creatures during his reign. Into this brazier, he set the serpent feather, and it lit with an eerily comforting greenish flame that produced no discernable heat. Into the next brazier, adorned obviously with reptilian monstrosities surrounded by throngs of fervent sacrifices, Qualthalas laid the tooth necklace. The Neihwe'un assisted with the third selection, its ropy new tendrils twisted around one of the heavy iron bowls to reveal the etching of a vase matching the canopic jar they possessed. Summarily, the creature snatched the item from the elf's fingers and dropped it unceremoniously within. Three braziers lit, two remained.

Try as he might, Qualthalas could recall no clues about the two remaining rulers. Scepters and claw-rings were both common icons of the Western monarchs of Ral-Qariin; it seemed one must have specific knowledge of the Emperor or Empress' dynasty to discern the proper offering. Qual put a hand to his slightly prickly chin (facial hair grew extremely slowly upon a moon elven face, a full beard was nearly a decade's achievement for the few Sillistrael'li patient enough to cultivate one) and mused, humming to himself. Fifty-fifty odds, the elf narrowed his eyes at the gamble, thinking it a very foolish game to play, but apparently the Primordial liked playing the odds, for it boldly plunked the last two objects seemingly at random into the remaining two braziers and cackled in its familiar, eerie way. It shook and rustled its vines triumphantly as the last braziers lit and they heard the gratifying, grating noise of metal scraping upon stone from the other end of the room.

"I'll take you to my next game of cards after this little diversion is over with," Qualthalas laughed and clapped the Neihwe'un upon its (loosely termed) shoulder and eyed the now familiar creature reflectively. It was singularly the strangest friend the bard had ever acquired in his many storied travels. They waltzed upon the chamber floor like two misfit kings, narrowly avoiding decapitation by axe blade once and taking more care as they continued, advancing to find the sarcophagi sunken further back into the alcoves. All five appeared to have slid upon ingenious tracks hidden within the tilework, and the stonework of the walls behind must have shifted to deepen the passageways. Qual moved to inspect the changes closer, but a mass of vines shot up in front of the elf to block his path. "Caution, Aelyph'en. Something yet stirs within the alcoves – vibrations of a mystical nature."

To be sure, something significant was forthcoming; all five sarcophagi emanated a dim, indigo illumination that rose in intensity to a brilliant violet hue, and Qualthalas could feel the air of the chamber rushing past him as if into a vacuum. A loud crashing noise like a miniature thunderclap issued from each alcove, causing both Qual and the Primordial to retreat a few metres and shield themselves. The moon elf opened his eyes just in time to witness the five sarcophagi glowing in the last moment before they vanished entirely from the chamber, whisked off by teleportation magic to Gods knew where. Qualthalas would have paid a shiny golden crown for that knowledge, but as he knew, gold could not buy him anything of real value in this world. *Maybe I am growing wiser in my old age*, he thought, chuckling to himself, and seeing a passage revealed in behind the alcoves, he led his Primordial friend on, likely into the next trap-filled chamber, his mood restored. Qualthalas was resolved to get to the heart of the Citadel, rescue Kaira, and somehow foil the Darklord's plot after successfully returning to Sillis-Thal'as with information his grandfather could use in defense of Antiqua.

If the moon elven Prince would pay a crown to know where the sarcophagi appeared, he might have paid a king's ransom to wipe the dreaded consequence from his mind. Within specially prepared chambers, constructed under the largest cities on each of Antiqua's five continents, the ancient mummies' burial tombs coalesced, and their magical seals unraveled. The ancient beings stirred in their sarcophagi, babbled in unfathomable tongues, and invoked terrible pacts, released finally from the binding spells which had suppressed their dark magic for so long. With vengeant wrath, compounded by sheer insanity from entombment, the subsequent havoc these horrors would wreak became the Darklord's open declaration of war upon the surface world, and sparked what history later recorded as, *"the beginning of the Eighth Cycle of Antiqua."*

Epilogue

REACTIONS

Ithrauss Suh'Min Tenebril-Durath reeled within his towering arcane spire upon Sillis-Thal'as. Abject horror washed over his wizened face as he retreated from the dread vision revealed within the Sanctus Orb. The impending repercussion of five, millennia-old, entombed dead roaming the planet unchecked was unthinkable: it would shake the foundations of Antiqua. The ancient sage's psyche was wracked by sheer panic, yet, as the ramifications of this vile act assaulted his mind, he found focus and acted swiftly. His pale blue robes fluttered as the old moon elf enacted a spell formula that pierced several planar barriers simultaneously. Unrestricted communication opened between the sage and his scattered, distant peers: those who departed to strange realms throughout the cosmos. In moments, he issued a distress call to every executive officer of the Twisted Strings, with the imperative order to assemble in their secret hold, hidden on the faraway continent Aguoyd'Hraug. Several missives were sent to other key members of the guild who lay tucked away in locations so deep and secret that scrying upon them was rendered impossible.

The sage's mind worked to estimate how long it would take the ancient, entombed undead to rouse themselves enough from their ages-old torpor to wreak supreme havoc upon the world, as they had millennia past. Ithrauss knew their various histories; all were bloody, despotic, and tyrannical – if he chose words that profoundly *understated* the socio-political climate during their respective dynasties. Several historical texts, lost to Antiqua's modern libraries, inadequately described the atrocities these creatures had committed in life, so terribly diabolical were their dominions. In ages past, *Archmaster Ithrauss* had fought alongside Drakhanic and Celestial paragons, and barely prevailed against the savage, myriad powers possessed by the ancient Kings and Queens. He and the formative agents of the Twisted Strings staged covert sabotages against the strongholds of these dark powers, their campaigns were responsible for the eventual demise of two of the five monarchs now risen through Zhiniel's necromancy. To confront such evil again exhilarated and terrified the sage equally. Countermeasures sprang to his thoughts, but most involved mitigation of the impending disaster; the attacks loomed so imminent that prevention of the ensuing cataclysm... was arguably *impossible*.

For centuries, the Sanctus Orb remained enshrined upon its amethyst and platinum stand, yet Ithrauss laid a hand upon it with urgency and issued the command word, "Exe'espalloc-Nur." In response, the diamantine facets of the orb separated to reveal visible, crackling, energized fields of blue mana which sizzled as the entire artifact shrunk to the size of an egg in his palm. Ithrauss clutched the relic to his robed chest tightly, took an arcane stance upon legs shaking with adrenaline, and closed his eyes in supreme meditation to steady himself. The next spell he cast empowered through Drakhanic breathing techniques learned from a sect of Sand Monks, and his silver eyes flared when the incantation burst from his dry, caked lips. "*Kanas-Doiah'Noh Suvarius Kura-Throe'Assat-saku!*" The resulting 'BOOM' shook his laboratory and set off an arcane alarm that echoed through his empty chambers – Ithrauss was already inside the secret hold of the Twisted Strings. He, the one to issue the call, was also the first to arrive, and it fell upon the ancient Diviner to unlock the veils of protection which had hidden the fortress from any assault or prying eyes. Even the Darklord below had no prior knowledge of its existence, nor presently would Zhiniel care; its location merely would have been catalogued for destruction or careful manipulation. As of now, it only registered as an afterthought in his perfectly wrought schemes.

Moments after Ithrauss lifted the protective enchantments, vibrant lines of Drakhanic script bathed the chamber in orange light; runic circles of conjuration materialized in spherical patterns beside the wizened guildmaster. Warm breath escaped his lips and his shoulders relaxed. Ithrauss' ancient tutor was the second to arrive, and the first to heed his desperate transmission. Raising his hand to shield his eyes from the sudden radiance, Ithrauss felt a warmth upon his fingers and cheek as intricate trigrams assembled the physical body of his professor within their centre. The reptilian form, clad in deep purple raiment, stepped forth, and blinked at its long-time friend. Nictitating membranes in its amber-yellow draconian eyes retracted as Ouren the Convincer held up a gnarled wooden staff in greeting to its former pupil. "We've much work, yet again, old friend," came the hissing, sibilant speech from between its pursed lips, which revealed yellowing, ancient fangs. The Naga'Zhi Psion curled its clawed fingers around a scintillating amethyst sphere, similar in appearance to the Sanctus Orb, which it held up before Ithrauss, reassuringly. Together, they would combat this threat with forces from several realities combined. Soon the hall was filled with beings of myriad origins: the officers of the Twisted Strings assembled for war.

Y'Tasziah Camylla Devilsbridge sat in momentary comfort upon a velvet chair in the meeting hall of House Devilsbridge. Her mind worked through the stunning revelation that her missing elven contact had taken pains to lead her to. One single son of House Zennitarr had *survived* its obliteration, and he lived behind an illusion, adopting a false identity within the Gilded Hammer's Guild Hall. She awaited her father's swift return from a Chamber meeting of little import, however, the House's prime seneschal she had dispatched to summon Orion a half-hour prior had yet to return. As if summoned by Y'Tasziah's troubled thoughts, Daime Khylienne Jhi-Panthras suddenly burst into the room and nearly collapsed from exertion.

The lady's hands went to her knees and sweat dripped from her soaked brow onto the grey fur rug at the entry to the hall. Y'Tasziah stood in alarm as the lady sputtered, with a hoarse and cracking voice, "Lord Devilsbridge is no longer in attendance at the meeting, *Seignorine.*" She drew another ragged breath and continued, "Ravantheos himself motioned me over and informed that, without warning or cause, your father abruptly stood and approached the bench to excuse himself, then marched out of the chamber hall." Seeing her struggle for words and noting her discomfort, Y'Tasziah urged Khylienne to take a seat and rest before continuing. The Daime took to an ornate chair and sipped from a nearby cordial of water to cure her parched throat. She resumed speaking in an even, stable voice while she regarded Y'Tasziah gravely, "Estedar slipped me *this*, then bid me fly to your side and deliver it to your hand directly. He was *covert* with the exchange."

The middle-aged Daime produced a *writ-pouch* – a specially sealed document in leather wrap – which was pre-enchanted to convey sensitive materials between specific Houses and would alert the sender if tampered with or opened by any but the intended recipient. Y'Tasziah gathered the document with trembling fingers and unraveled the strap which held the pouch shut, then carefully removed the small scroll it contained. She worried profusely about her father's irregular behaviour – at times he would take a moment to collect himself if something bothered him, but to *leave* a meeting without warning or cause was unheard of.

The ink still drying upon the pristine parchment, the flowing script of her father's unmistakable handwriting read, "*Y'Tasziah, dearest daughter, there is no time to explain in detail. Some cataclysmic force has appeared beneath Morningmist – one I must personally investigate immediately with the aid of my trusted Companions in the city. In the event I do not return, I formally declare you as Head of House. In the interim, assemble Vanguard-One and maintain a presence at the main gates. There may be imminent attack. Ravantheos is aware of the peril, however we hope to contain the menace without public alert. I regret the gravity this must instill in your heart but understand your role and remain vigilant. I love you, my daughter.*" The bottom of the scroll was smudged with a wax seal bearing her father's signet ring stamping: a sure sign of his haste. She detected something else though, when her eyes scanned the bottom of the paper; the faint magical emanation of Night-Ink, indicating a secret message only she might recognize.

That midnight, Y'Tasziah read the concealed script to discover that the heir to the former House Zennitarr's destroyed legacy was the only clue in the intricate web of deceit her father charged her to uncover. The secret message revealed Orion's suspicions surrounding *seven* of the Ruling Houses of Morningmist and their collaboration with a powerful force beneath the surface of the planet.

Cazares Seraszar Aeth'Akir paused in his pacing with a malicious smile upon his lips. He flipped his signature ebon dagger between deft fingers, and again threw it whistling past his prisoner's ear to embed itself in the wall beside the chained half-orykan woman's cheek. Kaira just narrowed her eyes at the pathetic display. Intimidation tactics roused no fear in the stoic barmaid;

she had been interrogated before. Even guard captains balked at her resolve (though the event she now reflected on involved Qual, of course, and her ire at the time focused on that damned bard so furiously, the captain swore that she was madder at the elf than himself.) She smiled at the recollection, and Cazares, conversely, frowned at the unwavering look of defiance the woman practically radiated.

The cursed traitor slid towards Kaira and ran a hand through her curls while he retrieved the dagger. She jerked away with such force, the neck-manacle holding her in place buckled and bent. She spat at his feet and sneered. Kaira strained against the heavy steel around her throat, but it held for the time being, and a line of blood made its way down to her breasts from the gash her struggling produced. The fury boiled inside her. A savage urge to snap this weakling's neck coursed through Kaira's veins, and she growled at Cazares while he stared back at her through his strange goggles.

The Gravewalker analyzed blips and readouts superimposed on his vision by the complex circuitry embedded within his chrome eyes, hidden from his prisoner's view. A wicked idea slithered through his terrifying psyche like an insidious smoke seeping throughout a deeper darkness. The little bitch had no inkling of his master's power, nor of the capabilities the Darklord bestowed. "I will show her, bring her to despair," he whispered aloud, "and make her hurt, just like *he* hurt me so long ago." This hatred knew no relief, it twisted inside the sociopathic conscience and festered there, just knowing that the little bastard prince had found love in this woman. Cazares was determined to present Kaira to his cousin, broken and tortured, before killing her in front of Qualthalas' eyes. Cazares lifted his goggles and cackled at the shock and revulsion that the half-oryk could not hide when she saw underneath, and he licked the edge of his dagger. *Yes, sweet revulsion.*

Zaeliar'a emerged from the nebulous portal within the sub-plane of the Fae Spring Court. The vibrant, life-infused energy of the realm momentarily blinded and sickened her as its positive force clashed with the negative energy that suffused her body. She recovered quickly, thanks to the infusion of life-force donated so graciously by Lady Pelein: her skin adapted and took on a darker hue, ebon amid the golden radiance of the trees and alien plants surrounding her.

A shimmering avian creature, resplendent with crystalline tips on its wing-feathers, shrieked above her, and Zaeliar'a extended her hand skyward. It was time to test her new powers on the strange plane. The Dreadheart could already feel vibration within her palm, and she tightened her grip into a fist, then reached out with her mind as she thrust downward to the aqua-blue grass at her feet. The bird let out a piercing call of panic as the air currents keeping it aloft succumbed to the greater force of gravity exerted by the vampiress. Zaeliar'a's unliving pulse quickened as she felt the plummeting paradise bird's brittle bones crunching in her otherworldly grip, even before they shattered when it struck ground. The once-beautiful creature lay in a crimson pool before her, its wings in a crumpled mess, and she watched it die silently; saw its last breaths escape its beak past its quivering tongue.

Satisfied, her gaze turned to a nearby hillock, where a vaguely humanoid figure peered around a gnarled, leafless tree. The thing flexed a clawed, metallic appendage, wrapped around one of the lower branches, and Zaeliar'a heard the tree limb crack while a low, clicking sound issued from the creature's mandibles. It bore a striking resemblance to a praying mantis with hard, creaking chitinous armour that covered its arms, legs, midsection, and oval head. Deep umber, compound eyes sat to the sides of its open maw; the thing cocked its head sideward to regard her, as it wound its way out from under the tree. The fae mantis advanced with unquestionable menace, its frontmost appendages dug into the soft earth of the hillside, scissor-like, propelling the monster toward her at remarkable speed.

The Dreadheart drew her claymore and brought it to bear moments before the creature was upon her and, with a critical eye, she noted both its mandibles and terrible claws dripped with a red ichor that sizzled and bubbled upon its shell-like exoskeleton. With a sinful smile and glowing crimson eyes, Zaeliar'a swung the *Soulthorne Blade*, her namesake, in a vicious downward arc...

Qualthalas merrily wound his way through dark passages and trap-filled corridors with the Neihwe'un in tow, ignorant of the fact that he had unwittingly pulled the Darklord's first lynch pin. Somewhere deeper below, with a burst of laughter before his octagonal scrying screen, Zhiniel Al-Nistir Szord'Ryn awaited the moment he could reveal to the moon elf what he had done. Though the Darklord would have eagerly sent the sarcophagi himself, it was deliciously satisfying to know the irony that Qualthalas' progress into the labyrinth spelled doom for the surface world he fought so valiantly to protect.

As the image in the huge crystal faded away, Zhiniel was left staring at himself in its glass-like mirrored surface. In a bizarre moment of introspection, or perhaps foresight, his thoughts turned to the deciphering of the tablet left in the magmic gnome's possession. Inevitably the wretched creature would betray him; surely the clever thing would attempt to secret away the knowledge, hoping to foil the Soulharvester's well-laid plans. From the folds of his woven-chain robes, Zhiniel withdrew the real, original device and held its clear lens to his own eye. It winked to power, still displaying the image and profile information he had read tens of times to commit the knowledge of his adversary to memory. How the creators of the tablet knew of Qualthalas, of his capabilities, his thoughts; he had theories, but no solid understanding.

Yet, there it was in entirety: every aspect of the moon elven prince explained in illustrated detail upon the screen: his strengths, weaknesses, entire volumes written about his character flaws, his goals, and aspirations. Zhiniel analyzed charts and graphs detailing statistics that involved the 'Four Cornerstones' and 'Twelve Pillars' – the same terms uncovered in carvings and other devices found in mostly destroyed facilities beneath D'zurien-To'th.

Conveniently omitted from the copy of the tablet delivered to Galflagwindel the Maguscientist, Zhiniel recalled to the screen his own dossier. By speaking his name clearly in the indigo elven dialect, and in similar fashion, there it was in black and white:

Zhiniel Al-Nistir Szord'Ryn: a.k.a. The Soulharvester, The Darklord, Chainbreaker, and more. Offspring of an omniscient, paradox creating Archdevil dwelling within a black hole at the centre of Gaia, the Paradise Planet. Descriptors: Ruthless, Terrifying, Evil, Nefarious, Self-Serving, Megalomaniac. Harbinger of the Eighth Cycle of Antiqua, Zhiniel realizes his goal for domination of the planet in 99.1 percent of all divergent timelines recorded, ascending mortality after departing for the <redacted> Solar System where he uncovers the Gate of Death. Further study required beyond incursion of the God's domain. Timestamp: 11:02:37.

Once the gnome successfully reconstructed the one piece of missing information Zhiniel had cleverly left in the storage system of the edited device: this 'redacted' solar system, the Soulharvester would ensure his prince-pawn escaped to safety on the silver moon, with that final puzzle piece. The result would be predictable. The Maguscientist would surely entrust the moon elf with the location he needed, and Qualthalas would instinctively relay the information to his grandfather. From there, Ithrauss' powerful organization would spare nothing to make travel there possible, in hopes they could reach the Gate of Death before the Darklord, to prepare for his inevitable assault.

A smell of moldering decay, acrid and bitter, permeated the scrying chamber, and Zhiniel turned to greet Axelay DeVentis, the ancient fae lich, who nodded in respect to his master. The undead creature spoke only three ominous words, "All is prepared." Zhiniel's robes lightly jingled as he motioned to the giant onyx scrying mirror. The pair observed as, oblivious to the real peril they faced, Qualthalas and the Neihwe'un wandered his devious labyrinth. They would be funneled into his snare, and then he would acquire all the information locked in the moon elf's fractured psyche, thanks to the preparations now completed by his undead associate. The vine creature would serve too, as a living specimen of original primordial life. The research potential was worth the havoc it would predictably wreak while being subdued and captured. Once more, Zhiniel looked closely at the pale flesh of his moon elven counterpart and almost felt a fleeting pang of pity for Qualthalas.

Somewhere else in time, across the cosmos, a young man smirked and began practicing his sword technique, honing his skill with the blade physically and mentally. He continued to focus until time itself looped at his command, leaving him with years of mastery in the space of a single moment. He studied with samurai, ninja, soldiers throughout history, tribesmen and amazons alike. He stepped out of the freezing sphere at the same moment he had departed; passers-by nodded at him, and continued upon their paths, unaware of what had transpired. This was his practice for so many years of his existential life: in his youth he had no inkling of the special power he possessed, having always thought himself strange but not knowing he was unique.

Though only in his early twenties, the young man's experiential existence numbered tens of thousands of years, and the more he mastered this unexplainable ability, the longer he could stay suspended in solitude within that paradoxical, anachronistic realm. He could traverse time into the past, reaching with his genetic memory further and further through his bond with creation itself. He met ancient masters of the arts, developed friendships and rivalries; he learned all he could from these forays into his birthworld's past. The young man sought to understand and connect with the creatures that inhabited his planet; he visited ancient periods filled with rare and extinct creatures: giant and terrible lizards, flying creatures not unlike winged phoenixes, and even his peoples' predecessors – apelike and possessed of an instinctual cunning and growing intellect. They would prosper under his tutelage, for to them, he was as a promethean mentor – bringing fire to the terrified yet curious Neanderthals who understood they held a commonality. Grunts and gestures turned to articulation and codification under his guidance. *The Boy Who Would Be God* understood that his physical form held a piece of infinity, and through that connection, he forged a history in every moment he spent encapsulated in those time-dilated shifts. He surmised that if a God existed, someone must take the steps into infinity to attain that supreme omniscience. He intended to persevere and meet himself at the end of time to take his place upon the throne.

The Balancer shifted, and the Omniverse moved in response, swirling within the formless form of a being that knew no end. It could sense the ambitious youth's yearning, deep within the folds of its infinite dimension, and considered. The entity knew the answers to the paradoxical riddles infused throughout reality. The boy possessed the capacity to affect The Balancer's thoughts and intentions, perhaps he would make a suitable disciple – if he could withstand the tribulations requisite to mastery of the Four Cornerstones. The Balancer collapsed inside itself to enter the boy's mind, with devastating effect. He demonstrated existence as a singularity and buried the terrible knowledge deep within the DNA structure of the pre-embryonic child. Timeless as the entity was, it waited to see if the seed would grow.

About the Author

Ryan McLeod, a life-long voracious reader, has been creatively writing since the age of six. As an avid gamemaster of several pen-and-paper roleplaying games, he has crafted countless worlds suitable for adventure, including Antiqua, the setting of *Both Sides of the Blade* and his upcoming project: *Crucible RPG*. Alongside his writing, Ryan has also developed a love of painting and illustrating – all the artwork featured in the novel was produced by the author himself.

Ryan has a long history of martial arts experience, which he has drawn extensively upon to describe the combat in *Both Sides of the Blade*. He has trained with many of the weapon types mentioned in the book and several of the techniques described were developed in practicing the craft.

Among various other fighting and societal traditions, Ryan has studied ninjutsu and bushido – the samurai warrior's way, cultivating a fascination with occultism and spiritual beliefs. He trains in his own martial art and philosophy, Jade Serpent, at home and at local parks, where he is often observed practicing forms with a (wooden) katana.

Although he has authored hundreds of poems, *Both Sides of the Blade* is his first published work. The initial novel in *The Qualthalas Quandaries Quadrilogy* will be followed by *The Busty Barmaid's Boudoir*, then *Rogue, Vagabond*, and *Crown Prince*, and finally, *When the Song Ends*.